Shadows Of Lyonesse

Ravek Hunter

First Edition, October 2019
Copyright © 2019 Ravek Hunter Literary LLC
All rights reserved.
ISBN:
      978-1-948782-12-8 (paperback),
      978-1-948782-02-9 (ebook)

www.WorldsOfAtlantis.com

For Mrs. Wife,
who gave me two incredible boys
that I hope will be proud to read their father's work one day.

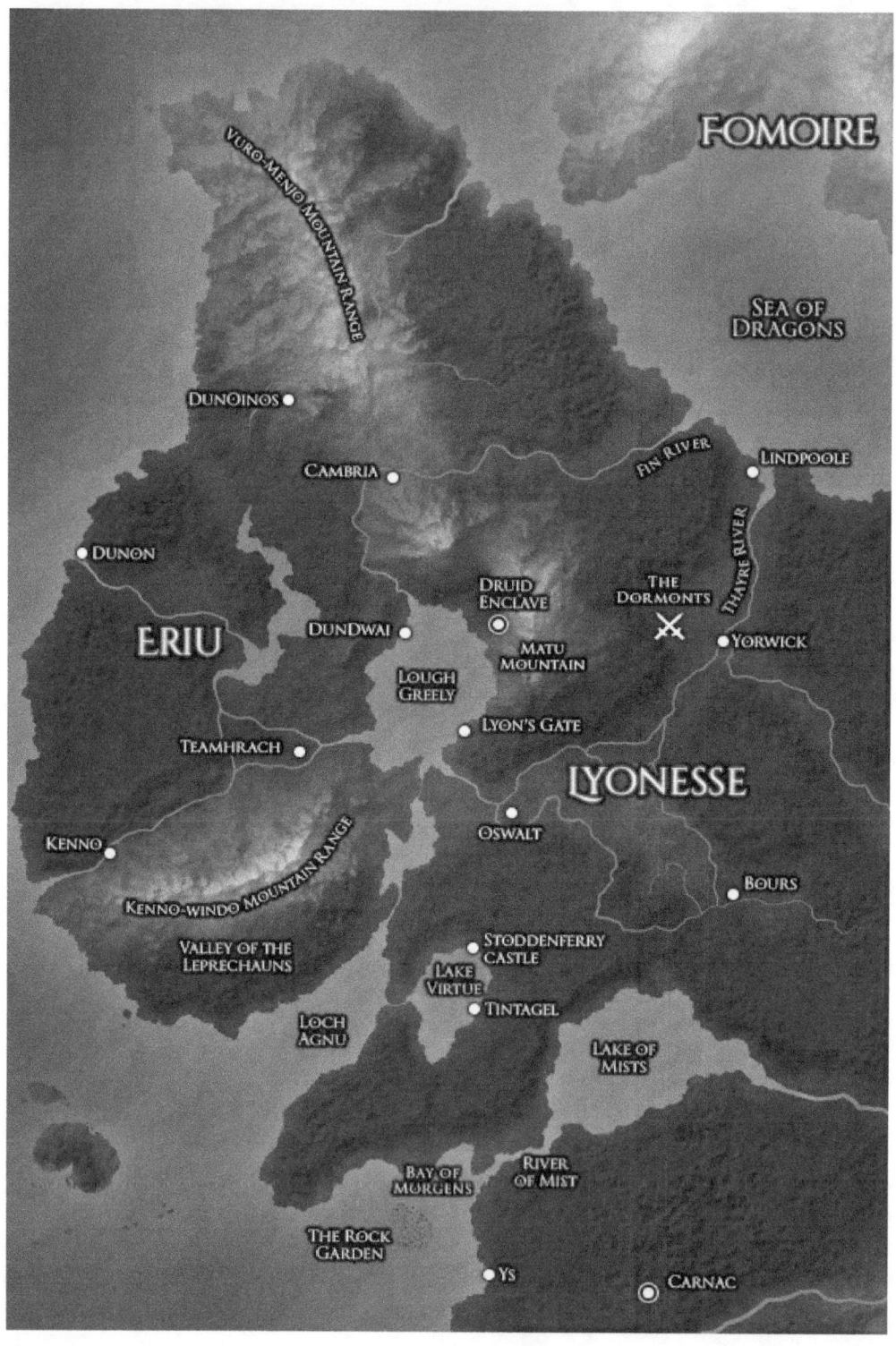

First Edition, October 2019
Copyright © 2019 Ravek Hunter Literary LLC
All rights reserved.
ISBN:
      978-1-948782-12-8 (paperback),
      978-1-948782-02-9 (ebook)

www.WorldsOfAtlantis.com

Shadows Of Lyonesse

Ravek Hunter

Fantasy Novels by Ravek Hunter

Red Wizard of Atlantis

The Fallen

Saving Eridu

The Imaziɣen Druid

Shadows of Lyonesse

Beasts of Courth

Ys (Coming in 2022)

If you enjoy reading books by this author, please remember to leave a review at your favorite bookseller!

To learn more about the backstory, mythology, and character development in these stories or to view world maps visit us at:

www.WorldsOfAtlantis.com!

TABLE OF CONTENTS

Children of Atlas

It was from the stars they came, out of the vast darkness of the Primeval Cosmos, plunging from the sky in a great wingless beast consumed by smoke and fire. It fell with a thunderous crash upon the earth plowing a long black rift across the open plain before it came to rest in a final shudder of sparks and lightning. The smoking shell of the massive creature lay shattered, yet from its broken maw came hundreds of odd-looking figures that crawled through the acrid haze and stumbled disoriented onto the lush green grass of a new world.

The Sylvan watched the arrival of the newcomers from the quiet repose of the forest. They scrutinized these strange bi-pedal aliens with blue-tinted skin and elongated heads and large almond-shaped eyes that had come uninvited to their tranquil isle, until now isolate and protected from intrusion by the vast expanse of the Primal Sea. They observed how the slender forms worked as a collective to remove the shiny scales of their battered host piece by piece to make shelters, how they buried their dead, how they mourned their passing.

When that was done, they brought red glowing crystals that shown bright even in daylight from the metallic frame of the silver beast's remains. The crystals they handled with great care and reverence, depositing them in caverns deep in the earth near an inlet on the coast. It was there too, that they began to build with stones.

These were a people with no hope of return or rescue, determined to survive and resolute in their struggle to make a place for themselves. A permanent place that would bring irrevocable change the Isle. To the land, to nature, to a way of life that had existed since time began.

Still the Sylvan watched.

The prophesies spoke of events such as these that would herald the beginning of the Fourth Age, the Age of the Golden Aspen, the Age when the winds from the north would bring an icy chill even in the summertime. And end the elves isolation from the rest of the world forever.

In time the Sylvan learned that the unusual blue-tinted people called themselves the followers of Atlas, the one who had risen among them and offered up hope for a new future. They would name the spine of the island in his honor and build a shining city on the sea that would become known as Atlantis.

And they thrived.

Recorded in the Fourth Age of the Golden Aspen
by Watcher CrellianRafkarSil of Avalon

CHAPTER 1

Origin of Evil

Sylvan Year (SY) 5488

"Summon my brothers."

The jailer backhanded the First Prince of Vradesti across the face, causing a thin trail of blood to run from his left nostril.

"You may demand nothing, dead man," the stout man sneered, wiping his hand on his creaking black leather smock with matching arm sleeves. "Your days of rights and privilege ended when you murdered your parents. And if your brothers want you tortured slowly for your crimes, I will indulge them gladly."

Zracul's long tongue instinctively moved to stem the flow of blood cascading over his lips . . . Or to taste. He reveled in the pleasure of it. The pain was nothing. Certainly, nothing close to what he could endure, and he doubted that the jailer, or any man, could push him past his threshold.

If he had one.

With his wrists and ankles chained to the wall, Zracul had just enough slack to move forward about an arm's length allowing the jailer to see him clearly in the torchlight of his dank cell. He was taller than the jailer, much taller and more powerfully built, but the stupid oaf did not seem afraid, not with the chains in place. He stared arrogantly at Zracul, waiting for him to test the limits of the thick links and realize how powerless he was and beg for mercy. Zracul would die under torture before he gave the fool the satisfaction.

He closed his eyes and allowed his body to relax. The chains that bound Zracul forgotten as a mere inconvenience while he focused on entering the mind of the pathetic sack of rancid flesh in front of him.

"What are you playing at, dead man?" The jailer barely managed to utter the sentence before the arrogant expression melted on his face, replaced by the blank gaze of an imbecile.

Fully in control now, Zracul laughed; there had been no resistance whatsoever. He issued the jailer instructions to retrieve his brothers, tell them he had to say something of grave importance and impressed upon his mind the argument that would make them come. Then he issued his last instruction, the one that gave Zracul particular pleasure – *Blior do ialpvrg*.

The jailer began to walk out the door submissively, then as an afterthought, Zracul called for him to close the door to his cell before sending him on his way again.

It wouldn't be long now.

He sat with his back against the wall and adjusted the chains for his comfort. If his brothers brought guards, this could get messy, he thought. Not that it mattered really, Zracul was covered in blood.

His parents' blood.

It was still sticky and stinking on the expensive black velvet robes that he imported from TaMehu, an exotic land over five hundred leagues away. Zracul would get new robes, more expensive robes next time. He was nothing if not a slave to the finest fashion of the day.

Zracul relaxed and considered what he had done. He thought it would have been difficult, murdering his parents, but once he surrendered to the darkness that consumed him, it was much easier than he would have expected. He'd loved them very dearly—he still loved them—but they had grown old and incompetent, allowing their kingdom to languish in poverty, ignoring opportunities for wealth and expansion. Now it would be up to his brothers and him to put things to right.

If they ever arrived.

He would wait a while, and if it seemed the idiot jailer could not convince them to come, he would find them himself. Zracul shook the chains, testing their weight. He wouldn't even be a prisoner if he hadn't been so overzealous and passed out from exhaustion after the slaughter. He had planned to find his brothers afterward. Instead, he woke up chained in a cell. It didn't matter. Fewer witnesses to what he would do next might work out better for him.

Zracul took in his surroundings. He was the sole occupant of the large cell, but his acute hearing could easily pick up the sounds of rats skittering here and there a few cells over, looking for a place to nest or something to eat. He ignored them. It was the footfalls approaching from beyond the thick wooden door at the top of the long flight of stairs that led to the castle prison that got his attention. Three were approaching.

Good, no guards.

The bolt unlatched with the click of a key in the lock, the heavy door creaked open, and the steps grew louder. Finally, there they were, his brothers Vadim and Fain, standing with the jailer in front of his cell.

"Open the door," Vadim ordered coldly, and the jailer moved to comply.

Within seconds the cell door stood open, and the brothers walked in to face him. They looked angry and hurt, their faces traversed with lines of tears streaked across their faces and their fine jackets over tight-fitting trousers stained with sticky crimson. Zracul could imagine the tragic scene when his brothers came upon their parents' bodies – the shock, the horror, the final embraces, and the ultimate realization that they were lost. They'd loved their parents as much or more than he did and all three brothers, along with their two young sisters, had been a close family. It must be painful losing so many people you love at one time, Zracul mused. He would remedy that shortly.

The jailer quietly retreated along the line of cells. He had one last instruction to carry out. Zracul almost stopped him, he might have been a good servant, and he *had* managed to get his brothers here. But he decided against it, considering the blood that still trickled from his nose.

"What is it that you want?" demanded Fain. "You were laughing hysterically over the corpses of our parents when last we saw you."

"Yes," Vadim added vehemently, "what do you have to say now that you couldn't say then?"

Zracul regarded his brothers for a moment. They were so innocent, so beautiful at that moment. He hated himself for what was about to happen; he hated the thing inside of him that had forced him to make the deal. With all the choices and compromises he had to make, this was the best way for everyone.

Because he loved them.

With a swiftness that none save himself knew he possessed, Zracul ripped the chains from the walls, sending a spray of stone bits and dust into the air. Before either brother could blink, he had them each in a powerful grip, sending them flying into the wall he had just vacated. They landed in a heap with the dust settling on their still forms never reaching the floor beneath them.

He had not killed them, but now he would have full control and their undivided attention when they regained their senses. His brothers were students of magic, like himself, and quite accomplished in their skills. He closed off that part of their minds when they started to come around; Zracul didn't need the inconvenience of dodging spells while he attempted to have a civil conversation with them.

Vadim was first to open his eyes and glare up at him. Blood matted the hair near his temple and saturated the fabric of his white shirt and jacket collar. "What are you, brother? What thing have you become that you can cast us around like dolls?"

Zracul waited.

Fain stirred then, although he did so quietly; he was a crafty one when he wanted to be. Then he gasped. "I am cut off, brother," he whispered urgently to Vadim.

"You both are. We need to talk." Zracul motioned for them to sit up and he sat on the floor opposite.

There was a scream then, from far off in the depths of the castle — a desperate scream filled with pain and agony.

Vadim stood. "What is that?"

Zracul calmly motioned for him to sit. "The jailer. He is standing in the incinerator. He should be dead soon."

"Why would he do that?" Fain demanded.

Zracul shrugged. "Because I told him to. It was his reward."

"Reward? Reward for what?" Vadim sprang to his feet, his eyes wild with disbelief.

"He struck me earlier. I am yet a prince of nobility. It could have been worse for him."

Vadim sank to the floor, and they all listened to the jailer's suffering. It went on and on to the point that Zracul wished he had just snapped his neck. It was so distracting he couldn't continue speaking with his brothers until the screams stopped. Why couldn't the man just die?

Finally, after what seemed like an interminable eternity, it ended.

Tears were running down Fain's face. He had always been the emotional one of the three of them. "There is something evil in you, brother."

"Good of you to bring that up. That's why we're are all here today – to discuss what I am now and what effect that will have on your futures." Zracul tried to keep a normal tone, not cheery, not somber. He wanted them to understand the pragmatic nature of everything he had done for them.

Vadim and Fain remained silent, looking at him for all the world as if he were insane. Maybe he was and didn't know it yet. Maybe it was all a dream. Whatever it was, they would be part of it now.

"Do you remember how sick I was recent? For weeks I lay in my bed sometimes lucid, sometimes not, but always struggling with something unseen. It was a sickness that would pass, Mother would say, and they brought in healers from every part of the kingdom. But I did not get better, and it did not pass. Father was at the point that he could not take the screaming anymore and was on the verge of sending me off to a temple bedlam convinced I would never get better. He would have been right to do so."

"Are you mad, brother?" Fain's eyes held fear when he asked. And hope.

"I wish it were so brother; everything would be so much simpler if that were the case. What I am now is much more than what I was before, and I must admit, the power is addicting."

Vadim looked skeptical, "Power?"

"Yes, Vadim. For weeks, it whispered to me in dreams and at the edge of consciousness. I listened not knowing what it was or where it was coming from until it almost had me convinced and that's when it struck. To my horror, the attack came from inside of me." Zracul wiped the remaining blood from his face as he spoke. "I struggled for weeks to repel what I could not see and only feel. It was inside my head trying to take control, but I sensed that I was much stronger than it expected."

Fain's features darkened and he appeared upset by the memory of that time. "The things that you screamed . . . were profane. Our sisters heard the words not knowing what they meant; the household heard them and there were whispers."

"I feel the worst for our sisters. They should never have endured what I put them through, but I will save them as well." Zracul paused while he pried open the metal clasps on his wrists and ankles with his newly acquired unnatural strength. His brothers watched him with wide-eyed fascination as he broke the locks and bent back the metal as if it was made of parchment.

"To everyone else, I was sick or going insane. To me, it was a terrible battle for my mind, my sanity, myself. If I lost, it would control me, and if I won, it would be forced to flee. Every day we fought to a stalemate, but I was losing my strength little by little until I resolved that I would let myself die before allowing it to take me. That got its attention."

"What was it, brother?" Vadim shifted uncomfortably. "Did it force you to do these terrible things?"

"It was something terrible, far more terrible than even I could have imagined. And when I decided to die, the struggle ended. We spoke then, a civil conversation you could say. It wanted something, and so did I. So, we came to an agreement."

"What sort of agreement, Zracul? Some mad deal with the devil that has taken your soul?" Vadim's face reddened with anger. "How will you save yourself after what you have done? There is no redemption!"

"But there is, brother." Zracul slowly crawled toward them on his hands and knees. It was time. "And there is power beyond what you could ever imagine. The choice is no longer yours, or our sisters. I have saved the family, our legacy. Our lineage will continue immortal. And at such a small price! The blood of an aged monarch and his queen!"

The heavy doors leading to the cell block that were carelessly left open by the jailer all slammed shut at the same time, echoing deafeningly through the prison vaults followed by a chill, unnatural wind. Zracul decided then that it was indeed good fortune that he had been dragged to the dungeon, no one would hear the screams of his brothers through the thick stone walls.

~~~

Zracul sat in the small throne room attended by his two

brothers and young twin sisters. The blood of his parents that so recently stained the floor, carpets, and furniture had been cleaned or burned, while the servants and guards who knew the truth about their deaths were dispatched with equal efficiency.

Despite efforts to keep news of the tragedy within the confines of the palace, rumors flew on swift wings to the furthest reaches of the kingdom. Within hours, all knew that the king and queen were murdered by an assassin in the dead of night. The story described the murderer as a tradesman angry about high taxes and poor living conditions. Starving and unable to provide for his family, he was driven to madness. It was a tale concocted by Zracul soon after he freed himself, knowing that there was enough truth in it to make it believable. There would be no trial since there was no real assassin and the disfigured body of a middle-aged man that no one could recognize was displayed to the public. It was a gruesome end to the killer that fit nicely with the corpses of half a dozen guards and servants silenced for what they had witnessed.

As the First Prince, Zracul was next in line for the throne, but it was a mantle he was unwilling to be burdened with until he was much further along with his plans. Instead, he announced that he and his brothers would co-rule until a year passed in honor of their fallen parents. That would give him the time he needed. The crowds had reacted favorably and embraced their new sovereigns, just as Zracul knew they would.

That was not why they gathered together this night.

It was late, and all the servants and guards had been sent away for the night. Dim light flickered eerily off the sizeable portraits of the royal family going back generations. They were spaced around the room between tapestries depicting scenes of the hunt and ritual celebrations. The artful fabrics served to insulate and conceal all but the large double doors standing opposite the throne.

His throne.

Zracul's brothers, Vadim and Fain, had been difficult to tame in the beginning but they eventually accepted his dominance and came around. His sisters, Daria and Jaria, were far less of a challenge. They were young, and their minds not disciplined by years of magic study. All they had to endure was his lust to corrupt their bodies and his bite to subjugate their will.

Now they were all one big happy family again

Zracul told them of the demon that shared his body, he knew it as Ornias but had no power to utter its name to others. To do so would give mortals power to send it to the Infernal Planes, which the demon would never willingly allow. Tonight, Ornias would speak to Zracul's family directly through his host. He was going to transform them into more than what they were now, more than they had ever been, by fusing their unique abilities with his darkness and create a new race of immortals to dominate the world.

He called them Vampyr.

It was not the first time Ornias tried to father a new race; he had failed more than once in the recent past, leaving creatures of the night to be hunted and afraid in the places he had been. This time would be different. This time he had the power of his host joined to the power wielded by his brothers. He had never had access to so much power at one time before. Zracul knew all of this and more. Much more. His mind was one with the spirit of darkness that had become his personal demon. Now they were gathered together to make an unholy beginning that would reign until the end of days.

Zracul stood from his father's throne, ready to allow Ornias to address his family. "None of you here is unique in your circumstance. I have fathered others like you throughout the world. They feed on their own kind and hide in the shadows of the night." Zracul paced the room between them as the demon spoke with his tongue. "Those others will never survive."

The voice that came out of his body was deep and

rumbling like an animal trying to speak through a snout designed to rip and tear flesh rather than articulate language, and yet the words held power. Zracul could see and hear and smell, but it was the demon that controlled his form. He passed by a large mirror set in the wall and was struck by the glimpse of what he saw –black velvet robes, leather boots, long black hair that hung below his shoulders, deep angular features that women always favored, close-cut beard and mustache along with dark eyebrows and pale skin. These were the parts he recognized as himself, but it was his eyes, once soft and inviting, that were now black and so engulfing that for a moment Zracul was startled not to find familiarity with his own face. Had the demon purposefully given him this glimpse just to prove how inseparable they were now? He never wished to see that image again.

The demon continued, "But that is all about to change. You will no longer fear the sunlight. You will enjoy greater strength and endurance far beyond even the mightiest human. The night will be your friend and during the dark hours your physical abilities will be enhanced – your vision, your form, your mortality. Power over creatures of the night and more I will grant to you. Never will you want for nourishment, as everything that lives around you will feed your immortality. Human blood will sustain you longer than the blood of any animal or conjured creature, but beware the Sylvan, as their blood will kill our kind."

Zracul stopped pacing and faced his family; they were much like him already without the demon and the promised augmentations. They were still animals. If left to their own, they could hunt at night and feed on the living. And they would age and die as easily as any living creature.

"Now, open yourselves to me. I command it! I will take from you what I require to make you all my immortal children!"

Zracul could feel his power forcibly drawn into his dark consciousness where the demon dwelled. At first, he worried that he would be overcome by it, scorched and overwhelmed by the enormity of so much of it at once, but the power flowed into the void within him and was . . . Consumed. Then Ornias drew on the power from Vadim. He could feel it race through him and again into oblivion, like a black hole that swallowed everything and gave back nothing.

"From Vadim, you will all learn to transform into a creature or element, cause darkness around you even in daylight and beguile those with weak minds!"

A black tendril snaked between Vadim and Zracul undulating slowly, drawing the power deliberately. Vadim did not move, not even a blink and Zracul wondered if he could. Then power was rushing from Fain, and he could see the undulating tendril connecting them as well.

"From Fain, you will learn to bring forth and control the dead and lesser demons to serve your will! They will be your consorts, your servants and your protectors."

The tendrils went out to the twins at the same time connecting them both to him.

"Daria and Jaria will contribute their youth and reproduction! You will never grow old and any child of your union with a mortal will be born as we are, despising their weaker parent for who they are."

The room began to spin around him. If his brothers and sisters felt the same, they surely did not show it. Zracul was at the center and it spun faster and faster.

"You will become immortal! But beware your vulnerabilities! You will die to fire, dismemberment, decapitation, the blood of a Sylvan and a shaft through your heart. Avoid these things, and you will live forever!"

The room suddenly stopped spinning. They all stood at the point of a perfect pentagram, the black tendrils forming the lines, Zracul at its northern point, the others facing him.

"I am your Father! I am your God! Where I go you will

follow unto undeath as we remake the world in the image of our choosing!"

Power, unlike anything Zracul had ever felt before in his life suddenly and surprisingly surged from the black void that was the demon inside his mind. Through him and into the tendrils that connected their life forces, first into Daria and then Jaria. They fell dead to the floor; he could feel their life slip into nothing.

Zracul screamed and tried to stop the flow but he was powerless. He watched horrified as Fain and then Vadim died where they stood. Then it was rushing into him, and his vision went black, his breathing stopped. He felt the cold hand of death wrap around his heart squeezing the warmth of life from him.

Such pain!

"Damn you back to your hell, demon!" he screamed with his final breath before his body fell to join the corpses of his family on the cold stone floor – dead.

Undead.

~~~

Count Terril Djago stood atop the highest crenelated tower of the inner keep overlooking the green expanse of Cambria that stretched out before him. This land was his home and he was proud of what his family had made of it over the centuries. Although he ruled a mere county with a single fortified city, his power and influence rivaled that of the grandest Duchies in the kingdom of Lyonesse. Even now, he hosted the king's brother, Duke Banfield Eldorath of Yorwick, a man he had known for years and counted among his closest friends.

"The view of Cambria from this height is astounding, Terril!" the duke exclaimed. "Why have you never invited me to take in this wondrous sight in all the years I have known you?"

Count Djago effected a look of effrontery and then slapped his friend on the shoulder, punctuating the move with a rolling laugh. "Because we have always been too drunk to climb so many stairs!"

Laughing with him, the duke sloshed the half-filled wooden tankard. "Well, I certainly cannot begrudge your reasons for staying mostly sober this time. Have you had any luck with your endeavors so far?"

"Lady Genestra has made me very lucky nearly every night," the count smiled slyly. "But for our purpose, we have not had the success we wish for yet."

"There is no complication?"

"No, no," Djago shook his head. "The druids assure us it is simply a matter of time and persistence."

The duke elbowed Djago playfully. "Just be satisfied with all the practice then. After the duchess squeezed out two of our own, I am lucky for a visit from her once in a fortnight!"

"You have an heir! Her work is done!"

"That is true." Banfield nodded in agreement. "Now show me all the fabulous points of interest in Cambria so that I might recognize them from here."

Although it was hours into the night, Cambria was alive with the glow of torches and light-globes along every street. Count Djago pointed toward a domed building surrounded by a cluster of smaller structures. "There is the Temple of Sunna." Pointing south of the temple was a series of buildings set in regular rows surrounding a long open patch of ground. "There is the Military College." He shifted his arm toward the north near the center of the city and indicated a high tower with a smooth exterior and several balconies along its length. Most notable was a crimson pyramid-shaped crystal that rotated slowly at its apex radiating its light far into the distance. "And, of course, the Atlanteans."

Djago slowly cast his gaze over the city. Cambria was surrounded by a high crenelated stone wall that extended into the waters of the Fin River where the port was bustling with trade vessels sailing in and out at all hours of the night.

"How are the borders?"

Frowning slightly, Djago spat off the side of the tower. "The usual. Strange creatures from Fomoire are somehow finding their way across the Sea of Dragons and into our villages and settlements. I must have half an army patrolling the Fin between here and the coast, and still innocent lives are lost. I fear it will always be so."

"Lindpoole has it worse," the duke replied. "The king would be grateful if you would send another company of swordsmen to help them on the land side."

Djago sighed. "Is that the true purpose of your visit, Banfield? If Lindpoole would use their resources less on ships and more on soldiers they wouldn't need our help."

"We are men of position and politics, Terril. There are always ulterior motives in our business. We are exceptional in that we have maintained our friendship despite who we are." The duke shrugged. "And you know what Lindpoole faces on the Sea of Dragons – monsters from Fomoire, raids by the Vikja, not to mention the eternally frigid weather. I do not envy Count Temprest."

"He is a good man," Djago agreed. "Assure your brother that we will send a company to Lindpoole right away."

Duke Eldorath lay his hand on Djago's shoulder. "You are a good man as well, like your father before you, and I pray that you will sire a strong heir to follow in your family's footsteps."

CHAPTER 2

Rise of Kumida

Fomoire translates as 'The Place of Fire and Ice' in the language of the Tuatha Dé, and it is an apt description indeed. I've walked its treacherous land and witnessed the ice avalanches in the mountains and rivers of molten rock that flow through the flatlands. And there are terrible places where both exist together – volcanic explosions that rip through the ice and seas of noxious mists where not even the hardiest of creatures can survive. As if that weren't enough, more than three thousand years ago the Tuatha Dé inhabited this hell on earth with some of the most magnificently vile monsters of their own making. True horrors isolated from the rest of the world as a result of a civil war that became known as the 'Breaking.' The Tuatha Dé thought themselves compassionate. They thought themselves humane. They thought they would find redemption in their act of kindness for not simply exterminating the abominations they created. Perhaps they should have thought it through a little more.

Wodanaz the Wanderer

"Hey, Kumida! Where you off to?" The man who spoke was the largest of three huddled around a fire. His gruff voice dripped with mockery and disdain as if he were speaking to a slave about to be while a single eye under a thick brown bushy brow glared at loathing.

da stopped in his tracks. Frikok and his two friends had y times in the past. He hoped that it was too cold for o again today. Cyclops, even those of his clan, had eir weaker brethren. And these three were the worst. He tried to think of something clever to say that would distract them from hurling more insults at him, or worse, make them angry enough to abandon their warm fire and beat him for the fun of it. "Huntin'," was all he could come up with.

"Huntin'?" Frikok elbowed the man next to him as if he were about to tell a great joke. "What you gonna hunt? More of them scrawny rabbits? Why don't you bring us a fat boar that we can roast on the fire? We might even share some with ya!" The other men laughed at that.

Kumida wondered if they really would share this time. Whenever they saw him return with his rabbits, they always took them and beat him harshly if he complained about it. "OK."

"OK?" the man repeated. "What are you gonna hunt 'em with? That scrawny spear?"

Kumida glanced at the spear in his fist. He thought it was a fine spear, fashioned from a limb of oak and sharpened to a fine point. Maybe it wasn't as large as the ones they carried or have a metal tip, but . . .

"Take this one!" Frikok shouted gleefully.

Kumida looked up just in time to dodge the lethal projectile, and his quick movement caused him to stumble into a passerby.

"Hey! Get off me boy!" The Giant cuffed him on the shoulder sending Kumida face down into the icy mud.

Frikok and his friends roared with laughter while the one who sent him sprawling walked on in disgust. Kumida staggered to his feet, covered in a cold, rancid sludge. He was raging inside. He wanted nothing more than to stick his dagger into the single eye of these hateful men. But he couldn't show it. To do so would surely get him a beating on top of the humiliation he had already endured.

"There he is!" Frikok announced to no one in particul "Kumida, the great boar hunter!"

The laughter renewed, and all Kumida could do was wipe the grime from his face and eye. He considered running away, but if he did, they would find great sport in chasing him down. It was miserable living this way. He was smaller than most other Cyclops even a year younger than himself, and he had no living family or friends who might offer protection from the daily harassment. Worse still, he knew that Giants of his size brought shame to the clan, a sign of weak breeding. Eventually, he'd be shunned or killed outright. Maybe he should leave his clan before it came to that. He idly wondered if he could he survive alone in the wild.

Kumida was still cleaning the filth off his tattered clothing when he heard Frikok speak again. "Lugal! What's that you have over your shoulder?"

To Kumida's relief, his tormenter was distracted for a moment. The Cyclops Frikok spoke to was carrying what appeared to be the naked form of a human. It was odd how nearly hairless they were.

"Another hero," Lugal replied without stopping.

"Save me a leg, would ya?" Frikok laughed.

Lugal didn't even spare a glance in Frikok's direction. "Get yer own."

Frikok laughed as if the joke were on Lugal and then set his angry gaze on Kumida once more. "What are you doing here, boy? Get going and don't come home without that boar or we'll pound you to pieces this time!"

Kumida picked up his spear and didn't stop running until he was out of sight of the village.

The rocky terrain of the evergreen forest was well known to Kumida. He had spent as much time in this wilderness as in the village while growing up. These days even more so. There were many caves in the nearby foothills that he enjoyed exploring and often used when he camped overnight. Of course, he had to chase out the occasional bear or saber-toothed mountain lion, but even the largest of them was merely an annoyance. Aside from his people and Giants from neighboring territories, his only fear was the humans from the south. If they came alone, then they were easy prey. It was when they came in groups that they were dangerous. At least twice in his life, Kumida had been chased by their hunting parties. They came with weapons, wore armor and sometimes rode four-legged beasts he learned were called horses. And they were hunting for the sport of it. That's how his father died only a year before – murdered by a pack of humans. They dragged his remains across the Sea of Dragons never to be seen again. Kumida swore from that day to kill and eat as many humans as he could get his hands on. All Giants, Cyclopes included, hated them.

Kumida glanced around nervously. He had never killed a boar before. They grew very large in this forest and could kill him as easily as Frikok and his friends if he wasn't careful. The only reason he knew anything about killing them was from watching his father. But his father was a large Cyclops who could stand his ground against the inevitable charge. Kumida was sure that he could not. He would have to think of a different way of going about it. Otherwise, he might as well stick to trapping rabbits and never return to his village to face the wrath of Frikok and his friends.

Frikok had never demanded anything other than a rabbit from him before. Now he wanted a boar. Kumida knew nothing about tracking them or what they ate to bait a trap. Maybe this was Frikok's way of getting rid of him for good.

Kumida walked deeper into the forest with no particular destination in mind. If he was lucky, he might come across a bush with sweet wild berries. They should be in season now that the worst of winter was over. With that thought driving him, he decided to go further south and search for the elusive berries near the banks of the Arges River. There would be more wildlife near the water as well, possibly even a boar.

The Arges River was a few days south of Kumida's village, and he was looking forward to the journey. It wasn't often that he went anywhere or did anything with purpose, but today would be different, and the idea of it put a spring in his step. He had no obligations to concern himself with at the village. No one would wonder where he went or why he was gone so long. No one would miss or look for him. Kumida doubted that anyone would even notice his absence. Given his circumstances, it was probably better that way.

The crack of a branch in the still forest drew his attention. It came from somewhere ahead of him. Kumida knew that no animal would be so careless. Monster or beast, it was probably watching him already. He proceeded cautiously.

The rustle of leaves and a sharp twang alerted him to a presence in the bushes. A second later he was jarred by a sudden jolt and a sharp sting in his left shoulder where a shaft with feathers had sprouted.

"Got him!" a voice from the bushes exclaimed.

"Good shot, Wilfred!" another replied. "Hit him with another!"

A second twang and something buzzed past Kumida's head.

"Missed him!" the voice spoke again. "Was aiming for his blasted eye!"

"Good try. Was that your last arrow?"

"Yes . . ." the voice moaned.

Kumida still couldn't see them, but he knew where they were, and they sounded human.

"Well, Wilfred, let's finish him off. You can have his head as a trophy since this is your first time out."

Two human men stepped out of the bushes twenty paces from where Kumida stood. One appeared older than the other, and they both wore leather armor under thick furs. Each carried a long steel sword in one hand and a travel pack in the other. They looked like every human who had ever chased him in these woods, except that there were two of them. Kumida needn't run from just two.

Grabbing the shaft of the arrow in his shoulder, he jerked it out roughly. It hurt. Badly. Rage flooded through him at the pain and for the one who put it there. He stared hard at the humans and roared. It was a deep, feral sound that echoed off the trees around him. Startled, the humans took an involuntary step backward.

"You said you've killed these things before, Geralt?" the younger one asked his companion nervously.

"It . . . it's been a while . . ." Geralt replied weakly.

Kumida charged.

The men's eyes widened with fear, and they dropped their travel packs and raised their swords in front of them.

It didn't take long for Kumida's long legs to cover the distance between them. Considered small for a Cyclops, he was still easily four times the weight of the humans and he charged them with a spear they would consider the size of a small tree. Courageous as the men were, they were nearly in full flight when Kumida barreled into them. The younger man was thrown a good distance to the side while the older human fell under the crush of Kumida's weight.

Pressing on the man with his massive hands, Kumida got to his feet. There was a sharp pain in his abdomen with blood saturating his shabby tunic and trousers. The human was still on the ground. His body twisted and broken, he tried and couldn't stand, yet he still lived, eyes darting around fearfully as if looking for something. His sword lay on the ground next to him, coated in Kumida's blood.

"Run, Wilfred!" the man on the ground screamed.

Movement on his left, Kumida swiveled to face the young human, sword held high.

"Get away from him!" the boy shrieked. "Run, monster!"

"Wilfred, no! Leave me!"

Kumida roared in pain and anger at the young man, then ran his spear through the boy's chest.

"Nooo!" the older human cried out, desperately struggling to move.

With tremendous effort, Kumida pulled his spear from the body of the human called Wilfred and sat heavily on the ground. His abdomen was bleeding badly, and it hurt to move. He would need to find a place to rest soon.

He glanced over at the man called Geralt sobbing where he lay. "I will eat that one" Kumida gestured toward the human Wilfred. "You, I leave to the beasts in the forest. They will be hungry after such a long winter."

The man struggled to move but did not speak. Kumida wasn't sure if he could. Blood was running from his nose and the side of his mouth. He was gasping more than sobbing now, clearly experiencing some trouble breathing. Kumida didn't care. Nor did he have the energy to finish him off.

Standing with the help of his spear, Kumida slowly walked to where the young human lay. He grabbed one of his feet and slowly dragged the body behind him. There was a cave nearby that he had used on several occasions. He hoped it was still empty. In his current condition, he might not be able to dislodge its tenant.

An hour later, Kumida stared into the dark interior of a small cavern. To his relief, it was unoccupied. He dragged the dead human to a corner of the cave and then found a flat, dry spot to lay down. Pulling his thick fur cape around himself tightly, he lamented that he didn't have the strength to build a fire. The night would bring below-freezing temperatures. He knew that he was going to die in this cave. Whether from loss of blood or freezing to death he did not know. It hardly mattered. The human had killed him. He smiled. At least he took them both with him.

Time seemed to pass slowly as he watched the morning light turn to afternoon through his barely cracked eyelids. He was so tired. Then suddenly it was dark, and the chill was so stark that he thought he might freeze right then. Had he fallen asleep and awakened to the night? Or could he be dreaming? His eyes closed, and he felt himself falling. Darkness swallowed him, and in his last moments, he knew that he was not alone.

~~~

The Cyclops that was once Kumida awoke in the dark. It was night. Only three days earlier he had killed two humans hunting trophy beasts in the forest. One was in the cave with him now. The stink of the rotting corpse filled his nostrils and made his stomach growl with hunger. He sat up and looked around with his single eye, somehow capable of seeing clearly in the dark.

That's not all that had changed. Memories flooded through him.

His body had grown muscular and massive, far larger than any Cyclopes he had ever seen and nearly as large as the mountain Giants in the north. There were certain other magical skills as well, but far fewer than he had hoped. This body had a stupid intellect and the Chaos Demon that now possessed it was limited by its host's natural potential.

It would have to be enough.

Even the brightest of the Cyclopes would pose little challenge to him. He smiled, the memories of Kumida's life with his clan spinning through his mind. They had not treated his host well. What a surprise they were in for when he returned. First, however, he had to eat.

Kumida lumbered over to where the remains of the young human lay. Not bothering to start a fire to cook it, he pulled apart the bloated limbs and pried open the chest cavity with his bare hands to eat the choicest parts raw.

When he finished, only a little fat and splintered bone remained. So famished was he from the physical transformation he had even sucked out the marrow. He was hungry still but satisfied for the moment.

Kumida picked up his spear, it appeared small and brittle in his hands, unlike his previous memories when he considered it his most valuable possession. He snapped the hardwood in half effortlessly and discarded it on the cavern floor. It was a useless thing now.

He strode from the cave into the chill night air. Fomoire was dangerous during the day, but the danger paled in comparison to the foul creatures that hunted at night. Kumida was unafraid. He briefly thought about the human hunter he left in the forest and wondered if he had survived until that night. He hoped he had. The human deserved to witness the horrors that would fight over his flesh.

Taking a few deep breaths to prepare his lungs for the long run ahead he set off in the direction of his village. His plan was simple. By morning the clan chief would be dead, Kumida would have taken his wives, and Frikok and his friends would be his slaves—if he allowed them to live. After that, he would find a way to sow blood and turmoil across this land like nothing seen before. The thought of it brought joy to a body that had never felt the emotion until that moment.

~~~

Kumida sat in a massive rough-hewn stone chair padded with pillows at the center of the Great Hut that was considered the ruling place of his clan. He was alone and it was late. His wives were asleep, as were nearly everyone in the village except for two of his guards that stood outside.

Waiting.

He was awaiting the arrival of Steropes, chief of the Cyclopes clan known as the Melanochroti, a powerful clan that would be essential to Kumida's designs for the future. He could have waited until the morning to receive the chief, but Kumida was impatient and would have the loyalty of Steropes or his head before the sun came up.

In the quiet cold night, Kumida thought back to his triumphant return to his clan. It was bitter for some, maybe most, but he didn't care. From the start, they'd tried to mock him, notwithstanding his astonishing new size, and he ripped their throats out until there was no one left with a voice to complain. He pronounced himself the clan chief, and none dared dispute his authority. It was a claim achieved by right of combat, the survival of the strongest, and his ascendance brought with it rivers of blood and death.

Frikok and his cohorts were among his first victims. Kumida planned to enslave them, but his anger got the better of him, and he bled them on stakes for days before they died. The family of the previous chief was the last to die – wives, brothers, sisters, and heirs. He killed them all. It was a pleasure for him to indulge his sadistic nature. Many of them did not receive a quick death.

Now, nearly a year later he was negotiating with the other clans, Cyclopes and otherwise, to secure their loyalty before he invaded the south. Lyonesse, Eriu, Ys and eventually Courth, would all fall to the Giants of Fomoire. The Western kingdoms would be his before he set his sights further south or east. Nothing would stop him.

Light from torches set around the room flickered with the breeze that rushed in when the thick hides that covered the doorway parted and a guard walked in. "He is here."

Kumida snatched a clay mug from the stone pedestal next to his chair and hurled it at the man, its contents spraying across the floor before shattering on the guard's chest. "Then bring him here, you idiot!"

The guard nodded, completely unaffected by the occurrence of the mug, and departed the hut. Kumida did not have long to wait. Shortly, the flaps opened again to reveal a massive Cyclops, nearly the size of Kumida himself, filling the doorway.

Kumida waved him in. "Sit, Steropes."

The Cyclops chief strode into the room and stood defiantly two paces away. He was an unusual looking Cyclops with ebony skin, long black hair tied in a high ponytail and a single green eye under a heavy brow. It was said that he was the most powerful and dangerous of all the Cyclopes in Fomoire. Kumida would change that.

"So, it is true." Steropes surveyed him like some strange animal. "You have changed from the sniveling midget I saw last time I was here." Contempt coated the words that spewed from his enraging smirk. "At least you washed the mud off your face."

Kumida sprang from his throne and grasped Steropes by the neck. The Melanochroti chief's eye widened and filled with fear at the shock of the sudden violence and clutched vainly at Kumida's arms to break the chokehold. Kumida wanted to crush his throat and display his head on a spike outside the Great Hut, but doing so would cause open warfare among the Cyclopes tribes and right now he needed allies. Loyal, obedient allies. With overwhelming strength, he pushed Steropes to his knees, delighting in the bulging eye and dark shade of purple that crept over the clan chief's face.

"You will sit when I command it!" Kumida spat in his face and released him.

Steropes fell forward, gasping for air, while Kumida calmly returned to his chair. When he finally regained his breath, he stared up at Kumida with a rage-filled glare, but he did not stand.

"What sorcery possesses you?" Steropes' voice was hoarse and dry. "No Cyclops has such speed and strength."

Kumida laughed at the irony of his statement. "Don't you see, Steropes? I am blessed by Arges."

"Arges?" Steropes sounded uncertain. "Arges lives in Aitva. How can he bestow such blessings from so far away?"

Kumida shrugged. "He is a god. I do not question how the gods work their magic."

"What do you want."

"I want you to submit and swear loyalty to me."

Steropes shifted to sit with his legs crossed. "I swear loyalty to the Fir Bholg king, Cug, as we all do."

"No more!" Kumida's rage was rising again. "I will be the first King of the Cyclopes and eventually Cug will bow to me or die from the effort!"

"You are mad. There will be war among the Giants."

"Perhaps," Kumida nodded, "but not among the Cyclopes. You should know that Brontes declared for me yesterday."

Brontes was chief of the third Cyclopes clan in Fomoire. Kumida nearly had to kill him to gain his submission. In the end, Kumida took Brontes's eldest son as a hostage to ensure his loyalty.

"The Fir Bholg are much larger than us and they have shamans. Our people are farmers. If you confront Cug, you will kill us all."

Kumida leaned forward. "That is true. But we have numbers and their shamans magic can do little to harm us. Most importantly, you have me."

"What if I refuse to follow you?"

Kumida scratched himself, then leaned forward until he was eye level with Steropes. "I will take your wives, kill your children and put your flayed body on display for your entire tribe to see."

"My people would rise against you!"

"And they would die horribly for it. Is that what you want for them?"

Steropes started to his feet and then stopped.

Kumida gestured indifferently. "You may rise."

Steropes stood and bowed stiffly. "I swear the loyalty and obedience of myself and clan Melanochroti until the day that you die."

Smiling broadly, Kumida rose from his chair. "Be careful not to pray for that last part, Steropes. Arges may hear you and bring your own instead.

~~~

"You must find the Mad Wizard known as Geoffrass. He has the tome we are looking for. But beware! He is talented in the magical arts and his apprentice, a Dvergr Dwarf called Firolin, is said to be no less capable."

Vadim dropped the body of a dead servant at the base of the

elevated throne where Zracul sat regarding him coldly. Then, he glanced at his brother Fain before he responded. "Brother, you know what we are now. Do you have such meager confidence in us?"

Prince Zracul felt heat rise inside his head and with deliberate cadence, set his fierce gaze first on one brother and then the other. "I know your black hearts, and I own your dark minds. My confidence in the two of you is absolute as long as you do not fail."

"Do we kill him, or make him one of us?" Fain's question caught him by surprise. He had not considered the Mad Wizard as a possible ally.

But too much was at stake.

"Try not to kill him if you can. I need answers about the tome."

"Perhaps you should send Jaria and Daria to accompany us," Fain spoke with a hint of jest.

Prince Zracul did not find the humor in the suggestion. "They serve me, alone. Now go; I will follow soon."

Bowing low, Vadim and Fain exited the throne room.

"Do you love your brothers more than us?" Jaria strode seductively from the shadows behind the massive, high-backed throne where Prince Zracul sat. Daria, an identical twin to Jaria, strode from the opposite side. Both women betrayed supernatural beauty barely hidden by their sheer gossamer gowns.

Zracul snorted unappreciatively. "My lust is for you; my love is for my brothers."

Jaria traced a long fingernail along the bone-line of his jaw, pricking it at the very end and drawing a drop of blood which she lightly set upon her long tongue. "How can we earn your love, brother?"

A smile twisted the features of Zracul's face, never reaching his eyes. "With your service and your lives."

Jaria and Daria converged on the throne and leaned in to kiss his lips. Zracul felt the thrill of pleasure in their touch and allowed himself to succumb to it. If nothing else, he would be distracted from his worries for the next few hours and diverted from the fresh corpse whose blood stained the purple porphyry before him like so many others before.

CHAPTER 3

Fast Changes

"A little closer . . ." Perault muttered quietly to himself.

He watched the silhouette of a man silently glide from one tree to another while occasionally stopping to strain his neck, listen and peer through the shadows in every direction. The man knew he was being pursued. Soon the dogs would pick up his scent again, and there would be no more creeks to throw them off his stink. It was dumb luck that Perault had guessed which direction the scoundrel would take to circle back to the game trail where he left his horse tied to a thicket. Now Perault waited patiently out of sight, knowing that the man would show up to reclaim his mount to make a swift getaway.

Perault had other plans for him.

One thing Perault was not, was stealthy, and he knew that if he moved from his hidden position, he would likely be detected. The one he watched, however, had skills. The man moved with care through the forest, knew where to step and more importantly, where not to step. He barely made a sound. Perault studied his mannerisms and noted the contrast between his fine dress and practiced maneuverings. There was a sword on his waist, and a long dagger in his boot like a woodsman might wear. But Perault doubted he was any woodsman. What he did know was that the man was a thief.

Just an hour earlier, a servant in Sir Aldeman's household had raised the alarm. Jewels once belonging to the old knight's deceased wife had been taken and a man no one knew fled through the kitchens only moments later. Perault happened to be attending his horse in the stable and witnessed the thief disappear into the forest. Learning what happened a few moments later, Perault raced after him in quick pursuit.

It wasn't long before Perault realized he had no idea which direction the thief had taken once he was in the forest and little aptitude for tracking him. Fortunately, Sir Aldeman's dog-handler was also nearby, heard the commotion and quickly assembled a few of his best canines. The chase was on. So far, not much had gone right for the hapless thief.

Now Perault sat and watched. Seconds passed and he lost sight of the man. The sun was near to the horizon and the shadows were thick in the forest. He wasn't worried. The thief would be along for his horse soon enough.

"Waiting for me?"

There was a sharp pressure between his shoulder blades. Anyone else might have panicked and died right then. Not Perault. He was patient and rarely startled into brash action.

"Are you going to push that blade through and finish this or may I turn and face my assailant?"

The pressure grew slightly at first and then pulled away altogether. "Stand up." The thief commanded.

Perault got to his feet and slowly turned to face the man. He was holding a slender long sword a hand-span from his chest.

"What is your name?" Perault asked calmly.

"None of your affair. Now tell me, why are you hiding in wait to ambush me?"

Perault scoffed. "I would never stoop to ambush or run a man through the back. I assure you that my face would be among the last images before you died."

The insult was not wasted on the man. "Looks like the tables have turned then, haven't they?"

Bile rose to Perault's throat – not from fear, it was disgust, and he spat on the ground between them. "You have made many mistakes today, thief, and allowing me to face you will be your last."

"Is that so?" the man laughed. "From where I stand, the future looks rather dim for you."

The baying of dogs rose in the distance. They had found the thief's trail again and would soon arrive. The same thoughts must have been going through the thief's mind, and he began to back away toward his horse.

Perault took a step forward. "Give up now, and it will be up to Sir Aldeman to hang you or send you to the mines. If you try to run, I will kill you."

The thief barked a laugh and continued to move toward his horse. "I don't think you will get the opportuni . . ." The words stuck in his throat, literally, as the hilt of a dagger sprouted neatly below his Adam's apple. Eyes wide in shock, he slowly sank to his knees, dropping his slender sword and falling before a trickle of blood could exit the wound.

Tentatively, Perault rolled the sputtering thief onto his back and retrieved the dagger lodged in his throat. Blood bubbled from the wound and down the sides of his neck as his body shook violently in a final spasm. The sight of the blood sickened him, and Perault's stomach churned, nearly spewing up his breakfast. This was the first man he had ever killed, and he felt rage at the thief for putting him to it. Placing a booted foot heavily on the thief's chest to keep him from flopping around, Perault cleaned his blade on the dying man's brown jacket. When the body stilled, he searched his pockets and soon found what he was looking for – a wool bag containing the jewels stolen from Sir Aldeman's house.

Perault waited patiently for the dogs and their handler to arrive. By the sound of their loud barks and howls, it would not be long. He considered the corpse but felt no remorse. The man was a thief after all and deserving of no respect or honor. The only emotion he felt at the moment was relief that he caught the scoundrel before nightfall.

Glancing through the branches, he observed that the sun was low to the horizon and would set within the hour.

Three hounds burst from the dark forest restrained by long leashes held tightly by their master. At the sight of the dead body, they broke into a howling frenzy. "Settle down you useless mutts!" the dog-handler yelled; his command reinforced by the snapping of their leashes. Immediately they calmed, if just a little, and set their attention to circling and sniffing the corpse.

"It was better I should follow you than this hopeless crew to find our man." The dog-handler was a gruff man of late years and little manners. Despite his admonishment of his hounds, they were known to be the best hunters in the Duchy.

"Don't be so hard on them, Bale," Perault was always amused by the dog-handler's bluster. He knew how much Bale loved his dogs. On the coldest winter nights, he would bring them from the kennels into the warmth of his own home, to the constant displeasure of the old man's wife. "I just happened to guess the right direction."

"I expect my mutts to guess as good as any man," Bale grumbled.

The rapid clip-clop of hooves on the narrow trail seized their attention, and presently a man rounded the bend wearing long blue robes and a white gold-fringed cloak clasped in the front by a shiny gold medallion in the shape of the sun. He was an older man with sun-darkened skin and close-cut gray hair that matched his short beard under a sharp nose and blue eyes. It was Sir Aldeman, and he was trailed by two armored men-at-arms in surcoats reflecting his house colors.

"Is this the man who took my wife's jewels?" Sir Aldeman demanded when he rode up. He did not bother to dismount.

Perault handed him the bag of jewelry. "These were on him, my lord. I expect he will no longer be troubling us."

The old knight peered at the thief. "He refused to surrender?"

"I gave him the chance," Perault assured him. "He declined."

Sir Aldeman looked around at his men. "Does anyone know this man?"

One of the guards spoke up. "His name is Tifton, my lord. He lived in a village to the north where my wife's sister is from. He is known to contract for special jobs – not all of them legal."

"An opportunist and a thief," Perault added. "He has no honor and should be treated like a dog." He cast an apologetic look over to Bale.

Sir Aldeman locked his gaze on Perault while he called to the guard, "Does he have any family?"

The guard nodded. "I believe he has a wife and two small children, my lord."

"Very well. Return his body to the family and pay the expense for his burial."

"My lord," Perault protested, "he is a thief who deserves nothing more than to be buried face down in an unmarked grave in the forest. He should be an example to any others who would consider his profession."

Sir Aldeman leaned over his saddle and smiled at him. "He is also a husband and a father. Poor Perault. You have been my squire for twelve years, and I have endeavored to instruct you as best I am able. Have I neglected to teach you compassion?"

Perault felt abashed. "Of course, you are right, my lord."

Sir Aldeman laughed. "You will make for a virtuous knight, Perault. Although I am sad that next year you will be leaving us. Now, bring the man's horse and accompany me to the house, we have much to discuss."

~~~

The druids suggested to Count Djago that for Lady Genestra to conceive, they must increase their efforts naturally. This advice they had been following rigorously with pleasure.

Djago lay in his bed after one of these active occasions next to his lovely wife in fitful slumber. He dreamed of a time when he would father a child, boy or girl he did not care, and know the joy that only others with children knew. The three of them would stand together on the balcony that overlooked the lights from the city that expanded toward the north and reflected on the glittering ripples of the Fin River just beyond. They would watch the beauty of the setting sun behind the snowcapped mountain peaks in the west and sometimes a sunrise above the vast forests at dawn.

But not this night.

The flicker of a shadow and slight movement of silks hanging in front of the double doors leading to the balcony nearly awakened him. Maybe it was the wind, except that the doors and windows were closed to keep out the nights chill. No, something unnatural was present in his room. It was an oppressive weight that caused his breathing to quicken and his body to sweat. His subconscious struggled to calculate the danger. Was it real or just a dream?

~~~

Morning light filtering through light-blue gossamer silks covering the wide windows stirred Lady Genestra from her restful slumber. Today she felt different somehow as if Sunna had bestowed upon her a secret blessing. It was a fleeting impression that she reveled in for as long as it would last.

Then she was aware of heavy warmth next to her. Her husband. She was surprised that he was sleeping in. Usually he was up and about his work much earlier in the morning. With a wicked smile on her lips, she wondered if he had lingered in bed until she awoke to punctuate the activities of the prior evening. She turned, snuggled closer and placed a hand on his chest. His body was oddly rigid as if he were very tense. She could feel his rapid heartbeat and became alarmed by his hasty breathing.

Propping herself up on one elbow, she looked at his face. To her horror, her husband's expression was frozen and contorted in terror; his eyes wide open and dry, his mouth open wider than would seem possible as if contorted in a silent scream. Lady Genestra scrambled away from him quickly and out of bed terrified that her husband had fallen to some terrible disease or poison.

She ran to the door of the room and called for the guards. Almost immediately, two armored men entered with hands on the hilt of their swords.

"Send for a druid!" she commanded. "The count is ill!"

Without hesitation, one of the guards bolted out of the room while the other strode to the door to the bedchamber and peeked inside. "Does he have a fever, my lady?"

Lady Genestra found herself wringing her hands uncontrollably and stopped, forcing them to smooth the sides of her nightgown. "I don't know. Don't go in—it might be catching."

The guard turned to look at the count lying stiff in his bed. "His face . . . The expression is . . ."

Unable to support herself any longer, Lady Genestra sank to her knees and began to sob. What was wrong with her husband? He was sound the night before, and they were so happy. What had happened in the night to cause this sudden change?

Before the guard could attempt to comfort her, two of her ladies-in-waiting burst through the door and fell to their knees beside her. They asked questions, hugging her tightly, but she could not respond. The thought of losing her husband left her feeling despondent. Still, she had to regain her composure. She was the countess after all and must represent the count in a dignified manner.

Slowly, she arrested her weeping and allowed her ladies to dry her eyes. She would be strong for her husband. Lady Genestra rose to her feet as elegantly as any queen and sat neatly upon a nearby chair. "I'm sorry for my outburst." She told the clearly uncomfortable guard. "I am fine now."

Her ladies sat next to her, each holding one of her hands while the lone guard stood nearly at attention against the wall desperately looking anywhere except at her. The situation was growing awkward when Sir Reynfrey, Commander of the count's Personal Guard and Minister of the Military, rushed through the door. At least twenty guards crowded the hallway behind him.

The commander was wearing his nightclothes with a sword buckled over them and his always perfectly combed jet-black hair in disarray. Despite the weight of the moment, she nearly burst out laughing.

Holding up a fist to stave off the entry of the guards behind him, he crossed the distance to the lone guard in the room in two long paces. "Report," he commanded quietly.

"Sir. The count appears to be alive, but in some state of illness and . . . distress," the guard responded.

"Have you checked all points of entry to the room for any disturbance?"

The guard broke into a sweat and began to stutter.

"Sir Reynfrey," Lady Genestra spoke up. "I forbade your man from conducting a proper search of our chamber before the druid arrived. I will not have him ill as well if the count's sickness might be spread."

The commander shifted his intense gaze to the countess and visibly softened. "You are right, of course, my lady. We will wait for the druid to judge his condition before we investigate further."

"Is the count alive, commander?" a calm voice inquired. A lean man squeezed his way around the guards choking the open doorway. He wore a long brown robe adorned with colorful feathers and beads dangling freely on lengths of leather thongs. His hood was up, but the light from the room illuminated the strange blue and white tattoos visible on his forehead and around the edges of his heavy gray beard. It was the druid Taudrick.

"It appears so," the commander replied.

"Attend to me then." The old druid strode purposefully into the room. "And you too, Lady Genestra."

The three of them stood at the side of the count's bed. Djago was laying perfectly still with his arms on top of the sheets covering him. His position would have been considered typical for a man at rest except for his face. His features were disproportionately contorted with such an expression of terror that Lady Genestra could hardly breathe at the sight of it. His eyes were open and unseeing, adding to the horror of the image. For the first time she noticed an excessive current of fluid and sweat that ran from his nose, eyes, and hairline that soaked the pillow under his head as if he were exerting tremendous effort.

Taudrick first placed a hand on his chest and another on his forehead. The druid's brow furrowed and he spoke a few words that sounded as if it were part of a song. Then he pulled the sheets down to the count's feet.

Lady Genestra gasped. Her husband's nightclothes were soaked-through with sweat, and his back was arched, matching the tension in his arms and legs. "Terril." She barely held in a sob. And her hands, shaking with fear and shock, descended to hold his rigid, cold forearm.

The druid sighed. "This is not a physical affliction. There is a terrible conflict waging inside the count's mind. I don't know how to describe it as I have never experienced anything like this before. All I can tell you is that he will either get better or die when his struggle ends."

"Is there nothing you can do then?" Lady Genestra felt desperate. She was watching her husband suffer, and she was powerless to do anything about it.

"There is one thing." The druid nodded. "I will sever the link between his subconscious and his physical body. I would not see his body broken if he survives the ordeal."

Taudrick placed his fingers on the count's temples and began to chant again. Slowly, Djago's body began to relax and his mouth and eyes closed. When the druid finally stepped back, Count Djago appeared relaxed and asleep as if nothing unusual was happening to him. The only indication of his continued affliction was his rapid breathing and occasional twitch.

"That is all I can do until he awakens," Taudrick announced. He turned to Sir Reynfrey. "What do you know about how this happened?"

Before the commander could reply, Lady Genestra spoke up. "We had a perfect evening and then we slept." There was no need for specific details of their adventurous hours of lovemaking. "I awoke this morning to his condition." She reached over and grabbed the hand of the old druid. It was the hand that had removed her from her mother's womb decades earlier. "Whatever it takes, whatever it costs, whatever you have to do, bring my husband back to me again. Do it."

Taudrick dropped his gaze and gently placed his other hand over her own. "I will do everything within my power, even at the risk of my own life, to bring him back to you - to us all - my lady."

"I will be here as well, countess." adjoined Sir Reynfrey. "May we inspect your rooms now?"

Lady Genestra nodded and then added, "Please do so with quiet consideration for the count."

Commander Reynfrey took a step toward the door and motioned to his men to enter, followed by additional hand-signals to keep it quiet. The guards entered and scattered about the chambers inspecting every corner for any detail that might provide an inkling of information.

Taudrick led Lady Genestra into the sitting room where her ladies-in-waiting anxiously rushed to hug her. The druid shooed them away quickly and took her to a chair away from all the others. "I have important news for you as well, My Lady."

"There is something more about my husband I should know?" Her heart was nearly beating out of her chest. Whatever he had to tell her in private couldn't be good.

The druid leaned close. "When you took hold of my hand, I felt something from you."

Lady Genestra nearly shook with dread at what the druid might say next.

"You are with child, my dear, and it will be a boy."

~~~

It was over and he was firmly in control now. Such a rare thing to encounter so strong a will from a mortal being. Still, it ended as expected, despite his weakened state from being imprisoned for so long. The count was no longer himself. He never would be again. His outward appearance did not betray any change as far as anyone who knew him could tell, yet everything that he was before, on the inside, was gone forever. Only Count Djago's memories remained to feed a new hunger. The ravenous hunger of a demon.

It started as an epic battle of control that waged for unendurable days and endless nights. There was the back and forth momentum of gains and losses, massive surges and counterattacks that nearly lost or saved the count. And there were heroic stands behind a wall of fortitude that rebuffed every attack until the last. It was a battle worthy of songs and poetry to pass down through the ages eulogizing the fallen heroes and espousing the valiant glory of the victors.

If anyone had noticed. If anyone *could* have noticed. A silent laugh rippled through the count's mind.

To the shadows that hovered over him, Count Djago must have looked like a body at rest, the perfect portrait of serenity and restoration while the war for his mind raged. When it was finally over only Mamon, Greater Demon of Greed, remained, in possession of a new puppet with which to carry out his dark schemes. There was much to do and Mamon was enthusiastic about getting to it; however, his new body was exhausted and he needed to get to know it better to maintain the façade that would be necessary to preserve the illusion that nothing had changed with Count Terril Djago.

For now, he would listen and learn from those gathered around him.

"The struggle is over." The voice of Taudrick sounded relieved and exhausted. "His mind is at rest now."

Sudden movement, the ruffle of fine fabric and the scuff of wooden legs betrayed the noise of Lady Genestra jumping from her chair in a move that had to be far from graceful. There was the sound of a slight stumble and the tear of silk as she must have nearly tripped over her skirts rushing to her husband's bedside. When she was beside him, she breathed a long sigh of relief. The air she exhaled smelled sweet of mint.

"Will he awaken?" she asked the druid nervously.

Mamon knew these people from Djago's own memories. Both of them were held in high esteem, especially his wife, Lady Genestra. The many vivid images of her in his mind portrayed her as a beautiful and elegant woman. And passionate, as revealed by their most recent exertions together striving to have a child. Mamon smiled inwardly at that thought. He would drink deeply of her sweet nectar before he broke her.

Taudrick was standing above him with Lady Genestra. "Yes, but in his own time. I believe he has survived the worst of it."

"What was 'it', Taudrick? Don't you know?"

The old druid exhaled a long breath that hinted of raspberries. "I can interpret the physical signs as a struggle in his mind. It is like nothing I have seen before. There are those among the Atlanteans who can delve into another man's mind and ascertain their condition. The Wizards of the Yellow Hall, I believe they are called."

"Then let us summon one of these Yellow Wizards to evaluate the count's mental soundness."

A bolt of fear and rage crackled across the demon's consciousness. He didn't need one of those damned Enlightened One's peeking in on his new tenancy. Mamon would surely be found out and summarily ejected from his powerful host. Maybe not by the first Yellow Wizard, but certainly by the many that would follow. Mamon knew he would need a few days to fully absorb the experiences and memories of Count Terril Djago and make them his own. However, he would awaken earlier to avoid the Yellow Wizard and simply deal with the disadvantages of not entirely knowing his host if it came to that.

Taudrick replied in the calm, soothing voice that he was so well known for, "If he does not awaken by tomorrow, we shall do so. Right now, I believe he needs rest and quiet."

"I suppose that is best," Genestra sounded reluctant.

There was a swish of silken fabric on the wooden floor accompanied by receding steps and the countess addressing someone, probably a guard standing at the wide double-doorway that led into the bedchamber. "Inform Sir Reynfrey that Count Djago is at rest and recovering."

"Yes, my lady." It was a dutiful response followed by the clang of a gauntleted fist slammed against metal chest plate and swift, heavy steps marching away.

"Genestra," the druid lowered his voice to almost a whisper. "It has been days since we spoke about your condition. When are you planning to share the news publicly?"

The countess was close again, her warm hand caressing Count Djago's cheek. "Not until my husband is awake. I wish for his ears to receive the news before anyone else. It will be a joyous day."

Mamon nearly rolled Djago's eyes. If Genestra were pregnant, then he would have to be far more careful with his cruelty toward her. An heir would serve as an easy host to transition to when Djago grew old or became dispensable. Mamon could keep the line of succession going for generations if he was clever enough.

"There is good news?" Mamon recognized the voice of Sir Reynfrey from a distance. He must have just arrived in the doorway.

An awkward silence followed until Sir Reynfrey spoke again. "About the count? I am told that he is improved?"

The druid coughed. "Yes, yes, good sir. The count has made a turn for the better. He no longer suffers seizures and his temperature has returned to normal. It is my opinion that he has overcome the malady he has endured and is only in need of rest."

The demon's chuckle echoed inside Djago's mind with no fear of reprisal.

"That is terrific news, Taudrick!" Sir Reynfrey was always an honorable man full of optimism and cheery disposition. Mamon knew a little of the man already from the strong impression he made on Djago's mind. If the benevolent commander were unable to be corrupted then the demon would dispense with him for another. Certainly, there were many contenders for the coveted position of Commander of the Guard and Minister of the Military. Perhaps Mamon would grant that last title to himself in either case.

"We are all relieved, commander." Countess Genestra's voice took on a more formal tone. "While we remain hopeful, the count has yet to come around. Until then, we must wait to find out if there are any lasting effects beyond fatigue."

"Of course you are right, countess." There was genuine sadness in his reply. Mamon wanted to wake Djago that very moment and strangle the pathetic man. "I will take retreat in the Temple of Sunna tonight and pray for our good lord. If he has any further improvement, you can find me there."

"Thank you, commander."

Booted footfalls with the occasional scuff of a heel signaled Sir Reynfrey's departure. Mamon could visualize the sardonic smiles that were shared between Taudrick and Genestra behind the commander's back. Reynfrey would be among the first whose departure Mamon would manipulate and there was no more bitter betrayal than the silent judgment of those thought of as friends.

Chapter 4

Small Victories
Late Summer – SY5489

Flashes of colorful light accompanied by explosions of energy rocked the ground. They were discharged from the broken windows of the otherwise featureless stone tower. Outside, near the single shattered entryway, lay several bodies ravaged by appalling violence. Some were guards, others were servants. Whatever they had been in life, they were nearly indistinguishable from each other in death. The sharp fang and claw of massive dire wolves saw to that. Ignoring the ferocity of the battle inside, they continued to rip apart the cooling flesh of their victims in search of the tenderest parts.

Prince Zracul watched it all dispassionately. He found no joy in what he witnessed; rather, he was becoming impatient with his two brothers' inability to bring their quarry under control. The longer it took for that to happen, the more desperate Vadim and Fain would become, increasing the likelihood that Geoffrass would be killed without divulging the answers Zracul sought. Worse yet, the object of their search could be damaged in the brothers' haste to please him.

Zracul couldn't let that to happen. He needed the Mad Wizard alive. Especially after the hundreds of leagues of travel over mountains and dangerous wilderness to get there from Vradesti. The Mad Wizard's tower, cloistered in The Wilds, had not been easy to find.

Spitting a curse, Zracul marched purposefully toward the tower, not caring where he stepped or on what. The dire wolves complained only through whines and whimpers, heads down, backing out of the way and submitting to their master's dominance. Trying hard not to let his rage rule his actions, Zracul stepped through the door.

Inside, blinding light reflected off smoke from small fires in every direction. The tower was hollow, except for a wide stairway separated by curved landings that led to a room at the top. There, near the ceiling high above, hovered a man in what amounted to nightclothes wildly gesticulating with his arms frequently releasing crackling branches of lightning at a lower landing or targeting a shot of fire at the floor. Squinting through the hazy light, Zracul observed his brother Vadim dodging the attacks on the landing and Fain doing the same between furniture and crates on the floor. Both were injured, with torn and burned clothing, but he could not tell how badly.

"What is the problem?" Zracul shouted at Fain over the commotion.

Fain had a panicked look on his face and appeared unsure how to respond.

"Well?" Zracul demanded.

"Watch!" Fain stepped from behind a burning wardrobe and cast a small ball of fire high into the air. It sped, fast and true to his intended target and exploded when it impacted sending a slight tremor through the foundation of the tower. When the light faded, the Mad Wizard emerged unaffected and responded with a fiery ball of his own that destroyed what remained of the wardrobe as Fain dove behind another piece of furniture.

"Where is his Dwarf apprentice, Firolin?"

Fain shrugged. "Not here."

Zracul was losing his patience. "Do you at least have the tome?"

Fain pointed about halfway up the tower to a landing. "Vadim has it."

Zracul sighed and began to ascend the winding stairway.

"Brother, no!" Fain yelled while scrambling to find something else to hide behind.

A few steps up, lightning tore into Zracul's body, spidering over his extremities and knocking him to the floor. Geoffrass must have noticed his ascent. He rose slowly, his body wracked with spasms, and continued to climb the stairs. Zracul walked casually; he would not run or attempt to avoid the expected assault. He had to prove a point to his brothers, although it angered him to suffer so much for their ignorance. When he was done, *they* would suffer in return.

Just as he reached the landing where Vadim huddled behind a thick pillar that supported the stairway, a ball of fire nearly blasted Zracul off the ledge. It was not the first one cast in Vadim's vicinity; the entire ledge was scorched and nearly devoid of anything else to burn. Taking most of the force of the blow, Zracul controlled his wobbly legs. "You have the tome?"

"Yes, brother, here." Vadim touched a thick leather satchel enchanted to resist fire.

"Good, keep it safe. It is worth more than your life." Zracul flashed his brother a cruel smile, stretching the horribly burned skin that remained attached to his face, and continued his trek up the stairway.

Vadim gasped at the sight of him. "Hide, brother! He will destroy you if you continue!"

Zracul did not need to gaze upon his reflection to know how badly he was injured. He could feel the intensity of the burn. The entire right side of his body was scorched almost to the bone, revealing blackened muscle and tendons in places where his clothing was burned away. The stench of his charred flesh was disgusting, but he blocked it all out; the pain, the agony, everything. His brothers had to learn by his example.

Another charge of electricity coursed through his body. This time Zracul did not fall, his body numb to the shock and pain of it, and after only a brief pause set his foot upon the next step. He was close.

"Who are you? What do you want?" Geoffrass screeched when Zracul reached the final landing. The Mad Wizard was still out of reach, hovering in midair and shielded from magic.

"I have the tome."

Confusion passed over the Mad Wizard's features. "What tome?"

Zracul walked to the edge of the landing. Geoffrass floated a span away facing him at eye level. "The Tome of Elements."

Geoffrass inhaled sharply. "How do you know about that?" he demanded, simultaneously casting another arcing flash of lightning at point-blank range.

Zracul took the blast and stumbled a few steps before falling into a sitting position with his back against the inside of the tower wall. There he sat gasping, breathing in the smoke from his own singed flesh and clothing.

The Mad Wizard drifted to the edge of the landing, a look of triumph on his face. "I don't know how you discovered I had it, but you won't be finding anything with that tome now, will you?"

Zracul's breathing calmed, and he felt the flesh on the left side of his face turn up in what must have been a grotesque smile. Their eyes locked for a moment and the Mad Wizard's expression slowly faded from triumph to fear, but time was up for Geoffrass and in the space of an instant Zracul was standing at the edge of the landing with one hand around the Mad Wizard's throat. At first, the old man struggled and tried to speak. There was no use, Geoffrass couldn't even manage to get a spell off without a voice to cast it. A thrill of pleasure drowned out everything else for a brief moment – Zracul held one of the greatest wizards on the planet like a rag doll on the edge of life and death with only the twitch or stay of his fingers to define which it would be.

"Are you ready to tell me what I want to know?" Zracul loosened his grip just enough for the Mad Wizard to speak.

He spoke one word, *"Prge,"* and fire exploded all around them.

What was left of the flesh on the front of Zracul's body melted away almost instantly, and he fell to his knees, the pain nearly overwhelming him. Then he felt the presence of Ornias, and he took strength from it. Somehow, he retained his grip on the Mad Wizard without killing him or allowing him to utter another word.

To his credit, Geoffrass managed to maintain his anti-magic shield, deflecting the fire away and leaving him unharmed. He struggled against Zracul's grip again, no doubt assuming an easy escape, but it was not to be. Zracul slowly regained his feet and looked through the fog of scorched, lidless eyes. The expression of terror that stared back at him was enough to tell him how bad he must appear – *like death itself* – he thought with some amusement.

"All that is left to decide is how you will die." To what remained of Zracul's ears, his voice sounded muffled and inarticulate. "Tell me where to find the Sphere of Elements and you shall die quickly. Refuse and you will die slowly. Either way, you will tell me."

"Brother?" Vadim touched his shoulder. Zracul glanced over to see Fain standing beside him. Both had looks of horror on their faces at his condition.

"Silence!" Zracul demanded. Neither brother spoke a word of protest.

"Which will it be, wizard?" Zracul loosened his grip once more, fully expecting to be assailed by flame once again. He almost hoped for it with his brothers standing with him now to share in his agony.

The Mad Wizard did not call down more fire. "I . . . I do not have it," he croaked. "The sphere is cradled by the hands of a god and hidden in a place where the likes of you could never retrieve it."

Zracul shook him violently in anger. "Where?"

Geoffrass began to laugh, his long white beard abrasive against the tender meat of Zracul's hand.

"Where?" Zracul repeated more forcefully.

The Mad Wizard laughed harder, sputtering and choking on Zracul's tightening grip. "No place for the bloodless!! It is hidden in the City of Mist!" His laughter rose in pitch until it abruptly stopped altogether and his eyes glazed over. Only then did Zracul realize that his grip had tightened in uncontrolled rage, thus ending the legendary life of Geoffrass, Mad Wizard of Tintagel.

Zracul threw the limp body onto the landing, then turned on his brothers. "Fools. Look upon me and see how I suffer. For you!" He reached out and grabbed the brothers by the front of their embroidered tunics and drew them close. "Know yourselves!" With the strength of a Fir Bholg, he threw them screaming from the landing.

He watched them fall to the bottom of the tower. Their flight terminated suddenly with the crush of bone and breaking necks that gave him more than a little satisfaction. They stared at him from where they lay, unmoving, with undead eyes, stiff and disfigured.

"Get up, you idiots!" Zracul demanded. "You are immortal!"

He picked up the satchel holding the tome that Vadim had dropped before his sudden flight and descended the steps to the bottom of the tower. By the time he reached the bottom his flesh had already begun to heal and regenerate itself. It would be another day or two to full recovery. Until then he would rest and prepare for the next leg of their journey. Vadim and Fain were waiting for him.

"You both live." Zracul could hardly hide the amusement in his voice.

Vadim appeared particularly unappreciative. "We are still exploring the limits of our new 'condition'."

"There will be time for that," Zracul assured them. "You two are going to Tintagel and I am going to Lyon's Gate."

"Lyon's Gate?" Fain repeated with surprise. "Tintagel?"

"The lake south of here is known as 'The Lake of Mists'. That cannot be a coincidence. There are ancient archives at the library in

Tintagel where the two of you can research any ancient cities that once graced its shores. Meanwhile, I will join the Tourney in Lyon's Gate to give us a story." Zracul put a hand on each of their shoulders, causing them to flinch noticeably. "I have suffered greatly for you today, brothers. I suffer still. Do not fail me again."

~~~

"The Orks make piss for ale." Cug, king of the Giants, made a face. "When will the Vikja bring more of their brew?

Aengus, an aged Fir Bholg clan chief with long silver hair that fell over a dark brown fur cloak looked dubiously into his own mug. "Next week."

Cug coughed a bitter laugh. "The good thing about that is we don't have to waste any on this upstart Kumida."

Laughter rippled through the assembled crowd. Cug was standing with several chiefs and shamans from all over Fomoire. They were gathered around a roaring bonfire at the center of his village. Thirteen clans of Giants called this foul land their home and ten were represented here that evening. Only the Cyclopes had yet to arrive and they were expected soon. The chieftains came because Cug summoned them. From the hills, marshes, and mountains they traveled from near and far every year to pay homage to their king and discuss trade and the state of their affairs. This year was expected to be a little more entertaining as all of them were eager to meet the new Cyclops chief that was calling himself a king.

"Here he comes now," someone said.

Cug peered through the smoke and haze that obscured the darkness as much as the night itself. A form approached, large and menacing, flanked by two others much smaller. Entering the light of the fire, Cug was shocked to see the largest form was a Cyclops – the biggest Cyclops he had ever seen, nearly as big as a Fir Bholg. It had to be Kumida. He dwarfed the Cyclopes clan chiefs Steropes and Brontes that walked beside him.

The imposing Cyclops walked over to King Cug. He did not bow as was the custom; there was no greeting at all. "I am Kumida," was all he said.

Cug tried to take the measure of the mysterious Cyclops. No one had ever heard of him before this year. All they knew was that he claimed to be blessed by Arges and had proclaimed himself King of the Cyclopes.

"Where is your clan chief, Kumida?"

"Dead."

"Tragic. How did he die?"

"I killed him."

Kumida's black eye reminded Cug of a corpse. "Why would you do that?"

"He refused to submit to my rule. I am now King Kumida of the Cyclopes."

Cug noted that Steropes and Brontes had the look of men desperately wishing they could disappear.

"And to whom does the king of Cyclopes bow to?"

Kumida had not blinked the entire time they spoke. Not once.

"I bow to no one. We meet as equals." Kumida said it, boldly confident that Cug would simply accept his self-coronation.

Cug's first impulse was to beat the arrogant Cyclops to near death then throw him in an icy pit in the mines, but something inside cautioned him to stay his hand and proceed with Kumida carefully. If he were truly blessed by Arges, the god might not look too favorably on Cug for killing him.

Cug merely nodded and smiled. "We shall see about that."

Kumida smiled as well, but it was not a genuine smile that reached his eyes. Cug was sure he was smiling at his remark for a very different reason.

"I am told you have come here for my help, not my approval. What is it that you want, King Kumida?" Cug tried hard not to stress 'king' sarcastically, but he was sure that he failed.

Kumida's expression tightened. "I plan to lead the Giants south into the Western kingdoms."

The shamans and chieftains gathered near Cug and Kumida erupted in a cacophony of shouting.

"You're a fool, Kumida!" Cug bellowed above the noise, quieting everyone around them. "What do you think will happen if we invade the south and begin burning villages and murdering their people? Eriu and Lyonesse will unite behind the druids and destroy us once and for all! You know the reason they have not done so was because of the peace agreement forged years ago by the druids and our shamans."

Kumida's voice was like the low growl of a saber-toothed cat before it pounced, "You are the fool, Cug. All of you are! You have forgotten who you are; descendants of slaves to the Tuatha Dé. And what are we now? Nothing better. We might as well live in a frozen cage with no hope of ever rising above the icy mud where we are stranded, slaving away to survive in this harsh land. If we unite, our numbers will overwhelm the kingdoms of the south and we can find warmer lands to settle."

Cug couldn't believe what he was hearing. "Even if we succeeded in forcing our way past the might of the Western kingdoms, which is doubtful at best, what do you think would happen? The Tuatha Dé would hunt us down, perhaps with the help of the Aes Sídhe."

Kumida's face was a portrait of rage. "You and your Sack-People have become too comfortable behind your stone walls carrying bags of ore from your mines to trade with the humans." He threw his hands in the air and shouted to the crowd, "What about the rest of you? Don't you wish for the life of comfort that Cug can offer in Fomoire? Come with me, and you shall have it!"

Before Cug could respond, Aengus interrupted. "There is some merit to what Kumida speaks. I suggest that we consider the matter very seriously and meet again in one week. The days will give us all time to reflect on what is best for the future of our clans."

Cug could see what Aengus was doing. He needed to speak with the clan chiefs and shamans when Kumida was not present. "You are wise as always, Aengus. We should think deeply on this matter before making a decision."

Kumida seemed a little confused. He must have expected to bully them into invading the south or force a confrontation. "Very well," he grumbled. "We will meet again in a week. Just remember; I am not here to explain myself or ask forgiveness. I am here to demand that you join me!" Glaring at Cug once more, he turned and walked into the darkness followed by Steropes and Brontes.

Cug was not at all happy with this turn of events. After so many decades of relative peace, this Kumida was expecting the Fir Bholg to give up everything they had and rush south to make war on the humans. A war they could not survive, let alone hope to win.

Cug addressed Aengus. "Come with me to the Great Hut, we have much to discuss." Leaving the bonfire, the two Fir Bholg trudged through the snow-covered streets. Even though most of the buildings in the village were constructed of gray stone and timber, the clan leader's home was traditionally referred to as a "Hut". Few villages in Fomoire had the luxury of stone construction and Cug's village was the only one surrounded by a wall. Half of it anyway, in the shape of a crescent backed up against the mountains where they mined ore for trade.

Arriving at the Great Hut, servants quickly rushed to take their heavy cloaks and offer warmed Vikja cider before leaving the two men alone to talk.

"There is something not right with that Cyclops," Aengus commented. "You've heard the reports about how he took power?"

Cug nodded. "Yes. He was a nobody for years before disappearing into the southern forest to hunt rabbits. When he returned a few days later, he had grown larger and aggressive. He took control of his clan and then the other two Cyclops clans within a year. Three clans in a year! He wields power now rivaling ours combined."

Aengus agreed. "There must be sorcery involved somehow. Is it possible that druids are manipulating him to convince us to go to war, thereby giving them the excuse to be rid of us?"

"Druids are human and it's hard to know the aims of humans, but I doubt it. That's not in the druids' nature according to my shamans. Something else is motivating him."

"Send your best warriors to invite him on a hunt this week." Aengus had a sly look on his face. "While he is gone we will meet with the other clan chiefs and decide how to deal with him."

~~~

"Kumida and most of the Cyclopes that came with him have joined a number of our warriors on a hunt while we debate his demands." Cug addressed the Fir Bholg chieftains and a handful of elder shamans seated in the Great Hut. "Our choice is simple – we agree to invade the Western kingdoms, which means war with the humans, the druids, the Tuatha Dé and others, or we refuse and go to war with the Cyclopes. He will expect a response from us either way when he returns."

"Why should we cow to the demands of this dung-hole?" One of the chieftains demanded. "We should kill him and his men when they return."

Cug shrugged. "I wish it were that simple. Aside from the fact that he is unusually large, Cyclopes are unaffected by most magic and all three of his clans are camped less than a league from this very spot. If we failed, they would surely kill us all."

Phaos, the young chieftain of the Logger Giants jumped to his feet. "Then we should gather our clans together and rid Fomoire of the Cyclopes altogether!"

Aengus, standing next to Cug's throne, responded, "That would take time, Phaos. Time we don't have. It would be impossible to muster a large enough force to defeat his clans before he returned."

"So what do we do?" A shaman cackled from the group. "Invade the Western kingdoms with him? Even if we managed to overcome the metal-clad humans and the druids that would surely join them, what about the Tuatha Dé?"

"Bah! The Tuatha Dé are few and far between since The Breaking," a chief of the Mountain Giants replied. "They are more concerned with playing god to the humans than with us."

Aengus shook his head vigorously. "The Tuatha Dé are few but powerful and their human-hybrids are still formidable with their magic. We should not underestimate them."

"I don't know," the Mountain chief replied. "A tribe of Orks escaped Fomoire into The Wilds a few decades ago and what did the Tuatha Dé do about them?"

A shaman supplied the simple answer, "Nothing."

"Not to mention the dragons, griffins, and other flying beasts that have left these lands over the centuries with no repercussions."

"What if the Aes Sídhe intervene on humanity's behalf?" a shaman called Thrakel pressed, her cracked voice a reflection of her advanced age.

Phaos barked a laugh. "Who among us has seen them in decades? Do they ever leave their mountain in the sea anymore?"

The room erupted into a heated debate with one Fir Bholg trying to outshout the next. Cug let it go on a while, he needed them to get it all out before he told them what they were going to do. He and Aengus had agreed earlier that faced with two impossible choices, there was one way to save their people from annihilation.

Before the deliberation degenerated into violent discord, Aengus raised his hands and shouted them into silence. "King Cug will speak now!"

Cug stood and leaned on the heavy cudgel propped next to him. "No matter what is decided, we will need time to gather our forces together. Each of you must send messengers to your clans today telling them to gather your warriors for battle. When they are ready, bring them here."

"To what end, my king?" Phaos looked confused. "As you say, our warriors could never arrive in time to challenge the Cyclopes."

Lifting the cudgel, Cug drew his heavy brows together as if inspecting the dangerous weapon closely. "We need time," he muttered to himself.

"What was that, lord?"

Cug shifted his gaze to stare hard at the gathered Fir Bholg, most of whom he had known their entire lives. They had to trust him. "When Kumida returns from the hunt, I will tell him that we have agreed to join him."

~~~

The Fir Bholg warriors sent with Kumida returned to the village unexpectedly only four days after departing on the hunt. They were immediately brought before Cug.

"They went south?" Cug was surprised. He would have expected Kumida to return early and press for an answer to his invasion demands, not head further south. "Do you know for what purpose?"

The Fir Bholg warrior shrugged, "The Cyclopes were very drunk and one of their warriors suggested they cross into Lyonesse and fleece a dryad. Kumida got very excited and immediately broke camp and headed south. I don't think he even noticed that we stayed behind."

This was shocking news. Kumida was determined to start a war one way or another. "You and your warriors stay out of sight until Kumida returns. I don't want anyone from his clans thinking you murdered him and left his body in the wilderness."

After the warriors departed, Cug poured himself a cup of ale and fell into the pillows padding his massive stone throne. Kumida's latest actions could be a huge problem for the Fir Bholg, for all the Giant races for that matter. Cug needed the council of his closest friend and advisor. He would help him think clearly on this matter better than anyone.

"Find Aengus," Cug called to a nearby servant.

CHAPTER 5

Count Terril Djago

"Look what I have brought from the forests of Lyonesse!" Kumida gestured to a line of seven diminutive Sylvan women shivering under sheer frocks not at all suitable for the harsh cold of Fomoire. "Aren't they beauties?"

Cug had no love for the Sylvan, but these represented far more than just seven Dryads near to freezing to death. "Aengus, find furs to cover them. Quickly!" He took a moment to draw a deep breath and calm his anger while Aengus swiftly exited the room.

"Surely I have kept them warm enough these few nights." Kumida turned to smile wickedly at the Dryads.

"You should not have brought them here, Kumida," Cug kept his voice measured. "It is bad enough that you raided Lyonesse, but to return with these women? Do you know what you are risking?"

"The ire of the druids!" Thrakel screeched.

Kumida turned on her, "Quiet old hag!" then back to Cug. "As a gesture of my goodwill I present two of my coquettish friends here as a gift to you. They will no doubt warm your bed as enthusiastically as they did mine."

Aengus returned with the furs and covered each of the miserable Dryads. He then took a pot of warm ale from a nearby table and dispensed it into a cup for the women.

"Thrakel, take charge of the Dryads, feed them and find a warm place for them to stay. Above all, keep them alive." Cug ordered.

The Elder shaman moved to gather the Dryads. "It is their magic, and the tree that they are bound to that sustain them. The longer they are away from their home the weaker they will become until they eventually wither away and die like a fallen leaf." She herded them out of the room. Steropes held the hide covering the door open for their exit. Cug noted that the look on his face was one of concern and uncertainty – he understood the grave situation Kumida had put them in.

Cug glowered at Kumida. "When the druids catch wind of this abduction, they will rally the Temple Knights of Lyonesse to seek retribution. They will burn our villages one by one until they find those Dryads. You should return them to the forest immediately and pray to Arges that the druids are satisfied with their return."

"Ha!" Kumida's bawdy laugh filled the Great Hut. "Do you know how valuable those wenches are to me? You will see."

"Kumida, you don't understand . . ." Aengus began.

"Enough!" Kumida roared. "I am not here to discuss these Sylvan whores. What have you decided? Will you invade the Western kingdoms with me or not?"

"In light of what you have already done, we may not have a choice." Cug stood from his throne. "You will have your answer at first light."

"Do not toy with me, Cug," Kumida seethed. "I will have your answer in the morning or consider you against me. Remember – we are Giants, born for battle and Giants have always followed the strongest leaders. King or no!" He nearly ran over Steropes when he stomped out of the Great Hut.

Aengus, standing next to the throne, rested a hand on Cug's shoulder to keep him from bounding from his chair after the infuriating Cyclops.

A short while later Thrakel returned. "I have put the Dryads in a warm place with food, although I do not think they will eat," she informed Cug.

He nodded and resumed his place on his throne. Cug was finally alone with Thrakel and Aengus. "We are about to find ourselves in a grinder between Kumida and the druids." He looked first at Aengus. "What do you recommend we do now?"

"Nothing has changed," Aengus replied. "We may be able to use one problem to solve the other."

Thrakel cackled hoarsely. "One thing has changed. Kumida's words have improved extraordinarily in the past week. Almost as if he were evolving . . ." The thought trailed off.

"Evolving into what?" Aengus sat heavily on the ground sloshing a little of his ale over the rim of the cup.

"That, I do not know," Thrakel shrugged. "In any case, I will contact the druids and tell them what has happened. Aengus is right. We may yet be able to use this to our advantage."

Hours later, Cug was awakened in the darkness of the night by screams of women who were not Giants. Rushing to the entrance of the Great Hut in nothing but his small clothes, he burst through the thick hide flap to find several of his guards on high alert in a state of confusion.

"What is happening?" Cug spun one of his guards around to face him.

"I don't know, my king. We gathered here to protect you in case the village was under attack!"

Several dozen warriors had arrived with the commander of the guard. He was calling out for the men to take defensive positions around the Great Hut. "Take two men and find out what that screaming was all about!"

The guard nodded and then led a pair of Fir Bholg warriors down the street. The village was alive with activity, lights igniting in every window, men and women nearly falling into the street with whatever weapon they could find within reach. The screams, though brief, had surely awakened everyone. This was no invasion, Cug was certain of that. This had something to do with the Dryads.

Minutes ticked by before he spied Thrakel loping up the road, followed by the three guards he'd sent earlier. She was wearing a thick wool night shift that did little to hide parts of her bouncing underneath that he was determined not to acknowledge.

She was sweating and nearly out of breath when she arrived in front of him. "Kumida took three of the Dryads and escaped with them into the forest before we could stop him."

"How many Cyclopes were with him?" Cug never wanted to kill another of his kind so badly.

"Just him," Thrakel breathed heavily.

"Be still, Thrakel." He put a hand on her shoulder. "I should have placed guards around their hut."

Her tired eyes looked at him. "Won't you take warriors and give chase?"

"Whatever he intended for those Dryads is already done. And I doubt we would ever find him in the dark forest at night." Cug was tired of being played the fool by this Cyclops. "Go hide the remaining Dryad, Thrakel. I don't want him taking any more. Kumida will face me in the morning."

Try as he might, Cug could not sleep. He sat on his throne drinking his warm ale and considered how he and his people had come to be in this predicament. It was Kumida. Only Kumida.

"Can't sleep?" Aengus entered the Great Hut.

"Waiting for the dawn. Kumida will be here then, and I will tell him . . . something." Cug poured Aengus a cup of ale.

"I thought we had worked all that out already." Aengus pulled a stool over close to his king.

"I want to kill him."

"We are not ready."

Cug slammed his fist on the edge of his throne. "When will the rest of the warriors arrive?"

"Three to six weeks, depending on the distance they must travel. We will not have enough warriors to challenge Kumida until then."

Letting out a long sigh, Cug closed his eyes. It seemed like he was always battling himself to control his rage when he should be killing Cyclopes. "Very well. I will try to be patient."

"You must, King Cug. No matter what. Our people's survival depends upon it."

The light of dawn had just cracked the horizon shooting fingers of dim light into the sky that brightened with every passing minute. Cug and Aengus waited quietly; there was nothing left to say, for the man they knew would come.

They didn't have to wait long.

With the sun not yet completely above the horizon, Kumida strode confidently through the entrance to the Great Hut. His fine leather armor creaked from being worn too long, and his fur cloak revealed recent blood spatter.

"I am pleased that you are up and eager to give me your answer this morning, Cug."

Cug was in no mood for clever conversation. "Why did you take the Dryads?"

Kumida had a genuine look of surprise. "For their treasure, of course."

"What treasure? They had nothing when you paraded them in front of me yesterday."

A sickening smile revealed blood-stained teeth as Kumida reached into a small pouch that hung around his neck on a leather thong. What he produced nearly made Cug forget everything and kill

Kumida right then and there. Three small seeds, the size of acorns still coated in blood, sat like ruined innocence in Kumida's palm.

"The Seed of the Dryad." The Cyclops rolled the seeds around with his thick finger. "They contain certain magical protections and strength of constitution, so I am told."

Regaining his composure as best he could, Cug barely hissed, "You killed them for a seed that you heard a rumor about?"

Cug was far less concerned with the death of the Dryads than how the druids would react to the news and what that could mean for the lives of his people.

"There are still four of them left if you want seeds for yourself."

"I don't want the damned seeds!" Cug leaned forward and bellowed.

"Then what do you want!" Kumida raged. "The longer you keep me waiting for an answer the more I must find ways to amuse myself! Give me your answer!"

Cug seethed, furiously caught between what he wanted to do and what he must do. Either way, he might lead his people to destruction. Desperately he controlled his impulses and formed the words that he didn't want to speak.

"We will join you, Kumida. We will join you invading the Western kingdoms whatever may befall us. The combined might of the Fir Bholg clans will meet you on the Ice Coast the first week of spring."

Kumida stood arrogant and proud as if he had willed this thing to happen, once again displaying the crimson pearls of his grotesque smile. "You have made the right choice, Cug! Cyclopes and Fir Bholg united under a banner of war that will lay waste to the Western Kingdoms and all who oppose us. I will inform my clans!"

Cug watched the powerful Cyclops depart his hut with trepidation. For the first time since he had been crowned king, he felt the icy chill of fear in his bowels. Doom awaited him; doom awaited them all.

~~~

The body of Terril Djago opened his eyes, and Mamon, Demon of Greed, beheld a crowd of people filling the bedchamber.

"Welcome home, my love." Smiling broadly, Lady Genestra kissed him on the forehead.

Behind her stood the druid Taudrick, Commander Reynfrey, several council members and guards and servants. All of them wore joyous expressions that appeared sincere. It sickened the demon inside him. If it were up to Mamon, he would throw them all out, kill the druid and Reynfrey, vigorously bed the countess and begin to set into motion his plans to conquer the world. Unfortunately, he probably wouldn't get far with that strategy. They would likely deem him unfit to rule and strip him of all his powers. These humans had no imagination. He would have to be clever and manipulative, make a few things happen and quietly kill those that needed killing before he achieved what he desired. It would take time and he would have to be cautious.

"I am glad to return." He smiled at Lady Genestra. "How long was I asleep?"

"Two weeks, my dear. But don't worry, Taudrick has assured us all that you will recover fully."

Taudrick leaned closer, fixing him with an intense, unwavering gaze. Mamon wanted nothing more than to look away. This druid might be able to see into his soul and know the truth of what he was. Reluctantly, he held the druid's steady scrutiny and determined that this man would be the first to die.

"Do you know what affected your mind so?" The druid placed a hand on his forehead and then his cheek.

Completely under Mamon's control, Djago shook his head. "It was like a fever dream to me, with visions of battling monsters and all manner of strange creatures. Perhaps I am becoming a prophet?"

The room percolated with polite laughter.

Taudrick was not laughing. He squinted and probed with his mind. The druid sensed something, Djago was sure, and it only confirmed his resolution to cut his throat.

"Now I think I would like to take a bath, which perhaps I could do on my own!" Djago announced with a hearty laugh and a smile, but it was clearly a dismissal. The druid pulled back.

With many well-wishes, everyone filed out of the room except for Taudrick and Lady Genestra.

"I will stay close in case you feel faint or have a relapse," Taudrick assured him before he too departed. To Djago's ears it almost sounded like a warning.

When they were alone, Lady Genestra took his hand. "I was so afraid you would never wake up."

Djago kissed her hand gingerly. "I am here now, feeling stronger by the moment. You have no more worries."

"Then I will send for hot water and bathe you myself. We have so much to talk about."

Mamon had a strong desire for this beautiful woman, but Djago's body was still too weak and he certainly did not want to listen to her prattle on for the next hour. "No dear, you have had a rough few days with little sleep. You can rest now, knowing I am recovering." He leaned forward and kissed her on the cheek. "Please just tell the bathing attendants to prepare a bath for me."

For a moment he thought she might argue, but then she smiled. "Of course dear. I will see you for dinner then. I have news that you will want to hear." Humming a happy tune, she glided out of the room.

While waiting on his bath to be prepared, Mamon willed Djago's body to get out of bed. It felt good to possess a strong body again, and even better that his host held power and influence. He would go far with this one. Donning a thick robe to fend off the chill, he strode over to Djago's writing desk. There were important documents that he was aware of through his subjugated mind that needed replies. Mamon found cruel delight in the fact that the responses would now be very different from what Djago had planned. There would be many things different from what Djago had planned.

Mamon paused, leaving his host staring blankly at a paper in his hand. The demon would have to change the way he thought about the relationship with the body of Djago. The count's mind and soul were gone, never to return and only his memories remained. Mamon focused his energy on strengthening the bonds that connected him to the body, memories, and mannerisms of the count. He went further to integrate with his host than he had ever done before and when it was done, he not only controlled Djago, he had *become* Djago.

~~~

The evening meal was usually attended by two or three dozen guests and friends of the count and countess. To Djago's relief, Lady Genestra had orchestrated a private affair for the two of them, excusing her husband's fatigue and need to recover before returning to their usual social festivities. This pleased Djago, as he was in no mood to entertain a bunch of half-wits he was probably going to dispose of anyway. Even his wife was an annoyance to him, despite her incredible beauty, for his mind was absorbed with a desire for power, greed, and domination rather than wasting time playing the role of a devoted husband.

"You are quiet tonight, my husband." Lady Genestra's concern was apparent on her face. "Are you feeling unwell again?"

Djago gently placed his hand over hers for reassurance. "I am feeling fine, love. Just a little tired from my ordeal. I'm sure that my strength and wit will recover fully in a few days."

"Shall I send for Taudrick and his healers to attend to you? Perhaps they can help?"

"No, no." He kissed her hand. "They are such a nuisance prodding here and there, with endless questions and putrid concoctions. I would prefer they leave me to rest."

"Very well, then," she agreed. "I will tell them to leave the watch to me tonight."

"That would be a relief." He smiled weakly.

"I have something to tell you that shouldn't wait." Her tone was a mix of seriousness and excitement.

"Yes, I remember," Djago replied. "Please tell me."

Genestra brightened visibly and with barely contained enthusiasm announced, "Our prayers are answered. Husband, I am with child."

Mamon felt nothing. Less than nothing. But he had to keep up the pretense and allow Djago's appropriate human emotions to respond. "I am so happy! We have tried for so long, and now the gods have answered." He kissed her hand again and squeezed it tightly.

"Taudrick is sure that it will be a boy. I want to name him after your father, Pen Djago." Her excited eyes waited for his approval.

Djago reflected her excitement, "That is wonderful!"

Genestra stood and hugged him tightly. "I was so lost without you. How could I bear the thought of having our child without you by my side? I am so happy now. We will be such a wonderful family."

"That we will, love, that we will."

~~~

"Lonsh zien a nanaeel oddooain ol iolcam aboapri fafen priaz!" Djago lowered his arms and stepped away from the center of the flaming pentagram that dominated the open space of his official office. It was the only place where he could lock himself away in complete privacy without drawing suspicion of his motives. The guards were steps away beyond the sound-proof doors and there were no windows through which his activities could be spied. Best of all, the hour was late. Far too late for his most decent wife to intrude upon his profanity.

Smoke filled the area occupied by the pentagram and presently the vague shadow of two humanoid forms began to resolve. Quickly the air cleared, and the two naked figures stepped forward toward their new master. One was a male, the other was female. Both were incredibly beautiful despite the bat-like wings that protruded from their spines and the sharp fangs that jutted over their full, red lips.

'Come forward and speak your names." Djago commanded.

The woman did not hesitate. "I am your servant, Naamah."

Djago admired the Succubus's form. She was full-breasted with strong curves around the waist and hips that excited his senses. Her long blond hair framed sharp features that promised slow, lust-filled kisses that would excite his pleasures and promise death to mortals.

The male was less than a step behind. "I am your servant, Ouza."

No less lovely than his female counterpart, the Incubus was the perfection of the male anatomy. With his long, soft blond hair and strong features, Ouza lured countless women into sacrificing their lives to feed his appetite.

Summoned from the Infernal Planes to do his bidding, they would serve his purposes with loyalty and unquestionable certainty. Unlike himself and the Chaos Demons, summoned demons could not possess another life-form. They relied on illusion for their deception and if they died by any means their tortured essence would immediately return from where they came. Djago had the entire night to discuss the role he had in mind for each of them. First, he would enjoy the pleasure of their perfection.

"Come to me." The unnatural flames subsided cloaking the room in a dark shroud. It didn't matter; all of them could see well enough in the darkness. Djago allowed the pair to remove his clothing and press close to his naked skin before he sank to the cold, stone floor to appreciate their pleasures.

Hours later, Count Djago lay on the bare floor between his two new servants enjoying a glass of fine Mekali wine. He could have continued their activities for the entire night. His lust was insatiable, but for the mortal flesh he inhabited. Despite his fine physical condition, his body would always tire far sooner than he wished.

Djago released a long sigh. It was time to issue instructions to the demons he had summoned. They would need clarity of purpose to keep them focused on his objectives. An idle demon was a dangerous and unpredictable thing that could disrupt his schemes regardless of his strong hand of control.

"Ouza, you will take the form of a dashing young noble from the outlands near the Matu Mountains. I will prepare the proper pedigree for your fictional family." Djago idly ran his fingers through the Incubus's tender locks as he spoke. "I want you to join the cavalry and become a soldier's soldier. By the end of the summer, I will ensure that you rise quickly in the ranks to at least commander before we retire Sir Reynfrey."

"Yes, Master." Ouza nodded. His face held a smile that was not reflected in his dead eyes. Djago knew that no matter how well he treated his minions they would always have an intuitive hatred for him. Given half the chance, they would happily murder him in his sleep.

It was a good thing greater demons never slept.

With slow, languid movements, Djago rolled in the opposite direction to face his beautiful Succubus. "And you, my dear, will present yourself to the druid's Enclave in the guise of an elder druid from a secluded settlement deep in The Wilds." He softly caressed her supple lips with his fingertips. "You will call yourself a healer, devoted to Sunna, eager to learn new methods and means of magic to help your community stay well and prosper."

"Yes, Master." Her seductive nature pulled at his desires prompting Djago to consider whether or not the exhausted body he inhabited had enough left for another round with this beautiful, yet deadly creature.

It did.

~~~

The summer days dragged long and unusually warm with rains that never seemed to end. It didn't bother Djago, he could care less what the season was. Cold or warm, it would never be anything like the searing heat of the Infernal Planes. It was during these months that he took the opportunity to carefully institute subtle changes within Cambria that most considered common-sense choices or simply went unnoticed altogether. He consolidated his power by placing people he could control or influence in important positions of authority and those that would oppose him met with untimely accidents or vanished altogether.

As for Lady Genestra, he had his way with her for a while and he was gentle and kind in his treatment. He abhorred every moment of it, never allowing his true nature to reveal itself. Djago could have been cruel, but she was beloved by the people and a sour word from her could destroy everything he was working for, plus he genuinely valued the child that grew within her. He would endure her presence as long as it benefited his agenda.

Toward the end of the summer season, he and Lady Genestra attended the wedding of Duke Maruk of Tintagel to Princess Eselt, the youngest daughter of the Eriu High-King Cadeyrn. It was a strange affair, with the princess stealing glances at the duke's son, or adopted son or some such, and the duke's captain of the guard always looking on disapprovingly. It didn't matter to Djago, he enjoyed the intrigue of chaos and betrayal that bubbled below the surface and suspected that it was the same in every noble house in the Western kingdoms.

Returning to Cambria, the daily charade of a loving husband and doting father-to-be began to drain upon him and soon enough, Djago even tired of their mundane coupling. Finally, he suggested, for

Lady Genestra's sake, that they spend their nights in separate chambers. He convinced her that they would both sleep better, and more importantly, she could be cared for more diligently by her ladies-in-waiting over the final term of her pregnancy. Reluctantly she agreed, and just like that, he was free to do as he wished during the night.

The night.

That was his time to send and receive communications with his spies outside of Cambria and manipulate his operatives within. Djago lay plans to accumulate massive wealth and power, that was the true nature of Mamon, Demon Greed, and he would control the whole of Lyonesse before projecting his power into Eriu, Ys, Courth, and realms beyond. He controlled everything that mattered in Cambria except for one thing – his wife. Lady Genestra was the wildcard that could disturb his intrigues, but he couldn't kill her. Yet. At least not until the child was born and that would be soon.

Djago would set his most significant deceptions into motion in the fall. Cambria would be ready then. He would have a son and the heightened emotion and celebration by the people could be channeled to his advantage. Fall would herald the shadow that would cover Lyonesse like a shroud and when he was done, not even the power of the Enlightened One could save them.

"My lord, I have received a message from a Fir Bholg shaman in Fomoire." Naamah entered Djago's private study without so much as a knock. Only she and Ouza had that kind of access to him. The guards knew it well and wouldn't dare challenge them. A rumor circulated that one had tried recently and summarily dismissed from service.

"A Fir Bholg?" Djago looked up from his desk just as she dropped the illusion hiding the beautiful woman standing before him. He would have her stay with him a while tonight.

"Indeed." She pulled down her hood, revealing smooth pale skin and long blond hair. "With news you may find interesting, maybe even important."

Djago admired her fine features and pouty red lips. Everything about her was beautifully seductive until he looked into her eyes. He had seen other men captured by that empty gaze to their demise. Orbs so black, like wells of pure darkness impossible to escape, that could see into a man's soul and own it. Fortunately for him, he had no soul. "You have read it, so summarize."

"An upstart named Kumida has taken control of the Cyclopes clans and demands that the Fir Bholg follow him. He intends to invade the Western kingdoms, but he has recently committed an abomination."

"So far, I like this Kumida." Djago laughed. "What sort of abomination affronts the Fir Bholg?"

"He has taken several Dryads from their home in Lyonesse." Naamah's neutral tone minimized the act as if it were inconsequential, but Djago knew better.

"Are they still alive?"

"Three are dead by Kumida's hand, the remaining four have been hidden by the Fir Bholg."

Djago rose from his desk and began to pace. "Do the druids know what you know?"

"Not yet, master."

"See that they don't," Djago commanded. "Tonight, you will open a portal so that I may speak with these shamans. Perhaps I can use this information to our advantage."

Over the spring and early summer, Naamah had fulfilled her duties well by infiltrating and ingratiating herself to the druids of Sunna. Even Taudrick had taken a liking to her before a freak accident involving a carriage took his life. It was so violent that not even the druids healing magic could save him. The old druid had been suspicious of Djago's recovery from the beginning, even going as far as suggesting that Lady Genestra bring in an Enlightened One to examine him. Djago couldn't have their kind anywhere near him if he hoped to preserve the anonymity of the count's possession. Taudrick was too close to Lady Genestra and too dangerous to have access to the household because of her.

Of course, Lady Genestra was devastated by the loss of her friend, but Djago wasn't bothered by her distress, she would get over it eventually. He used her anguish to convince the Enclave to send Naamah as a replacement for Taudrick and they had no choice but to agree. Quickly, she became the family healer and liaison to the Enclave of Sunna for the Count. Djago was quite pleased with himself for orchestrating such an improbable move.

The door to the study opened and Ouza strode in. He was as handsome as Naamah was beautiful. To look at them together they might even be considered related. Like Naamah, Ouza had light skin and long blond hair, his tied in a ponytail, over glistening dead black eyes. Half the women in Cambria swooned over him wherever he went and half again of those likely ended up in his bed. Djago didn't care, as long as his commander was discreet and consumed those who wouldn't be missed. Perhaps he would invite Ouza to join him that night.

"Ah, good timing, Ouza," Djago called to him.

Ouza walked to stand next to Naamah, wet clusters of melted ice stained his cloak. "Greetings, master. The first snow is upon us."

Djago shook his head. "I noticed. And do not call me master. If anyone overheard, there might be unfortunate talk or questions. Refer to me as lord or count. Do not make me correct either of you again."

"Yes, lord." They both answered in unison.

Ouza had pleased him as well in the execution of his responsibilities. Literally. By late summer Sir Reynfrey, the Minister of the Military and Commander of the Elite Guard went missing. A young noble woman disappeared at the same time and it was speculated that she and Sir Reynfrey had run off together to escape his wife and children. No one that knew Sir Reynfrey believed the rumors, but it didn't matter, the general public did not know him and the story seemed plausible. It wouldn't have been the first time forbidden love caused tragic failures in judgment.

As promised, Djago replaced the commander with Ouza cloaked in the illusion of a male human to act as a spymaster within the household and maintain a tight grip on the military. Ouza would be a key player in Djago's plans to dominate Lyonesse and he anticipated that the Incubus would eagerly implement his agenda with unerring loyalty and fervor

"Now listen carefully." Djago ran a hand through his thick black hair and scratched his neck. He was pleased to realize that the motion was a well-known characteristic of his host. He was settling into his new form well. "It is time to invent a crisis that will give me a reason to send Lady Genestra away – she is an unrelenting annoyance nearly every hour of the day – and manufacture an adversary for the people of Cambria to fear and hate."

Djago pulled a small vial filled with white powder from the top drawer of his desk and handed it to Naamah. "This is what we are going to do . . ."

~~~

"What is your name, shaman?" Djago peered through the hazy portal at the Fir Bholg staring at him. It was the first time he had seen a shaman of the Giant race and found himself surprised at how normal she looked. He knew the Fir Bholg were quite large creatures, easily four or more times larger than the average human, but the view through the portal was deceiving considering there was no size perspective. Other than her rough features, this one might have easily been mistaken as a typical druid. Her layered brown robes could not conceal the lean frame underneath and the feathers, bones, and beads that adorned her clothing resembled closely the ones worn by Naamah, who stood nearby keeping the portal open.

"I am Thrakel, Elder shaman and advisor to Cug, King of the Giant clans. You must be Count Terril Djago of Cambria." The shaman seemed to study Djago just as curiously.

"Well met, Thrakel. Now, please tell me what you know of this Cyclops named Kumida."

The shaman smiled, displaying a row of broken, jagged teeth stained yellow and brown from decay. "He is strange and one to be feared, Count Djago, and not just for his remarkable size."

"What else is there, Thrakel? Can he wield powerful magic?"

"To our great fortune, Arges has not blessed him in that way. Rather, he is ambitious. Already the Cyclopes clans have united under his rule, and many among the Fir Bholg are swayed by his promises of glory. As it stands, he expects my king to assemble his warriors and meet him on the Ice Coast next spring. From there they would launch an invasion into the Western kingdoms."

Djago did not see an advantage in what he had heard so far. In fact, just the opposite. If the Giants invaded, it would unite the Western kingdoms in common defense and completely disrupt his plans for the foreseeable future. "The fact that you are telling me this must mean that your king is not so enthusiastic about war with us."

The shaman raised one dark eyebrow. "You are perceptive, Count Djago. However, as your druid Naamah probably told you, we have a larger concern than Kumida. It is that of the dyads he abducted. Three are dead, four are alive and under our protection, all have been mistreated by Kumida and his men. If the druids were to find out . . ."

"I understand now." Djago smiled. There was an advantage for him after all. Significant advantage. "Assure your king that we will help each other. Naamah will contact you again in a few days to discuss the details."

The shaman nodded and the portal faded until it disappeared altogether.

Djago stared into the absent space where the portal once hung contemplating his options. The strange happenings with the Cyclopes and the Fir Bholg could advance his scheme exponentially if he could manage to control the Giants and keep them from fighting with one another.

He turned to face Naamah. "It is time for you to approach the Atiod-Bherto. Promise them whatever they want, reveal yourself if you have to. I need them to disrupt the druids of Sunna when the time comes."

"Yes, lord." She bowed. "I will go immediately."

"And Naamah, use them to find out more about Kumida. There may be another angle here I should be considering."

CHAPTER 6

An Heir

"Genestra!" Count Djago rushed to his wife's side. She sat on a small couch situated in a sitting room adjacent to the main dining room. Her face was flushed and she was holding a damp kerchief trimmed with delicate lace that she used to soak the tears that ran down her face.

"She is dead, Terril. Someone poisoned Tala, my lady-in-waiting, my friend." Her slender shoulders shook with the effort to speak between sobs. She rested her delicate head on his shoulder. Djago didn't know why, but he felt a powerful lust for her at that moment.

"I know" Djago held her close and stroked her hair to comfort her. "And I feared that you might have been harmed as well."

Genestra squeezed his arm and regained a measure of calm. "I am fine, husband, but why would anyone want to hurt Tala?"

"I do not believe Tala was the assassin's target. She was an unintended victim."

"What? Then who?"

Djago lifted her chin and looked deep into her eyes. "I do not want you to be afraid, but it was an obvious attempt on your life and the life of our unborn child, the heir to my title and lands."

Genestra gasped. "What enemy have we made that they would make an attempt on the life of an innocent? We have lost so much this year – the scandal of Commander Reynfrey and the tragic death of dear Taudrick – now Tala. I feel as if I have become surrounded by strangers."

"It is true," Djago shifted on the couch to face her more directly. "So much has changed since my recovery and little for the better, except that we will soon have a son. With that in mind, I have decided to send you to our summer house until our child is born."

"No!" Her reaction was immediate. "I cannot leave you here alone." Genestra's thin eyebrows came together sharply above eyes lit with the fire of determination. "Who will look after you when I am gone? How will you look upon our son when he arrives?"

Djago pulled her to his chest and held her tight. "I will miss you and lament every moment I am away from your touch. And I will regret missing the birth of our son. But you will be safe. Both of you. That matters more than anything else."

"What about you?" She pulled back a little to look him in the eyes. Djago could see that fear replaced the fire in her gaze. "How will you stay safe?"

Djago laughed softly. "I have Commander Ouza to protect me, and I am confident that he will find the assassin and uncover the plan behind their attempt on your life."

Genestra snuggled into his embrace. "Commander Ouza seems loyal enough, but I have never felt very comfortable around him. Maybe it's because his personality is so bland compared to Sir Reynfrey."

Squeezing her tight – he wished he could squeeze the life out of her and be done with it – Djago kissed the top of the head. "Don't worry, my love, he is a fine commander and very diligent in his work. Don't allow yourself to be dissuaded from his professional mannerisms because he lacks fluffery."

Genestra giggled and slapped him on the chest playfully. "I never considered Sir Reynfrey's poetic conversation, 'fluffery'. I would say he was charming." She sighed then and her tone saddened, "I will go to the summer house to protect our child. But as soon as you find those responsible for Tala's death you must send for me."

"I promise I will. When it is safe again." Djago lay his cheek on the top of her head and held her close. He was tired of the pretense.

It was a maddening sham but if everything went according to his design, she would not return until after the baby was born.

A few hours later Djago stood in a cold, damp subterranean chamber below the fortified Keep of Cambria. Ouza was with him and one other who was shackled to an inclined rack with arms and legs stretched far apart by the tension of iron chains. Aside from the dank odor of fungus and mold that hung heavy in the air, there was the stink of bile, feces, and blood that filed Djago's nostrils, exciting his senses with the craving for more.

"This one is strong-willed," Ouza observed. "He may die before he confesses."

Djago shrugged. "We have three confessions already and at least a dozen more interrogations after this one. I expect to lose a few. Who is this one?"

"The cook."

"Ummm," Djago studied the unconscious man closer. Before he arrived in the dungeons, Ouza had already beaten the cook severely, removed his fingernails, and stripped the skin off his feet. Blood still trickled from his ghastly wounds. "Careful not to deform the ones who confess. They are less reliable as a witness when they go to trial visibly mangled. The people must believe wholly in their testimony and cry for rebellion."

'Yes, my lord. Should I wake him?"

"Please do."

Ouza hefted a large bucket of water and effortlessly dumped the contents on the cook's head. He jerked forward, limited by his restraints, sputtering and coughing from the near-drowning before his swollen eyes widened in terror.

"Lord Djago." The cook reflexively pulled at his chains, "You know me. I have been a loyal servant since your father was the count. Please tell Commander Ouza that I could never have had a hand in this terrible scheme! Please!"

Djago leaned close. He could smell the fear and desperation. Good. He wanted the cook to admit to the crime and point to another.

What better claim could there be than the lifelong loyal servant, tempted by greed, performing one small service in exchange for a life of wealth?

"I know you poisoned the porridge," he whispered near the cook's ear.

"No, my lord! It wasn't me! I swear on my life!"

Djago moved to his other ear and whispered again, "Swear on your life? Would you swear on the lives of your wife and children that you are innocent?"

"Yes, my lord! I would swear it!"

Moving to stand in front of the cook, Djago fixed the man with an intense, cold stare. He knew it was an intimidating look having practiced it for hours with a small copper mirror that sat by his bedside. "Very well, take him down."

"Thank you, my lord. Thank you!" the cook cried with relief.

Djago did not move. "And bring this man's wife and children. He swears on their lives, so let's test their innocence on the rack as well."

"No! No, my lord, please! I will do anything; say anything you wish! Please don't hurt my family!" The cook futility pulled at his chains, tears carving trenches through the blood and grime on his face.

"Now the truth is clear!" Djago shouted. "You did, in fact poison the porridge!"

"Yes, my lord!"

"And the poison was intended for Lady Genestra, was it not?"

The cooked sobbed and sputtered, nearly hysterical.

"Was it not?" Djago slammed his fist against the rack.

"Yes! Yes, my lord!"

"Now tell me, who instructed you to poison my wife?"

The cook appeared confused, uncertain what to say. Djago knew he would not have the answer and nearly laughed at the mental contortions the man was going through to find one.

"It was the ding's brother, wasn't it?" Djago bellowed.

Startled by the outburst, the cook vocalized his confusion. "What?"

Djago grabbed him by the blood and sweat-stained collar of his tattered shirt. "Duke Banfield Eldorath of Yorwick," he hissed.

The cook slumped in his chains and bowed his head in defeat. He knew his confession would send him to the hangman's noose. "Yes, my lord."

Djago released the cook and took a step back. "See? That wasn't so hard now was it?"

The cook did not respond.

Turning to Ouza, Djago spread his hands as if expecting applause.

"Very good, my lord," Ouza indulged him.

"Put him in a cell and have him washed and fed." Djago strode toward the exit while he spoke, he had other things to do. "Then have a witness watch him sign his confession. Do the same for the rest."

"Yes, lord."

Djago left the dungeon to the tune of his own footfalls and quiet sobbing of the broken cook. A smile stretched his lips. He hoped he would get the chance to break a few more if time permitted.

~~~

"You have a son, my lord." Ouza delivered the news without emotion. Why wouldn't he? Djago had mixed feelings about it as well.

The trials had resulted in nearly two dozen men hung for treason. Each one of them confessed and pointed to Duke Banfield Eldorath, ruler of Yorwick, as the mastermind behind the attempted assassination of Lady Genestra. The duke's motivation was fuzzy and unclear of course, but the reasons for it didn't matter, only the outrage of the citizenry of Cambria. Djago did his best to fuel the anger of the mob with further plots and rumors of plots that stirred the imagination. He nearly had them openly calling for warfare when it was announced that his son was born.

And outrage turned to celebration.

On the one hand, the demon inside Djago was glad to have an heir to possess when his current host eventually died, but the timing couldn't have been worse. Now he would have to devise another scheme to get the people stirred up once again. Whatever it was would have to be even bigger, perhaps an attempt on his own life, an invasion, or both.

Bells began to ring from all around the city. News traveled fast, it seemed.

"Send word to the summer house to have Lady Genestra and the child brought to Cambria when they are ready," Djago sighed reluctantly. "Plan a week of celebration and feasting when they arrive." He hoped that the child would keep her occupied and distracted from pestering him to spend time with her. It had grown so bad before he sent her away that he'd nearly strangled her just to remove the annoyance.

The slight sardonic smile on Ouza's face nearly triggered the minor demon's death. The Incubus continually gave the impression that he delighted in other's misfortunes, even if it was that of his own master. Fortunately for him, Naamah walked into the room, and Djago allowed the small affront to pass.

"Go now," he ordered harshly. Ouza's smile disappeared, and he swiftly exited the room.

"All is ready with the Atiod and the Fir Bholg." Naamah was always to the point. Djago liked that about her . . .among other things.

He sat in the wood-framed chair behind his desk. "And what about the Dryads?"

"The Fir Bholg returned them to the druids outside of Lindpoole, just as you arranged. The Arch-druid, Filberzh the Risen, was furious about the abduction, vowing to punish Kumida and the

Cyclopes until he read your message. He has since returned to the druids' Enclave near Oswalt."

"Has Thrakel and her king agreed to the rest?"

"They have, my lord."

Djago paused a moment to revel in his delight. The past few weeks had been kind to him. Even the minor setback with his son's untimely birth didn't seem so daunting any longer.

Then he remembered, "What about Kumida? Did you discover the truth?"

"He is as you expected." She smiled, a rare thing that nearly always meant death was nearby. Djago smiled at the thought of it. He had witnessed her process with a prisoner, a common thief, a few weeks ago. Djago was fine with it. She had to eat. The memories excited him.

"You have done well, Naamah." He rose from his chair and took her hand. "Now, join me in my bedchamber, and we will discuss other ways you can serve me closer to home."

Two days later, Terril Djago watched from the balcony of his bedchamber as Lady Genestra arrived in Cambria with their infant son, Pen. She exited the carriage by which they came with the small bundle in her arms and waved to him joyfully. Djago returned the happy greeting and left the balcony to prepare to reunite with his wife and meet his new son for the first time.

"Get up and get out." He roughly shook Naamah from her late slumber. They had been awake most of the night. "My wife is here, and the sheets will need to be changed."

Without a word, Naamah found her clothing and departed. There was no love between them; there never would be, just the carnal acts to satisfy their mutual lust. The demon inside Djago often wondered what it would be like to love, but the closest he would ever come would be the memories of love that he could glean from his host. He knew there was something soul crushing about what he lacked, the void within and a brief melancholy that would recall the echo of an ancient memory from a time before he was a demon. Djago had no time for such thoughts, his wife and child would soon be waiting in the sitting room for him.

Washing the stains of the night from his body, he called for a steward to help him dress as he mentally prepared to step into the character they all expected. He hoped he wouldn't have to tolerate the charade longer than necessary; he didn't have the patience for it and there was much he wanted to do before the day ended. Maybe Ouza would find him sooner than late.

Djago strode into the sitting room, smiling from ear to ear. "Genestra, my love, I am so pleased you have returned! I have missed you dearly. Now, show me the special surprise that I've been expecting!"

Lady Genestra stood when he entered, the folds of her emerald-green dress falling smooth, she held a tightly wrapped bundle to her chest, and she returned his broad smile enthusiastically. "I missed you too, husband."

Djago carefully leaned in and gently kissed her cheek before he stepped back. "You look well."

"I am well." She lifted the bundle and turned it so that he could see its tiny face. "I present to you Pen Djago, the next Count of Cambria."

Unsure of what to do, Djago bent to kiss the child on the head, before announcing to the room, "I claim this child as my son."

There were several people in the room – friends and nobles that he barely noticed. They all clapped and cheered the declaration then gathered around them to offer congratulations. As if on cue, servants entered with trays of wine and platters filled with delicacies, and Djago suddenly found himself at the center of a celebration. It was a completely unexpected turn of events that filled him with fury and it took every ounce of restraint he had within him to keep it in check.

Minutes passed and then an hour. Just when Djago was sure he couldn't take it any more Commander Ouza burst into the room. "Count Djago, you must come quick! Soldiers from Yorwick have ransacked a village on our side of the border! Only a few of the farmers managed to escape and live to tell the tale!"

Djago felt relief run through his entire body. "I must attend to dangerous affairs of the land! Forgive me, Genestra," he exclaimed and departed with dramatic urgency. The stunned looks of shock and fear from everyone in the room nearly made him laugh.

Once alone in the corridor Djago patted Ouza as they walked. "You couldn't have come at a better time. I was near to the edge of murdering the lot of them."

Ouza remained quiet, but Djago could see well enough the sardonic smile that crept over his face. The same smile that made Djago want to kill him once before. This time he found humorous. "Where did you get the uniforms?"

"We discovered a Yorwick patrol camped on their side of the border. It was late, and they were drunk." Ouza's smile widened. "It was a fortunate find."

"I'm impressed with your resourcefulness, commander. Hit a few more border villages over the next few weeks. I want the citizens of Cambria screaming for war before I declare it."

They walked into Djago's study. Naamah was waiting, cleaned and dressed. He nodded to her and sat behind his desk while the other two remained standing. So far, the pair had served him well. Yet they were just at the beginning of a long and winding road of manipulation, intrigue, and deception with most of the tricky parts still to come. Djago found it unfortunate that he only had the power to control two of his summoned creatures at a time.

He recalled the day Dhroghan and his cursed Tuatha Dé trapped him and others of his kind in Metis's pithos. In those days he could summon and control hundreds of unearthly beasts, his power was vast with an ego to match. That ego was what had eventually allowed them all to be captured. He and his brethren were imprisoned for centuries in that damned pithos where their power decayed considerably. Ever since their recent and unexpected escape, Mamon was determined not to make the same mistakes again. Still, he was stripped of his true form with no possibility to retrieve it, unless he returned to the Infernal Planes. Nothing was worth that sacrifice.

"Ouza, I want you to dispatch riders to King Praeter Eldorath in Lyon's Gate and to the rulers of every major city in Lyonesse. Have them carry the same message of protest regarding Yorwick's recent aggression on our border and the trials that concluded assassins were sent by Duke Banfield Eldorath himself."

Djago shifted his gaze to Naamah. "You, my dear, stay in communication with the Fir Bholg shaman Thrakel. If they deviate from our agreement, I must know immediately. Secondly, inform the Atiod-Bherto to have their part ready by next spring and make sure their Arch-druid Cateteric understands that if he fails me the consequences will be dire."

Neither Ouza nor Naamah moved to leave. Djago appreciated their discipline and devotion, although he knew they would rip him to shreds if they had the power to do so.

"You may go." He waved them away and turned his attention to the numerous papers scattered over his desk. They departed in silence.

Over the next few weeks reports arrived from villages along the eastern border. Survivors claimed that soldiers and wizards dressed in the colors of Yorwick wantonly attacked their villages, killing citizen and soldier, burning their homes to the ground. Another report described the assault on a small Cambrian garrison, killing all the defenders except for two squires who somehow managed to escape to tell their tale. One of the squires recounted that the leader of the group not only had the colors of Yorwick, but also the household crest of the duke's own household!

The people of Cambria were incensed. They called for justice, they called for intervention by the king, they called for everything just short of war. Of course, Duke Banfield Eldorath denied it all, blaming bandits in stolen uniforms or a subversive group bent on causing strife in the kingdom. From the communications Djago received from King Praeter Eldorath, it was clear that his majesty supported his brother. Djago was frustrated. What would he have to do to instigate an escalation? Stage a mock invasion? Himself become a victim of assassination? At least the crisis provided an excuse to minimize the time he spent with Lady Genestra and their child.

The answer arrived in his bedchamber in the middle of the night less than a week later. Djago knew the man was there as soon as he entered and was impressed by his ability to move with blade drawn in absolute silence. This was no amateur.

Djago lay still, giving away no movement to indicate that he was awake. Slowly he probed the man's mind and was surprised to discover the absence of intent to kill. He allowed him to approach closer. Then the sharp side of the blade was pressing against Djago's neck. He opened his eyes slowly and without reaction to the disconcert of the assassin who clearly expected a far more startled response. Perhaps even an attempt to scream.

"Why are you here?" Djago asked calmly.

The assassin quickly recovered himself. This one was good at his profession, thought Djago. "I am here to kill you, of course."

"No you're not," Djago coughed a laugh. "You are here to give me a message. Otherwise, I'd be dead already."

Uncertainty flooded the assassin's eyes and he pulled back his knife. "I am from the Arid Fellowship." He paused for a reaction but got none. "My master knows that you planned the assassination attempt on your own wife."

Djago sat up in his bed and placed his hands on his lap. "Why would he think that?"

The assassin snarled. "Because no one in the Western Kingdoms would dare carry out an assassination on a political figure without the permission from the guild master of the Arid Fellowship."

"Do you have a point?"

Djago could not see the assassin's face but he knew that he was scowling. "Because you are a noble and possibly ignorant in what you do, the master proposes that you do not repeat the mistake. There will not be a second warning."

An idea was forming in Djago's mind and rather than just kill this fool he thought to use him as a messenger. Instantly he clamped down on the assassin's mind preventing him from the ability to move or speak. Then he wove threads of persuasion through his mind that would lend weight to Djago's words when they were re-spoken.

"Tell your guild master that I have a job for him. If he accepts there will be a horse's weight in gold and my promise not to undertake any further . . . trespasses on your profession." Djago paused to cement the thoughts of his plans in the man's head. "Now ride quickly back to him, do not stop to rest your mount, steal another one along the way if necessary."

Djago released the assassin's mind and watched him silently turn and disappear from the room. He was pleased with this unexpected gift. If the guild master of the Arid Fellowship accepted his proposal, then the people of Cambria would have to rise up with him. And just to be sure, he had a second plan in mind that would horrify the entire kingdom. Djago didn't expect to receive a response either way. He would have to wait and be patient, for if the guild master did as he asked it would likely just happen. It was almost thrilling to contemplate.

CHAPTER 7

Broken Expectations
SY5490

Kumida stood unmoving on the plain that abutted the Sea of Dragons called the Ice Coast. He stared toward the northern horizon, his singular dark eye searching the distance for any movement that would herald the arrival of his Fir Bholg allies. Cug had promised to meet him here with his army the first week of spring and still Kumida waited. They were already a month late and every day that passed without their arrival only soured his mood further.

"Any news from our scouts?"

Brontes shifted his weight in the icy sludge behind him, Kumida could sense his unease and fear. "No, my king, none have returned."

Over the past three weeks, they had sent a dozen scouts north to report on the progress of the Fir Bholg. At least one should have returned by now.

"Where is Steropes?" Kumida growled.

"He is at the water's edge inspecting the ships after last night's storm. Should I retrieve him?"

Kumida barked a laugh. "No, Brontes, let him go about his work. Those ships need to be ready when the Fir Bholg arrive. Lindpoole will never expect an attack by Giants from both land and sea!"

Giants knew nothing of building ships, but the demon inside Kumida did. Before he found the Cyclopes, the demon had possessed a Vikja shipbuilder until he drowned in a sudden storm at sea. The

Vikja's knowledge proved useful over the winter. Kumida instructed several Cyclopes in the art of building and sailing the Vikja ships and put Steropes in charge of the small fleet. They had enough to sail two hundred Cyclopes warriors anywhere along the coasts and riverways of the Western kingdoms and he planned to use them to their best advantage. The remaining Cyclopes and Fir Bholg, if they ever arrived, would march and attack from the land side.

"What of the humans to the south?"

Brontes stepped up to stand beside Kumida. "A few hunters near the Arges River. None have crossed over into Fomoire yet. Even if any did, they would stay well west of the Ice Coast since there is little to hunt here."

Kumida's stomach growled at the thought of fresh meat. "Double the foraging parties and bring me a human or two if you can. I crave the taste of marrow. Just don't allow any to escape and give us away."

"I will lead the foragers myself and return with plenty of meat in a few days, King Kumida."

"Make sure of it, Brontes, I expect a few hundred more hungry warriors to feed by the time you return."

Brontes nodded, then turned to sludge through the wet snow toward their camp. Kumida watched him go. He didn't trust that one. Brontes was a smart Cyclops and the hardest of the clan chiefs to break in the beginning. He would bear watching closely.

More days passed while Kumida waited for the Fir Bholg to arrive from the north and Brontes to return from the south. Both would be a welcome advent. Then, on a particularly crisp cold morning at dawn, a night sentry burst into Kumida's tent.

"My king! The Fir Bholg have arrived!" He was practically in a panic.

Kumida was relieved and didn't see the need for alarm. From the horizon, it would still take them several hours to reach their camp. "Wake me when they are close."

"That's what I mean, my king! They will be here in minutes."

Kumida bolted out of his cot and grabbed his thick fur cloak to ward off the chill. Why would Cug march the clans through the night to arrive at their camp at dawn? Brushing by the uncertain sentry, Kumida ran to the northern edge of camp.

There they were.

Hundreds of Fir Bholg less than half a league away. But they were not marching in a casual column, they were advancing in battle formation.

Kumida knew he had been betrayed.

"Sound the alarm!" he bellowed to the closest Cyclops. "Form a line to the north! We are under attack!"

Rams' horns sounded, piercing the tranquility of the early morning.

Cyclopes warriors began falling out of their tents, some with bits of armor strapped on and others barely clothed at all. Each one of them held a war club, spear, or battleax. Kumida knew that even with all the Fir Bholg clans gathered against him, he still outnumbered them. However, he did not feel the advantage. The Fir Bholg were much larger than the average Cyclops and worse, they were organized and prepared. The demon mind inside Kumida recognized that the battle was already lost yet still sent his warriors against them knowing nearly everyone would die.

Gathering twenty of his best warriors, Kumida fled toward the water where his ships were beached. When he arrived, most were gone, and others were damaged so badly they would not stay afloat. It dawned on him then that both Steropes and Brontes were part of the deception, abandoning him at this final hour to leave him for dead.

Kumida did not doubt that they had either colluded with Cug or guessed his intent when the Fir Bholg had not arrived when expected.

Kumida was furious. How could he have missed the signs of their subterfuge? "Steropes!" he roared to the wind.

One of his men approached at a run. "My king, one of the ships is still seaworthy!"

Kumida wasted no time getting his men onboard and shoved off. If they went north, the Arges River would dump them into the open waters of the Sea of Dragons, and south would take them along the eastern border of Lyonesse into The Wilds where few humans settled. Kumida chose south.

From his vantage on the river, Kumida could see that the battle continued to rage at the camp nearby. Soon the Cyclopes would realize that their king was not with them and many would retreat to the ships expecting to escape safely. It was not to be. Before they were a quarter of a league down the river, Kumida observed dozens of Cyclopes crowding the beach with nowhere to go. Within an hour they would be so many rotting corpses among the scuttled vessels.

Kumida felt nothing for them. He was incapable of compassion.

"Leave the sail and continue under oar until we escape into The Wilds," Kumida ordered. "We must be well down the river before an alarm can be raised."

The Cyclopes pulled hard, picking up speed. They were poor sailors, but their strength behind the oars would give them an advantage over any pursuers.

"Where will we go, my king?" the warrior guiding the ship with the tiller asked.

Kumida considered the thought for a while before he answered. There was only one place he could think of where they would be safe from humans. A place close to their god where they would live to kill another day.

"We will travel to Aitva."

~~~

"The Fir Bholg have routed the Cyclopes clans on the Ice Coast of Fomoire, my lord." Naamah delivered the news as cold and impassive as always. She might as well have been informing him that his porridge was getting cold. For that matter, Djago was sure that the only time his Succubus showed any passion for anything was when she killed . . .and in his bedchamber. He looked her up and down. She had been away for a while, carrying out his orders to prepare the Atiod-Bherto to aid him in the conquest of Lyonesse. Her blond locks fell seductively over her smooth, pale shoulders and he longed for her sharp nails to trail bloody lines down his back.

That would have to wait until later.

"What about Cateteric? Will he be a problem?" Djago knew well the reputation of the arch-druid as a betrayer and manipulator. He supposed that's how he and his cult had survived so long after the Oak War.

Naamah's dead eyes stared straight into his own. "Cateteric is mine now. He will do as you ask, and more if necessary."

Djago was amused. "You bedded the arch-druid?"

"Is that a problem?" Djago was sure that he detected a hint of humor in her reply. Remarkable, she might have a sense of humor after all.

He shrugged. "Just asking." The truth was that he loved the idea of the master manipulator being manipulated. "Come back tonight, and we will discuss your techniques in greater detail." He waved her out, then sprawled in his high-backed chair to look upon the bloom of spring in the valley outside his window. Djago was disgusted by the beautiful scenery around Cambria – high green hills carpeted with colorful wildflowers, clusters of small birds darting from the crenelated walls of the city to copses of leafy trees, clear blue skies no longer obscured by winter's dreary overcast. To Djago it was a disheartening reminder that he was in the thick of spring, sitting in his gloomy keep and not trampling his enemies into the mud.

A week earlier Cambria hosted the Tourneys in the north. Knights from all over northern Eriu and Lyonesse came together to compete. Conspicuously missing were the knights from Yorwick. Djago wasn't surprised by that, but he was a little disappointed. It could have been another excellent opportunity to visit more travesties his good people would have blamed on the Yorwick knights. As it was, the games ended without incident, and the semi-finals moved on to Oswalt. The champions would conclude in a few weeks at the Grand Tourney in Lyon's Gate.

Djago lifted a parchment from his desk and studied the flowing script in the hazy light that filtered through the window for the hundredth time. It bore the king's seal and a command that he come to Lyon's Gate the week before the Grand Tourney to discuss Cambria's grievances with Yorwick. Duke Banfield Eldorath would have received the same summons.

Unless he planned to defy the king openly, he would have to go. Djago hated the idea of protesting Yorwick's aggression in open court and awaiting the political judgment the king and his advisors would make. He already knew the outcome— the king would rule on his brother's behalf, blame the continued raids on brigands, or some such, and likely send troops from Lyon's Gate or another neutral city in Lyonesse to occupy the border. It would set Djago's plans back at least another year.

Djago slammed the parchment on his desk. Where were the damned assassins? He was sure the Arid Fellowship would have acted already, assuming their damned guild master had agreed to his proposal. Did a cart full of gold mean nothing to them?

There was still one more trick up his sleeve that Djago planned to put into motion before departing for Lyon's Gate. He rang the small bell sitting on his desk, and a servant immediately rushed in from outside the door.

"Yes, my lord?"

Djago barely looked up from a list of Cambria's military assets he was studying. "Find Commander Ouza. Tell him to come to me immediately."

~~~

The Sun Goddess Sunna entered the realm of the sky, her radiant gown brilliant and gold. She brought life-giving light into the world and kissed her dear sister on the cheek to wish her a pleasant slumber. Eriu, the Moon Goddess, reflected her sister's luminosity and retreated with the darkness.

Perault awoke to the dawn. His mind was already awhirl with thoughts of the week to come. He was in the final year as a squire to Sir Aldeman that would culminate in a special ceremony where he would receive the silver-fringed cloak. It was the mark of a Provisional Knight -one who was searching for an Act of Heroism or Service that would earn him the coveted gold-fringed cloak. He would have exactly three years to complete such a quest and he had no idea where to begin. If he failed, then he would have to give up the cloak and take up a trade or join the military as an officer.

Of course, he could avoid all that and elect to endure The Testing, a grueling trial of body and soul designed to determine his fitness to serve Sunna and win the right of the gold-fringed cloak without an Act of Heroism. He would probably elect to take The Testing anyway, just for the badge of honor that it conveyed, but first, he wished to seek the occasion to perform an Act of Heroism and prayed that Sunna would grant him the fortune and opportunity to do so.

He lounged on his goosedown pillow and reflected on the past decade in service to Sir Aldeman. From the time Perault could carry sword and shield he had been squired to the great knight. It was because of the close friendship between Perault's father, Earl Fineas Eckert, Lord of Stoddenferry Castle and Sir Aldeman that he became his squire.

The knight was old when Perault was sent to him, yet in those first few years Sir Aldeman would still compete in the Tourneys, always finishing in the top five before he reluctantly retired from them altogether. Sir Aldeman once told him that he would be the last squire the old knight would accept into his service and for that Perault was eternally grateful.

Under Sir Aldeman's tutelage, Perault excelled in nearly every combat technique there was to learn. Whether it was with lance, sword, ax, or flail, Perault was better than any that came before him. And it was with these skills that he entered the Squire's Tourney with the expectation that he would win or place in several categories. No matter how he finished in the Tourneys, he did not doubt that Sir Aldeman would recommend him for the silver-fringed cloak, but as the legendary knight's squire, he was determined to finish at the top to honor his master.

Perault had to get out of bed.

His mind was running wild with what needed getting done before departing for the beautiful lake-side city of Tintagel, where the first Tourney of the season would take place in the south. Sir Aldeman's estate was southeast of Tintagel and if they left by noon he would have his master settled into the inn reserved for knights and lords outside the fairgrounds before nightfall. Perault was fortunate that Sir Aldeman was a very wealthy landowner who didn't mind spending his coin on comfort. There were many squires that slept with their horses in the stables, even in their graduation year.

Washing and dressing quickly, Perault sped to the kitchen for bread and warm cider. The servants were busy preparing for the short journey as if they were taking a six-month expedition. They greeted him as warmly as a favored son. Sir Aldeman never had children and knowing full well that Perault would be the last squire to serve the aging knight, the servants looked upon him as almost an heir. Never had Perault thought of them as servants either, rather, they were more like a large family. More than one of the kitchen maids had chased him from the kitchens with a spoon or cuffed him on the shoulder for getting into trouble when he was a boy. He thought back on those days with fond nostalgia knowing that in a few weeks he would be leaving the household, the people he had grown up with, and the memories he cherished forever.

Nearly the entire household would be traveling to the Tourney. They would enjoy large tents at camp that would be nearly as comfortable as the inn where he and Sir Aldeman would be staying. It was a mark of pride and the honor of the household to bring them to the Tourney if a lord could afford to do so.

As luck would have it, they managed to depart almost precisely at noon. No doubt due to the Head Steward who made it a point to always stay on schedule. That was fine with Perault. He would leave with them and then ride ahead to make sure Sir Aldeman's accommodations were in order by the time his master arrived.

A long train of carriages and wagons snaked onto the main road outside the estate. To Perault, Sir Aldeman's entourage looked all the world like a small parade. Every servant was dressed in matching livery and a few carried pennants on tall poles that shone brightly with Sir Aldeman's coat of arms – the silhouette of a horse and lance on a field of white and gold. Bards were dispersed along the line playing lutes, beating drums, or strumming viols in a happy cadence. Sir Aldeman himself chose to ride his warhorse, at least the first league or two before inevitably retiring to his carriage. On this day he was resplendent in a silken white tunic under a gold riding jacket, matching pantaloons tucked into high riding boots and a gold-toned wide-brimmed hat set with a fluffy white plume. Behind him rode two dozen men-at-arms in full chain armor with surcoats displaying the house crest and matching pennants atop tall spears.

An impressive sight if Perault had ever seen one. It seemed to him that every knight of Lyonesse prided themselves on their pageantry as much as their combat prowess.

He pulled his mount up next to Sir Aldeman. "I'll leave you now and make haste to Tintagel."

"Get on then boy! I want my favorite chair and a warm mead when I get there!" Sir Aldeman crooned to him jubilantly.

Perault laughed and put his heels to his warhorse. He had no fear that the famous knight's chair would be waiting for him in the common room when he arrived. A dozen old knights would make sure of it before Perault ever got there. The servants joked that Sir Aldeman was holding court with his peers at the inn whenever he was in residence. It was becoming an annual tradition even when there was no Tourney since his master had retired.

Following the stretch of road that led from Sir Aldeman's estate to the main road, Perault passed leagues of farmland and forests that stretched to the horizon. Winter was officially over but a biting chill still hung in the air as a reminder that spring was slow in coming. Despite the cold, farmers were at their labors in the fields tending to their diversified crops and paid him little mind. Perault could not recall a year that had gone by in his life when the harvests in the kingdom were not abundant. Lyonesse was the breadbasket of the Western kingdoms with enough of a surplus that agriculture was its primary export and none within the realm would go hungry. This year was expected to be no different.

On the main road, hours passed with a few travelers here and there that Perault cheerfully greeted. He was in a fine mood today and looking forward to the Tourney. He allowed his thoughts to wander, conjuring images of his successes in each event, leading to the honor of receiving his silver-fringed cloak from Duke Maruk himself. He laughed out loud at the idea and considered how foolish his fantasies must be.

Rounding a bend, he was surprised to see three men on horseback blocking the road. He had been riding through the forest for some time now, and in this particular area the light was dim from the thick canopy of branches overhead. Perault never wavered or considered turning back. Rather, he confidently rode up to face the men who blocked his way. They looked like city folk whose clothes had seen better times mounted on horses that appeared underfed. Perault would need to be cautious.

"Is there a hazard ahead?" Perault needed to ascertain their intention quickly. If they were highwaymen then it would be up to him to dispatch them, even if they allowed him to pass. It was not in his nature to leave a threat to prey upon the next weaker man or family.

The man in the middle had a scar running along the left side of his face; he was the apparent leader. "There is a hazard all right, and we are here to collect a toll to ensure the safety of all who pass."

"A toll on the king's road? There has never been such a thing." Perault laughed at the men. He wanted to force their hand if they were intent on holding him up. "Besides, we are only a few leagues from Tintagel. Surely the duke would send his own men to secure the passage!"

The two men flanking the one who spoke rode a few steps closer to Perault. He knew they were attempting to intimidate him, but he was not going to tolerate that. They probably saw him as a rich mark wearing expensive threads, sitting on a fine horse and likely considered the sword that hung from his waist nothing more than a decoration.

The man with the scar was not amused. "We are here until the duke's men arrive. Until then, we will take whatever you have in your purse."

Whatever happened to the poetry of a good highway robbery, Perault wondered. In the books he read by Vyvyan or Boeger Penhallow there was always a much more creative dialog with the vagabonds. It ultimately resulted in the realization that they had chosen the wrong path in life and begged for repentance. That would not be the case today it appeared.

Perault pulled on the reins of his warhorse and fluidly removed his sword from its sheath. The sharp hooves of his mount battered the startled bandit on his left, crushing his skull with a few well-trained kicks while Perault struck the bandit to his right, slicing through the man's collarbone nearly to his spine. Both men were jerking spasmodically in the dirt by the time his horse had all four legs firmly on the ground again. Without pause, Perault spurred his horse forward to charge the remaining bandit.

The man with the scar, stunned by the unexpected violence, barely cleared his sword in time to deflect Perault's first blow. It wasn't intended to kill as much as it was to distract. Expertly turning his horse into his adversary, the massive steed nearly knocked the bandit off his mount, leaving his flank open for Perault to plant his sword deep between the man's ribs.

The bandit stared at him in disbelief, the light of life leaving his falling body. Perault watched with morbid fascination. There was nothing honorable about these deaths, and he certainly did not feel triumphant for taking their lives. He also felt no remorse. Strange how killing a man was nothing like how he'd imagined. Where was the glory? Where was the satisfaction? The men were dead and could never be redeemed.

Only a year before he had killed a thief who had stolen Sir Aldeman's late wife's jewels. The Temple Knights investigated the crime and determined that he was nothing more than a man down on his luck looking to make quick coin. It was likely they would never know how he found out about the jewels and their location within the house. Servants gossiped innocently about things like that sometimes, and the thief probably overheard and took advantage of his new-found knowledge.

His stomach abruptly churned with sickness. Perault pulled his horse away, dismounted, and heaved everything he had eaten for a month onto the ground. When he was done, he glared at the three immobile corpses on the ground.

"Such a waste of life," he lamented and in a fit of rage kicked the body of the man with the scar until he heard the distinct crack of the corpse's ribs break. Moments later, Perault composed himself and mounted his horse once more. There was no time to bury them, as he had to get to the inn.

Perault plucked a handkerchief from his sleeve that was sewn with the heraldic symbols of his master's house and dropped it on the ground near the bodies. Sir Aldeman's entourage would come across the butchery soon enough and know that it was he who had done this.

Suppressing his anger, Perault kicked his warhorse forward without a backward glance. Killing and battle were nothing like the fairy tales.

CHAPTER 8

Tintagel

Perault skirted the crowded southern gate which served as the primary point of entry into Tintagel. Behind those high walls rose the marvelous towers and inner citadel, known as Valiant Keep, where resided Duke Maruk and his family. He was glad that Sir Aldeman kept to his usual lodging outside the city where he was well known and away from the intrigues of the duke's court. His master often said that politics was a clever man's game that he had no interest in joining. Perault held no doubt that Sir Aldeman was clever enough for it, but his temper likely would have separated too many nobles from their heads in their disagreements.

Chuckling to himself at the thought, Perault knew that Sir Aldeman had no patience for liars and braggarts. To the accomplished knight, there was simply little honor in it, and Perault had to agree. He deserved a quiet retirement and had reached an age that he didn't have the energy for more than moderate physical activity. These days Sir Aldeman preferred to entertain at home and drink his ale with other retired knights trading tall tales from their youth.

The Tourney in Tintagel would be unique in that it was the last one Perault would compete in as a squire to Sir Aldeman. The Squire's Tourney was no different from the Grand Tourney that the knights competed in – the events were the same, and they took place in the same arenas. Perault was confident he would represent his master's household well in the events he intended to sign up for, he knew most of the other squires well and their capabilities, and few of them could measure up to his prowess in several of the events.

He thought back to the years that preceded his current circumstance. Sir Aldeman's training historically produced some of the finest men-at-arms and lancers in the realms and Perault was proud to count himself among them. Now, the focus of the final months of his training was devoted to understanding the Code of Sunna, how to conduct oneself with honor as a Temple Knight and lessons in humility. That last part was most certainly tailored specifically for Perault's tendency toward haughty arrogance that was said to be part of his natural character. Perault never denied it, it was who he was, and as far as he was concerned, he was determined to be the greatest knight Lyonesse had ever known.

Presently, Perault found the inn, turned over his horse to a stableman and went inside to ensure everything would be ready for Sir Aldeman's arrival. He took his duty to the old knight very seriously, especially now that Sir Aldeman was advanced in his age and merely asked for a little comfort during the twilight of his years. Perault would make sure of that and more. He owed his master an eternal debt of appreciation for preparing him for the station that he would soon be ascending to. Not just the combat training, that had come easy to him, but more importantly the state of mind required to always conduct one's self with honor and integrity.

A few hours later, Sir Aldeman and his retinue arrived at the inn. The Tourney would begin the next morning and last for a week before they would travel on to Oswalt for another week of Tourneys. After that, would be the Championships in Lyon's Gate where knights from not only the Western Kingdoms, but for the first time, the Eastern Kingdoms, would compete. All the kingdoms would be sending their best to compete in Lyon's Gate. Occurring every three or four years, the Grand Tourney had become the most significant international event in the Western Kingdoms.

The next morning Perault rode to the Tourney field to register Sir Aldeman's House banner in the Squire Tourney. There were a number of different events to choose from including single combat elimination events like jousting, archery, mounted melee, and dismounted melee. There were also team events for many of the same. It was not unusual for a competitor to enter two or three events for the week and Perault, true to his form, always pushed himself to do more than the others.

"Greetings, Perault!" A good-natured voice called from behind.

Perault knew that voice well. He turned and smiled. It was squire Davin of House Jeutemont descending upon him with one of his patented bear-hugs.

Perault endured the embrace with as much dignity as possible before he was released by the massive squire. Davin was the same age as Perault and also in the final weeks of his service as squire to the aged Sir Grethin. He knew Davin through their masters, who were the best of friends for decades. The squires often hunted and sparred together when they met on social occasions and had built a close friendship over the years.

Perault slapped his old friend on the shoulder. "What events have you registered for, Davin?"

Davin shrugged. "The usual, ya know. Archery, ax-throwing, and jousting. How about you Perault? Or should I say which events did you not sign up for?"

Perault laughed at that. "Not as many as last time, I fear. I'm committed to single and team joust, archery, single melee, and mounted melee. That's about all I can handle, I think."

"More than most, as usual, my friend. And archery this time, eh?" Davin shoved a meaty elbow into Perault's side playfully. "We may be against each other in the finals if you're any good, ya know."

"If we do I might concede outright!" Perault couldn't help but recall the last Tourney they competed in together. Squire Davin had only entered the melee competitions at that time and was feared by everyone he was set against. That all ended when he broke a fellow squire's spine in one-on-one combat, killing him instantly. Davin was devastated. He refused to compete in the melee events again. That was three years ago, and Perault shared some hard times with his friend before he finally forgave himself, including an attempt to end his own life. Davin was a big, muscular man far quicker on his feet than most would guess and his strength could only be described as unnatural. He was also a sensitive man who cared about others beyond the skills measured at a Tourney. Perault thought that, beyond anything else, was why he liked Davin so much.

"Has Sir Grethin finally prevailed over his frugal nature and allowed a room for you at the inn for your final Squire's Tourney?"

Davin laughed heartily at the supposed joke. "I'm in the tents as usual, like all the other squires. None of us has enjoyed your luck to have a master remotely concerned with his squire's comfort."

"Don't worry, my good friend!" Perault announced grandly. "The quickest cure to a fellow squire's envy is through a keg of ale that will be dispatched immediately to your tent!"

"Does that mean you will be joining us this evening?"

Perault slapped Davin on the chest and turned to leave, calling over his shoulder as he walked away, "Do you even have to ask?"

The rumble of Davin's laughter followed him.

In all the years Perault had traveled to Tourneys with Sir Aldeman, they had never stayed in tents. There was always an upscale inn or some forgettable noble begging to have the great knight at their residence for a few days. Nevertheless, Perault would always find himself in the squire's tents drinking and swapping stories with his peers. It was the one thing that kept him grounded, and he cherished his friendships. If not for them he surely would have been hopelessly pompous and insufferable in any social encounter and shortly shunned from polite society.

Perault mounted his horse and soon found himself riding through the tent city created near the Tourney grounds. Each tent was an expansive enclosure that connected with the next. It was something like a single massive tent with multiple soft-sided chambers and entrances. Outside, the livestock and horses roamed within picketed corrals next to covered wagons where blacksmiths went about their work repairing horseshoes, armor, and weapons. Occasionally, he passed large open squares surrounded by a maze of tents with enough room to provide for an open-air tavern, complete with long tables, servers, and cooks just like the finest halls on the other side of the walls in Tintagel. Perault knew his way around both worlds equally well.

The explosion of colors representing each house as evidenced by the banners and corresponding tents was nearly overwhelming. Worse still was the matching livery the squires were compelled to wear. Perault also wore his master's colors and did not feel the specter of appearing ridiculous in this environment. However, once he left the boundaries of the squire's camp, the colorful display of his surcoat made him stand out like a peacock among ducks. It was a discomfort that, for some reason, only he appeared to endure.

Perault's route brought him into a second tent city. This one was far less organized and colorful with zig-zagging avenues occupied by various merchants and enthusiasts unable to find or afford proper accommodations within Tintagel. Here, the stink of mud and manure was a potent reminder that he was among the general populace. Perault never understood why the basic difference between nobility and common citizenry was the inclination to excise their excrement. Considering that he was the son of an earl, he supposed it came down to breeding and good fortune.

As swiftly as possible, Perault escaped through the southern gate into Tintagel. Unsurprising, the streets were clogged with people moving like a river in one direction or another. During the Tourneys, the population swelled to more than double, spilling out beyond the walls into several tent cities similar to the last one he had traversed. Perault's father explained that it was an economic windfall for the merchants of the city that occurred only during the Tourneys. Perault didn't think much of that, his concern was winning every event and giving the crowds . . . How did his brother put it? . . . the highest possible degree of entertainment.

The smell of the city filled his senses with aromas of cooked food, boiling laundry and animal defecate all at once. At least it was marginally better than the merchant's tents. Despite the smell, the streets were reasonably unpolluted and Perault nodded with respect to the cleaning crews he passed. To a man they hailed him and shouted words of encouragement. His success in the Tourneys as a relative local had earned him an acclaim among the common folk that he would never admit he secretly relished.

Perault was certain in his course through the upper city. He was going to the home of a wealthy wheat and barley merchant who owned an estate outside of the inner wall of Valiant Keep. The merchant, Erol Brigham, and his family had been close friends to his own since before he was born. Often, Perault would stay at the Brigham Estate when Sir Aldeman allowed him a day or two off from his duties. Mr. Brigham had two sons near his age that were as close to him as his own brothers and a daughter that he didn't think much of when he was younger. To their parents' credit, the boys were well educated and benevolent. Perault thought they envied his physical prowess as much as he envied how knowledgeable they were about the world. It was a good match, as he made sure they were never bullied or intimidated by other children and they told him incredible stories about life outside Lyonesse. The Brigham girl was two years his junior and loved to recite poetry, display her pretty dresses, and constantly torment him with her clever tongue. Never having sisters of his own, Perault supposed that she was the most annoying thing to walk the earth.

And then one year, not long ago, Perault went to stay a few days with the Brighams and began to see her differently. Somehow, she had grown curves in places where there were none before and she spoke softly and without the bite of insults he was used to when she was younger. Her long brown hair had grown longer and she smelled nice. Oddly, he spent more time with her on that visit than with her brothers and more peculiar still, they did not seem to mind. Even Mr. and Mrs. Brigham approved and simply smiled a lot at him and each other. That was two years ago. Somehow, the annoying girl had become the beautiful woman he knew as Melisende Brigham and she was nearly the entire reason he visited as often as he could manage.

Perault was looking forward to seeing Melisende, even if his visit would be brief. He was here for the Tourneys and there would be no time for walking on the beaches and exploring the caves and coves on the coast, speaking their feelings through poetry in the evening firelight of the hearth, or attending the local theatre. They usually did everything together, enjoyed each other's company and stole a few kisses – but that was it. Perault would take his passions no further unless he married Melisende. And he did want to marry her, but not until he earned his gold-fringed cloak. Perhaps that was why her parents trusted him to accompany their daughter, unchaperoned. They knew Perault would never dishonor his family name or jeopardize his opportunity to become a knight with a scandal. He thought maybe Melisende understood as well, but he was not sure about that.

Over the past two years, his feelings for Melisende had grown significantly. Her brothers, Elian and Yorlik, only a year apart, assured him that their sister felt the same way. In fact, the whole family, Perault's as well, were hoping for a match. This was news to Perault. News he embraced whole-heartedly, assuming Melisende was willing to wait.

They had never spoken of it, and he wondered if they should.

The path that Perault followed to earn his gold-fringed cloak was destined to be perilous and fraught with many challenges that might well leave a new bride widowed in their first year of marriage. He was not willing to put Melisende in that position. He would be firm about that when they dared to have the eventual conversation.

He guided his mount down the broad avenue that led to the gates of the Brigham Estate. The crowds had thinned out considerably since he turned away from the market and toward the affluent row of estates that lined the way to Valiant Keep. It was well known that to own one of these prestigious properties was to thrive in the good graces of Duke Maruk and the king.

The Brigham Estate was expansive with multiple levels, towers, and enclosed stables. It was situated along the west wall with a premium view of Lake Virtue and the closest estate to Valiant Keep itself. It was clear by the grandeur and opulence of the manor that the Brigham family was one of the wealthiest in Tintagel if not the whole of Lyonesse. The largest of four of the granaries that provided their fortune was further to the south at the edge of the trade district where the Brigham wheat was converted into bread or sold by the bag in the markets while the barley was distributed to the local taverns. The Brigham granaries were the largest suppliers of bread and flour to the city with an enviable surplus that was exported throughout Lyonesse and into Eriu.

Perault was aware that Erol and Lyra Brigham had come onto the political stage years earlier when, as a wedding gift, they honored King Praeter Eldorath and Queen Penelope by donating ten percent of their production to the orphans and homeless of the kingdom. Their donation became an annual tradition that had since virtually eliminated hunger in the realm. It was rumored that the royal couple was so touched by the humanitarian effort that King Praeter offered Erol Brigham vast lands and the title of a duke in the unsettled territory south of Castle Bours. Perault's father confirmed the rumors and also divulged that Mr. Brigham declined the honor. The thought of it still brought tears to Perault's eyes. As a duke, the Brighams would have enjoyed enviable power and influence in the greatest realm of the Western kingdoms. As a low member of royalty himself, Perault did not dare search his soul to know whether or not he would have made the same choice. The answer would likely leave him disappointed with himself and only elevated his esteem of Erol Brigham.

Although the Brigham Estate was a fortified structure constructed with a creamy-gray, fine-textured limestone, there was no gate to impede Perault from riding to the heavy set of oak doors that served as the manor's main entrance. Nevertheless, he knew that a servant would always be keeping watch for visitors and by the time Perault dismounted, there was a young man waiting to take charge of his horse.

Barely a second later, one side of the grand oak double doors opened, and two men about his age stepped out, both smiling from ear to ear – the brothers Elian and Yorlik.

"It's good to see you brother!" Elian exclaimed and embraced Perault in a familiar hug.

Yorlik, the taller of the two, joined in making it a group hug. "But I'm sure it's not us you came to entertain!"

"Fortunately for the two of you, your sister grew up to be the prettiest of your lot!" Perault jested. They all laughed together, slapping his shoulders heartily.

Then his gaze shifted to a figure coming down the stairway beyond the doorway. Yorlik or Elian, he wasn't sure which, was saying something else, but his attention was fully diverted. It was Melisende. She wore a pale blue dress with her long brown hair spilling over her bare shoulders in wavy curls. Her skin was creamy white like pure milk and her lovely eyes blue as the lough itself. When she saw Perault standing in the doorway with her brothers, she smiled with radiance to rival that of Sunna.

Her brothers stopped speaking and turned to see what distracted Perault.

"Yorlik, we've already lost him."

"My eyes confirm it, brother. Let us leave them to their reunion."

Perault felt a rough pat on his shoulder and then their laughter receding behind him. Without further hesitation, Melisende quickly crossed the space between them and they embraced tightly, sharing a long kiss.

"Hello, lad!" A booming voice called out causing them both to jump and pull away from each other. "We've all been on pins and needles expecting your arrival." It was Erol Brigham, with his wife Lyra brushing by her husband to embrace Perault warmly. Erol was a large man, tall and wide. He was not so much fat as he was stout. In his youth he carried bags of heavy flour in the granaries and was quite muscular before time settled and softened him a bit with age and ale. Lyra was a slight woman with brown hair and comely looks that she clearly had passed to her daughter.

"Let us go to the sitting room for refreshments," Erol suggested jovially.

Perault felt like he had come home. The truth of it was that the Brigham Estate was more home to him than Stoddenferry Castle considering that he hadn't had the opportunity to visit his family home so often since he had with Sir Aldeman. It had been only two months since his last visit to Melisende, but to him it felt like an eternity.

When they were all seated with glasses of fine Mekali wine from Atlantis, Mr. Brigham rose to offer a salute. "This is your last Tourney as a squire to the honorable knight, Sir Aldeman. In a few weeks, no doubt on the heels of many victories, you will be presented with the silver-fringed cloak and honored as a Provisional Knight of the realm! We are all proud of you, Perault."

The big man raised his glass high. "Salute!"

They all stood and responded in unison, "Salute!" before sitting once more.

Perault felt a little embarrassed and was about to offer his thanks when Melisende squeezed his hand she was holding and hissed at her father playfully, "Father, tell him."

"What? Oh, yes." Erol Brigham smiled broadly. "In honor of your impending accomplishment, my family and I have decided to follow your progress in the coming weeks in both Oswalt and Lyon's Gate." He looked over and smiled proudly at his daughter. "Melisende wishes to witness the fine cloak laid upon your shoulders, as do the rest of us."

A thrill of excitement rushed through Perault. Not only would he be able to spend a little time with Melisende during the entirety of the Tourneys, but he would have the honor of demonstrating his skills in the various events he would participate in under her watchful gaze. "That is excellent news!" Perault responded.

"Tell him the rest, Father."

"Of course, daughter." He cleared his throat and smiled again. "Well, it seems that your family thought that it was such a good idea that they have decided to join us!"

Another thrill went through Perault. He had not seen his family in over a year. What a reunion it would be to have everyone together once again.

"And don't forget the last part." Melisende chimed in a sing-song voice.

"Ha-ha, the last part indeed." Mr. Brigham snickered. "You're not going to believe this, boy. In a highly unexpected break from usual protocol, the Master of Ceremonies, Duke Maruk, will not be knighting the squires at the end of the Tourneys in Lyon's Gate."

"Has the duke fallen ill?" Perault was concerned.

"No, no. Nothing like that."

"Then who will it be, Mr. Brigham?"

Pausing for obvious dramatic effect, Erol Brigham gazed around the room before he finally made the announcement. "Why, the next best thing, King Praeter Eldorath of Lyonesse himself!"

~~~

"I missed you," Melisende whispered snuggling her cold nose into the soft creases of Perault's neck.

He was glad that they were finally alone given the small amount of time that they would have together over the next few weeks. The Parade of Champions kicked off the Tourneys at first light the next morning with combat events commencing immediately afterward. The knights events would begin first, with the squires filling in the time between them.

"Of course you did, my dear," he chuckled. "You know that I missed you too."

Shifting her head to lay on his shoulder, she smoothed the wrinkles in her skirts with the palms of her hands. "Are you ready for tomorrow?"

Perault was touched by how unnecessarily nervous she was and he attempted to assuage her fears. "Have no worries, dear. I know the field of competitors quite well and there are few who give me the slightest concern."

She appeared to relax and after a moment raised her hand in front of her. "Why don't we take a stroll?" As well as she tried to conceal it, Perault detected a slightly wicked smile on her face. He stood without hesitation, took her offered hand and then strode arm and arm through the darkening halls of the estate.

They didn't talk much, it was enough that she was so near and he could smell the floral fragrance she had applied to her skin. It was intoxicating. Soon they came to a steep stairway which ended at a cozy observation courtyard on a landing in one of the tallest towers of the estate. From here, Perault could see over the high curtain wall that surrounded the upper city of Tintagel and far across the turquoise blue waters of Lough Greely just beyond. The cool spring breeze chilled further by the cold waters of the lough felt good to Perault considering his rising internal temperature with Melisende so close.

She led him to a shallow cove carved into the side of the tower out of sight of the entry where they had sat many days during his unofficial courtship to her. Mostly they would converse about everything under Sunna or read short stories and poetry to each other, but on this occasion, Melisende had something very different in mind.

For the better part of an hour, she kissed him passionately and pressed his hand against the fabric covering her breast. Perault allowed himself a few satisfying squeezes and nothing more. To his relief, Melisende did not press him further. The women of Lyonesse were known to be strong-willed and passionate in their love once they accepted a man. Despite his intense desire for her physical touch, Perault loved Melisende deeply and could think of no other who could dominate his thoughts so completely. He would marry her one day, Sunna willing, and endeavor to make her proud to be his wife.

These were the moments he would someday wish he could have frozen in time.

Later that afternoon Perault joined the Brigham family for an early dinner before the inevitable farewells. With the family present, the best he would receive was the press of Melisende's lips on his cheek before he was riding alone to the Knights Inn. His thoughts were awash with his love much of the way. He could still feel the place on his skin where her lips had pressed when he caught sight of the inn in the distance. At that moment he decided it would be best to put all thoughts of Melisende away for a while so he could focus on the challenges ahead in the Tourneys without distraction.

Inside, the inn was congested with servants ferrying platters of food and ale from the kitchen, and pages running endless streams of messages from their masters. It was the way of the Tourneys. A frenzy of drinking with the knights sending good-natured taunts to their adversaries or words of encouragement to their allies. It would go on like this much of the night leaving those competing in the Tourneys swaying in their saddles the next morning. Perault would have none of it. He wanted his wits about him. Davin and the other squires would have to drink without him tonight.

Before finding his room, he sought Sir Aldeman, who was sitting near the large hearth for warmth. He was surrounded by a host of several other retired knights and nearly as many younger ones. They were all enraptured by his tales. Perault knelt quietly next to his master until he was noticed.

"Ah, Perault, so good that you are here. Did you have a nice time at the Brighams today? Of course, you did! That young lass of theirs certainly turns a head or two." There were chuckles of agreement from the nearby onlookers. "Now, tell us what events you registered for at this Tourney?"

Hiding a smile of embarrassment, Perault did his best to sound humble. "Yes, Sir Aldeman. I am registered for six events this week, and I am feeling strong."

One of the old knights sitting next to Sir Aldeman let out a long low whistle. "That is a lot to take on, young man. I hope you are more sensible when you are competing in the Knights Tourneys in a few years."

Before Perault could answer, Sir Aldeman cut in. "Sir Mordecain, this boy could probably best most of the knights in any Tourney we've ever been in, including us!"

Sir Mordecain laughed, "Agreed Sir Aldeman, they breed them stronger and faster than they used to. What do you say, Perault?"

Perault stood and bowed. "You are correct, Sir Mordecain. I have probably bitten off more than I can handle, but I hope to win as many events as possible to impress the king since I will be fortunate enough to receive the silver-fringed cloak from his hands in Lyon's Gate. And this way, even if I lose a few I'll still win more than anyone else."

The knights around him laughed heartily. "And I thought he was a humble lad, Sir Aldeman," another knight shouted with laughter.

"Never humble in combat or love, Sir Grethin!" Sir Aldeman shouted, and the knights erupted in more laughter.

"Bring a drink or ten for the lad," Sir Grethin called to a server.

Sir Aldeman winked at Perault and whispered, "In their eyes, you're a knight already. You've done well my boy."

Perault allowed himself only one hour and one drink before he excused himself from the jovially drunk knights and retired to his room for the evening.

Finally at rest, he lay in the darkness of his room thinking about the journey that had brought him here. Sir Aldeman was a good man and good to him. And not because Perault's father was an earl, it was the nature of the old knight.

The first few years were tough. He'd missed his family and had to learn the duties and discipline of a squire. Sir Aldeman only had to cuff him a few times before Perault fell in line and learned his job. Soon he began to love the work and the excitement of serving an accomplished knight. Even if Sir Aldeman was late in his career, he still placed well in the Tourneys and commanded great respect from the other knights.

As the legendary knight grew older, weaker, and slower, there came a time for him to hang up his shield. This was about the time that Perault became old enough to compete in the Squire Tourneys. Sir Aldeman pushed Perault to enter, and he did, only to get completely smashed in every event. From then on, Sir Aldeman poured all his energy into Perault's training, and three years later he began to win the events he entered. At first, only one or two and then more and more with each passing Tourney. The previous Tourney he had entered five events and won all but the archery competition. Perault had shown great promise once he had encouragement and Sir Aldeman married skill with Perault's natural talent to perfection.

In his youth, Sir Aldeman was a legend of the Tourneys. In fact, he was the only knight to ever win six events in a Tourney and he did it five times in his career. Many of the other knights were not surprised that Perault possessed much of the same skill and determination of his master, but Perault had something else – a focus or intensity that was far beyond anything Sir Aldeman had ever enjoyed. Or so he said. Not to mention that Perault was so much bigger and stronger than Sir Aldeman, even when the knight was in his prime. Sir Aldeman actually feared that Perault could accidentally kill or do permanent injury to another participant if he did not constrain himself. Fortunately, Perault already realized this in previous practice matches and as a sad witness to his friend Davin's tragedy. Since then, he was careful to let up a little when striking sensitive areas of his opponent.

Over the last two or three years, Sir Aldeman had been so concerned with Perault's training that he relieved his squire of all his usual duties. Instead, his master assigned the household servants to those responsibilities. Yes, Sir Aldeman had been good to him, and Perault had done his best to exceed his expectations. The next few weeks would be important not only to him, but to his family and to the legacy of Sir Aldeman. Perault was confident in his abilities but wary of being overconfident as this year was expected to field some of the best talent in years. He was determined to make his master proud.

Thoughts of glory and victories yet to be won spun in Perault's head until they became vague images under heavy eyelids until the darkness took him.

CHAPTER 9

The Tourney

Waking with the dawn, Perault felt refreshed and energized. Today would be a good day. After washing and dressing quickly in a surcoat bearing Sir Aldeman's House colors, he strode into the common room to join a score of other knights and squires up early in preparation for the day of competitions. Many of them hailed him cheerfully as he took a seat. The table was laden with a traditional breakfast of warm crusty bread with sweet molasses, soft cheese, and hot spiced ale. For generations, this was the meal that all knights partook before competition, combat, or battle and today the custom was open to the squires who were competing in the Squires Tourney that day.

Perault let his gaze pass around the table while he poured himself a mug of steaming ale. None of the older knights were present. He smiled to himself, not really expecting them to rise so early. He knew Sir Aldeman wouldn't be awakened and dressed by his steward for at least another hour, just in time to join the spectators at the Tourney grounds for the Parade of Champions.

The chilly morning breeze stirred his short brown locks of hair and gently brushed by his cheek when the front door of the inn opened. Perault glanced up to see his two squires Hanlin and Dorlik walk in. The two men glanced around the room and then smiled broadly when Perault waved them over to sit next to him. They were squires in name only and for only as long as he was competing in the Tourneys. Both were on loan from the king's army where Hanlin was a groom in the cavalry originally from Bours and Dorlik was an apprentice to a blacksmith and hailed from the northern side of Eriu. More than that, Perault considered them both friends that he had grown to know well over the years and often visited whenever he traveled to Lyon's Gate where they were stationed. This would be the second Tourney that they "squired" Perault and he knew that his horse and armor could be in no better hands.

Before they sat, Perault stood, and the three traded bear-hugs and slaps on the back. "I see you have kept Sir Aldeman's colors in good condition." Both men wore surcoats similar to his own.

Dorlik ruffled Hanlin's short sandy-blond hair. "I had ta remind this one not ta wear his while mucking about shoveling horse dung. We have ta look respectable representin' the next champion o' the Squire's Tourney, ya know!"

"Leave off, you fat-headed lout." Hanlin shoved the much larger man's arm away playfully with little effect. "You're too busy braidin' your hair to take notice of my shovlin'!"

Perault laughed and motioned for them to sit. "You two haven't changed since I saw you last year! Sit with me and shake off the morning chill with a bit of spiced ale." He called for mugs and poured them both a few swigs.

"Are ye ready for the games then, Perault? You been keepin' fit and fine for 'em?"

"I have, Dorlik." Perault slapped the big man on the shoulder. "You think just because Sir Aldeman is getting on in age he lets up with his training? I think this year has been the most exhausting because it's my last."

Hanlin laughed at that. "We'll see the results on the field, I'll wager!"

"You know how it goes, Hanlin. You boys keep the dents out of my armor and my horse strong and healthy and I won't leave any effort unshed in the arenas."

Dorlik lifted his mug into the air, it looked tiny in his meaty hand. "Here's ta leavin' nothin' on the field o' battle. Especially yer head!"

Perault spent a few more minutes laughing and catching up with his friends before it was time to leave for the parade grounds. He was not surprised at all when they walked outside to find his horse fully saddled and covered in a caparison with Sir Aldeman's coat of arms and colors. Nearby stood his squire's horses, lances displaying matching pennants and a fourth horse hitched to a wagon carrying Perault's weapons, armor, and repair equipment. Dorlik and Hanlin must have risen before dawn preparing everything in advance.

Perault smiled to himself. Good men, these two.

Without delay, they all mounted and headed toward the jousting grounds where the opening ceremonies were to commence a couple of hours later.

"Did ya hear 'bout the new babe born to tha Duke an' Duchess o' Cambria?" Dorlik rode on one side of Perault with Hanlin on the other.

Perault nodded. "I heard there was an heir but not the name. It was last fall wasn't it?"

"The boy's name is Pen," Hanlin chimed in. "Pen Djago. He was born in the winter."

"Perhaps we will watch him in the Tourneys one day," Perault noted the congestion building on the road ahead and spurred his mount forward at a quick pace. "Let's get off the road and go around all these people. I don't want to be late."

The Parade of Champions would take place on the largest Tourney field outside the walls of Tintagel. Temporary benches twelve deep and several spans high were erected all around the field to give paying spectators the best advantage viewing the jousting and mounted combat that would be taking place there later in the day. Already, seats were beginning to fill up. Early on in the Tourneys there would be many events occurring at the same time with so many competitions. Smaller fields surrounded by benches were visible nearby as well. The arenas within the city walls would be in almost constant use.

Perault sent Hanlin ahead to speak with the Tourney officials about their position in the Parade of Champions. Four years prior the officials determined the order by a House's social rank in the kingdom, however, that resulted in so many objections and petty squabbles that King Praeter announced that there would be a change for this Tourney.

Hanlin rejoined them a short time later. "It appears that the Houses will now be arranged in the parade by their success in the prior Tourney. That means that for the knights, House Talowin will lead and for the squires House Aldeman."

Hanlin led them to their appropriate position on the field to the cheers of onlookers who were already settled. There they would wait another hour for the competing Houses to find their places and the remaining spectators to filter in. Of course, Perault knew that no matter how quickly that happened, the parade would not begin until after the Duke of Tintagel arrived.

As it turned out, the Tourney officials were surprisingly efficient and sooner than Perault expected, trumpets blared and Duke Maruk led Lady Eselt to their noble seats atop the largest and highest of the constructed stands. The masses surged with cheers at their entrance. The duke and duchess were obviously beloved by their people. The duchess looked as young and radiant as ever smiling and waving to the adoring crowd, but as they passed close, Perault's sharp vision detected a hint of sadness in her features and her smiles almost appeared forced and unnatural. The last time he had seen the duchess was when she married the much older duke right here in Tintagel the previous summer. It was then that he foolishly taunted Sir Drystan for his love of the duchess as only a week before he had found him embracing Eselt atop the highest landing of his own family's castle in Stoddenferry. The image was still vivid and haunting, and he hoped for their sake that the affair had truly ended when Eselt became the duchess.

A quiet anticipation settled over the masses once the duke and duchess took their seats. Tintagel had not hosted anything larger than local Tourneys in nearly eight years, but the people had heard stories about the pageantry of the major Tourneys and expected high entertainment. Perault competed in the major Tourneys four years before in Bours, Yorwick and Lindpoole and knew the people were about to get exactly what they wanted.

As if the conclusion of his thought was the cue, several dozen brightly clad riders charged into the middle of the field and formed three counter-rotating circles one inside the other. Each rider trailed vibrant fabric ribbons of green, red, and yellow that fluttered wildly behind them in the circular formations and each held a longbow from which they fired arrows almost straight up in the air towing a matching ribbon. Just as the arrows reached their apex they exploded in a display of colorful light and smoke and a loud gong echoed across the flat landscape. At first there were cries of fear from the startled crowd that quickly turned to screams and shouts of delight. Then, as the smoke from the arrows began to dissipate, bells from Tintagel began to chime vigorously and the gold-cloaks of House Talowin led the parade of knights around the perimeter of the field.

"By order of Duke Maruk and Duchess Eselt of Tintagel, and with the good blessings of King Praeter Eldorath and Queen Penelope of Lyonesse, the games of the Tourney are declared to begin!" The disembodied announcement reached every corner of the field and beyond through some magical enchantment. Perault was no wizard but he could recognize the signs of magic when employed in so obvious a fashion.

The parade marched far around the edge of the field with each House announced to the crowd as they passed dipping their lances in salute to the duke and duchess. By the time Perault joined the parade leading the squires, House Talowin was on the opposite side of the field with a long line of knights stretching between them. Still the crowd cheered and he was especially proud when he passed the duke and duchess to see his family sitting with Sir Aldeman, the Brighams and Melisende just a level below the royals as honored guests. The look of pride on his father's face so closely matched that of Sir Aldeman, that Perault was almost overwhelmed by his emotions and his eyes welled with tears of joy. It was for them that he was determined to be a champion even if it was merely a champion among squires. He would not let them down.

~~~

Two armored squires, mounted and riding hard with lances thrust before them, met in the center of the small arena brutally shattering their wooden shafts violently upon each other. The crowd roared at the impact that sent one of the metal-clad combatants careening dangerously over the back of his horse to land hard on the earth below. The other squire, nearly as precarious, managed to stay upon his mount by some miracle and regain control. He would be named the victor in this round.

Perault watched in fascination from a discreet location near the stables where Dorlik and Hanlin were preparing his horse with a specialized saddle and various pieces of metal armor to keep the powerful beast from getting injured by an errant thrust or shattered shards of a lance. There would be one more match before it was his turn to take the field. Just above him and to his right, a father was explaining the rules of the joust to a young boy who must have been his son. It reminded Perault of the first time he attended a joust with his own father who explained the concept of the match in much the same way.

"Jousting is a fast-paced, violent game with a simple set of rules." The boy's eyes were on the field, but Perault could tell his ears were hungrily taking in every word his father spoke. "Two adversaries take positions some distance apart at opposite ends of those lanes yonder separated by the barrier."

"What is the barrier for, Pa?"

"The barrier is there to keep the riders from crashing their mounts into each other and guide them straight and true to their opponent. When the herald drops a flag they start off as fast as they can toward each other, and it is up to the skill of the rider to find his mark on the other with a wooden shaft called a lance."

The boy had a look of confusion on his face. "What's the mark?"

His father smiled. "That's the place on his opponent where he thinks he can knock him off his horse if he strikes it."

"What if he misses?"

"Well, most of the time that is the case, and it becomes a game of points. If one of the riders shatters his lance on the shield, chest, shoulder, or helm of his opponent then he gains one point. If they both shatter their lances then it is considered a draw and no points are awarded. If one rider knocks the helm off the other, whether or not the lance shattered, two points are awarded. And if one is lucky enough to knock the other from his horse by hitting his mark then three points are awarded."

Perault was pleased to see excitement fill the boy's eyes. "How does one win the game?"

"They charge each other up to three times and the first combatant to win a majority by the third run or gain three or more points will be announced as the winner. If after three runs the riders are tied then the joust is considered a draw."

Perault had experienced every one of those scenarios several times over and although jousting was not his best event, he was considered to be very good at it. The only thing that irritated him about jousting in a Tourney was that the identity of one's adversary was not known until they were face to face and ready to charge. This eliminated any opportunity to develop a strategy unless his opponent was extremely well known to him.

"I want to be a knight one day and joust. Can I, Pa?" The boy was at that age when dreams and fantasy were possible. Perault envied his innocence.

The next duo of squires took to the field and began their runs while Perault regarded the mass of spectators with almost passive disinterest until his gaze fell upon his family, Sir Aldeman, and the Brighams seated together anticipating his appearance. It gave him confidence and determination seeing them there to support him. He was fortunate that there were so many in his life cheering his success.

Especially Melisende.

She was almost like a beacon among the stars, outshining them all with her beauty. Perault tried not to look at her, he tried to refuse the distraction, but it was hopeless. She was there drawing his eye to her as effortlessly as she ran her fingers through his hair . . .

A hand from behind firmly grasped his shoulder interrupting Perault's brief diversion. "'tis time," Dorlik spoke softly.

"I am ready." Perault rubbed his face to cover the flush of embarrassment that attended his cheeks and walked with his friend to the stables.

The armor that he donned for the battle was specially designed for jousting. It was heavy and ponderous to move in with certain areas reinforced to lessen the impact of a strike that might otherwise kill a man. Likewise, the lances were designed with blunt tips that would not penetrate an opponent's armor for non-lethal jousting. Still, there was always the danger of breaking one's neck or serious injury from strike or fall if Sunna did not bestow her blessings.

The clash of battle sounded distant in the arena. Another pass and then Perault would be called to take position. Dorlik moved a heavy three-tiered block into position next to his horse to allow for easier mounting and held Perault's arm until he was steady in the saddle. Hanlin held the reins.

"Everythin' feelin' fine? Nothin' pinchin' anywhere?" Dorlik was busy pulling straps and testing the hinges on Perault's armor nervously. He always overcompensated the first battle of every Tourney.

"I feel tight as a clam, Dorlik. Don't worry." In truth, Perault could hardly breathe. "Lead us out, Hanlin."

Hanlin pulled the reins and Perault's powerful mount responded enthusiastically. His horse was a finely bred warhorse from

Bours that was trained well enough to know what would soon occur once he was strapped with metal plates. Perault barely had to utter a command; the horse knew so well what to do.

They stopped in the shade at the edge of the arena. The previous battle was over and the field cleared of debris, yet they would go no further until called forth.

The herald stepped to the middle of the arena and raised his voice loud and clear, "This is the third round of ten with the winner advancing to the semi-finals! From my right, I call the reigning champion of the Joust from four years ago in Yorwick, Squire Perault of House Aldeman!"

The crowd cheered wildly, as Hanlin led Perault into the light of the arena and positioned his mount along the line of the barricade separating the tracks. He held a hand up in salute of his countrymen and women who had taken the time to come and watch him joust.

"From my left," the herald continued, "comes a squire known and loved as a son of Tintagel and a favorite of the Tourneys! Squire Edwin of House Talowin!"

The crowd roared with approval at the name spoken. Squire Edwin was a local who'd nearly beat Perault in the Yorwick Tourney. His master, Sir Geremy, was the current Knight Champion of the Tourney and no doubt had pushed his squire hard to improve.

Hanlin handed the reins to Perault. "Looks like you're gonna be tested right off this year."

Perault nodded slowly, "That is truly the case. Edwin nearly beat me with lance in Yorwick." He smiled at Hanlin. "But not today."

Both squires in position, the herald moved off to the side and raised a white flag with the silhouette of a boar emblazed upon it — the duke's coat of arms. In quick succession, Perault lowered his visor, saluted Squire Edwin, took a lance from Dorlik, and readied himself for the signal. The crowd went eerily silent.

Then the flag dropped.

Perault's mount nearly jumped into a sprint at the bare touch of his heels and raced down the line toward an equally eager opponent. Faster and closer they charged, Perault was in a near trance-like state of focus. He knew precisely when he would drop the tip of the shaft and exactly where it would impact Squire Edwin's body. It would be a perfect strike that would knock his adversary off his horse and grant Perault a quick win.

Simultaneously both lances shattered on the squires' armor with enough force to bend them over their horse's haunches, but neither fell off.

"Draw!" the Herald cried, and the crowded responded raucously.

Recovering quickly with the aid of Hanlin and Dorlik, Perault readied himself in position for a second charge.

"He hits harder than I remember," Perault spoke between heavy breaths.

"Then don' let 'em hit ye." If Perault had enough breath, he would have laughed at Dorlik's simple wisdom.

Moments later, the flag dropped again.

Perault rushed ahead, this time calculating a different spot on Squire Edwin's armor to abuse. He stood forward in the stirrups and the two came together a second time with nearly the same results as the first pass.

The crowd roared to life again nearly drowning out the Herald's pronouncement, "Draw!"

Perault was frustrated. His opponent had indeed improved since the last time they met.

When he passed Squire Edwin on return to his position, Perault raised his visor and spoke loud enough for those in the crowd nearby to hear. "Hold onto your breeches this time, Edwin." The response was a throaty growl.

Back in position once more, Hanlin quickly checked over Perault's mount while Dorlik pulled the straps even tighter on his armor. Perault barely noticed any of it; his mind was analyzing the previous passes, working through solutions to overcoming Squire Edwin's defenses and discarding them just as quickly. By the time the flag stood high and erect, Perault knew he had one play if he were going to win this joust. He would have to take a chance that would either win the joust decisively in his favor or result in utter failure.

The flag descended for the final time, and the crowd held its collective breath.

Perault urged his mount faster, much faster than was prudent for a joust. If his mount stumbled, it would likely break a leg and send him flying like a steel-clad turtle into death's embrace. It didn't matter, all that mattered was victory.

When they met, it was near the center of lanes and Perault's mind faintly registered that Squire Edwin must have been pushing his mount just as hard. The thought was replaced by the immediacy of a lance shattering on his chest plate pushing him upward and back while he instinctively clinched his knees tightly against his mount's flanks. At the same time, Perault's lance connected low, just under Squire Edwin's shield near his waist. Rather than immediately shattering, the shaft bent with the force of the blow before it exploded into a million pieces and all the concentrated energy collected in the bend released at one time.

Squire Edwin's body ejected off his horse with the intensity of a catapult, the power of it causing his mount's legs to buckle and roll ten strides before it came to a halt. The squire's body landed roughly some distance behind, where it lay still and unmoving.

Perault gained control of his horse and wheeled it around to where the squire had fallen, but by the time he was by his side Squire Edwin's retainers were already attending to him. Unable to dismount safely on his own, he waited impatiently for the men to do their work. The last thing he wanted was to permanently injure the squire or worse. Squire Edwin was an adversary at a jousting event, but he was not an enemy, and Perault held him in high esteem.

A moment later, Squire Edwin's attendants had removed his armor and he was standing looking disheveled and a little disoriented, but alive. Perault was relieved and so was the crowd. Silent moments before, they cheered enthusiastically at the squire's recovery.

Perault removed his helmet. "Are you well, friend Edwin?'

Edwin glanced up, exhausted from his ordeal. "I'll be fine Perault. Good move on your part. You guessed I was timing your charges, eh?"

Satisfied there was no permanent injury, Perault gave him a sly smile. "I would have been a fool not to catch on a third time around." He pulled the reins and spun his mount toward his own men.

Dorlik and Hanlin led Perault, still mounted, into the stables where they helped him dismount and remove his armor.

"You have a sword and shield single melee event in two hours. Better get some rest." Hanlin informed him.

"Right now, I think I need a drink and I can rest well enough sitting in an alehouse as well as anywhere."

Dorlik nearly knocked Hanlin over with a slap on his shoulder. "Ya see there? Just like I always told ya, Hanlin. Someone was gonna knock sense inta our ol' friend here one day!"

~~~

Perault stared across the small arena at the brutish-looking squire he was about to face in his final one-on-one melee event of the day. He flipped his blunted sword nervously and silently calculated how he would counter the younger man's size and strength advantage. His name was Squire Rambert, and rumor was that he hit like a falling boulder.

"Begin!" Perault was startled by the Tourney Official's command.

Rambert was clearly ready, as he immediately began to charge across the ten paces between them. Reacting more than thinking, Perault swiftly side-stepped the assault, pushing off his opponent's shield with his own which caused Rambert to lose enough balance to spin around and fall hard on the arena's packed soil.

As hastily as he could manage, the squire regained his footing only to find the flat side of Perault's broadsword finding firm purchase against the side of his open-faced helm. With barely a twitch, Squire Rambert returned to the earth, out cold.

"Winner! Perault of House Aldeman!" The Tourney Official shouted to the crowd cheering excitedly at the quick bout.

Perault removed his helm and offered a flourishing bow to Melisende before retreating from the arena. After the morning joust and four single-combat events, he was exhausted and ready to find a warm meal and an early bed.

"Well, that was fast." Hanlin remarked.

Perault gave him a withering look. "Good thing, too. My arm nearly went numb when he ran into me. I don't think I could have taken many hard blows from that fellow."

Dorlik laughed and unbuckled Perault's armor. "You did him a kindness, ya know. He'll no be runnin' like a ragin' bull inta tha next man he meets!"

"You look like you need rest if you're going to stand up straight tomorrow." Hanlin looked him over like he was inspecting one of his horses. "Back to the Knight's Inn with you. Dorlik and I will have your horse and equipment in proper shape by morning."

Out of his armor for the first time in several hours, Perault washed the dirt off his face and pulled on a dry shirt. "My thanks to you both. I couldn't do this without you."

"An' we know it!" Dorlik chuckled amiably.

Taking the reins of his horse from Hanlin, Perault rode through the congested streets out of Tintagel and into the wide plain beyond the walls where the temporary stands were erected to view the jousting and archery contests. It was late afternoon and the Tourney was still in full swing, with spectators swarming from one event to the next. Not until the last light of day would the action move from the arenas to the taverns. Perault was glad his day had ended early.

A short while later he entered the nearly empty common room of the Knight's Inn. Not even the elder knights had returned to gloat about their winnings or wail over their losses. No longer physically able to compete in the Tourneys, they would feed their competitive lust with wagers of coin and bragging rights. He knew that Sir Aldeman always bet on him, so he anticipated that his master would be in a gleeful mood that evening.

Perault sat alone at a long table and dined on a healthy portion of hot stew and warm, freshly baked crusty bread with ample servings of ale to numb his sore aches. He had five combat events scheduled for the next day and he was going to need every ounce of strength he could muster to win them all. His fatigued mind mulled through the details of what he faced and found his heavy eyelids had other ideas for his attention.

It was the sound of someone walking through the front door of the tavern followed by a comfortable warm breeze that startled him from his half-doze. He glanced up to see if it was someone he knew. Beyond the haze of filtered light through dusty windows Perault spied a curious figure approach his table. He was a lean, middle-aged man with long raven-black hair under a traveler's hat and dressed in blue-gray layered robes that billowed behind him as he strode closer. In his hand he held a knobby staff that he didn't appear to need and a pack over his shoulder that had surely seen better days.

Without pretense, the man sat quite deliberately on the other side of the table across from him. No longer dozing, the man had Perault's complete attention.

"Hello, Perault. I understand you had a good day at the Tourney."

Perault blinked in surprise. "Greetings, good sir. Have we met before?" Perault was certain they had not.

"Never, lad, but I know you quite well. You are a great knight destined to attain honor and glory and all that you knightly sorts cherish."

A serving girl appeared with a flask of red wine for the strange man. Perault did not recall ever hearing the man order it.

Perault shifted uncomfortably. "Good sir, perhaps you mistake me for someone else. I am nothing more than a squire to House Aldeman. I will not even become a provisional knight for a few weeks, let alone a great knight. And I certainly have never done anything truly great, unless you consider the Tourneys such an accomplishment."

The man poured himself a cup of wine and drained it just as quickly then filled it again. "Passable," he muttered. Then he leaned forward and focused eyes on Perault that seemed to blaze with intensity. "Whatever you are now, a great knight you will be. Greatness is inside you, waiting to be discovered. Time and events to come are the details that will fill the spaces of your story."

Perault leaned back, feeling invaded. He was now sure this man was crazy and didn't want to say anything that might upset him. "I pray you are right sir. Nothing would give me more satisfaction in life than to serve the duties of my station with honor and integrity."

The man burst out laughing. "There will be that too, after a time. Remember our meeting, lad. Our paths will cross again, and when that time comes it will be important that you remember what we discussed here today. Mind getting this?" The old man gestured toward his empty cup as he stood and started toward the door.

Perault shrugged. "Of course. But may I ask to who I owe the pleasure of today's discourse?"

Without turning the old man called over his shoulder, "Myrllin," and walked out the door of the inn.

Perault stared hard after him, mouth fully agape.

CHAPTER 10

Turmoil in Cambria

Black soil clumped under bright green grass flew from the hooves of Perault's charging stallion in a controlled sprint across the wide field. Ahead of him charged twenty squires fully armored with lances leveled, intent on unseating his line. Perault was at the center, the captain of his group by unanimous vote, gripping his shield and lance tightly. It was almost time.

"Hold the line," he shouted to his left.

His men were spread dangerously thin with at least a span between one another. It was important that he present the illusion of inexperience if his rival, Squire Duncan, were to be overcome by the stunning arrogance that he was so well known for. Perault would not underestimate his adversary in any case. He knew full well that Duncan was considered a talented young field commander destined to lead cavalry units in the army. Worse still, Duncan had never been defeated in a mounted battle no matter the size of the Tourney.

Perault planned to end the squire's winning streak.

"Stay with me!" he cried over the beating sounds of hooves and roar of the crowd.

He was waiting for Duncan to make his move toward his center, the only logical action any commander would make. Especially one whose ego had no room for the slightest creative thought. That was Perault's singular advantage in this contest.

They were not far away, closing fast, when Duncan called the command Perault knew would come, collapsing into a tight line half the length of his own. Duncan would expect Perault to order his side into a crescent to effectively surround the smaller line and when they did, they would be completely ineffective, like an ocean wave crashing on a rocky shore.

"To me! To me!" Perault gave the anticipated signal and nineteen riders converged into a tight wedge behind him.

The look on Squire Duncan's face when they collided was one that Perault would never forget. They came together like a thunderclap of metal and screaming horses, the sound echoed across the field, stunning the masses to silence with the raw violence. Two groups became one and then Perault's group broke through the other side and split into two lines each curling back around to the right and left. To their credit, Duncan's tattered group formed professionally as a single unit and turned to face them for a second charge. They were less than half their original number to Perault's with a loss of only five on the first pass.

"Wedge!" Duncan called to his men, but they were too few and too late.

Perault's men closed in from both sides in a classic pincer move, while Duncan's compressed closer together, his lancers losing speed and beginning to panic. It was clear that Duncan was doing everything he could to keep his formation together. When they crashed together for the final time, more men fell from the jarring impact and Duncan emerged with only three of his men intact. Perault had not lost a single lancer.

He formed his men up for one more assault, but to his surprise, Squire Duncan turned to face him with lowered lances, conceding defeat. Perault and his team saluted them in turn.

"It seems you are destined to become the perfect knight," Duncan's tone was mordant and openly scornful. "Where do your talents end, I wonder?"

Perault was struck by the squire's attitude, future knights were not supposed to act this way. "Where do my talents end, you ask?" He fixed Duncan with a severe stare. "Forgiveness."

Without waiting for a reply, Perault spun his horse around to face the crowd and thrust what remained of his lance upward in salute to the crowd. The response was energetic, calling his name, "Perault! Perault! Perault!" until he departed the field.

As soon as Perault rode into the stables, Dorlik and Hanlin were there to meet him.

"That's it, Perault." Hanlin took the reins of his horse to keep it steady while Perault dismounted. "You have managed to champion five out of six events in Tintagel, not a bad showing."

"Well done!" Dorlik agreed enthusiastically.

"I suppose my archery skills could have been better, placing fifth was a bit of an ego buster." Perault held his arms out straight so Dorlik could remove his battered chest plate. "Davin of House Jeutemont ran circles around me in that one." He glanced over to Hanlin and winked. "But I suppose I can live with winning the other five."

A few hours later, Perault found himself on the field again, except this time it was without his armor and shield. He stood among his peers facing the stands where the duke and duchess were once again applauding the competitors. The ceremony was really a celebration for the knights who had overcome their colleagues in each event and been named champion. Sir Geremy was among the top competitors again, this time winning four events, more than any other knight.

Still one less than he had won, even if they were against squires. Perault smiled to himself.

The ceremony went long with each knight acknowledged by name, receiving a silver circlet from the hands of the duke himself and a few words of congratulations. For the squires, their recognition came at the end, with their names read by the herald to the crowd and each man stepping forward. No circlets for them. Not yet. Despite the quick tribute, Perault was gratified by the thunderous cheers he received from more than just his family, the Brighams, and Sir Aldeman.

With a little more pomp and circumstance, the Tourney at Tintagel ended. The next Tourney would take place in Oswalt sixty leagues to the north in a week and conclude with the finals in Lyon's Gate two weeks after that. Perault was confident he would make it through to the end, but he was under no illusion that the competition would get any less challenging – in fact, it would be quite the opposite.

That would be a worry for another day. Tonight, the city was in celebration and soon he would seek out Melisende for an evening of dancing and feasting at Valiant Keep by invitation of the duke and duchess. It was an invitation to all the champions, knight and squire, as well as the nobles, wealthy merchants and influential of Lyonesse.

He missed Melisende. Not once since the Tourney began had he the chance to more than wave to her in the stands. That evening would be sweet in many ways since his parents and brother would be in attendance as well and he had not seen them in many months.

"What do you boys have planned tonight?" Perault asked on his way to the inn with Hanlin and Dorlik.

"We got an eye on a certain pair o' servin' girls at a tavern in tha city." Dorlik's smile was as infectious as his northern Eriu accent was appealing to the young women of Lyonesse.

Hanlin, on the other hand, was smooth with poetry and prose. The pair was infamous for leaving a string of broken hearts during the Tourneys.

"Well, don't go off and get married. We have two more Tourneys and I'm going to need you both unhindered if I'm going to win five more events in Oswalt!" Perault knew the first part of his comment was stupid the moment it left his mouth. Hanlin and Dorlik were absolutely incorrigible when it came to relationships with women beyond the haystack. For their part, they let Perault off easy with nothing more than outrageous laughter as a reply.

When Perault walked into the common room, he was surprised to find Sir Aldeman had made it back before him, and was in his usual place next to the fireplace, surrounded by a dozen of his old cronies.

Without hesitation, he knelt next to his master and waited to be acknowledged.

"Get off your knees boy and stand like a man!" Sir Aldeman bellowed jovially. "You may still be a few weeks away from your silver-fringed cloak, but as far as I'm concerned you're as good a man as any of us here!"

"Hear, hear!" The old knights around them added their approvals.

Perault slowly stood. The unspoken meaning of Sir Aldeman's words was not lost on him. His master, mentor, father-figure, and idol was publicly releasing him from service. It was unofficial of course, as the law required that he either earn the right to wear the silver-fringed cloak or be dishonorably dismissed to leave the service of a knight.

"Quit gawking, lad!" Sir Grethin called from nearby. "You did well winning the championship in five events, although my boy Davin trounced you convincingly in archery! A hard lesson in humility was it?"

The rest of the group made low instigating sounds at the gaff.

Perault knew that the playful insult was meant more for Sir Aldeman than for him. In their old age they found many subtle ways to continue competing against each other and probably would until their last breath. That was the way of the Temple Knights.

Sir Aldeman did not miss a beat. His mind was still as sharp as the blade that almost never left his side. "Or maybe he was doing your boy a charity!" He shot back.

The old knights roared with laughter.

"Pull up a chair, have a few drinks and give us all the details of your triumphs in the Tourney!" Another knight called to him.

Feeling a little desperate, Perault had precious little time to get changed before he was supposed to meet Melisende at Valiant Keep. He worried that if Sir Aldeman wanted him to stay awhile as well then how could he refuse?

Before he had a chance to speak, Sir Aldeman saved him once again. "This one has an invitation to feast with the duke tonight and on the arm of a pretty girl I would wager. Get on with you boy, you don't want to keep her waiting!"

In that moment, Perault was sure Sir Aldeman was the wisest man he had ever met. "Thank you, my lord." He bowed formally to Sir Aldeman and then to the rest of the old knights, "My lords, may you not find yourselves rooted too deeply where you sit to find your beds when the ale drips from your empty cups!"

They roared with laughter and spirited insults as he retreated to the stairway that led to his room. He earnestly hoped that one day he too would be sitting among his elderly friends trading jests and jabs with a young generation of squires. There was no better way to enjoy the sunset of one's life, in his opinion.

An hour later Perault was standing arm and arm with Melisende laughing with his parents, the Earl and Lady of Stoddenferry Castle. He missed his home and the life he once knew there and looked forward to one day returning, perhaps with another by his side. He squeezed Melisende's arm familiarly. It was hard not to continually steal glances at her with her hair high above her seductively bare, pale shoulders and yellow bodice that formed her shape so well. Perault was sure every young man in the hall was stealing glances at her as well.

"Where is Reginald?" Perault asked after his older brother.

His father smiled and gestured toward Melisende. "He is with this one's brothers, no doubt flirting with some young heiress in a pretty dress."

"Ah! Look who it is." Melisende was looking over the earl's shoulder. They all turned to see Melisende's parents walking over to join them.

"Good evening Mr. Brigham, Mrs. Brigham," The earl greeted them.

"Good evening to you all," Mr. Brigham replied distractedly.

"Is there something the matter, Father?" Melisende's sounded uncharacteristically worried. Perault knew her father as a man of whimsical charm and charisma.

Her father furrowed his brows and lowered his voice. "Not to spoil this wonderful night, but there is more troubling news out of Cambria."

"What is it, Erol? You must tell us." Perault's father whispered.

"Well, it seems that the trials have convicted a number of conspirators and they all have a strikingly similar story about who was behind the attempted poisoning of Lady Genestra."

"Who has been named?" The Earl's serious tone was unmistakable and Perault knew that whoever it was had to hold a substantial position within the kingdom for Lord Brigham to be so upset about it.

It was Mrs. Brigham that answered, "Duke Banfield Eldorath of Yorwick, the King's brother!"

Everyone gasped.

"Lyra, that can't be true!" Perault's mother had a look of shock on her face.

"I'm afraid it is, Rhoswen. It is terrible news for the kingdom." Mrs. Brigham replied while her husband confirmed the truth of it with slow nods.

Perault's father had a grave look on his face. Somehow, he appeared to understand more in those words than the rest of them. "The king will have heard the news by now as well. It will be up to him to clear this matter quickly. He must. Otherwise, circumstances may take on a life of their own and we could find ourselves in a bloody civil war."

They all stood in quiet contemplation for a few moments at the horrifying prospect and then Mr. Brigham tried to lighten the mood. "So, Perault, what do you have planned for Oswalt?"

Perault appreciated the attempt, but his enthusiasm had been drained by the bad news. Suddenly, the Tourneys seemed trivial in comparison to events transpiring in the real world. His generation and his father's generation had been fortunate never to know the experience of war, but they all knew the awful truth of it even though the Temple Knights so often glorified the occurrence in songs and poems. Just when he was about graduate into a world he thought he knew, everything was changing.

~~~

Waves pounded the cliffs over Lough Greely where Perault stared at the massive, polished granite walls that surrounded the glorious city of Lyon's Gate. Beyond the ramparts he admired the spiraling towers and elevated palace encompassed by more fortifications that were as beautiful as they were functional. In the bright sunlight every wall and every tower sparkled an iridescent silvery-white that was almost magical. Maybe it was, as far as he knew. Despite its beauty, the undisputable impression he had the first time he came to this place was power and Lyon's Gate was the undisputed seat of power in Lyonesse. It was also the residence of the royal family and arguably the grandest city in all of the Western kingdoms with the possible exception of Ys far to the south. He had visited Lyon's Gate many times with Sir Aldeman in the past but never had the fortune to meet the king. This time would be different, and when it happened, he was determined to have a collection of championships associated with his name.

Perault glanced toward the port a half-league outside the southern gate of the city. Ships were still arriving from Oswalt and parts of Eriu ferrying in nobles and commoners alike arriving late to the first day of the Tourney. Soon, the sun would cast its last rays upon the walls of Lyon's Gate turning them from silver to gold. It was a spectacular sight that only reinforced his belief that there was some sorcery involved with their construction.

He pulled the reins of his mount to slowly pace toward the east gate which was the closest entrance to the Games District where his inn was located. It was where Sir Aldeman and the old knights usually stayed. Lodging at an inn inside the city was convenient. This one was a stone's throw away from the arenas where Perault competed in the melee events, far closer than the inns outside of Tintagel and Oswalt, and allowed him greater opportunity to rest in comfort between competitions.

Reluctantly, he steered his mount toward the crowded road leading into Lyon's Gate. Perault appreciated the quarter-league of open fields outside the walls in every direction except the lough. No structures of any type were permitted in this zone, temporary or otherwise. It was a measure of security that, even in peaceful times, was never compromised. The air was clean and it was peaceful there, giving him the opportunity to exercise his horse and think without distraction.

The day had been a good one for Perault. He won three individual events and one team event sending him to the next round in each. It was unfortunate that his jousting team had lost in Oswalt, leaving him with only four events in the finals there. Oswalt was far tougher than he expected and he felt rather lucky that he had come through with four championships in the end. Fighting well-trained squires on the verge of earning their silver-fringed cloaks was much different than the less experienced adversaries he faced four years ago in Yorwick.

Once through the gates, the crowd dispersed in several directions, and the press of bodies thinned substantially. Despite the dramatic swell of population boom, Perault was impressed by the diligence of the work crews keeping the streets clean of animal feces and debris. There wasn't a street he traveled day or night that wasn't well-lit and cared for. The Tourney in Lyon's Gate was an international affair, and he was sure that King Eldorath meant to make an impression on friend and rival alike. And not just with the impressive scale and power of Lyon's Gate, but with the high standard of living his subjects enjoyed as well.

"Perault! Perault!" Someone was calling his name in the street. Perault glanced around to see Hanlin and Dorlik sitting at a table outside a tavern. To his surprise, Squire Davin was sitting with them.

He dismounted and handed off his horse to a groom employed by the tavern and joined his friends.

"I see you boys wasted no time getting to your relaxation, where did you find this one?" Perault clapped Davin on the shoulder, nearly causing him to spew his ale across the table.

"We have ta fortify ourselves fer another day of watchin' you get beat near ta death, ya know!" Dorlik smiled over his mug almost empty of ale.

Hanlin filled an empty cup from a pitcher beading with sweat and handed it to Perault

Perault laughed, "That you do, my friend." He turned his attention to Davin. "How did you do today, good sir?"

"I won, of course," Davin smiled. "Although with you not there I had little to inspire my brilliant skills as a bowman and nearly quit from boredom."

"Didn't go so well with yer bow-master though, did it?" Dorlik did a bad job trying to hide his impish grin behind his mug.

Davin shook his head sadly. "It is true. Sir Geremy was defeated in the first round by some prince from the Eastern kingdoms."

Perault knew Sir Geremy as one of the finest bowmen in the kingdom. He had once been squire to Davin's master, Sir Grethin, and often did his old master the service of training his younger squires with the bow. Sir Geremy had been Tourney champion in the bow event for at least sixteen years.

Perault was astounded. "The Eastern kingdoms? We have never had anyone from the Eastern kingdoms in a Tourney. What do you know about him?"

Davin shrugged. "Only that he is strange and talented with a bow."

"Strange how?"

"He wears blood-red armor and a long sword with a slight curve to it," Davin offered.

"He's from a city called Vradesti that no one has heard of," Hanlin chimed in.

Dorlik had something to add as well. "The crowd calls him the Red Knight or the Blood Prince, depending on the event."

"Quite the mystery," Perault conceded. "I should like to see him in action. What are his events?"

"He has only entered two other events – single melee combat and single jousting. So far, he hasn't lost." Davin refilled his mug.

It wasn't unusual for foreign knights from as far away as Courth to compete in the Grand Tourney and when they did, they were generally among the very best their kingdom had to offer. Perault was sure that was probably the case for . . . "What did you say his name was?"

"I didn't," Davin teased. "But I heard it as Zracul of Vradesti."

"Any idea when he will compete next?"

"As it happens," Dorlik was drinking directly from the pitcher now. "He'll be fightin' in tha shord 'n shield an hour afta you tomorra."

Perault nodded uncertainly, not sure how much he could count on his drunken friends' information.

"It's true, except that it will be a jousting match an hour before your own," Hanlin corrected. "We won't have to point him out, he's obvious enough."

Perault decided it was time to change the subject. "Any news from Cambria?"

"No . . . gud noos . . ." Dorlik said between hic-ups.

"Easy there, big fella." Hanlin slapped his friend on the back. "I'll have you sleeping in the stables with Perault's horse if you don't slow down!"

"He's right," Davin interjected. "The word is that Count Djago was utilizing outlawed methods, torture and the like, to gain information from the suspects he rounded up."

Perault wasn't convinced. "Count Djago has always been regarded as a well-liked, respected man with an impeccable reputation for honor and integrity. I met him once a few years ago and I would be inclined to agree. Sometimes rumors are evil things not to be trusted."

"It seems like they are more than just rumors," Davin took a swig from his mug. "I heard Sir Grethin tell Sir Hapsig that Count Djago was in such a state after the attempt to poison his pregnant wife that he began arresting anybody and everybody that might have a remote connection with the poisoning no matter who they were or what position they held. And he said although there was little evidence of torture those he interrogated were strangely eager to admit their part in the plot when they came to trial."

"That is concerning," Perault agreed.

"Moreover," Davin continued. "My master mentioned that the king was so concerned that he sent messengers to Count Djago protesting his disregard for goodness and human compassion."

"Perhaps the rumors are true then, although I would wish them not to be." Perault placed a hand over his mug when Hanlin offered to fill it. He had had enough for the evening. "I wonder if any of us would act differently if we were trying to protect our own family from assassins."

"It's a hard question," Davin stood from the table and tossed down a coin. "Best of luck tomorrow my friend. I'm calling an early evening."

Perault clasped Davin's arm in friendship. "Sunna guide you, Davin. I anticipate meeting you next in the champions circle."

CHAPTER 11

The Trouble with Leprechauns

A tall man with jet-black hair, pale skin, and sharp, angular features some might call ruggedly handsome sat astride his mount preparing to ride into the arena. The armor he wore was notable by color and style – blood-red and marked with striations leaving the repulsive impression of exposed, raw muscle. The man was speaking harshly to one of his three attendants, the one who held his javelin flying a pennant that displayed a white fang on a crimson field, with a look of dire fear on his face for whatever it was he was being reproached for. The others wisely kept their eyes on the ground.

"Would you say he was a cruel man?" Melisende sat with Perault waiting for the knights to be announced. From their vantage point low in the stands with only a short barrier between them and the action on the field, they could easily see the man in red armor waiting in the shade of the arena.

"I do not know him, my dear," Perault couldn't stop watching him, "but I would say his servant probably thinks so, by the look of him."

The herald strode to the middle of the arena and raised his voice for all to be heard. "It is my privilege to announce the challenger, a man from the lands of Eastern kingdoms far across The Wilds called Vradesti. A prince of nobility, Zracul! The Blood Prince!

Zracul came pounding into the area, circling the perimeter twice before he stopped at its center next to the herald. The crowd cheered and clapped politely, although he was almost completely unknown to everyone so far.

"The prince will be challenging one of our own! A man who is considered a legend in jousting having won the Tourney Championship twice in his career and placing second in the Yorwick Tourney only four years ago. A native of Lyon's Gate and commander of one of the king's elite cavalry units, welcome Sir Beldham!"

In striking contrast to Prince Zracul, Sir Beldham rode into the area at a proud and stately pace, almost arrogant, with polished metal armor that shone like silver in the afternoon sun and long blond mustaches that defined his strong square jaw. He took his place on the other side of the herald to the wild excitement of the crowd. There was no doubt who the popular choice on the field was that day.

As demanded by tradition of the Tourney, the herald quickly outlined the rules of the joust and then sent each knight to their own starting lane. When they were set, he held up a white flag and cried, "Ready?"

In response, both knights closed the visors on their helmets indicating that they were and a second later the flag dropped to the ground. The stands vibrated with the sudden roar of excitement from the crowd and Melisende gripped Perault's arm with fearful anticipation.

Not hesitating a second, both knights spurred their mounts, gathering speed with every step. It was clear to Perault that Prince Zracul had the faster horse in this contest, but that hardly mattered since they were not racing. What did matter was the placement of their lances on one another's armor; that demonstrated the skill of the victor.

Seconds later, lances found their mark, shattering wood splinters in every direction. Neither knight lost his seat, but it was Sir Beldham who swayed a little after the impact, confirming that it was he who had taken the harder hit in their first pass.

"Draw!" The herald called out barely perceptible over the loud cheers.

There was little time to rest before the herald held the white flag high to start the second pass. Each knight had a new lance and as quickly as the flag hit the ground, they were off again, barreling toward each other and perhaps their destiny.

To most spectators, the crash of a wooden shaft on metal armor looked much the same every time, unless one man was dismounted, which would not be the case on the second pass, but Perault watched through the experienced eyes of a competitor and he could tell that this time, Sir Beldham was hurt.

"Draw!" The herald shouted once again.

It wasn't until the knight was back in his starting position for the third pass did it become obvious. Sir Beldham was slumped over the front of his saddle in obvious pain, a noticeable dent in the left breast of his armor that should not have been there. Not with Tourney lances. They were designed to shatter on impact, delivering the energy of the charge into their opponents' body without doing any serious damage. Yet, the Blood Prince's lance had shattered, leaving no reason to doubt anything underhanded had occurred.

The herald stood holding the white flag for a final pass that would never occur. Sir Beldham's squires had already removed his helmet and chest armor and the herald would not drop the flag without first receiving a ready signal from both competitors.

Sir Beldham took a lance and slowly rode to the center of the arena where he stopped, tipped his lance to Prince Zracul and then turned and tipped his lance to the crowd, drawing appreciative applause.

"Winner, Prince Zracul of Vradesti!" cried the herald to further ovations.

"What happened, Perault?" Melisende was a novice when it came to the games of the Tourneys. "Why did they not go again?"

Perault patted her hand, still clutched tightly to his arm. He never wanted her to let go. "Sir Beldham was hurt badly on that last pass. His armor took a serious blow, probably broke a rib or two and he couldn't breathe with it on. He was forced to either concede the contest or risk death in a final pass without armor to protect his torso."

"These games are not worth one's life," Melisende agreed.

Perault snorted a laugh. "You would be surprised how many knights have chosen differently. Some would prefer to risk death to the prospect of losing an ounce of dignity."

"You're all savages."

Squire jousts would soon begin in the arena, one of which Perault would be competing in a couple of hours and he still needed to see Dorlik for a fitting in his repaired armor. He was sure the blacksmith would be pacing and aggravated that he was not already at the king's forge getting it done. Dorlik was one who took his time in his work and did not like to be rushed to complete a job.

Perault took Melisende to her carriage waiting outside the arena and kissed her fondly goodbye. "Will I see you in the stands later?"

"Of course." Her lovely smile stretched across her face. "My father will accompany me this evening since my lover will be otherwise engaged. Good luck!"

She kissed Perault's fiercely blushing face and rode off toward the estate of the wealthy merchant that was hosting the Brighams and his family during the Tourney. He missed her the second she entered the carriage and knew he would have to put her out of his mind so that he could mentally prepare for the jousting event later. For just a moment, he allowed himself the joy of imagining that she would be his wife one day with a family of their own to follow not long after. He whistled to himself as he rode to the forge and realized that he was living the best time of his life.

~~~

Two single-combat events and a joust completed Perault's second day of the Lyon's Gate Tourney. He left his horse with Hanlin and his armor with Dorlik, both of whom would be up late making sure everything was ready for him the next morning. It was a short walk through the Gaming District to his inn and for once he was disappointed. Adrenaline had converted to anxious energy that he needed to burn before he would be able to get a good night's rest. Instead of taking the most direct route back to the inn, he decided to go through the local market and along a row of inns and stables where many of the Tourney knights were staying.

Like most districts in Lyon's Gate the streets and avenues were wide, well-lit with light globes and lined with tall trees and pruned shrubbery balanced with the occasional water fountain or marble statuary. It was the time of evening when the street vendors were closing shops for the day and the socialites were calling for carriages to ferry them to dinner or entertainment. Despite the many invitations, even for a squire, Perault always politely declined. He wouldn't allow a night of free-flowing drinks and little sleep to compromise his performance in the slightest. Most of the serious competitors he ever met shared the same philosophy when it came to the Tourneys.

It was a cool evening with a slightly brisk spring breeze that made the air delicious to breathe and easy to sleep. He felt his heightened level of vigor begin to normalize the further he walked, confident that by the time he found his inn he would be ready for a quick hot meal and a soft bed with thick blankets.

Along the way, he passed several couples strolling and conversing quietly about intimate things. They smiled and nodded as he passed. None of them knew who he was and if they did, he was glad they didn't make a fuss about it. He had enough of that outside the arenas where a small group of his most ardent followers often gathered to meet him or offer congratulations or advice. The couples on this night appeared graceful and genteel, reminding him of Melisende and the thousand reasons he should be strolling with her right now. Still, his quest for knighthood ruled his life right now, and he feared that would never change. It prompted him to consider his future again, and he struggled with the idea of whether or not his way of life would be fair to her.

They had spoken after the Tourney in Tintagel. They had a wonderful time and he professed his love to her father. Lord Brigham was more than approving, even eager for the match and before Perault departed his parents congratulated them on their eventual nuptials. So much for keeping his intentions discreet. He still hadn't officially asked her for her hand, and worse, he knew from the look in her eyes that she was expecting it. If he didn't ask her soon, she would be lost to him forever.

The problem was that she would expect them to marry after he received his silver-fringed cloak. It would seem logical to her since he would no longer be a squire and could start a household of his own. But that was just the beginning. To obtain his gold-fringed cloak and become an official knight he would have to either endure The Testing or achieve an Act of Heroism within three years.

The Testing had something to do with getting thrown into a dark hole for a period of time and enduring many unspeakable, soul-exposing trials. Or so the rumors went. He wasn't afraid of that, but what he really wanted was the title of Hero to earn the gold-fringed cloak and that could take time and would certainly be dangerous. So what was he to do? Marry Melisende and then run off to be a hero somewhere or die trying? That probably wouldn't be the best way to begin their marriage. And that's where his mental debate always ended leaving him nothing, no logic, to go with from there. Yet, still his heart urged him on.

Perault stopped and looked around. He had wandered further than he intended to and now stood at the edge of the Gaming District where many of the foreign knights were staying. From a nearby inn he could hear the raucous singing from the patrons inside. It was an old Eriu tune about fighting all day and carousing all night. Whether the patrons had heard the song a hundred times or for the first time that night the lines brought roars of laughter. Perault smiled to himself at the camaraderie and lifelong friendships that would be built on a night like this.

He walked on a little further intending to pass a pair of two-story inns with a stable between them and turn down the next street to angle toward his inn. As he passed, he was startled by quick movement near a stall in the stable and a diminutive creature silhouetted against a lantern hung on the wall. It was such an odd-looking thing that Perault immediately stopped to get a better look. In the dim light he was just able to make out a small humanoid creature dressed smartly in a coat and breeches with a brimmed hat atop his shaggy head and bulbous nose. If his eyes were not deceiving him, the little man could not have been over waist high. At first Perault thought it might be a child dressed for dinner, but it was alone in a darkened stable at an hour most children would be in bed. He didn't have much time to gawk as it noticed him almost immediately and ran off further into the stables, out of sight.

Perault was compelled to take a closer look and walked a few steps into the stables. Everything was quiet, almost too quiet. Normally in a stable full of horses there was movement—their great bodies shifting, a whiny or a huff, maybe a stomp or kick if they were nervous. Not so, here. The two dozen or so horses stood quietly in their stalls strangely calm as if they knew something he couldn't begin to guess at. Perault continued to the spot where he first saw the creature standing. The dried straw and dirt on the ground had been disturbed by something moving quickly away from a stall where a huge warhorse stood coolly. Small tracks led him out of the back entrance of the stables. It led into an open corral occupied by several more horses. To his disappointment, the tracks were lost in the multitude of boot and hoof marks of men leading steeds in and out of the back entrance to the stables earlier in the day. Whatever the thing was, it was lost to the night.

Out of curiosity, Perault backtracked to the stall where he first saw the creature. "Hello?" he whispered into the darkness. The warhorse eyed him critically, but made no sound. This was a very well-trained steed. Without getting too close to the horse's sharp hooves, Perault peered around the stall to see if anything was amiss. Along one wall, on stands and pegs, hung the full accouterments for a knight's mount – metal armor plates, tack and bridles, leather saddles along with several lances stacked upright in the corner. The banner of the knight's house was hung on the opposite wall – a white fang on a blood-red field. This was Prince Zracul, the Blood Knight's mount.

It suddenly occurred to Perault that there should be at least a dozen stable boys attending their master's mounts during the night, but not a one was to be seen. He navigated his way through the stables searching for any clue to their absence. He found a small hearth, still hot, that many of them would have been huddled around for warmth and the telling of ghost stories. Perault continued through the stables. There was a sound, like a scuff or scrape against a wooden partition not far away. He followed the sound to a darkened stall that had been left unoccupied. Perault pulled a light-globe he always carried from a small pouch at his side and let the bright illumination flood over the enclosed area.

He gasped.

A dozen or more small bodies lay nearly on top of one another at the back of the stall. They were young, probably second- or third-year squires barely away from their mother's skirts. Perault's eyes welled with tears at the sight of them. What fiendish devil could have done this to little more than children? He took a step forward to check them for any sign of life. Maybe one was lucky enough to survive. If he could find out what did this he would make it his mission in life to track it down and avenge these poor souls.

Perault inched forward and extended his hand toward the nearest body. He touched the boy's cloak first, then his soft brown hair until finally the flesh of his cheek. It felt warm. Hope and relief flooded through Perault, and he gently turned the child over. The young squire expelled a long breath and a quick cough before resuming what appeared to be a deep slumber. Perault shook him gently, and then his eyes opened glassy and confused.

"What?" the child demanded groggily.

Perault went to the next child and shook him, this one stirred as well and then he went on to the next and the next. Before long, sixteen young boys sat staring at him angry and uncertain. One of them, a lad with red hair and too young for whiskers, finally spoke up.

"Please don't tell our masters we fell asleep. They will punish us for the offense, twenty lashes at least!"

The other boys agreed heartily with the redhead.

Perault smiled. "Don't worry. Your secret is safe with me as long as you tell me what happened. Truthfully."

It took a while to piece their stories together, but in the end none of them remembered falling asleep in the first place. Perault found this more than a little odd and suspected the small creature was at the core of it. He did not let on about that bit of information as there was no reason to frighten the boys. They were already in a near state of panic that the knights they served would find out about their dereliction.

Perault looked them over carefully, none of them appeared maltreated. "I believe you, and so your masters shall not be informed of what has happened here tonight." He pressed his brows together in what he presumed would be taken as a serious expression. "Now return to your duties and make sure they are well done before morning!"

Without the slightest hesitation, they all bounded from the empty stall eager to get on with their chores. Perault smiled to himself when they were gone. He had learned a thing or two from Sir Aldeman after all! Yet even his humor at the situation could not shake the eerie feeling that something malicious had occurred that night; he simply had nothing to base it on other than the shadowy figure and his instincts.

Be that as it may, it was gone and the young squires were attending to their business. There was nothing left for him to do and the spike in adrenaline paired with the longer than expected stroll left him tired and ready for his bed, hot meal or no.

CHAPTER 12

Champions Ball

Perault was in a mood. Four hours earlier his melee team had lost in the finals despite his personal heroics of clubbing seven of the opposing team nearly to death before they took him down. Now he stood in another arena facing an opponent in single combat for yet another championship. The best he could do now was to win four championships this Tourney and he was relieved that all of them were single combat. He hated relying on the skill of others to help pull his team through considering that so often they disappointed him.

The man he fought in this final was a squire named Sefrick. By all accounts a good man, Perault pitied him for the beating he was about to receive. Why the fool would face him with spear and shield in battle instead of a sword was anyone's guess, he supposed. Still, he reminded himself not to underestimate his adversary. This was the finals after all and Sefrick must have possessed considerable skill to make it this far.

The arena was filled to capacity with the expectation that even squires would put on a good show for the championship. Their loud buzz lowered to a still murmur when the herald walked to the center of the field. He announced each of their names and Houses to boisterous cheers and then moved to the side of the arena to begin the match. Unlike jousting that included up to three passes, single-combat melee only ended when one of the men could no longer stand or yielded to the other.

"Begin!" the herald shouted and the crowd rose to their feet with a roar.

Perault met Sefrick in the center of the field and they began to circle each other while looking for any opening to exploit. Sefrick found his opening first and struck with a quick side-step thrust of the blunt-tipped spear inside Perault's shield. It banged hard against his chest plate sending him stumbling.

He's quick with that stick, Perault acknowledged to himself with some reluctance.

Perault realized that he had to get an angle on Sefrick's right so he could see those dangerous thrusts coming. His strategy paid off when he deflected the next thrust with his shield. Perault continued to dance to his left, forcing Sefrick to pivot to his right in a constant circle. The spear lunged forward a third time, but Perault was waiting for it. He slapped the spear to the right and spun into Sefrick's vulnerable right side open for a moment due to his awkward extension. Flipping his sword in a swatting motion he pummeled Sefrick's helmet in a move that must have caused his ears to ring. Sefrick reared backward, trying to retreat far enough to bring his spear between them again, but Perault would have none of it. He countered by following close before charging into Sefrick's spear arm and planting his left foot behind Sefrick's right resulting in his opponent falling to the ground in a tremendous clatter of metal armor. Not losing the slightest momentum, Perault kicked his adversary's shield away and planted his sword at the base of Sefrick's neck. Holding his spear ineffectively above his head, Sefrick dropped the weapon and shouted, "I yield!" loud enough for all to hear.

"Winner! Perault of House Aldeman!" declared the herald followed by shouts and praises from the stands for his victory.

"Champion at last!" Dorlik's great bear hug lifted Perault off his feet.

"Congratulations!" Hanlin chimed in.

"Thank you, good sirs. Now get me out of this barrel of metal and let's go watch the Red Prince's next bout. He is jousting for the finals today and from what I have seen of him so far he could easily be the next champion."

After changing into his regular attire, Perault and his companions rode over to the jousting arena. The match was about to begin and it was crowded without a seat to be had, leaving the three to stand with the stable hands and squires at the gate separating the field from the stables. The view was quite good, if at eye level where he knew they would feel as much as hear the thunder of hooves and crash of wood and metal.

The herald had just finished going over the rules of the joust when they found their places. Prince Zracul enrobed in his blood-red armor sat mounted next to his opponent, Sir Meldecamp, they saluted the crowd and casually rode to their respective places in preparation for their first pass.

"What happened to Sir Geremy?" Perault had been too busy with his own event to keep up with the latest Tourney ranks. As the champion of the last major Tourney in Yorwick four years ago he was favored to win this year as well."

Dorlik grunted. "The Blood Prince there put a proper finish on 'is chances fer champion, is what."

"Yeah, He unseated Sir Geremy pretty hard on the second pass this morning," Hanlin laughed. "His squire, Edwin, told me this afternoon that his master was still laying in his bed sore and bruised."

Perault chuckled. "I wish I could have seen that."

Sir Meldecamp was from the rugged mountain city of DunOinos in Northern Eriu and known to be a flawlessly technical jouster with no imagination whatsoever. Before Sir Geremy beat him in Yorwick, Sir Meldecamp had been champion the three previous Tourneys. Perault had seen him joust a few times before in local Tourneys he often attended with Sir Aldeman over the years and admired his patient execution that often lulled his opponent into underestimating him and making a critical mistake. It would be exciting to see how the so-called Blood Prince would fare against him.

The white flag fell to the earth, and both knights charged relentlessly toward each other. Drawing closer, Perault carefully watched their nearly identical technique - weight forward in the saddle, one hand tight on the reins – closer now, nearly there – they stood in the stirrups and lowered their lances marking their target only seconds away from victory or defeat. Then something unexpected happened. Prince Zracul's weight fell down and to his left with a broken stirrup. To his credit, in the second before impact, the Blood Prince lifted himself back to his original position with the strength of his right leg alone. An impossible feat in Perault's experience, he should have fallen off his horse and tumbled to the ground, most likely trampled by Sir Meldecamp's warhorse killing him instantly.

In spite of his heroic effort, luck was not completely on his side. With Prince Zracul's desperate shift, Sir Meldecamp's target was no longer center mass and his blunted lance impacted Prince Zracul's left hip solidly. The lance shattered when it struck but the force of it pushed the Blood Prince high off his saddle, spun him around and launched him off his horse into the air. Prince Zracul, still holding tight the reins of his horse, caused its head to swing backward as its bulk continued with forward momentum. There was a resounding crack followed by the twisting stumble of the horse's body, while Prince Zracul landed roughly onto the hard-packed earth of the jousting lane with the reins ripped from his mount's bridle still firmly in his grasp.

Sir Meldecamp charged through and turned. Behind him lay the bodies of the prince and his horse twitching in the dust. The crowd was completely silent from the shock of it all; even the herald neglected his duty to call the match.

The prince's squires rushed to their master and removed his helm, there was nothing they could do for his broken mount, and it was left to the convulsions of what had to be its fatal injuries. At the same time, Sir Meldecamp called to his squires to help him dismount and go to the aide of his fallen opponent, but there was nothing he could do, and they held him back and out of the way while a healing priest rushed in from a sheltered section of the arena.

Before the priest could take ten steps, the Blood Prince was miraculously on his feet with the help of his attendants. The crowd roared their approval. At first, he appeared unsteady and confused, and then he held a fist aloft to show that he was well enough to walk away from the calamity he had endured. The crowd rewarded him with accolades fit for a champion.

Perault was never sure whether or not the herald ever officially called the joust for Sir Meldecamp, he was nearly dumbstruck by the impossible recovery of the Blood Prince after his terrible fall. It was a fall that should have killed him, yet by pure luck or the divine intervention of Sunna, he survived and walked away from it. And there was something strange about the way the stirrup failed at the most critical moment that nagged at Perault. It didn't seem natural . . .

He turned to Dorlik and Hanlin. "Go about your business. I will meet with you in the morning. I need to speak with this Prince Zracul."

The two of them still bore the stunned looks of men having witnessed a miracle.

"We'll have a tale fer tellin' at the tavern this eve an' a lap fer tha lasses!" Dorlik found his voice quickly enough and grabbed Hanlin firmly by the shoulders to usher him in the right direction. "This one needs a' drink."

Perault smiled as they left, knowing what a night they would have and then turned on his heels to seek out the prince.

He didn't have far to go, but pushing through the congestion of the masses leaving the arena took him considerable time to reach the prince's stables. He arrived to find Prince Zracul speaking harshly to his three squires over the body of his once impressive ebony warhorse. He recognized the youngest squire as one of the boys he had encountered the night before asleep in the empty stall. To see him in the light of day gave Perault pause for concern over the boy's physical condition considering he looked quite a bit paler than he remembered, with gaunt features and bloodshot eyes. The other two squires appeared in no better condition. It angered Perault to see them in this state and it would offend him greatly if he found the prince was not keeping his squires within the acceptable standards of the Western kingdoms.

The Western kingdoms.

Perault reminded himself that they were from the Eastern kingdoms and not subject to the rules and laws agreed upon in treaties between nations of the Western kingdoms. It saddened him to think how different the standards seemed to be across The Wilds.

The discussion halted abruptly and the prince turned to face Perault expectantly.

Not waiting to be challenged, Perault quickly introduced himself. "Greetings, Prince Zracul, my name was Perault, a squire to Sir Aldeman and I may have information regarding your misfortune this day"

The prince waved his hand dismissing his squires and addressed Perault. His demeanor appeared to have changed completely. "Greetings, squire. I am sad to say that I do not know of your lord, Sir Aldeman. As you can see, my stirrup did not simply wear out and break." He held two ends of the left stirrup in his hands "These have been cleverly cut from the back so that it would not be noticed, and only so deep as to break when the stress was at its highest."

Perault took the stirrup and examined it himself. The prince had a very good eye for detail. "Yes, I see, my lord."

"Now, what is it you may know of this treachery besides what I have told you already." There was a slight edge of anger in the prince's tone that was not unexpected, considering that someone had deliberately tried to kill him.

Under the circumstances, Perault decided it was best to tell Prince Zracul everything he had experienced the night before in the stables, regardless of how fanciful it might sound. The prince never laughed or looked at him as if he had taken too much ale early in the day. Quite the opposite.

"What you were describing was a Sprite or Leprechaun." Prince Zracul had taken his story seriously.

Perault agreed. "Perhaps, but Sprites are said to have wings and not the strength to cut that heavy leather and Leprechauns are creatures from children's stories. I was thinking it might be one of those small monkeys from the fair that they dress up to do tricks."

Zracul frowned. "Leprechauns are real enough, although I would not expect to find one in the city as they are said to live only in the densest forests of Eriu."

Perault was skeptical. There had to be a more logical explanation than Leprechauns, Sprites, and tailored monkeys. "Shall I call the authorities and ask them to investigate? You could have been killed."

The prince shook his head. "No, thank you. I appreciate that you brought this to my attention first. I'm sure it was simply a joke taken too far among the squires or a jab from a jealous competitor. In any case, I will take care of this myself."

Perault bowed, sensing he was being dismissed. "If I can be of any further service or assistance, I am lodged at the White Horse Inn as part of Sir Aldeman's retinue."

Prince Zracul smiled but it appeared less than genuine "Thank you, Perault. Don't give it another thought."

The prince exited the stable and walked toward the inn leaving Perault with the distinct impression that he would find exactly who was behind the attempt on his life. It caused him to shudder to think what the prince might do when he found the culprit. Whatever it was, Perault was sure it would not be pleasant.

~~~

The wheels of the carriage bounced along the uneven cobblestone path that led up the steep incline to the front gates of the Royal Palace of Lyon's Gate. Perault, rarely the nervous sort, felt butterflies in his belly this evening. He was going to meet King Praeter Eldorath and Queen Penelope for the first time this evening.

Sitting next to him, Melisende squeezed his hand as if reading his thoughts. "You've earned this, Perault. No other squire has won more than a single championship, let alone four. There isn't even a knight who has won more than two this year!"

She was right. Although he'd missed his goal of winning five championships at the Tourneys, he couldn't be disappointed by his success. The great Sir Aldeman had won six in his prime, so many years ago, but those were different times and the competition was limited to knights and squires of Lyonesse. Now, as an international event, only the best of the best won championships. Not to take anything away from Sir Aldeman's accomplishments.

"I'm sorry your parents and brothers could not join us this evening. I would have liked for them to be here to share in the celebrations."

Melisende giggled. "This is a private affair that will be attended by only the nobles of the realm to honor the champions of the Tourneys. The king wanted to make an exception for my father, but you know him, he wouldn't have it. No need to engender petty jealousies with the nobles by accepting favors of special treatment."

Perault smiled at the thought of it. "He might as well be a noble. Most would probably be surprised to find out that he wasn't for all he does for the realm."

The carriage stopped, and the door was opened from the outside by a liveried footman bearing the gold crest of the rampaging Lyon on his chest. Perault exited first and then held out his hand for Melisende. She paused briefly at the doorway of the carriage, bright light globes illuminated her emerald-green gown and reflected off the ruby and emerald encrusted necklace adorning her bare neck. Her hair was up for the occasion, with narrow strands of curls falling around her face and lightly brushing the pale skin of her shoulders. Perault was spellbound, she was such a beauty, and he was lucky to have her on his arm this evening.

They joined the reception line that led through the high front entrance to the palace where they would be formally greeted by the king and queen. Melisende had met them both on several occasions, considering her parents' friendship with the royals, and reminded Perault that all that was required was a simple bow and curtsy on their part and not to expect much conversation.

It was probably the third time she had told him the same words and considering his nervous state he was glad for it. The line was long, but it moved quickly and before he knew it they were face to face with the King and Queen of Lyonesse. The pair wore all white with gold Lyons embroidered along cuffs or crafted on buttons and jewelry as the main accessory.

An unassuming man and unassuming woman stood behind the seated couple and whispered into their ears almost simultaneously as Perault approached with Melisende. He would almost prefer to face a creature from The Wilds than risk a misstep or wrong word that might be considered an insult or embarrass his family. There were so many people standing to either side, his parents among them somewhere, watching every move and listening to every word between the royals and their arriving guests. He had never heard much about palace intrigue, the people, even the nobles, of Lyonesse were not like that; however, they did enjoy the gossip.

Perault bowed to the royals as Melisende curtsied. His cheeks blushed a little from how awkward he must appear next to her calm grace. The king and queen smiled and nodded in polite response. Thinking that was all there was, Perault began to turn away only to have his movement arrested by Melisende's urgent, yet furtive snatching of his sleeve.

"Perault, son of the Earl and Lady Eckert and squire to House Aldeman, Penelope and I welcome you to our court." King Praeter was not an elderly man, perhaps in his mid-fifties, but his voice was deep and gave the impression of a depth of wisdom that few could match.

"Thank you, your majesty," Perault practically stammered.

"It seems congratulations are in order." King Praeter raised his voice so all could hear. "Four, you are the champion of no less than four events at the Tourney!"

The crowd of onlookers clapped loudly and briefly at the accomplishment. Perault didn't know what to say and very nearly wanted to throw himself off the walls after he heard himself say, "I expected to win six."

"Six!" King Praeter exclaimed with a laugh and the gathering laughed with him. "The boy has enjoyed success beyond imagining and still he expresses disappointment for not having done better!"

If Perault's cheeks were flushed before, they were absolutely flaming now.

"Hold out your sword hand, squire," King Praeter commanded. He was still smiling, giving Perault some assurance that he wasn't about to lose it. He did as instructed.

The King of Lyonesse placed his palm over Perault's hand and leaned forward. "You will be a great knight one day," he whispered, but not so low others around them couldn't hear. "I feel it in my bones. Remember this time of your life, savor the days that they do not pass so quickly, for they will never come again."

King Eldorath flipped Perault's hand over so that his palm faced up, snatched a golden button in the shape of a rampaging Lyon from his own jacket and placed it in his hand. "Keep this trinket as a remembrance of the day we first met, young squire. We will accomplish much together one day."

"Thank you, your majesty."

The king released his hand and placed it over the queen's sitting at his side. Melisende jerked his sleeve a second time as she curtsied and he bowed. Their meeting was over.

They stepped away from the royal couple, all eyes on them until the next couple stepped forth and pleasantries began anew. Perault was glad it was over and needed a drink. He found a servant carrying wine and removed two glasses from his tray, handing one to Melisende.

Alone at last, as much as they could be in a ballroom full of people clad in colorful coats and gowns, Perault could breathe again and looked at Melisende with new eyes. "You saved me from acting more of a fool than I was. I have always admired your beauty, but now I will enjoy admiring your brilliance as well." He kissed her lightly on the cheek.

She smiled demurely. "I was a nervous wreck the first time my parents brought me to meet the king and queen. I drove my mother nearly to fits over finding 'just the right dress'. Now that I have been to court a few times, it has become familiar and less heady. You will find it the same soon enough."

Perault was taken aback. "Should I expect to be here so often?"

"All Temple Knights are welcome at court anytime, so I imagine you will attend court out of respect for the crown whenever you are in Lyon's Gate."

"When *we* are in Lyon's Gate," he corrected. "I could never come here on my own. Imagine the trouble I would get into!"

Melisende laughed. "I will see if I can find time in my schedule. There are many suitors who attend court and will no doubt require equal attention."

Something in Perault cast all of his logic aside – the plans for his life after he earned the silver-fringed cloak, where he would travel, what he would do in pursuit of an Act of Heroism that would earn him the right to wear a gold-fringed cloak one day, all carefully considered and organized nearly on a schedule. He planned to marry Melisende as well, someday in the future when he was done with all the rest. Standing here now, he knew that her subtle insinuation was also a warning about how time would pass and circumstances would change.

Perault couldn't stand the thought of life without Melisende. He sat aside their glasses and took her hands. "No suitor will ever seek your attention at court."

She pouted playfully. "Have I become so unattractive?"

"Never." He looked deep into her eyes, and her expression turned serious.

"What is it, Perault?"

"I want you to marry me."

Her eyes widened in surprise. "What about all the things you want to do? After tomorrow you will no longer be a squire and you will have obligations. It would not be right for me to stand in your way."

"You will never be in my way. I will do all the things I have spoken of; I will do them all with you as my wife on a journey that we will share the rest of our lives."

Melisende's eyes welled with tears, and she kissed him fiercely. "Then we will marry, and you will earn the gold-fringed cloak of a full Temple Knight. My knight. And build a family together with many little knights to follow in your footsteps."

When they embraced Perault could feel her beating heart for the first time and he knew that he had done the right thing. For both of them.

"Celebrating a little early I see." Perault's family had found them, his father leading the way through the crowd with his mother and brother just behind.

"Father, Mother, Reginald," he greeted them. "We are engaged!"

"Well, about time," Lady Eckert kissed her son and hugged Melisende. "The Brighams will be thrilled at the news as well!"

His father and brother both clapped him on the back and shook his hand.

"You will be married in Stoddenferry, I hope?" His father was a stickler for tradition and always expected the important occasions celebrated by their family to take place at their ancestral home.

"If Melisende and her family will consent," Perault replied.

Melisende smiled. "There would be no better place to begin our union."

"King Eldorath will announce the knight champions!" a herald cried from the center of the ballroom. Squires did not receive recognition at the Champions Ball, they would receive letters of congratulations signed by the king and queen in a few days.

Like a parting sea, the king and queen made their way through the crowd to stand next to the herald who handed the king an unfurled scroll. A pair of servants carrying a heavy box between them walked up and stood beside the queen. In a strong, regal voice the king acknowledged the knight champions of each event while Queen Penelope presented them with solid gold badges of honor that could be worn on their jackets or ceremonial armor. The last to be announced was Sir Meldecamp, Champion of the joust and Grand Champion of the Tourney. Perault was aware that the Tourneys roots were in the sport of jousting with melee and archery events added centuries later. By tradition, the winner of the joust was also honored as the Grand Champion of the Tourney. A symbolic, but powerful honor to be sure.

When it was over, the king and queen opened the ball with the first dance. Perault thought the royals a handsome couple and wondered why after more than thirty years of marriage they never had any children. It further exacerbated the current discord between Yorwick and Cambria since King Praeter's younger brother, Duke Banfield Eldorath was the next in line to the throne upon the king's death. It was said that the duke wanted the king and queen to birth an heir more than anyone, considering that he was only two years younger than his brother, had no heir himself and didn't want the burden of running the kingdom in his late years.

Perault had his own worries to weigh on his mind without taking on those of a king and queen. Tonight would be a celebration of his accomplishments in the arena and a future with the one he cherished above all others, Melisende. Taking her by the hand, he led her onto the dance floor to join the king and queen, knights and squires, nobles and ladies in blissful turns of merriment that dispelled any thoughts of anything beyond their moment of joy.

CHAPTER 13

Endings and Beginnings

Zracul was going out for the evening. He should have been attending the Champions Ball at Valiant Keep, but due to the rumored nocturnal activities of a supposed Leprechaun, he had another dinner engagement in mind. Zracul was never one to linger on what might have been, he had lived too long and endured too many disappointments not to know that tomorrow was another day. Each day could bring new fortunes by chance and sometimes displeasure would encourage the making of one's own fortune. Such was the case tonight - it was fortune in the form of retribution.

Initially Zracul was puzzled why anyone would want to try and kill or injure him at the Tourney. This was his first time in the Western kingdoms, his first time in Lyonesse, and he knew practically no one. At first, he placed the blame on his competitor, Sir Meldecamp. It stood to reason that he was the only one who would gain from Zracul's defeat, but that was too obvious, and from everything he could find out about the knight, he was highly respected and honorable. A man like that was not going to suddenly begin sabotaging his adversaries for reputation he had already earned. There had to be someone else with a stronger motive.

So who then?

It was only after the end of the Tourney that he realized the truth of it. The objective had not been to kill him by cutting his stirrup; it was simply to ensure he lost in a very specific way at a very specific time. What were the odds that he would get knocked off his horse in the first round of the finals on the first pass? Only an expert in wagers would have the answer to that. Whatever the odds were, the payoff would be huge.

He set a plan into motion to infiltrate the underworld of Lyonesse. Yes, even the pristine city of Lyon's Gate had a vibrant and diverse underworld hiding just below the surface. Zracul owned the underworld in the Eastern kingdoms and he would do so again here. He sent his creatures out again and again with instructions to identify the person or persons that orchestrated his fall.

Normally, Zracul would have sent his brothers, Vadim and Fain, to seek out the truth and deliver death to his enemies. Unfortunately, they were over a hundred leagues away at the Great Library in Tintagel researching the location of a place called Kiltullagh, where legends whispered lay hidden the Sphere of Elements that he was after. If it weren't for the arrival of Ornias, the demon that was as much a part of him now as his own consciousness, Zracul never would have known about the sphere in the first place. Now that he did, he was driven to possess the artifact and use it to his advantage. It was only the ancient knowledge revealed by Ornias and the demon's desire to challenge the power of the gods that together they were on this journey. If they succeeded, the world would never be the same again; overcast by a perpetual cloak of darkness that he and the demon, as one, would rule over with the servitude of a race of their own making.

Not two hours earlier, one of his sisters returned with the answers he was seeking. Now he was on his way to pay a visit to a man named Arthfael, a bookmaker by trade and a very successful one at that. He was the one responsible for his humiliation. It wasn't only a matter of pride; in fact, Zracul was quite impressed with the whole deception. He especially wanted to know how Arthfael had managed to compel a Leprechaun to do his bidding. That would be quite a tale indeed.

Fully naked and alone in his dark room at the inn, Zracul willed his body into a rapid transformation that resulted in a gaseous form similar to the consistency of a thick oily smoke. In this form he could move quickly, nearly undetectable and almost anywhere that wasn't sealed or underwater. The most serious danger he faced would be wind and rain. Fortunately, the skies were clear and the air was still on this evening. The physical downside was that the transformation would only change his flesh, leaving clothing and objects behind. When Ornias first revealed the knowledge to alter his physical body, the demon had conveniently left that part out and Zracul found himself in a very awkward situation. It seemed the Demon of Greed had a sense of humor to match the black void that served as his soul.

Silently oozing through a separation between the window and its frame, Zracul moved like a dark shadow down the wall and into the alley illuminated only by the light of the half-moon reflecting off a shallow pool of water in the street. Arthfael would be in his office tonight, counting the revenue from a very lucrative Tourney week. This was the information brought to him by his sisters, Jaria and Daria. They somehow managed to locate a man that pointed them to a fat banker named Arthfael. After that it was simple. They seduced the man, gained the information their master wanted, spent the next few hours torturing the poor fellow and then consumed him. Zracul chided the girls for taking their time getting the information back to him, but he was not too harsh, the banker was their reward.

Zracul's nebulous form traveled quickly through the streets and alleys, keeping to the shadows and avoiding crowded spaces until he came to the door leading into Arthfael's home. It was located in the upscale banking section of the trade district only a block away from the home of the man who had betrayed him. Zracul paused a moment with silent pride that his sisters had not simply crossed the short distance to deal with Arthfael themselves, defying his implicit instructions. He wanted to deal with the mastermind of his humiliation himself.

The door Arthfael's home was thick and probably reinforced from inside with a bar or locking system, perhaps both. According to the dead banker, Arthfael took his security very seriously and would likely have never answered to a simple knock on the door. Zracul did not intend to knock.

Studying the exterior of the home with his mind's eye, Zracul noted that it was built of polished stone like most buildings in the city and extended two levels high with houses attached on both sides. The windows on either side of the front door were barred and shuttered. To anyone else, this would be a formidable obstacle to entry, but for Zracul in shadow form, he could easily seep through the narrowest gap underneath the door.

Once inside, Zracul resumed his human form. The entry was dark except for a small lamp that illuminated a hallway running off to his right. To his left stood a closed door, no doubt a closet for hanging hats and cloaks, and straight ahead rose a stairway leading to the second story which was also dimly illuminated from above. Zracul had no certainty about where Arthfael would be or if there were any servants about, but he reasoned that a man like Arthfael would have an office downstairs to meet with his clients and then a secret, smaller office near where he slept to count his money.

Following the line of the stairway, Zracul silently glided to the second level. As spartan as the lower level appeared, the opposite was true upstairs. Expensive furnishings, tapestries, and paintings adorned the hallway to his left and right while dim light globes illuminated a thick blue runner that insulated against the cold of the stone floor. Arthfael most assuredly enjoyed his comforts.

The hour was late, and so far he had not come across anyone else in the house. He suspected any that were usually about had already retired to their bedchambers. It was fortunate for them as he planned to kill any servants or family members during his search. He didn't need premature alarms raised that might allow his quarry to escape. Zracul wouldn't seek them out, he came for just one man, and he doubted Arthfael was asleep yet. Taking the shadow-filled hallway on the right, Zracul didn't have to go far before he came to a pair of large and ornately carved double doors gilded with gold flake. This must be Arthfael's room.

The doors were very thick oak and even Zracul's acute hearing was unable to detect any movement behind it. Assuming shadow form again, Zracul searched for the smallest crack or opening around the door to gain entry, but surprisingly there was none. It was the kind of door that was treated with a special oil and built to exacting standards that only the wealthy could afford. Its purpose was to protect the room inside from the intrusion of fire or smoke. Arthfael must be the type who kept his wealth close, rather than trusting it to a banker.

Zracul resumed to his normal form once again. There was only one way to enter the room beyond, and that would be through force. He rationalized that even if there were servants about and they alerted the guard, he would be done here before they arrived. Taking a step back, Zracul charged the door pressing the full power of his strength and body and focusing it on his leading shoulder.

The heavy double doors exploded inward with such force that they nearly broke off of their hinges. Inside, Zracul gazed quickly around what appeared to be a large sitting room elegantly furnished with plush chairs facing a wide fireplace and a wide table to one side stacked with small papers that he recognized as gambling ledgers. Through an open doorway, Zracul could see into an opulently appointed bedchamber. A door slammed shut from somewhere in that room. Someone was in there, probably Arthfael.

From the hallway from whence he came, Zracul heard a rush of footsteps and then a frightened gasp. He spotted a young woman in nightclothes with eyes bulging at the sight of a naked stranger standing in the debris of her master's doorway. In her panic she ran down the stairs, lost her footing and tumbled the rest of the way. Zracul could have caught up with her easily, but he had to catch Arthfael before he disappeared out some passage or secret doorway. Tracking him a second time might prove more difficult if he went into hiding.

Entering the bedroom, there was only one other door visible. It was another heavy oak doorway as stout as the first ones he'd broken. This time he kicked the door clean off its frame to land flat on the floor. There was a sudden click and the "thump" of pressure in the center of his chest. Glancing down, the butt of a crossbow bolt protruded from deep in his torso. Zracul admired the shot; it was a blow that would have killed any living man.

Across the room stood the origin of the bolt – a fat man holding a crossbow standing behind a large solid oak desk piled with over-flowing bags of silver and gold between toppled stacks of coins.

The man was wearing layers of expensive silk robes lined with fur dyed a vivid shade of purple; a very expensive textile color from the Mouillians or the Capsians, he couldn't recall which at that moment. What he did know was that the man before him could be none other than Arthfael. Almost sadly, there was a smile of victory on his wide face as if he expected Zracul to fall dead any second. He was so arrogant that he had not even bothered to set another bolt in his crossbow. It would not have mattered.

Then a fly landed on the crossbow.

Before the fly could flutter a wing to escape, Zracul was standing chest-to-chest with Arthfael; the crossbow slung to the ground in splintered pieces over the corpse of a dead fly.

Arthfael's smile evaporated, and his eyes filled with disbelief and horror. "T-take it, take it all, whatever you want. Even the precious gems in that chest over there," he vaguely gestured to a small chest against one wall.

"I am not here for your wealth," Zracul hissed in his ear.

"W-what was it that you want?" Arthfael stammered. "I'll give you anything."

Zracul grabbed the man by his collars and shoved him into the chair behind his desk, then he casually half-sat on the desk in front of him. "Why don't we chat for a moment?"

The fat man's eyes darted around the room as if expecting others. "But don't you want the gems in that chest yonder? They are worth a fortune!"

Zracul snarled, "Forget the damn jewels! I want to know where you found a Leprechaun to cut my stirrups."

Recognition filled Arthfael eyes. "You are Prince Zracul. Please understand that was just business! I never intended for anyone to get hurt! You were doing well in the Tourney and the odds were high against you falling to Sir, Sir. . ."

Zracul finished for him, "Meldecamp. Yes, I get that, but what about the Leprechaun?"

The man's eyes widened. "How could you know about that?"

"I make it my business to know things. Like how much you are going to suffer if you don't tell me what I want to know," Zracul growled.

Zracul felt a satisfying shiver from Arthfael before he spoke. "The Leprechaun was security for a wager a man lost a few weeks ago. Somehow, he had captured the little beast in the deep woods of Eriu. I didn't ask how. As you may have heard, a captured Leprechaun is required to perform three reasonable services for his capture to earn his freedom. This one had a single service remaining which transferred to me when the man lost his wager. I simply concocted a plan to maximize the profit of his service. You just happened to be the mark for this scheme. Forgive me, please, you are obviously sound and no harm has come to you," Arthfael pleaded. "I will gladly pay for any inconvenience I have caused you!"

"Where is the Leprechaun now?"

The man looked incredulous. "Gone! He performed his last service so it was impossible to hold him a moment longer. Believe me, I tried!"

Zracul was disappointed by that. "Too bad, I would have liked a Leprechaun. As for you, I will grant you a swift death."

Arthfael cringed into the back of his chair, "WAIT!" before the echo of his scream faded, his neck was broken and his eyes were glassing over in death. For a few moments, Zracul sat staring at the dead fat man. A waste of life. So many in this world wasted their short lives away for no purpose, he mused.

Just then his sensitive ears picked up the sound of men in armor clamoring down the street toward the house. The servant that escaped earlier must have alerted a patrol. He decided it would be wise to make this look like a robbery. No reason to cause lengthy investigation, especially when they were soon to find his mutilated friend who'd been Jaria's and Daria's playmate. That was going to cause enough of an uproar in the city in itself.

Zracul found a knife in the desk and cut Arthfael's throat so deeply that it nearly decapitated the dead man. It would serve to disguise his real cause of death. Then he scattered the bags of gold and silver coins all over the room; no one would know if any were missing. Almost as an afterthought, he lifted the small chest that Arthfael was so desperate to negotiate for his life and smashed it on the floor. It splintered into a thousand pieces releasing a spring mechanism that shot a score of darts, no doubt poisoned, in several directions.

How clever.

Had he opened the chest normally all those darts would have plunged into his face, blinding a normal man. At least a dozen beautifully cut gems glinted in the wreckage of the chest. Zracul would have liked to take them if he could have.

The soldiers were inside the house and pounding up the stairs. Zracul had only a few seconds to escape or he would have to kill them all. Quickly, he ran through the door leading into Arthfael's bedchamber and leaped through a shuttered and barred window two levels above the alley on the rear of the house. By the time the soldiers reached the sitting room, Zracul was only a shadow silently gliding through the night in the distance.

~~~

At precisely noon, Perault was assembled with a score of his fellow squires in the vast courtyard of the upper ward facing the open gates of the palace where a gilded carriage was making its way along the long cobblestone ramp. It was the king's carriage and behind him rode exactly one hundred Temple Knights in full ceremonial armor and gold-fringed cloaks with the symbol of Sunna on their backs. Each carried a long pole, symbolic of a lance, where fluttered a pennant with the colors and symbols of their households. There were few people on hand for the ceremony as it was closed to the general public with only about a hundred nobles, knights and family members in attendance to stand as witness. Perault's parents and brother were there, along with

Melisende, her parents and brothers and of course Sir Aldeman. It was a perfect day with all the people he loved in the world with him on one of the most important days of his life.

The carriage arrived with the king and he stepped out wearing an all-black jacket, tunic, and trousers accented with silver trimmings under a massive fur cloak with a gold fringe at its edges. On his side he wore a gilded long sword glinting with jewels that he was known to call *GohedPrge* that supposedly translated to *Everlasting Fire*, but from what language Perault did not know and for what reason he did not know.

The knights following the carriage split into two groups and lined the north and south edge of the courtyard. Six of them stayed with the king and forming a line behind him. They were the elite personal guard loyal to the king and queen alone, subject to their bidding until death or abdication. They were the best and brightest of all the Temple Knights voluntarily serving out of loyalty and devotion to Sunna and the kingdom of Lyonesse in what was often a lifetime appointment.

King Eldorath approached the double line of squires. Perault was in front with his friend Edwin Finbrat to his left and Duncan Pentager to his right. Davin of House Jeutemont stood directly behind him in the second line. The four of them had spent much of their lives together over the years. The knights they served knew each other well and often got together to tell tall tales and relive their youth together. Perault imagined that one day the four of them would sit together reliving their adventures as well.

"In the light of Sunna, I grant thee each the right to call yourselves a Temple Knight of Lyonesse by the grace of your king. The world will know you by the cloak you wear, marked with the symbol of Sunna and adorned with a silver edge." King Eldorath spoke loud and true for everyone in the courtyard to hear. "Once you wear the cloak for the first time it becomes a part of you for life and you are bound by the laws of kingdom and Sunna that govern its endowment." The king began to pace the line, his gait slow and purposeful, meeting every squire's eyes with his own. "There is the Temple Knights Sacred

Oath that you have all learned from your first days as a squire. It will guide your conduct for the rest of your days and if you choose The Testing, it will be the source of Enlightenment and Sunna's Wisdom that is imparted to you through those very words." He stopped and raised his hands high. "Say them with me now." Every squire spoke the words they revered more than any other.

"I hear the call from darkness and come into the light

Born once again unto Sunna, to bask in her radiant wisdom.

Pledged to defend her teaching and follow her faith

Hold close the secrets of the Order to which body and soul I am endowed

Ne'er to commit murder, deceit or lie

To honor and serve Country and King,

Upon pain of death and ruin upon my soul if ever I should fail.

In her Grace I shall serve with bone and blood and spirit

With every breath within me unto the end of days."

The king lowered his hands and slowly looked over the squires. "From this day forward, you have two years to earn your gold-fringed cloak by either an Act of Heroism or by undergoing The Testing. There is no other way. If the time passes and you have accomplished neither, then your status as a knight will be revoked and you must find a different path in life. But if you succeed, you may call yourself a Temple Knight of Lyonesse by the grace of Sunna and pride of your king and country!"

Perault and the other squires cheered. He felt so much pride to be soon counted among the Temple Knights that he nearly burst. It was exhilarating.

The king pulled his sword, holding high for all to see and called its name, *"GohedPrge!"* It responded by bursting into flames along its entire length without causing harm to the great man that wielded it. "Now come forward and receive your reward!"

The squires cheered even louder. It was the closest Perault had ever come to a rapturous event and for a moment felt overwhelmed with tears running down his face. The others around him were openly weeping as well almost making him want to laugh at the strange beauty of it all.

Two of the king's knights rode up and dismounted. One began arranging the squires in a line while the other retrieved a large chest from the carriage. Returning his flaming sword to its scabbard, King Praeter called forth the first squire. Almost hesitantly the young man approached and then fell to his knees. The knight standing next to the king retrieved a silver-fringed cloak from the chest and handed it to the king, who gently lay it over the squire's shoulders, speaking a few words too quiet for Perault to hear.

It went the same way for every squire until it was time for Perault to step up and kneel before King Praeter. He felt the cloak settle upon his shoulders held by the king's firm hands and then a soothing voice speaking in his ear. "Sir Perault of House Eckert, rise a Temple Knight of Lyonesse. May Sunna guide and protect you." Then lifting pressure on his shoulders prompted him to stand and face the king, who winked and smiled before turning his attention to the next in line.

Perault was sure he had stepped into a dream. He was no longer Perault the squire of Sir Aldeman, he was *Sir* Perault of House Eckert. The House of his family. A House with a rich heritage of Temple Knights going back generations, including his father and brother. Now his name would grace their regal roster along with all those before him. He wondered if he and Melisende might one day have sons that would also count their names among them.

After King Praeter laid the silver-fringed cloak on the last squire, he walked their line once again admiring his new company of young Temple Knights. Perault looked over at his friends and the other squires adorned in their new cloaks and to a man they were all smiling as broadly as he was.

"Sir Knights!" The king called and the newly-cloaked knights stood at attention. "You may go out into the world and follow your calling. Honor Sunna, honor your king and honor your family!" With a final salute, he turned and stepped into his carriage which headed to the palace without delay followed by the slow procession of one hundred Temple Knights of his elite guard.

When they were gone, the families rushed into the courtyard to embrace the graduates. Melisende was the first to reach him almost at a run, jumping into his embrace.

"I'm so proud of you, Sir Knight!" She barely got the words out before they were overrun by their combined families.

The next morning, Perault was packing his belongings to leave the White Horse Inn. He would be joining his family and the Brighams on the return trip to Stoddenferry where the two families would be organizing his impending nuptials to Melisende. He had already bid farewell to Hanlin and Dorlik and sent them on their way with promises to see them again soon. Before he departed the inn, however, he had one last sad task to carry out – saying goodbye to Sir Aldeman.

He went downstairs to the first floor where Sir Aldeman's rooms were located. His master hated stairs, said they made his bones creak to climb them. Former master, Perault corrected himself with a smile. He knocked on the door.

"Get in here, Perault!" Sir Aldeman called. Perault never could figure out how the old knight always knew it was him at his door.

Sir Aldeman was sitting in a chair with a sheathed sword on the table beside him. He gestured to a chair facing him and Perault sat with some trepidation. His old master was wearing his fine clothes bearing house emblem and colors, odd considering there was no formal occasion that day that he was aware of.

The old knight smiled warmly. "I would ask you to serve me one last time even though I no longer have the right to do so."

"Of course, my lord. What service may I offer?"

Sir Aldeman lifted the sword on the table, his sword, the sword he had carried since he was knighted decades ago by the current kings' father. "I would like to pass the care of my sword to you. You are the closest I will ever have to a son of my own and I can think of no one better to pass it down to." He caressed the sheath with momentary reflection before he continued. "This sword has been in my family for many generations, fought in many wars and conflict defending this land even before it was a land called Lyonesse."

Perault was dumbstruck at what Sir Aldeman was offering. "I have even come to believe that the Dwarves that crafted the blade added a little something more, a magic perhaps, which has helped our family survive for so long."

He held out the blade for Perault to take. Conflicted with emotion, he took it hesitantly and with reverence. "I swear to you Sir Aldeman, that for as long as I shall live I will properly care for your sword and carry it with the honor your ancestors would expect and deserve." He inhaled an unsteady breath. "Most importantly, I will never dishonor you, my lord, as I carry the sword in the commission of my duties as a Temple Knight of the realm."

Sir Aldeman stood and laughed. "Go into the world, my boy, and make a name for yourself. Then come back and entertain an old man with tales of your deeds!"

They embraced as equals for the first time and laughed together for a while before Perault slung the sword over his shoulder and prepared to leave. He would miss Sir Aldeman. The knight had been as much a father to him as his own, even more so if the truth be told. Not that his own father was neglectful in any way, it's just that his life as a squire started with Sir Aldeman at a young age and he had only occasional contact with his family in the years that followed.

"I will always love you like my own father," he told Sir Aldeman and then left the room. He barely kept his emotions in check not wanting to break down and cry in front of his old master. Outside the closed door, Perault stopped to take a breath and thought he heard the muffled sound from the other side of the door that would forever break his heart – the old man wept.

CHAPTER 14

Revelations

Lady Genestra ran as fast as her long skirts would allow through the darkened corridors of Cambrian Keep. She ran toward the nursery where Pen was cared for during the day and it took every bit of control she could manage not to lift her skirts and sprint like a farm girl. Behind her, a dozen soldiers clamored in their leather and metal armor anxiously trying to keep up.

Held tightly in her balled fist were words written frantically on parchment informing her of an ambush. Only a day out of Cambria, still within the bounds of their realm, her husband's carriage was set upon by assassins. There was only one survivor, a simple groom that managed to escape into the forest, who described a ferocious pitched battle between the count's guards and the assassins. There were many details of desperate heroics and last stands that Lady Genestra had gleaned over, with only a single line near the end that captured her attention and sent her running in panic; *Count Terril Djago is dead and his issue may also be in danger.*

She didn't care that the men who attacked the count's entourage were wearing the uniforms of Yorwick, nor even that five hundred Cambrian soldiers and druids had been dispatched from a nearby outpost to the scene. All that mattered was her child's welfare which she would defend tooth and nail to her death if necessary.

Finally arriving at the nursery, she burst through the door to find a young nursemaid on her knees holding her tiny child's hands in a walking exercise.

"My lady!" the nursemaid jumped to her feet in surprise. Young Pen, barely more than an infant and left free-standing for a moment and startled, fell on his bum and began to cry.

Genestra rushed over and picked up her child, holding him to her chest in a tight, protective hug. The guards pushed into the room a step behind her and immediately fanned out into the chamber, checking all the doors, closets, and windows. Jarl, one of Commander Ouza's under-captains was diligently barking orders to search every nook and cranny for dangers.

"What is it, my lady? What has happened?" Wide-eyed, the nursemaid was being restrained by a pair of Jarl's guardsmen.

"Let her be," Lady Genestra commanded. "Aine is innocent."

The guards immediately released the nursemaid and she hurried over to share in Lady Genestra's embrace with the now content child.

"Everything is fine now," Lady Genestra assured Aine, then she rested her cheek upon the top of Pen's head and stroked her nursemaid's hair to keep her calm. "Count Djago is feared dead in an ambush and there may be some danger to our child, his heir."

Shouting suddenly erupted from outside the east window of the nursery. Jarl and several of his men rushed over to look outside while the remaining guards circled Pen and the women protectively. Then there was a scream of pain that ended seconds later with a sickening thump and more shouts that sounded like military commands.

Jarl turned to Lady Genestra. "You are safe, my lady. A man was found climbing the ivy on the wall outside this very window and Commander Ouza had him shot down."

"Blessed Sunna," she muttered and held Aine and Pen tighter.

A little while later, Commander Ouza arrived in the nursery. He carried what appeared to be a medallion on the end of a leather thong that he twirled around his forefinger rapidly in one direction, then the other. Pen and Aine were again calm and playing under her watchful eye while the guards kept watch out the windows and down the corridor.

"The danger has passed, my lady." Commander Ouza's tone was bland and to the point as always.

"What about the man that was found on the wall? Is he dead?"

"My best marksman shot him through the leg, but unfortunately the fall killed him."

Lady Genestra sighed and nervously smoothed the wrinkles in her skirts. "What do you know of him? Will there be others?"

Commander Ouza held up the medallion. "He was wearing this. It bears the mark of Yorwick." His features changed to a chilling scowl "Undoubtedly there will be others and we will do everything in our power to protect you and the count's heir, beginning with the removal of all the ivy on the walls."

"That's comforting commander." In truth, she didn't feel comforted at all. Comfort was the last thing she felt whenever Ouza was around. "And what about my husband? Any word?"

The commander slowly shook his head. "We will not know anything further until the soldiers find the location where the count was attacked and send word through the druids."

"Was Naamah with my husband?" She disliked the strange druid only slightly less than Commander Ouza, but she knew her as a competent purveyor of druid magic and healing if the rumors were true.

"No, my lady. The druid was sent on a special assignment before the count departed for Lyon's Gate."

Heat rose within Genestra. Lyon's Gate. Her husband had been summoned to that city by King Praeter to work out a peace agreement with the duke of the very men that attacked him on his way there. Was the king a party to this treachery? She didn't want to think of it. What protections would they have if the King of Lyonesse was against them?

The next morning Lady Genestra was awakened by rapid knocking at the door. Initially disoriented, she surveyed her surroundings and remembered that she had stayed the night in the bedchamber adjacent the nursery. She wanted to be close to Pen, even though Commander Ouza assured her that the Keep was safe. Nearly one hundred guards were now stationed night and day at every doorway, window, tower, and rooftop connected to the nursery and the bedchamber where she lay now.

Even so, the night was long and full of fears real and imagined that she had barely fallen asleep when the knocking began. "What is it?" She shouted.

Wynne, her fair-haired lady-in-waiting, nearly ran into the room. The smile she wore stretched on her face nearly ear to ear. "I have news about your husband!" She knelt at the bedside and took Lady Genestra's hand. "He lives!"

"He lives?" Genestra was astounded. During the night she had finally taken the time to read the details of the attack from the message transcribed from the sole survivors account of the ambush. It seemed certain that after fighting heroically, the count died under the assassin's blades. She read it over and over and wept every moment of it.

"He lives!" Wynne confirmed. "Commander Ouza woke me to tell you. He said he would have come himself except that the hour was too early for him to disturb a lady."

Genestra nearly scoffed at the idea. Commander Ouza probably didn't want to stray far from whatever housemaid or kitchen girl he was entertaining. "Praise Sunna, he lives. Where is my husband now?"

Wynne kissed Lady Genestra's hand excitedly. "Commander Ouza says that the count is in the care of the druids and that he will be brought back to Cambria in a few weeks when he is well enough to travel."

Genestra smiled warmly at her lady-in-waiting. "Then we will prepare our bedchamber for his arrival. It must be bright and warm for him to convalesce. I will bring his papers and quills from his study to keep him distracted." She squeezed Wynne's hand affectionately. "You have begun my day with wonderful news. Now go tell the others, I will dress."

Wynne's eyes lit with excitement, and she practically sprang from the room. Genestra was very fond of her lady-in-waiting. She could not have asked for a more fitting servant to replace her beloved Tala. Young and silly at times, Wynne was devoted and cheerful even in the most difficult times. Those times had been more often than not since her return to Cambria with Pen.

Genestra suddenly wondered why she was so happy for her husband's return. Of course, she would never wish an ounce of harm upon him, but their relationship was not the same as it was before. They hardly had a relationship at all for that matter. Djago was always working, rarely shared a meal with her, and slept in the small bedchamber adjacent to his study every night. He had not even lain with her once since her return. And worse, he spent barely a moment with his son. It was not like him at all. They used to spend all of their free time together, love deeply, and dream of a family. Those memories were faded now, like it was a different life in a different time. It made her sad to think of it. Everything had changed after Tala was murdered.

Nearly every day Lady Genestra received an update on her husband's condition. Soon, the messages began arriving from the druid Naamah and she took small relief that her husband was no longer surrounded only by strangers. Genestra considered traveling to where he was, but Commander Ouza insisted that it would be far too dangerous, especially considering that the soldiers that ambushed the count had not yet been captured.

The mood of the citizenry changed markedly once word got out about the attack on the count. People were openly calling for warfare for the first time. The anger and tension in the streets, among the soldiers, servants and guards were palpable. Commander Ouza had the military conducting exercises in the fields just outside the city where the people could see them and the blacksmiths, bowyers and fletchers were working around the clock to fill his orders.

Lady Genestra realized Cambria was at a tipping point craving one final push to send them over the edge and into conflict with Yorwick, maybe even Lyon's Gate. If it happened, the bloodshed of thousands that would follow. She always knew Djago to have a cool head in these matters and they needed him in Cambria to reduce the tension and work toward a peaceful solution if one could be found. Genestra wondered if that was possible anymore. Her husband was angry all the time, furious at Duke Eldorath in particular and his journey to Lyon's Gate appeared to be the last best effort to find the peace between Cambria and Yorwick. That was ruined now and she was sure her husband was angrier than ever about it.

In the afternoon, Lady Genestra decided to take a walk in the gardens with Pen, Aine, and Wynne. They were enjoying a small picnic of sweet fruits and cheese on the bank of a small pond when Commander Ouza found them.

"I have news, my lady." He bent his neck in the customary show of respect, but made no effort to recognize that Aine and Wynne were even there.

Lady Genestra was wary. "Is it my husband?"

"No, my lady. He is getting stronger by the day and will return to us soon."

"Then what is it?"

The commander held a small parchment. "As the ruler of Cambria until your husband returns, I am required to inform you of major events in the Western Kingdoms that may adversely affect our lands."

Lady Genestra barked a laugh. "Thank you for reminding me of that fact, commander. I had almost forgotten that it is not you who rules Cambria until my husband's return."

The commander didn't even have the grace to blush. "I am doing the will of the count as he commanded before he was injured and as he commands now with written words."

"Very well, commander." She wasn't about to go down that rabbit hole with him. "What is the news? Or shall I just read the messages from your spies?"

He ignored that. "Teamhrach in Eriu is preparing to make war upon Tintagel, a conflict that could embroil the whole of both Eriu and Lyonesse if things get further out of control."

"Since when do things not get out of control when it comes to war?" It was a rhetorical question and the commander simply nodded his response.

She wondered if this could be the tipping point that she feared. "What has the king said on the matter."

"Not much. He has sent missives to all the cities in Lyonesse to be prepared and ready in case he announces a call to arms." The commander squatted to face her at eye level. "We do know that Lyon's Gate and Oswalt, situated virtually in between Teamhrach and Tintagel, have already called up their armies just in case."

Lady Genestra had friends in Tintagel and she began to worry. "What is the source of the conflict?"

Commander Ouza shrugged. "The Duchess Eselt of Tintagel was accused of the crime of adultery by Duke Maruk, a trial resulted in a guilty verdict and she has been sentenced to death."

"Ah, I see," Lady Genestra nodded. "And the High-King of Eriu takes exception to the death sentence because Duchess Eselt is his youngest daughter. Why the harsh sentence? Usually, foreign nobles are banished to their home country if they commit crimes short of murder."

"That is still unknown to us, my lady."

"Thank you for the report, commander. You are free to return to your duties."

With a curt bow, the commander strode along the winding path through the gardens that led to the Keep. Genestra watched his back until he was out of sight. When she turned to her companions, she was only mildly surprised to find the women's eyes locked in the same direction.

"He is the most beautiful man I have ever seen." Wynne blushed, clearly forgetting that she was with the Countess of Cambria.

Lady Genestra stifled her anger. Wynne was barely more than a child with little experience with men. "Keep clear of that one, dear. There is something off about him that I have yet to determine."

Wynne's head bobbed quickly with excessive nods. "Yes, my lady."

Quickly the tension passed and the women returned to chatting and entertaining Pen. Lady Genestra nodded and smiled when it was appropriate, but her mind wandered. She recalled a day the previous spring when she picnicked in the gardens with her husband. It was something they would do regularly on warm days with cool breezes. The times seemed simpler, with few concerns and . . . Hope for the future. She wondered what the future held for her now. Never would she have expected then how life would change or that she would be sitting with her servants rather than her husband. What would her life be like next spring?

From the day Djago fell ill nothing had been the same. If she walked the halls of her own Keep, her home, she rarely recognized anyone from before that time. There was hardly a person she knew then that had not retired, died, or just disappeared. She wondered why. Did they know something she didn't? Was she so consumed by her love and concern for her husband that it blinded her to the obvious malfeasance that must be taking place right under her nose? Genestra resolved to find out. She would not be the fool that was the last one to know.

A little while later Lady Genestra left Aine to put Pen down for a nap and sent Wynne into the city on a few errands. She had nothing in particular planned for herself so she decided to go to her husband's study and retrieve a few administrative papers to keep his mind busy once he returned.

The corridors in the keep near the count's office were oddly empty and devoid of human activity. The last time she was here the halls were alive with servants, messengers, and various nobles and foreign dignitaries crowding the way. They were all either in the count's service or pandering to gain his attention for the briefest of moments. Today, the silence was almost deafening.

When Lady Genestra arrived at the door to the study she was relieved to find it unlocked. Inside, the main chamber was dark save for the filtered light that entered through the westward facing windows. She walked about the room activating light globes that brought warm illumination to the sparse chamber before she sat behind the large wooden desk in her husband's high-backed padded chair. She had never sat in his chair before, it felt more comfortable than she would have imagined and it might have been her imagination, but she was sure that his scent lingered in that space. It should not have been a wonder, she laughed to herself, since he spent so damn much time there.

She thought about her husband for a while and imagined a time when they would be happy again together. Perhaps when this business with Yorwick was finally resolved. At least she could hope. Their boy was growing fast and would need the council of his father soon. Pen would learn to wield a sword, sing poetry, gain a proper education, and learn to rule. Almost all of those things would require diligent and persistent mentoring that only his father could provide. She knew in her heart that those would be happy times.

Genestra glanced at the papers neatly stacked on the desk and casually read through them. Most were documents related to trade, work orders, and requests for everything from making repairs to stables used by the cavalry to dredging a new well on the southern end of Cambria. Nothing too exciting and nothing that couldn't wait, which was probably why they were still stacked here.

The desk held three drawers. She pulled one and found blank parchment and extra quills. A second drawer contained the count's Seal of Office, small inkpots stoppered with wax, and a few gold and silver trinkets that were probably gifts from those wishing to do business inside the walls of Cambria. The final drawer was locked and there was no key anywhere that she searched. Looking closer, she spied a small gap between the drawer and the frame of the desk that she thought she might jiggle the lock loose if she had the right tool.

An idea came to her and she removed a narrow pin from the bun in her hair causing the dark locks to spill around her face. To her amazement, the plan worked and her success was announced by a distinct and satisfying click. Inside were more papers related to troop movements and strategic plans to attack Yorwick. There were also a number of pages devoted to cataloging locations on the border that had been attacked by Yorwick soldiers over the past few months. Oddly, there were villages and outposts on the list that had never been attacked. She wondered why. The last page in the drawer, at the very bottom of the pile, was a list of a hundred or more names that she would later wish she had never seen. On it were people that she knew, like the druid Taudrick whom she had loved so much, his name was crossed out. Then there was Sir Reynfrey, and her lady-in-waiting, Tala, on the list with their names crossed out. There were many, many more on the list that she knew who were no longer in the keep. Most with their names crossed out.

Lady Genestra's eyes began to well with tears. Was this a list of friends lost or a hit list marking those to be disposed of? What innocent purpose could such a list serve? Tears fell on the parchment. What had her husband done and why? *Who* had he become to perpetuate these evil deeds? And what about that other list, the one with locations never attacked on the border? Was that another hit list? Could her husband be guilty of causing death and violence upon his own people? Had he gone insane?

"What are you doing here?" a voice boomed from the doorway, cruel and angry.

Lady Genestra snapped her head around, startled at the unexpected sound, her tears running fluidly over her pale cheeks. "Do you know about this?" She held out the list of names.

Commander Ouza appeared annoyed. "Where did you get that?"

"In the drawer here." Lady Genestra motioned to the open drawer.

"That drawer was locked for a purpose. Those papers are for the count's eyes and only those he wishes to share them with!" The commander's face was red with anger. He took a step forward, his fists clenched at his sides as if restraining some primal urge. "You should not be here!"

"This is my husband's study and as he is not here this business is mine!" she shouted back. The tears slowed; she felt her own anger rising. "Why would my husband be killing his own people? Why would he be killing our friends?"

Her demands were met by the cold, dead stare of Commander Ouza's rage-filled eyes. "The count did not make those lists! We recovered them from spies and locked them away to use to our best advantage." Commander Ouza was seething. "Your leap to conclusions only proves that you are not competent enough to be trusted with sensitive information of this nature. Even from his bed in the druids Enclave he controls what happens in Cambria through me and it will remain so until he returns. Now get out!"

Lady Genestra was struck speechless at the manner in which he spoke to her. She was the Countess of Cambria and the legal ruler until her husband recovered from his injuries. This fool had no right! She looked again at the list of names. It was true, none of them were written in her husband's hand. She should have noticed that from the start. Maybe the commander was right. Maybe she was just being a foolish woman. Without a word, she fled the room.

For two weeks Lady Genestra confined herself to the nursery and the adjacent bedchamber. The events in her husband's study left her mortified and uncertain of her own judgment, gut feelings and intuition. She wouldn't be prepared to face Commander Ouza again so soon and instead distracted herself from her troubles with the delights of her child.

There was a polite knock on the door to the nursery. Lady Genestra knew it was one of the guards posted outside allowing the passage of food or a message. In this case, it was a message the guard passed to Aine who handed it to Wynne.

"It bears the seal of the commander." Wynne held the rolled parchment out for her to take.

A cold chill climbed up Lady Genestra's spine. This would be their first contact since the day she fled her husband's study. "What does it say?"

Wynne hesitantly pulled back the scroll and slowly cracked the seal to reveal the words inside. Lady Genestra watched her eyes scan the document and then incredulously a wide smile crept over Wynne's face. *What could the silly girl possibly be smiling about?* She thought to herself.

"Count Djago returns!" Wynne announced excitedly. "The druid Naamah is bringing him tonight!"

Relief, happiness, and excitement flooded through Lady Genestra at the same time. Finally, her husband would return and set everything right again! She kept her emotions to herself and simply smiled at the good news. "Thank you, Wynne."

"Everything is ready, my lady. I will run to your bedchamber and set the fire and turn on the light globes in preparation for the count's arrival!" Wynne started toward the door and then stopped. "Should I wait for you there, my lady?"

"Wait for me there, sweet girl. I will be along soon." Lady Genestra felt like she was walking on air.

Wynne attempted a quick curtsy while turning for the door and nearly tripped over her skirts. She recovered quickly and with a giggle dashed through the door. Lady Genestra could only smile at her lady-in-waiting knowing how well-meaning the poor girl was, if not exactly the most graceful in thought or foot.

"Should I keep Pen awake, my lady?" It was nearly the baby's bedtime and his eyes were drooping.

"No, no." Lady Genestra leaned in to kiss him on the forehead. "Let him sleep. We will take him to his father in the morning."

Aine carefully rose to her feet and took the baby into the next room, leaving Lady Genestra alone with her thoughts. The room felt cold and abandoned without Pen's laughter to fill it. She loved her son deeply, and despite all she had endured cherished the past two weeks of her life in the nursery. She resolved to spend more time with him in the days and years to come. She wanted to experience Pen's life with him as he grew, nurture him and make sure he knew how much he was loved.

With some measure of reluctance, she exited the nursery to await her husband in their bedchamber. Surely they would bring him there first so that he could recover in the comfort of familiar surroundings with his family close by. Lady Genestra imagined so many scenarios of their first meeting after so long and they all ended with him in her embrace. It would be a time for welcoming and reunion. Commander Ouza's disrespect would be dealt with another time.

She entered her bedchamber just as Wynne was completing her final touches. "Everything is perfect, Wynne, just perfect." She hugged her lady-in-waiting tightly before she left. Her servants had become her friends and confidants and she intended to make sure that they were cared for as well. It was another thing on a long list of items she intended to discuss with her husband when he returned. Until then, she sat alone in her bedchamber and waited.

An hour after sunset, the trumpets blared heralding the return of the count into Cambria. Lady Genestra, dosing in her chair, awoke immediately and nearly bounded toward the balcony overlooking the west gate. Far below, a procession of at least two hundred cavalry units escorted the count's carriage through the main gates. Just behind his carriage rode the figure of Naamah, so seductive and beautiful. As if she knew Genestra was watching, the druid looked toward where the lady stood and smiled. Lady Genestra favored her with a wave but received no response.

Genestra retreated into the bedchamber. The count would be brought up any moment now, and she wanted her face to be the first one he would see when they entered. Minutes passed and then more minutes. What was taking them so long? Should she have met him at the entrance to the keep? More minutes, then an hour and two. Lady Genestra was pacing wildly across the floor. Where did they take him if not his bedchamber? There was only one place – his study. Initially furious, Lady Genestra had to tamp down her anger. Maybe there was good reason that they took him to his study first. Maybe there was something urgent that he had to attend to. After all, she had been secluded in the nursery for the past two weeks and something significant may have developed in Eriu or Yorwick.

There was one way to find out. A secret passage that led through the walls from their bedchamber to the count's study. Her husband used it often when they shared the bedchamber, but that was before he fell ill. This circumstance would be as good a reason as any to use it once more.

Pressing a panel near a bookshelf, the wall opened to illuminate a dark corridor beyond. Lady Genestra picked up a light-globe from a side table and stepped into the narrow passage. She pulled her night-cloak tighter around her lean frame to ward off the chilly drafts from the night air that found its way into the passage devoid of thick tapestries for insulation. Slowly at first, she wound her way around small puddles of standing water and dense cobwebs. Other than the occasional drip of water and the sound of her own footfalls, it was eerily quiet and she was glad her husband's study was not far away.

When Lady Genestra arrived at the end of the corridor, she searched the corner for a small lever that would release the latch that held closed the concealed door into the count's study. It only took her a moment to find, and she deactivated the light-globe before slowly opening it the barest crack to see inside.

Dim light filled the study and she could hear voices speaking on the other side of the room where her husband's desk was situated. From her perspective she could not see any of the occupants directly without taking a risk to open the door further. She could, however, recognize their voices. The biggest surprise was that her husband had apparently recovered enough to sit at his desk. From the description of his injuries and the almost daily progress reports, she expected him to be confined to his bed for several more weeks after his return.

"Jarl, take your men to the eastern border with Yorwick, steal livestock, and burn a few more farmsteads." It was her husband addressing Ouza's under-captains. He sounded cold and angry and she was chilled to the bone by what he was saying. Why would he order the deaths of innocent farmers? It made no sense.

"Medes," he continued. "There are still many more on this list who need to die or disappear. See to it." Could her husband be referencing the list of names she found in his locked desk drawer?

"And Theod, you must keep the production of armaments on schedule." The sound of a palm or fist impacting the count's desk echoed through the chamber. "You have all grown lax and lazy while I have been gone. We should have completed all of these tasks by now. I will brook no more failures on your part. Dismissed."

A jumble of heavy footfalls hastily exiting the chamber followed and then momentary silence. Lady Genestra sensed that someone was still in the room with her husband and tried to remain still.

"My lord," Commander Ouza was there. "My captains feared that you were dead or would not recover. And although I control them all, there is still a piece within each of them that cries out at the idea of murdering their own people."

Lady Genestra gasped. Could everything she suspected in her previous visit to her husband's study be true? Had Commander Ouza lied about the lists originating with captured assassins?

"I did not expect the ambush myself." The count laughed. "The Arid Fellowship is a remarkable organization and the timing could not have been better. Had I arrived in Lyon's Gate as planned everything I have worked for would have been for nothing. After we conquer the Western kingdoms, remind me to meet with their guild master. I would like to control these assassins to better serve my agenda."

"There is something else, my lord."

"What is it?"

"Lady Genestra was in your study recently and found the lists that I wrote for you in the locked drawer. I'm not sure how she managed to open it." Commander Ouza's voice was almost a hiss.

Lady Genestra was so startled by the admission that her foot slipped on the wet floor. She caught herself quickly, but the noise had not gone unnoticed.

"Someone is here." She heard her husband say. Then, booted steps were making their way toward where she hid. Hastily, she pulled at the concealed doorway. The last thing she heard before the door silently closed was her husband's voice, "Ouza, wait . . ." Genestra re-activated the light-globe she held, hiked-up her skirts and ran for her life back toward her own bedchamber. If she hurried maybe they would think it was just a rat.

Back in her own rooms, Genestra fell upon her bed sobbing. It was true. Everything she guessed at before was true. What had become of her husband? Why had he changed into the evil, murderous creature that placed his own greed above all else? She kicked off her slippers and curled up in her bed. She would have to leave with Pen, seek refuge with her family in Oswalt or the Queen in Lyon's Gate. They had to know the truth of what was happening in Cambria. For a long time she wept and planned her escape. She resolved to escape with her child at the first opportunity. Until then, she must be strong enough to play the part and show no outward signs of her distress.

If she was strong enough.

Their lives depended on it.

CHAPTER 15

A Quiet Murder

"It was nothing, my lord." Ouza strode from the shadows of the south end of the count's study.

"No, Ouza, it was something." Once the slight noise drew his attention, he sensed it was her. "Lady Genestra is no longer there."

"The countess? Where was she hiding?" Ouza looked around the room, clearly confused.

"There is a passage to our bedchamber behind the wall," Djago gestured vaguely toward the east wall, "But she has gone."

"Should I fetch her, my lord?"

Djago slowly shook his head. "No. Whatever she heard will be useless to her. no one would believe wild accusations from a hysterical woman in the middle of the night. You and I still have much to discuss. We will deal with the countess later."

"Very well, my lord."

"In the meantime, you can fetch Naamah. I would rather not have to repeat myself to her later."

Djago watched Ouza leave and then sat back in his chair and smiled. His final plan to motivate the people of Cambria to scream for war with Yorwick would happen that night. It was a little sooner than he expected, but he couldn't take any chances, especially if his wife knew more than she should. He didn't need any more obstacles getting in the way; they seemed far too common these days.

When Ouza returned with Naamah, Djago spoke to them in detail for several hours about his strategy to take Yorwick before finally concluding the meeting. "The fortuitous conflict with

Teamhrach will keep the king's forces in the south, leaving Yorwick to stand on their own. With our military superiority, we should be able to overrun them quickly. Especially so with the help of our allies."

Both Ouza and Naamah nodded their agreement.

Djago took a swig of chilled ale from a nearby cup. His throat was still sore from the assassins attack a few weeks earlier. They had done their job well, almost actually killing him in the process. "It is nearly dawn. Ouza, can you find a body? A man who doesn't stink of ale?"

"I can, my lord." He had a perplexed look on his face. "What would you like me to do with it?"

Djago smiled for a second time that night, this time much broader and handed Ouza a small rolled parchment sealed with wax. "Place this in the man's pocket and wait for me on the east side of the tower. I am going to say goodbye to my wife." He glanced out the window and noted that it was still at least an hour before dawn; there would still be plenty of time.

Waving Ouza and Naamah leave to depart, he stood from his chair and made his way through the concealed door and down the dark corridor. He did not need light to see where he was going. Demons enjoyed the benefit of night-vision as clear as if it were daylight.

When he arrived in the sitting room outside the bedchamber, only the fire from the hearth illuminated his surroundings, casting flickering shadows on the tapestries hanging from the walls. The figures depicted in the weave seemed to come alive with imaginary movements in the firelight. It was a haunting, almost sinister illusion that he liked best about this room.

Further in, his sensitive ears noticed the slow, rhythmic cadence of his wife's breathing. She was sound asleep. Silently, Djago undressed to his small clothes and slipped into the bed with her. She was also in her nightclothes and warm to the touch. Briefly, she stirred and then settled into her dreams once more.

Djago lay next to her for a while, staring up at the painted images on the ceiling. It was a scene of various domestic and wild animals dressed smartly in colorful tunics, breeches, and hats. Many of the creatures played a different instrument and circled those without them who danced in the green grass of a forest glen. There was no purpose to any of it, just an absurd waste of expensive pigments. Perhaps he would have it painted over with scenes of battle and conquest that would be more inspirational. At least for him.

After a while, he sensed that Ouza had arrived where he was instructed. It was time. Djago had lain there long enough.

In one quick move, he rolled on top of his wife and covered her mouth with his hand. Genestra's eyes popped open, terrified, and she struggled to free herself, but he was too heavy and too strong to escape. Djago smiled at her until she calmed and lay still again, starring angrily into his eyes.

"I will remove my hand, but don't scream. Understand?"

She nodded that she did.

Slowly, he removed his hand.

"What are you doing?" She breathed heavily to catch her breath.

"There is about to be an assassination attempt on our lives," he smiled casually.

Genestra tried to lift her head, her eyes darting around the room. "Get off of me!"

Djago pressed his forearm on her chest to keep her from squirming away and reached over to his pillow to retrieve an item he had left under it earlier. "Be still," he commanded, "and show me your right hand.

Obviously confused, Genestra held out her right hand where he could see it. It was shaking violently from fear.

"Good. Now don't panic, I am going to hand you a dagger to protect yourself." He produced a small blade from under the pillow and pressed it into her hand. She gasped at the sight of it and then reluctantly closed her hand over its handle.

"You and I are both aware that I am not the same man you used to know." He spoke calmly but did not move to release her. Her hand lay on the bed over her head holding the dagger. "I'm sure your little evening walk behind the walls convinced you of it."

"What has happened to you?" Her eyes swelled with tears and he could feel the tension in her body relax under him. He almost felt sorry for her.

Almost.

"Your husband is gone, my dear. He is dead and can never return." Tears ran lines down the side of her face while he stroked her hair with his free hand. She squeezed her eyes shut and then opened them again, Djago wasn't sure if she believed him yet. That would soon change.

"Then, what are you that you can masquerade as my husband? A changeling?" Anger was growing in her eyes.

Good, he thought.

"I am no mere changeling. I am much worse. I am a Greater Demon from the Infernal Planes, a Named Demon, Lord of Greed, Possessor of Wills, and your husband is mine." He waited for the emotions he knew would slowly cloud her features – shock, disbelief, fear, acceptance, and anger. She rewarded him with them all.

For a long moment, he stared into the emotional torment behind Genestra's eyes. It was exhilarating to watch her suffer the realization of who her husband had become. He was inspired by her torment and thought to take her right then. He was sure it would be the most satisfying union he had enjoyed in a while, but there was no time. Dawn was soon upon them.

"Now, my dear, it is time to bring our little tragedy to an end. Make use of your dagger, although I fear it will not save you." He offered her a sympathetic smile.

Confusion flittered across her features. "What?"

Djago shifted his body to free his arms and placed his hands around her slender neck. Slowly he began to tighten his grip, taking care to compress in just the right way so not to leave a mark. "Stab me."

She stared at him in disbelief.

"Stab me, bitch."

Her air cut off, eyes bulging and no way to escape, Genestra apparently remembered the dagger he placed in her hand and plunged the small blade into his left shoulder. She stabbed again and again, much swifter than he expected in her desperation and although the dagger was quite small, the repeated blows were doing considerable damage to his arm.

Angrily, Djago ripped the blade from her hand, "That's enough!" he shouted and plunged the dagger into her chest, ending the struggle.

Heaving himself off her convulsing body, Djago felt dizzy. He was losing too much blood. He had to act fast. Stumbling over to the east-facing window, he peered into the dark grounds several stories below. There noted the shadowy form of Ouza, cloaked in a spell of darkness, holding a man-sized body in his arms. Perfect.

He sent a thought to his commander – *Drop it and go*. Ouza did not hesitate. He dropped the body unceremoniously at the base of the tower and then disappeared in the darkness.

As soon as Ouza was out of sight, Djago smashed his fist into the window with such force that parts of the frame dislodged with the shattered glass that sprayed over the body and the stone pavers below.

Losing strength rapidly, Djago sank to his knees and then sat with his back against the wall under the remnants of the window. "Guards!" he bellowed. "Guards!"

Seconds later the sound of boots pounding into the sitting room outside the bedchamber reached Djago's ears, then the double doors exploded open and several guards rushed in, eyes wide with fear at the bloody scene they encountered.

"We have been attacked!" Djago shouted at them. "Send for Naamah now. My wife needs healing!"

Two guards fled from the room at a run. A third approached Djago slowly, trying to look everywhere in the room at once. "Where is the assailant, my lord?"

Djago had found a pillow nearby and was holding it tight against his shoulder and arm to stem the blood. He nodded toward the window. "He escaped through the window."

The guard spun in the direction of two others standing nearby. "Raise the alarm and send for Commander Ouza. Then send a patrol to the tower grounds and search every corner!"

An hour later, Naamah and two other druids had healed the worst of Djago's wounds and bandaged his arm into a sling to limit its mobility while his body did the rest. They told him that even with the healing his arm would be sore and of limited use for the next several weeks. That didn't bother Djago, he expected to have some wounding from Genestra's strikes with the dagger, but he was surprised at her ferocity landing more than just superficial blows.

The corpse of Lady Genestra still lay on the bed where he left it, now covered by a sheet to conserve the lady's dignity, awaiting druids to take her body away and prepare it for burial. Djago played his part, alternately weeping at the loss of his wife and raging at those who conspired to kill them. He hated every minute of it, and for everyone in the room except for Naamah, it was a good show that those fools would spread from one to another across Cambria like ripples in a lake. Before the sun went down on that day everyone would know that Lady Genestra was dead, that her husband mourned her and swore vengeance upon those who caused it and much more. Except for the excessive nature of his wounds, everything was going exactly as Djago expected.

Commander Ouza entered the room followed by several druids. Ouza strode to where Djago sat slumped in a cushioned chair while the druids began to prepare Lady Genestra's body for removal.

"My lord, I have news regarding the assassin," Ouza spoke quietly, but not too quiet so that others in the room could overhear. "He bore a letter signed by Duke Eldorath." Now the rumors would be amended to include that Lady Genestra was killed by an assassin also meant to kill the count and worse, sanctioned by the Duke of Yorwick himself!

Djago dramatically waved the commander silent. "Not while my dear wife still lays here in this state. Wait until she is removed and we will talk further."

Commander Ouza nodded curtly and stood rigid against the wall next to his master, watching the druids wrap the countess's body tightly in heavy fabric. When it was done, the druids gently lifted the small shrouded woman and took her away to be cleaned and prepared for the burial ritual. Naamah sent the healing druids with them and Commander Ouza relieved the remaining guards. Only Naamah and Ouza were left with him in the room.

Djago dropped the pathetic charade and stood straight. "Prepare for war. We will be marching in less than a fortnight."

~~~

Lady Genestra lay wrapped in beautifully woven fabric imported from Ys, bearing the coat of arms of Cambria displaying a red rampaging stag on a field of green lined in gold. She was elevated atop a high platform constructed by the druids that was decorated with hundreds of cut flowers.

More than a thousand Cambria Temple Knights with fluttering gold-fringed cloaks and tall spears formed an honor guard around the perimeter of Cambria's main square. The remaining space was filled with thousands of citizens mourning the loss of their beloved matriarch. Her family watched from a low balcony on the western end of the Keep. Genestra's father, Baron Morcant was there, along with several sisters, brothers, nieces, and nephews, except for her mother who was too sickly and distraught to make the journey from their lands south of Oswalt.

The druids were there as well, at least two dozen of them. They wore their dark earth-toned hooded cloaks decorated with feathers and shells and chanted in a deep baritone that sounded more like a low rumbling hum. Each of them gently swung strange decanters emitting white smoke on the end of leather thongs as they slowly circled the platform that displayed the countess's remains.

Djago watched it all from a landing over the entryway to the Keep from which he would soon be addressing the solemn crowd. Commander Ouza stood on his left dressed in shiny metal armor under a long white cloak and carried a spear with a pennant just like the Temple Knights. Djago was surprised to realize that he had never seen his commander dressed so. Naamah was on his right outfitted similarly to the other druids and carried one of the smoking decanters that Djago found so irritating. His son, Pen, was too young for these spectacles and remained in the nursery.

The crowd stood expectantly anticipating a eulogy to his wife and fair words of farewell. That was the tradition. Djago had words in mind, but they would be a little different than what the citizens of Cambria were accustomed to. He waited for the druids to complete their hymn before he began.

"People of Cambria, nobles and family members of our beloved countess," Djago nodded briefly to Baron Morcant, "these are sad times in our fair land!"

The crowd murmured its collective assent.

"Dark days are before us. We have invasions not only at our doorstep but in our very homes!"

The masses stirred. Djago could feel their growing agitation.

He held his hands out toward the structure holding Lady Genestra, and his voice broke with pain and passion. "This beautiful child of Sunna struck down in our home in the dark of night! Not even I could protect her! If not for the grace of our lovely goddess, I should lay there next to her!"

Sympathy and anger rippled through the crowd. They felt the pain he projected even if he could not truly feel it himself.

"And what of our son, the heir to Cambria? What do I tell him? His mother will never again sing him a lullaby or hold him in her arms or feel her kisses on his face! How can I make him understand the evil that has taken her from us?"

The anger was rising all around him and Djago was feeding off every ounce of it.

"Where do I look to place responsibility for this travesty? Who do we blame?"

Djago knew full well that the rumor mill had worked overtime in his favor. All of Cambria and lands far beyond Cambria knew that a letter from Duke Eldorath was found on the "assassin" who murdered Lady Genestra. Even the contents of the letter had become public knowledge. The letter authorized the assassination of the Count and Countess of Cambria by any means.

A man at the front edge of the crowd stepped forward. A man Ouza had paid well. He raised his voice in answer to Djago's question. "Yorwick!" he shouted.

Another man repeated the call and then another. At least a dozen sprinkled throughout the crowd were paid to do so until the masses picked up the chant. "Yorwick! Yorwick! Yorwick!" It echoed through the wide courtyard like thunder.

Djago raised his fists in the air and shouted to his people, "And where is Yorwick?"

Thousands of fingers pointed and shouted almost in unison. "East!"

He surveyed the crowd with satisfaction. He had them. And then his eyes fell on a trio of Temple Knights wearing the coat of arms of Yorwick on their tabards. He almost missed it as they deliberately held their arms over their chests to hide it. Djago nearly laughed with glee. What a gift! They were emissaries sent by Duke Eldorath with peace overtures. He was expecting their arrival, and the timing couldn't have been better.

"No!" Djago nearly screamed with rage and anger. He pointed to the three emissaries. "There! There is Yorwick!"

The crowd surged toward the Yorwick knights. The concern in their eyes turning to fear and to their credit they did not pull their swords. Rather, they backed toward the Temple Knights of Cambria lining the perimeter. By every right, they should have been protected. By every precedent their brothers in arms, even from another city, should have held away the crowd — not today.

The mob pulled the trio away from the Cambria Temple Knights, not a one of the thousand moved to interfere. Screams of pain and terror rose from the crowd and then abruptly ended as their bodies were torn to pieces. Djago looked on with satisfaction.

When it was over the rabid crowd took up the chant again. "Yorwick! Yorwick!" and paraded the fallen knights' heads around the plaza on tall pikes. Oddly, Djago noted that the druids were gone although he had not seen them leave. *What matter?* He thought. The baron and his family had left as well. Surely they were not expecting a tribute to their daughter morphing into a violent political rally. Djago laughed and raised his fists into the air feeling the triumph of the moment.

He was going to war.

CHAPTER 16

Under the Mountain

"What in the infernal hells is that thing?" Myrllin was peering around a corner down a long, rough-hewn corridor at a strange creature that blocked the far end. From a distance in the low flickering light shed only by torches left mounted on the walls it was hard to ascertain the details clearly, but he was sure it was nothing like he had ever seen before.

A low grumble of anger rippled from the throat of the silver bearded man crouching next to him. "Dat be one of da Stone-Breakers our wizards make ta help mine da ore an' precious metals we bring'n from da tunnels below." It was the Mountain King, Sulyen the Breaker, Lord of the Dvergr Dwarves, Protector of Tirnan Yog that spoke. "Dis be a corrupt'd one."

"This is what you summoned us for?" Wodanaz, Myrllin's brother, stood close watching with them and he sounded wholly unimpressed.

"Don't ya be takin' dese tings lightly, ol' friend." Sulyen thrust a thick thumb behind him where at least a hundred of his best warriors stood silently waiting his command. The yellow light reflected hypnotically off the Dvergr steel armor they wore from head to thigh and the steel-reinforced round wooden shields they carried. "Why de ya tink I brought dem?"

"They are fine looking for sure, Sulyen. But they look more prepared to go mining with those giant hammers rather than a sharp blade for killing."

"Bah," the Mountain King spat. "Dem be war hammers meant ta crush. Ain't no blade gonna squash rock. You'll be see'n soon enough."

Ignoring the banter between his brother and Sulyen, Myrllin muttered a simple spell that granted him the benefit of far-sight. He looked closer at what they faced and nodded. "They appear to have stone for skin and a roughly humanoid shape. Something akin to the earth elementals I have seen the Atlanteans conjure from time to time."

"Dey be stone, tru as we be flesh."

Wodanaz sighed heavily and glanced again at the Dvergr warriors. "Will it take so many of us to overcome it?"

"Not jus dis one, but da ones dat come after."

Myrllin withdrew his gaze from the monstrosity down the corridor and placed it squarely on the Mountain King. "How many are there?"

Sulyen shrugged his massive muscled shoulders. "Dun know. Enough dat dey massacr'd twenty men afore da remainin' miners could 'scape." The powerful Dwarf clenched his fists in anger. "Good men dey wus. All a dem."

Myrllin had known Sulyen since he was a child and although there was no doubt that he was hard as rocks with a fierce temper, he cared deeply for his people and they loved him for it. "You were right to send for us, Sulyen. This certainly qualifies as unusual. Do you have any idea how your Stone-Breakers became corrupted?"

"Dunno dat either, 'cept one a' our most powerful wizards be missin' down der still."

Wodanaz stamped the butt of the spear he called Gungnir on the uneven stone ground between them. "Let's get on with it then."

Myrllin rolled his eyes. His brother was impatient as always, but in truth he'd also be glad to get this done with sooner rather than later.

Sulyen sniffed loudly. "Wut ya gonna do wit dat toothpick?"

Smiling broadly, Wodanaz hefted Gungnir expertly and walked around the corner. "Just you watch."

Myrllin thought that it must appear odd to anyone else to see a middle-aged man in travel robes assume the position to throw a spear. It might also have appeared strange to watch such a man step into his throw and cast said spear with such perfect grace and control to rival those who spent their lives mastering the endeavor. But that's exactly what Wodanaz did.

The Stone-Breaker stood easily one hundred paces along the wide passage. Certainly not too far to reach with a well-thrown spear, except that the ceiling was low and there was not height for the spear to follow a natural arc in its travels. Instead, Wodanaz had thrown the spear straight down the corridor as if shot from a bow with power and speed that seemed impossible. Seconds later there was the deafening impact of shattering rock and a cloud of dust and debris erupted in the place where the Stone-Breaker stood.

Wodanaz turned, Gungnir—unblemished—instantly returned to his hand and smiled at the Mountain King. "*Some* blades shatter rock."

Sulyen's eyes were wide with astonishment at the impressive feat. The only hint of the Stone-Breaker's former existence was a pile of small rocks on the ground where it had stood guarding the entrance to the lower passages. Recovering quickly, the Dwarf unstrapped the massive war hammer fastened upon his back and held it easily in one hand. "Well, let's be about our work den. Dey no be facin' miners now."

Wodanaz laughed and slapped the Mountain King on the back. "To the gates of hell we go!"

Myrllin glanced at his own staff and felt a pang of envy. He was good with blades and fair enough with throwing knives, but hammers and rock-splitting spears were not in his repertoire. For this fight he would rely on his supernatural skills and lead from behind. He followed his brother and Sulyen into the depths of the darkness below trailed closely by the contingent of Dvergr warriors. Whatever was corrupting the Stone-Breakers had to be powerful and dangerous with an agenda that did not include wizards, minstrels, or even Dwarfs. He feared what they were yet to find.

~~~

"Close ranks an' protect yer brother's flank!" Sulyen's booming voice rang clear over the din of battle.

Dozens of Stone-Breakers had appeared from nowhere and now they were everywhere. It was everything the disciplined Dvergr warriors could do to form up with so many of the creatures already among them. They had just entered a wide passage that opened into a larger cavern where mining carts and supplies were strewn in disarray when they were ambushed. Even Myrllin was caught by surprise. He never expected them to emerge directly from the stone walls that surrounded them.

Chaos reigned through a cacophony of grunts, cries of pain and shouted orders made worse by the severe echo through the cavern.

Myrllin slammed a wave of force into the nearest Stone-Breaker, shattering it against the wall. He swiftly angled his way between the Dvergr warriors toward his brother. Wodanaz was hard-pressed to use his spear to any advantage in the close combat and was barely holding his own standing back to back with the Mountain King. The two were cut off from the rest of the Dvergr and surrounded by at least a dozen of the stone creatures.

Horrified, Myrllin watched as one of the stone beasts slammed a stone hand into the side of Wodanaz's head. Somehow, his brother shrugged off the blow and smashed the Stone-Breaker with the butt of his spear, cracking it in two. These creatures held no weapons, they didn't need them. The force of their heavy fists was enough to break bones, crush skulls, and dent even the Dvergr steel armor the Dwarfs wore.

"Hold on, Wodanaz!" Myrllin called to his brother. He was still a few paces away and too far to help with anything other than his magic. Sulyen, fully armored and using his war hammer to good effect, smashed the arm from one Stone-Breaker and the leg of another. Wodanaz struck hard with his spear, holding it like a staff, with less effect, but good enough to keep them off of him. In between, the monsters were landing terrible jolting blows where they found openings. The men wouldn't last much longer.

Myrllin prepared to cast.

Heavy boulders rose from the ground, many once parts and pieces from fallen Stone-Breakers that hovered in the air just over shoulder high. Myrllin partitioned his concentration and focused on the creatures around his brother and the Mountain King. Twelve targets and eleven boulders. With a mental push, Myrllin sent the rocks flying toward them.

Two Stone-Breakers shattered on impact and three others were crippled by the rain of stone. Myrllin cursed – somehow he'd missed the rest of them altogether. At least he bought the men a little time. He spoke the words to cast the spell again and watched as Wodanaz did something unexpected.

Gungnir glowed in his brother's hands and suddenly it separated into two pieces. Holding them apart, they instantly reformed into hammers each the size of Sulyen's one with a short shaft meant to be wielded in one hand. Wodanaz wasted no time putting them to use. He pulverized the closest Stone-Breaker and turned to block the attack of another. The men were not out of danger yet.

Myrllin had the next group of rocks floating in the air when his brother cried out to him, "Duck, brother!" Instinct alone saved his life as he threw himself to the ground dropping the floating rocks all around him.

Not a second later one of Wodanaz's hammers whistled over his head and smashed into the solid mass of the Stone-Breaker that was nearly on top of him, showering Myrllin with debris from the ruined monster. Had his brother *thrown* the hammer? Myrllin was on his feet quickly preparing his cast once more, but his intended targets were no more. Wodanaz and Sulyen stood exhausted in the center of an impressive pile of rubble that were the remains of several Stone-Breakers.

Turning, Myrllin was relieved to discover that the Dvergr warriors had managed to form ranks of several squares with the Stone-Breakers between them and they pummeled the formidable creatures from every angle. War hammers and maces expertly crushed the living stone until they moved no longer.

Moments later, it was finished.

Myrllin strode over to his brother while Sulyen went to see about his men. "Are you OK, brother?"

"They pack a punch, but I don't think they broke anything." Wodanaz rubbed at a dark bruise on his shoulder.

Myrllin studied the hammers that were now held tightly in his brother's belt strap. "Didn't know that spear could become hammers. A new skill of yours?"

Wodanaz chuckled and winced at the same time. "A few years back, I had a child with a Vikja witch. A red-haired boy she named Thunraz, or 'Thunder' in their tongue."

"Another child, Wodanaz?" Myrllin sniffed sharply. "How many does that make for you now?"

"Who knows?" Wodanaz shrugged. "Anyway, she prophesized some nonsense about him and bade me teach him combat with the hammers when he grew older. So, I found a blacksmith who favored hammers as weapons and spent a few years mastering their use. When the time came, I taught the boy, and the witch rewarded me by putting an enchantment on Gungnir that you just witnessed."

"Guess it came in handy," Myrllin smiled. "And is this boy, Thunraz, did he take to the hammers?"

"To my surprise, he is quite gifted with them. Perhaps I should ask his mother about that prophecy after all."

Myrllin laughed. "I thought you had enough of prophecy with my visions. Now you are getting prophecies from your lovers. And let me guess – long blond hair and easy on the eye?"

Wodanaz gave him a dark look.

Myrllin laughed harder. "So predictable!"

"I am not."

Just then the Mountain King joined them and Myrllin settled himself. "How are your men, Sulyen?"

"We lost four an' I'ma sendin' nine a da worst wound'd back to da surface."

Myrllin lay a hand on the Dwarf's shoulder and squeezed gently. "I'm sorry for the loss."

Sulyen nodded, but he had a hard look on his face. "Der be more afore we finish wit dis business I fear."

Myrllin nodded with him. "Then let's find the source of the corruption and end it."

Sulyen roared orders to his warriors to break into smaller groups and sent them further into the dimly-lit cavern to cover all the exits. If there were more of the Stone-Breakers waiting inside, the Mountain King was clearly determined to mount a better defense.

Striding into the cavern along with the Dvergr warriors, Myrllin took in all the details. They were well into the depths of the mines, at least a league by his calculations, and by the looks of it this cavern was a staging area for supplies and materials. Tools, once displayed neatly in racks, were scattered around the floor amid the remnants of huge wooden workbenches and mining carts that were nearly reduced to splinters. Dispersed throughout the rubble like handfuls of dice across a gaming table lay unprocessed gold ore that glinted eerily with the reflection from the light globes they carried. Worse yet were the random stains of blood, now a dry crimson that told the story of what happened in this room only a few days before. Myrllin had heard the tale from the survivors themselves of the horror they suffered. Only a dozen or so miners out of a hundred managed to escape with their lives. The most puzzling thing to Myrllin was why the Stone-Breakers would have removed the bodies. What had they done with them?

"You say that your wizards are the only ones capable of creating the Stone-Breakers, Sulyen?"

The Mountain King kicked at a mining pick on the ground. "Dat's rite."

"Is it just the one wizard missing since this all began?"

Sulyen's face flushed red with anger and pointed at the bloodstains. "No Dvergr would do dis ta his own people!"

Myrllin flashed a quick look at Wodanaz. His brother returned his gaze with an intensity that matched his own. They both suspected and feared what this must be. "Be calm, O'King." Myrllin gestured for the Mountain King to relax. "If any of your wizards are involved, it is likely that they are no longer themselves."

A long sigh that sounded more like an erupting geyser escaped between the old King's teeth. "We be missin' three wizards. But none a dem have da power to do dis."

"It's not their power we are worried about." Myrllin idly noted that all the tools in the cavern were made of Dvergr steel. Outside of Tirnan Yog it was as valuable as gold. Any worldly invader would certainly have taken the steel and left the bodies. "They have the knowledge that fuels the power. I suggest you send for a few of your wizards before we go further. We may need the help."

Sulyen took the heavy battle hammer that rested on his broad shoulder and placed it on the ground in front of him, holding the shaft like a walking staff. "Fraken!" he bellowed without taking his eyes off Myrllin's face.

What appeared to Myrllin as a middle-aged Dwarf with a long black beard just beginning to gray and a shaved head ran over to address his king. "Yes, Sulyen! I be here."

"Take ten men an' return to da Hall. Tell Turgik dat I be needin' him here wit me now. Tell him ta bring fifteen a' his best." Sulyen grabbed Fraken by the lip of his metal chest plate and pulled him close. "An git back quick. Drag da arch-wizard if ye need be."

Fraken slammed his fist to his chest in salute. "It be done, Mountain King." Then he ran off shouting orders to the other Dvergr warriors nearby.

"He be me best captin'." Sulyen watched Fraken as he quickly organized a company of warriors and departed for the surface.

Myrllin was almost amused at the way the Dvergr interacted with each other. "How long will he take to return with your wizards?"

"If not by da mornin' den dey probably be dead."

Myrllin knew that Captain Fraken and his warriors would have to run all night to get to the Hall and back by morning. The constitution of the Dvergr was as legendary as their ability to consume barrels of ale.

"Let your men rest then, Sulyen. Wodanaz and I will keep watch tonight."

Sulyen's face, lined with age and scars, cracked an unamused smile. "None be sleepin' t'nite."

Myrllin set about collecting scraps of wood to set a fire large enough to warm the cold cavern while Wodanaz and Sulyen took a team of warriors to retrieve the supply wagons that had been left behind during the ambush. By the time they returned and cracked a few barrels of ale, Myrllin had a roaring bonfire fortified with an enchantment that would keep it burning all night.

"We can rest. There will be no attack tonight." Myrllin sat next to the fire flanked by Sulyen and Wodanaz. All of them were feeling relaxed after more than a few tankards of ale.

Sulyen lifted an uncertain eyebrow, but it was Wodanaz that spoke. "How can you be so sure, brother?"

"There is no point to it." Myrllin shrugged. "Whatever manner of evil this is, it now knows we are coming to it and it has an idea of our strength."

"Wat do ye tink we be findin', Wizard?"

"Much of the same. I'm sure about that and something more. Something terrible and powerful with an appetite for destruction. And for reasons I cannot explain yet – our blood." Myrllin tossed a small splinter of wood into the magical fire where it burst into obscurity.

Sulyen reached over and pushed Wodanaz on the shoulder nearly knocking him off the barrel he sat upon. "I see ye foun' yerself a pair o'fine hammers. Wat happen'd to yer toothpick?"

Wodanaz laughed. "I didn't want to embarrass you in front of your men. Couldn't have them thinking all your friends too weedy to handle the weight of a good hammer!"

"Ha!" Sulyen nearly spewed his ale. "Der no be a ting a blade can pierce dat a gud hammer can't be smash'n!"

Boisterous laughter erupted from the men nearby and one of the Dvergr warriors raised his mug. "Sing us a tune, minstrel!"

"Well," Wodanaz rose to his feet and produced a golden flute from within the folds of his layered gray robes. "Since none of us will be sleeping tonight anyway I might as well entertain."

Myrllin stood as well and clapped him on the shoulder. "It seems you have a captured audience tonight."

"That I do!" Wodanaz waded into the center of the room and began to play a raucous, fast-paced drinking song the Dvergr knew well. The Dwarves shouted cheerfully in response and eagerly gathered in a wide circle around the bard. Within minutes he had them all dancing and drinking with the enthusiasm of men who could not be certain if they would live to see another dawn.

~~~

Myrllin was dosing when Captain Fraken returned the next morning with the Arch-wizard Turgik.

"'Tis 'bout time ye show'd up." Sulyen greeted them. "Wat be dat on yer face, Turgik?"

Turgik was a stocky Dwarf wearing fine blue robes with a heavy hammer tucked into his belt where the tip of his long gray beard ended. Most notably, he sported a fresh bruise just above his left cheek. The wizard cast a dark look at Captain Fraken. "Yer man here be a bit impatient wit our departure. He be lucky I didn't turn 'em inta a stone an' roll 'em back te ya!"

Sulyen roared with laughter and enveloped the smaller Turgik in a bear hug. "Why me little brother become a wizard I ne'er be knowin', but he come when I be callin' an savin' me hide on many occasions! Ye may be savin' it again soon!"

Turgik looked around the cavern as if seeing it for the first time. "I thot ye be just chasin' a few misguided Stone Crushers, but Fraken be tellin' me a story dat there be more to it."

"Tis more than I be tinkin' also." He cast a thumb toward Myrllin standing next to him and Wodanaz. "Ye remember me friend Myrllin?"

"Who be forgettin' Myrllin." Turgik smiled coldly.

Myrllin allowed a slight nod of his head. Turgik was a long-time critic of Myrllin's prophetic gift despite the friendship they shared with the Mountain King. He considered the Dvergr wizard a thorn in his side. A small thorn perhaps, but a thorn nonetheless.

"An' dis be his famous brother Wodanaz." Sulyen continued.

"Ah, Wodanaz!" Turgik smiled broadly. "Yer reputation do be precedin' ye. I hope ta be hearin' ya play soon!"

Wodanaz performed a dramatic flourishing bow. "If we manage to survive this ordeal, I would be happy to play for you and all the wizards of your order."

Turgik returned his gaze to Sulyen. "Why ye be draggin' yer friends down here wit ye? Me wizards and I can be helpin' ye track down da Stone-Breakers."

Sulyen pat his brother on the shoulder. "There be no doubt ta yer powers, brother. Myrllin here has de vision o' dark times ahead an' he asked ta be informed o' strange findin's so I be invitin' him ta see fer himself."

"Dark times, eh?" Turgik scoffed. "Der be always dark times 'erwhere."

Myrllin simply raised an eyebrow in response.

"Okay, Turgik," Sulyen's nervous laugh was entirely uncharacteristic of the noble Dwarf. "Let's be gatherin' da men an' be off." The two Dwarves walked a short distance away to speak with Captain Fraken.

Wodanaz leaned in toward Myrllin's ear and spoke quietly, "Are you gonna kill him?"

Myrllin was surprised at the question. "Turgik? No, he won't die by my hand and he knows it."

"Doesn't that make him more dangerous?"

Myrllin chuckled, "Only more arrogant."

In short order, Sulyen and Turgik had a Dvergr wizard assigned to each of the small companies of warriors, and they were ready to depart. One such company would scout ahead to ferret out any potential ambush along the way while the others would loosely follow keeping the company ahead in sight at all times. Myrllin appreciated the strategy, but he doubted that they would be tested again until they finally came face to face with their quarry.

For several uneventful hours they followed the narrow passages further and further into the dark depths of the mine. Many smaller rough stone corridors branched off of the main passage, but they did not explore any of them. It was unnecessary. Myrllin could sense the evil below, and he knew they would find it far beneath the surface in a space larger than any mine shaft.

"It be hotter than it should be at dis level," Sulyen commented.

Myrllin just assumed it would get hotter the closer they came to the core of the active volcano that formed the primary terrain feature of Tirnan Yog. Somehow the Dvergr had learned to control the volcanic activity and keep it from erupting. They claimed it was the secret to their mining industry considering that the constant flows of lava deposited vast quantities of precious gems and metals from far below for them to mine.

"Why would that be unusual?" Wodanaz asked.

"Der be no connections 'tween da mine shafts an' da lava tubes," Sulyen explained. "Tis always warmer here but ne'er dis hot. Somethin' be wrong."

"Tell your men to proceed cautiously then," Myrllin warned. "We must be getting close."

As if on cue, a scout from the lead patrol came running out of the dark passage ahead of them.

"King Sulyen!" The Dvergr warrior must have sprinted the whole way. He was flushed and out of breath. "A new passage be broken through da rock ahead."

The Mountain King showed genuine shock. "A passage ye be sayin'? Where do it lead?"

"Da patrol waits at da entrance fer yer orders." The warrior gulped and seemed to fear the words he was about to say. "Cap'n Fraken do believe it be leadin' straight to da core."

~~~

"Where be da patrol?" Sulyen was peering into the near-darkness of the recently excavated passage. Far into the distance, a hazy-red glow pervaded the gloom accompanied by an intense heat that was nearly unbearable where they stood.

223

"It be true den," Turgik's voice wavered with fear. "We must be protectin' da core or da whole a' Tirnan Yog be at risk!"

"Calm yourself!" Myrllin snapped at the arch-wizard. "Whatever is down there wants us to panic. I don't sense fear from it. Only rage and hunger . . . for something.

"Don't be tellin' me ta be calm, Myrllin. Dis ain' yer home in danger a' destruction. Do ya be knowin' how many Dvergr, women an' children, livin' above ye?"

Myrllin was trying to be calm and careful. It would do those Dvergr no good if they rushed in and died valiantly. Uselessly.

The Mountain King grabbed the folds of Turgik's robes and spun his brother around to face him. "Myrllin be right an' dis one, Turgik! Get ahold a' yerself! I be needin' ya, brother."

With what Myrllin believed had to be a monumental effort, Turgik folded his arms and kept his mouth shut. No doubt the arch-wizard would somehow see this moment as some kind of slight to his honor that he would blame him for later. He decided it would be better to extend the olive branch sooner rather than later to avoid future unpleasantries between them.

"Turgik, do you have a spell to protect us from the heat?" Myrllin knew that he must.

"I do."

"Then it will be up to you to keep us all alive while we find the source of this magic."

The fire back in his eyes, Turgik nodded. "Wit dis many I be needin' yer help."

Such an admission from the Dwarf must have taken a huge effort, Myrllin thought with some amusement. "It will only be the four of us, plus a half-dozen warriors and a matching number of your wizards. Sixteen in all. The rest will wait here. Can you handle that?"

"Dat be no problem." Turgik agreed. "But ye all must be stayin' wit-in fifty paces a' me."

Myrllin looked to the Mountain King. "Agreed?"

"Agreed." Sulyen hefted his heavy war hammer with one hand and slammed the butt of the thick handle into the stone floor for emphasis.

Wodanaz pulled Myrllin aside while Sulyen and Turgik selected the Dwarves who would accompany them into the core of the volcano. "If this is what we think it is, most of these men and women will die in there."

"Don't you think I know that?" Myrllin snapped. "*We* may well die in there. I don't need to explain to you again what the world is facing do I?"

"No, brother." Wodanaz eyes held a twinge of sympathy that angered Myrllin even more, but now was not the time for petty bickering.

Sulyen and Turgik rejoined them, a dozen Dvergr close behind. "We be ready."

Wodanaz pulled the hammers from his belt. "Let's get this done. There's a curvy Vikja woman awaiting my attention!"

They all laughed. Laughter that was abruptly cut short by a crash louder than thunder that vibrated through the floor from somewhere down the passageway.

"What in the infernal hells was that?" Wodanaz exclaimed.

Turgik features blanched pale. "No sound like dat should be comin' from da core."

"We be needin' ta get in der a'fore dem crazed Stone-Breakers cause da volcano ta blow. Let's go!" Sulyen waved for the Dvergr to follow and they all trotted at a brisk jog down the passage.

They were several hundred paces deeper when the heat became unbearable and they had to stop a moment for Turgik to cast the environmental spell that would keep them from roasting like ducks. When it was finished, Myrllin felt the heat melt away into a cool stillness that felt refreshing. He was surprisingly, and a little reluctantly, impressed.

"When we be enterin' da core, be sure ta be stayin' wit-in a few paces o' me. Even da Dvergr can only be lastin' a few seconds in da heat outside da barrier." Turgik warned.

From where they stood, they could see the intense orange-red glow of the massive cavern where they would find the semi-fluid flows of super-heated lava at the volcano's core. No longer jogging, they approached the entrance cautiously until they stood at the very brink of the hollow.

Myrllin stared in awe at the scene before him. If he ever imagined what the Infernal Planes looked like, this was it. The dome of the hazy, smoke-filled cavern was well out of sight and along the cavern walls at various elevations above them stood the open black voids of lava tubes that he knew ran for leagues under the mountain and out to sea. He shuddered at the ocean of slow-moving lava that churned in a clockwise rotation, interrupted by thick falls of more lava that emptied into it from smoky shafts below them.

Occasionally, a geyser of lava exploded from the surface of the pool initially startling him, but it was nothing akin to the thunderous sound they heard earlier. Broad ledges, like the one they stood upon, spiraled around the circumference of the cavern and into the darkness above. Myrllin was alarmed to see movement on some of those ledges – Stone-Breakers.

"They be keepin' da lava tubes clear," Turgik explained. "When da pressure be high, we be directin' da lava in-ta dem tubes an out da cavern here. Been keepin' our people safe dis way fer over tree-tousand years. Everythin' be lookin' normal an' dem Stone-Breakers up der don't seem ta be crazed."

"It's no illusion," Myrllin confirmed. "Everything may appear normal, but the evil is in here. I feel it stronger than ever."

Sulyen tapped the butt of his war hammer impatiently. "Wit way we be goin' then? Up 'er down?"

Myrllin paused a moment. It was difficult to ascertain a direction with the pervasive evil filling the room. He would have to rely on his intuition. "We go up."

CHAPTER 17

Phoenix Rising

A wild, feral scream echoed briefly through the vast cavern before it was abruptly cut off by a thunderous bang that shook the broad igneous rock walkway where Myrllin stood with Wodanaz and the company of Dwarves. There were no railings separating the edge of the walkway and the drop into the lake of lava several spans below and they instinctively grasped at the wall to steady themselves.

"What manner of creature makes such an utterance, I wonder." Wodanaz was peering upward through the haze as if the beast might reveal itself at any moment.

"That was no creature." Sulyen's voice was low and his shoulders flexed with barely constrained rage. Myrllin knew by the look of the Mountain King that he was making a titanic effort not to rush ahead in his anger, "It was the last breath of one of my people, a Dvergr."

Myrllin, too, guessed at the source considering there had been no sign of Captain Fraken and his patrol since they'd arrived in the volcano's core an hour earlier. "Keep moving then. If there are others alive then maybe we are not too late to save them."

The walkway continued to spiral upward around the inner perimeter of the cavern. Occasionally they would cross a wide landing where the entrance to lava tubes over twice Myrllin's height would wind away into the dark depths of the mountain. Sulyen had explained the previous night that every century or so the volcano underwent an effusive eruption – the lava in the core would rise and then drain through the dozens of lava tubes spread throughout the chamber. The tubes would guide the lava into the cold sea around the island where it would cool rapidly and safely. Keeping the temperature of the lava low was key to managing the volcano. If the Dvergr allowed it to become too hot, they would risk an explosive eruption that would destroy their home and all who lived there. Myrllin found it fascinating. He also feared that the evil they were stalking knew all of that as well and intended to destroy Tirnan Yog in just such a manner.

Another terrible scream and the collision of stone lent haste to their steps as they followed the winding walkway further into the haze above. Sulyen stamped the butt of his hammer on the ground sending a vibration through the stone that Myrllin could feel a few steps behind. He knew King Sulyen was becoming increasingly frustrated and angry at their slow progress on the hazy incline. It was troubling to Myrllin as well, good people were dying and there was nothing they could do about it.

Quickening their steps, the troupe pressed on.

An hour passed, then another, interrupted by three more abruptly final shrieks. Aside from that, everything seemed absurdly ordinary as they ascended, even the Stone-Breakers they encountered paid them no attention and continued to do the never-ending work of keeping the lava tubes clear of debris and blockages. Magic was present everywhere, yet in his mind's eye, Myrllin found no illusion or deception in what they saw.

"Do ya 'spose dat maybe dis evil ting be down one a dem lava tube's an' not in da cavern?" Sulyen grumbled.

"No." Myrllin was sure. "I can sense it ahead and much stronger than before. It will not be long now." He adjusted his pace to walk next to Turgik and spoke in a low voice, "Whatever we find ahead, you and your wizards must focus on keeping the heat shield in place. Without it, we all die. I suspect our adversary knows that already and will put emphasis on removing it." Myrllin grabbed the arch-wizard's thick arm roughly through his robes. "Despite what you may think of me, I will protect you."

Pulling his arm from Myrllin's grasp, Turgik spoke through snarled lips, "I be trustin' 'till der be cause fer no trustin'."

Myrllin smiled sharply. "Then we have an understanding."

Turgik nodded his agreement.

Another hour passed. Myrllin and Wodanaz had taken the lead with Sulyen and Turgik a step behind, followed by the twelve Dvergr warriors and wizards. Steam rose from the lake of lava below produced by the random trickle of water from melted ice seeping through the dome of igneous rock somewhere high above them. Aside from the violent pops of water instantly turning to vapor and the crack of rock from the industrious Stone-Breakers, the cavern was quiet.

Too quiet.

In Myrllin's mind the silence was a hurricane. He could feel how close they were to the source of evil, like they were right on top of it. Had there been less haze and steam, perhaps he could have seen it. As it was, his vision was obscured beyond a dozen paces.

And then something new began to resolve through the thick gray smog. A vague splash of crimson on the next landing. Still too far to see it clearly, Myrllin stopped.

"What's wrong, brother?" Wodanaz had his hammers in his hands, his eyes darting in every direction as if expecting an imminent attack.

"Be calm." Myrllin pointed to the crimson blemish ahead. "Do you see that?"

Sulyen and Turgik joined them peering through the thick haze.

"It do be a mark on da wall," Sulyen observed. "Maybe da red lava rock."

Turgik snorted. "You be out a da mines too many years Sulyen, an' yer eyes be goin' bad. Dat be no red lava to flow on da wall like dat."

"Let's get closer," Myrllin whispered. "But be on the ready, I believe what we are seeking is there, waiting."

Sulyen motioned to his warriors to be on alert and hefted his heavy war hammer. "We be ready."

Cautiously, the group continued up the slope of the walkway until they were almost on the landing. There they stopped as one, the haze dissipating enough for them to see more clearly. The stark reality of what lay ahead was so impossible to comprehend that it was like they walked into a nightmare.

The crimson stain originated from the base of a narrow ridge a span above them where lay the battered and beaten body of Captain Fraken. He did not move nor appear to be alive. Just as Myrllin thought to take another step, a stone monolith descended from the obscurity of steaming vapor and landed squarely on the small landing obliterating the Dwarf's body in a thunderous crash.

Bits of flesh and a cascade of blood flowed down the side of the wall.

"Fraken!" Sulyen roared and surged ahead.

Shards of rock burst from the wall on Myrllin's left and a huge shape barreled into him violently forcing him toward the edge of the walkway. Screams erupted from behind, the crunch of stone on steel, chaos of movement and the heavy stomp of boots was disorienting. Unable to stop his forward progress, he slipped over the side. For a second, Myrllin's eyes focused on his own two feet and the churning lava far beneath him. Then there was a crack of broken stone, more shards and something grabbed him by his robes, slinging him around and onto the landing once more in a heap.

Myrllin scrambled to his feet just in time to see a Dvergr wizard flail his arms wildly before falling over the side, rammed by a Stone-Breaker. His terrified screams diminished into the distance and instantly ceased seconds later. With barely a thought, Myrllin sent a wave of force into the elemental. It did not scream. It made no sound at all when it went over the side, other than a satisfying splash.

Pandemonium reigned around him. A roar of rage captured Myrllin's attention, and he turned to see the Mountain King on his back. Impossibly, he thrust a heavy Stone-Breaker off himself with his powerful legs and in an even more incredible feat of agility, he arched his back and sprung onto his feet. The momentum carried Sulyen forward, and in one smooth motion he brought his war hammer down upon the Stone-Breaker's chest, shattering it to pieces.

An unexpected wave of intense heat caused Myrllin's skin to burn and sweat to evaporate. A second later, it was cool again. The shield was failing. He spun around, searching for Turgik. The arch-wizard was nowhere to be seen. A cluster of four Dvergr wizards stood together desperately chanting, beyond them three Dvergr warriors were fending off blows from two Stone-Breakers. It wasn't going well for them.

"Myrllin!" It was the voice of Wodanaz. "Look after Turgik. I will take care of those monsters!"

His brother sped past him, sending his hammers ahead, one smashing the arm off one Stone-Breaker and the leg off another. Where was Turgik? There were piles of scattered and broken stone everywhere. Wodanaz and Sulyen must have demolished at least six of the creatures.

Oddly, Sulyen was standing and staring at the blood trailing down the wall. The blood of his captain.

"Sulyen!" Myrllin yelled to him. "Where is Turgik?"

Without taking his eyes from the wall, Sulyen pointed in the direction of a pile of rocks. *What was wrong with the man?* Thought Myrllin. *Had he gone daft from a rough blow from a Stone-Breaker?* There was movement under the rubble. Myrllin rush over and was relieved to find Turgik pulling himself from under the rocks.

"Are you injured?" Myrllin helped the arch-wizard to stand on unsteady feet.

"Me shoulder be shattered an' a broken rib or three. I be doin' fine." He caught sight of Sulyen, still staring silently. "Hey ye dotard! There still be Stone-Breakers ta kill!"

The Mountain King hefted his war hammer and marched purposely toward the bloody wall, ignoring the battle that raged between the Stone-Breakers, Wodanaz, and his Dvergr warriors. More of the elementals had joined the fray and one more warrior had fallen leaving Wodanaz and two warriors to defend the wizards keeping the heat shield in place. If they got through to the wizards, it would be over for them all.

"Sulyen!" Turgik called again urgently. "Wat ya be doin'?"

Sulyen paused long enough to glance back over his shoulder and thrust his war hammer in the direction of the crimson wall. There was unnatural fear was in his eyes. "It be da three-faced man."

Myrllin gazed in the direction that Sulyen indicated and was startled to see a Dvergr Dwarf, his entire body and robes the color of crimson. He stood against the wall where blood from the landing above slowly flowed down and over him in a nightmarish waterfall. Captain Fraken's blood. Most disturbingly, he appeared to have three distinct faces.

Turgik gasped. "It be da three-faced man, a demon from da Dvergr legends. An' he be usin' da blood magic!"

Myrllin was not surprised that they faced a demon. He suspected it from the beginning. But this one was very powerful for a Chaos Demon if that's what it truly was. Sulyen had said three of their wizards were missing. Could this demon be so powerful that it could possess them all and somehow merge them into one? Only a Named Demon could wield that kind of power. Maybe. And what was this blood magic Turgik spoke of?

The three-faced man's eyes popped open, all six of the bloody orbs set their gaze on Myrllin, and three pairs of lips curled into a grim smile. Then it spoke in three distinct voices simultaneously, *"Mer-lin. Gi biab ixomaxip pambt."*

Taken aback, Myrllin glared at the hideous thing. "How do you know me?"

The three-faced man stood perfectly still under the sprinkling of blood that continued to fall from the ledge as if to soak in every drop. "You and your brother slaughtered the witch Aja and captured the Chaos Demon within. Then you threw it into the Ourea and destroyed it forever. How clever and cruel. Even your father spared us an eternal end."

Myrllin's mind was spinning. How could it know all of this? "My father imprisoned the demons in the pithos because there was no other way to protect this world from you. He would have happily destroyed you all if he knew the way."

The three-faced man produced an eerie, mocking laugh.

Myrllin scowled in return. "We know the way now."

The laughter cut short. "You know nothing, mortal."

"I know that body is still a prison and soon I will know your True Name or destroy you as I did the others!"

"I have no name!"

It was Myrllin's turn for mocking laughter. "You will beg me to send you to the Infernal Planes when I am done with you."

Not a muscle moved on the three-faced man. He stood like a statue with only his mouth and eyes animated and alive. Yet his orbs were black and bottomless and cast a thrill of fear down Myrllin's spine if he allowed himself to gaze into them for too long.

"These little, ugly people will suffer and die horribly before you break me. I am the Lord of the Stone-Breakers! From this day forward, all Dvergr will live under the shadow of fear that will terrorize their men and women in a swaddle of death that will take their children. There will be no light! Only darkness! There will be night eternal! Every second of every day the Dvergr will pray for an end, and my laughter will echo through their proud halls. . ."

A roar of rage startled Myrllin from his focus on the demon. Sulyen was charging the three-faced man.

"Sulyen, No!" Myrllin cried, but it was too late.

The Mountain King's heavy war hammer crashed on the demon's head and the legendary unbreakable Dvergr steel shattered into a million pieces. A gong like a bell resounded from the impact sending vibrations so intense through the room that it knocked everyone off their feet and shattered the remaining Stone-Breakers. Cracks ran through the landing from where the three-faced man stood and he began to laugh.

"Sulyen!" Myrllin called to him. "Get off the landing!"

Still staring at the broken shaft in his hands, the Mountain King recovered from his shock enough to stumble off the landing. It was just in time. A few cracks splintered into many and soon the landing was falling away, piece by piece, into the slowly circulating lava below. The laughter from the three-faced man continued, even as he slid helplessly off the remaining edge of the landing to slip beneath the bubbling super-heated molten rock. *Why didn't it try to save itself?* Myrllin would have stood dumbfounded had he not been so busy trying to keep himself from falling over the edge.

The vibrations ceased with the passage of the demon and no more Stone-Breakers appeared to harass them. Relieved, Myrllin found his footing quickly and rushed to help Turgik and Sulyen. Soon, Wodanaz and the surviving Dvergr joined them.

"What in the unholy hells was that all about?" Wodanaz was covered in bruises and welts under a glistening sheen of sweat.

"We found the demon," Myrllin rumbled.

Sulyen was standing proudly with the shaft of his once unbreakable war hammer. "I killed it wit me hammer!" he smiled triumphantly.

Wodanaz shot Myrllin a skeptical look.

Myrllin shook his head. "I don't think this is over. He *wanted* us to destroy him."

"But I smashed me hammer on it!" Sulyen insisted.

"No, Sulyen. He was somehow trapped in his host's body. It probably happened when he tried to merge the three missing Dvergr wizards together creating what you saw as the three-faced man from your legends. He could create and control the Stone-Breakers with their magic still, but that was about it."

"It be da blood magic dat gave him da power," Turgik agreed gravely.

Wodanaz was pacing and juggling his hammers. "So what now?"

Myrllin shrugged. "If we are lucky . . ."

A deafening boom resounded through the cavern knocking them to the ground again. It was immediately followed by a rush of super-heated air and intense light. Turning to look at what lit the cavern, Myrllin was astounded to see a great bird of fire, ten times the size of a giant roc, hovering in midair before them. Fear filled him and he was sure they were about to die.

"*Micma, aziazor cnila, teloch, telocvovim, iadoiasmomar a iadoiasmomar!*" the creature seethed. "Fools! My home is the Infernal Planes, land of fire and flames. Some mortals call it hell, the Lake of Fire, Sheol, or Naraka. Do you think these paltry flames would be the death of me? Now I bring hell to your earth for all eternity. Death and suffering will follow, for I am the Phoenix rising from flame and ash, born again to rule all the lands. The world will tremble and kneel before me. All will know my image and fear my wrath!"

Wodanaz lifted his hammer to throw it, but Myrllin stayed his hand. "Wait, brother," he whispered.

The Phoenix cast its fiery gaze over them. "Your power is pathetic. I leave you to bear witness to what you have done."

With one beat of its blazing wings, it shot upward through the smoke-filled cavern, effortlessly bursting through the thick dome of igneous rock and out into the cold air of the open sky.

"Run!" Turgik yelled to them.

Myrllin didn't need to be told twice. The thick ice that covered the outside of the dome was falling inside the core and where it fell on magma it exploded, sending forceful jets of toxic scalding steam roaring into the air. If they didn't escape from the cavern quickly, they would be boiled alive or asphyxiated, despite the shield that Turgik held around them.

There was no time to go back the way they came. Instead, Myrllin led them into the first lava tube they came to. "You say these lava tubes lead to the Primal Sea?" He yelled loudly at Turgik to be heard above the pandemonium of explosions and hissing steam.

Turgik coughed violently from the fumes before he could reply. The toxic vapor was already filling the lower half of the cavern. "If da Stone-Breakers been doin' der job and clearin' da tunnels den ya. But it-a long way down!"

Myrllin grabbed a layer of Wodanaz's cloak and tore a large portion of fabric from it.

"What the hell?" Wodanaz protested.

"You need a new cloak anyway," Myrllin snapped. Then he lay the fabric on the ground and began to chant over it.

There were audible sounds of surprise from the Dvergr as the fabric thickened and grew. It grew until it was a large enough carpet for all of them to sit upon. Myrllin was the first to take his place and gestured for the rest to join them. "Sit down, quickly! Unless you want to call this cavern your tomb. Close together. I said close! Now hold on for your life."

Sulyen and Wodanaz tried to ask questions, but Myrllin brushed them off and focused on the task at hand. He spoke another word and the carpet abruptly lifted a dozen hands off the ground. Cries of shock and surprise assaulted his ears for a moment and then eleven butts spontaneously shifted in closer to the center until they were packed tight like fish in a barrel.

"*Now* we're ready to go!" Myrllin laughed. "If this ride ends abruptly, I apologize and hope you all had a good life."

No one said a word, except for Myrllin, whose utterance sent the carpet speeding through the dark tunnel. Several of his passengers released high-pitched screams at their rapid descent, and he couldn't be sure, but he thought one of them just might have been Wodanaz. The thought of it conjured delight at the many decades of teasing it would cost his dear brother. With another quick word, Myrllin conjured forward projecting light to illuminate the way. He had learned to control flying carpets years ago went he spent some time among the sky people of the Glass Sea. It was one of the most exhilarating experiences of his life. Now, his life and those with him, depended on how well he remembered his lessons.

Wodanaz raised his voice above the noise of motion and began to sing. It was a bawdy drinking song in the Dvergr native language. Myrllin briefly wondered if the Dvergr had any other kind of song. To his surprise, the tune was soon nervously taken up by the others, and Myrllin found himself on a surreal ride at break-neck speed through a dark twisting tunnel with no certain end and a bunch of crooning Dwarves. He supposed that if these were his last moments, at least there had to be a good story in it and he joined them in the next refrain.

For an hour they sped through the lava tube, the molten heat not far behind. Fortunately, there were no sharp turns and the drops were mostly gradual. It was a tunnel designed for keeping the lava flowing and not pooling to cool until it reached the sea. The air on their faces became colder the further they traveled from the core until it became nearly frigid, while the heat on their backs never diminished. Myrllin hoped that they had to be close to the water.

"How close do you think we are to the end?" Myrllin shouted to Turgik.

"I tink we be close now."

"And does the tube exit over the water or under it?"

"Might be under it, over it or half in it. Dependin' on da tube."

Myrllin slowed the carpet as much as he dared. Running into the surface of the water at high speed would kill them as surely as the magma shooting behind them. It would be tragic to get themselves killed nearly out of this fickle mountain.

They flew on for a while longer, mostly in exhausted silence, and soon enough there was light ahead. Daylight, to Myrllin's eternal relief. By the time they reached the lava tube's exit, the sun had fallen nearly to the horizon and the stars were visible in the crisp, cold night. It was summer in Tirnan Yog, but they were so far north it hardly mattered – unless it was winter, then half the sea would be frozen over. Regardless, it was still frigidly cold, and Myrllin found himself wrapping his cloak a little tighter around his thin frame. Wodanaz gave him a dark look, considering they were sitting on half of his cloak, which amused Myrllin more than a little.

"Look yonder, Sulyen." Turgik was pointing toward the southern edge of the island.

"By the gods." Sulyen's face was a study of remorse, guilt, anger, fear and a dozen other emotions flashing across his hard features. "Dat damn'd firebird has burn'd down da port!"

They were too far away to see details, but the orange glow south of the city could mean nothing else. The port of Tirnan Yog was mainly operated by a colony of Vikja who lived in houses made of hide and timber which was vulnerable to flame. Myrllin could only imagine the extent of the casualties after such an attack.

They all jumped with shock when an explosion of steam and heat erupted from the lava tube they had vacated just moments before as the lava flowed into the cold water. Myrllin hissed a curse, they had been so distracted by the devastation on the island, it nearly made his heart stop.

He turned the carpet toward the port and sped up. They were too late to help defend the city, but they might be just in time to save a few lives. Myrllin glanced over at Wodanaz and projected a thought. *Brother, follow this abomination. I will join you later. There is a hierarchy that I must protect.*

Wodanaz did not appear surprised, Myrllin knew his brother was aware he had a higher calling. *Go with my blessing, brother. I will thwart our adversary until you rejoin me for its defeat.*

Do not attempt to confront this evil thing on your own. Myrllin warned.

Have no worries, brother. At least the severe look on Wodanaz's face was a mild comfort to Myrllin, the last thing he needed was for his brother to become impatient and try and live up to his own legend.

Almost as an afterthought, Myrllin transferred control of the carpet to Wodanaz and then transported his physical body to the shore. From there he waved to the startled passengers he left behind and called for the Dragon he knew as Drago to take him south.

CHAPTER 18

Surrounded by Enemies

Stoddenferry Castle stood as a dark beacon against the clear blue sky. It was a modest keep elevated on the high cliffs overlooking Lake Virtue, surrounded by high stone walls featuring impressive tower platforms where huge catapults and ballistae could stand to defend when needed. That need had not come for several generations now to their fortune.

"We are almost home." Perault rode beside Melisende at the head of their small entourage. The Brighams and his family rode behind chatting idly while the baggage carts and servants brought up the rear.

"I have always imagined Stoddenferry as my home." She flashed him a quick smile. "It is so quaint and quiet compared to Tintagel."

It was true, Stoddenferry Castle did not encompass a massive city like Tintagel or Lyon's Gate. There was the equivalent of a small village inside the walls where a few tradesmen and merchants plied their trade, enough to support the residents of the keep and garrison of soldiers whose patrols protected the nearby villages.

"My father has set aside lands for me south of here. After we are married, we can live in the castle or closer to your family in Tintagel. I will not argue with whatever you decide."

Melisende cocked her head to the side in thought. Perault always found the unusual characteristic adorable. "Perhaps we can do both?"

Perault laughed. It was the perfect answer. "Excellent idea!"

When they approached the gates of the outer curtain wall, Perault's father took the lead cheerfully hailing the guards and anyone else they passed on their way up the steep incline to the keep.

"Welcome back, my lord." One of the guards greeted the Earl of Stoddenferry when he dismounted.

The earl clapped the guard on the shoulder. "Did the pigeons bring any news in the days we have been on the road from Lyon's Gate?"

The guard furrowed his brows, seemingly calculating the time it took to ride from the capital and what news they might have missed. "Did you hear about the attacks on the border villages in Cambria?"

"No," the earl responded. "The border with Eriu?"

The guard shook his head. "Nay, my lord, Cambria. Several small villages were burned in the night and witnesses swear the men responsible wore raiment marked with the emblem and colors of Yorwick. Tensions are running high in the north, my lord."

"That is distressing," the earl agreed. "Anything else?"

"You probably heard about the unusual murder in Lyon's Gate the morning after the last day of the Tourney?"

"No, we must have departed before the news got out. What happened?"

The guard shrugged. "Some wealthy banker was savagely dismembered in his home by something unspeakable. The authorities are still unsure if he was attacked by man or beast. The king issued a general warning to the population of Lyon's Gate to lock their doors and report anything unusual, but so far there have been no more assaults."

Perault felt a bolt of lightning run along his spine. Could the "beast" have been the same creature he spied in the stables? Prince Zracul was adamant about handling the matter himself, but Perault wondered if he should have alerted the authorities anyway. Would the banker still be alive if he had?

His father thanked the guard and called for servants to show the Brighams to their rooms where they could freshen and rest before the evening meal.

Melisende planted a quick peck on Perault's cheek. "I hear our parents will begin negotiations tonight. Should we have any worries?"

The absurd image of their fathers drinking and making jokes at their expense flashed through his mind. "Hardly."

"Good. See you tonight." Her scent lingered after her departure, Perault thought it might be White Ginger from the Far East. He inhaled the fragrance deeply trying to memorize its unique nature, but sadly it was soon forgotten.

Perault had been thinking a lot about Melisende, their impending marriage, and his journey to earn the gold-fringed cloak since they left Lyon's Gate. He would have to speak to her about it before she returned home with her family. After so many days he still wasn't sure what he was going to say.

Dinner that evening was filled with lively conversation. Perault recounted his most challenging bouts during the Tourneys, which were of course diminished by the trials of his brother Sir Reginald and then rebuffed by a tale or two from their father. They all knew their stories were ostensibly elaborative, but that just made them the more hilarious. When dinner was over both Perault's and Melisende's parents excused themselves to the parlor, while Reginald, Elian, and Yorlik went off to a game of stones leaving the young lovers conveniently alone.

"Walk with me?" Perault extended his hand.

"Of course, my knight."

Perault steered her through the keep to a tower that led far up to a landing overlooking Lake Virtue. In the daylight, especially at sunset, the view was breath-taking. In the dark hours of the night the beauty of the water was replaced by the reflection of the moon.

This was the landing where he had witnessed Drystan and Eselt engaged in an unholy embrace. Perault shuddered at the thought of it. He wondered briefly how it all must have ended for them.

"It is beautiful here." Melisende pulled herself into the folds of his cloak to share his warmth against the cold night breeze.

"You know I love you," he opened hesitantly, "and that it is my every desire to spend my life with you." Melisende pulled his arms around her. "But there are things that I must do before I can offer you a life worthy of your acceptance."

With these last words, he could feel her almost shrink against him and the measure of disappointment on her face when she twisted to look at him was heartbreaking.

There was nothing for him to do but continue, "If I don't have complete resolution without distraction to achieve the right of title for the gold-fringed cloak, how can I possibly have the integrity to ask you to commit yourself to me for life?"

He awaited a reply, but the minutes stretched on in silence and Perault worried that perhaps he had calculated her reaction very badly. "Please Melisende, say something. Can't you see that I want nothing more than to be with you forever, but I must be whole first to offer myself to you completely?"

He waited for what seemed another eternity before she quietly responded, her eyes swollen with tears. "I thought you were going to whisper sweet words to me tonight about our future together." She sobbed a moment against his chest. "I'm sorry, I know this is important to you and I am being selfish." She looked at him with a weak smile. "Go earn your gold-fringed cloak, Sir Perault, but remember that someone who loves you is waiting for your return."

She was hurt, he knew that, but this was the best way for both of them. Perault hoped that she would forgive him in the long run and he made a silent promise that he would do everything in his power to accomplish an Act of Heroism and return to her in triumph, with honor, sooner rather than late. With nothing left to say, they sat together long into the night without words and held each other tightly in the hope that somehow the night would never end.

In the days that followed, Perault bid farewell to Melisende and her family. It was time for them to return home to Tintagel and although there was not a promise of a wedding date, both families anticipated that it would not be long in coming. Perault echoed the confidence of that prediction before Melisende departed earning him tender kisses and hopeful affections.

Spring rains darkened the skies foretelling sad news nearly on the heels of the Brighams departure. It was news from Tintagel reporting that Duchess Eselt had been caught in an affair with the aging duke's adopted son . . . Drystan.

Perault was stunned.

He was aware of the dalliance while they stayed at Stoddenferry Castle the previous summer, but he had seen no sign of Drystan at the Tourneys in Tintagel. Thinking back on it, the few times Perault had seen the duchess, he thought she had a haunted look about her. Perhaps it was shame.

Further reports described a trial that left no doubt as to their guilt and in an unexpected move, the duke condemned them both to death. It was shocking news. More shocking than the crime itself. What else was going on that the duke would execute his wife and adopted son?

A day later another pigeon arrived with news that Perault found hard to swallow. The duke decided to have pity on Eselt and suspend her death. Instead, she was banished from Lyonesse forever and sent to live among the Leprechauns. Perault couldn't fathom how that would be a less worse fate than death, but he supposed it might assuage any retribution by her father, the High-King of Eriu. The stunning twist of the story was that Drystan had managed to evade his guards and escape Valiant Keep by diving from its walls into the rock-strewn, frigid waters of Lake Virtue.

No body had been recovered.

It was a sad story and not one Perault was entirely surprised about considering how the lovers carried on with little regard for anyone who might have seen them. He remembered when the duke and duchess were married. Drystan was a drunken mess during the entire celebration and Perault did not help the situation by mocking his better. It offended every sensible fiber in his being to know he had witnessed behavior unbefitting a Temple Knight and Perault's unfiltered moral judgment landed forcefully upon Drystan that night. Fortunately, things did not escalate further after Drystan had the good sense to pass out. Perault assumed, with Eselt married to the duke, that would be the end of it. Apparently, he could not have been more wrong.

Barely a week later Perault was summoned to his father's study. The room was located high in the northeast tower with tall windows that brightened the room and afforded a spectacular view of Lake Virtue. His brother Reginald was already there, and by the looks on their faces, they had not summoned him for pleasantries.

"What is it, Father?" Perault stood until his father waved him to a nearby chair.

"Your brother has brought distressing news from the pigeon rook. As a Temple Knight of the silver-fringed cloak, you are no longer a boy and should share in discussions that affect the security of our family, home, and kingdom."

Perault did not know what to say. His father had never spoken to him as an equal."

"We have news from both Eriu and Cambria," Reginald tossed the small notes he carried onto his father's desk. "One is no better than the other."

The earl flicked the notes with his forefinger. "It turns out the High-King of Eriu takes umbrage at the idea of his youngest daughter spending the rest of her life as a slave to the vile Leprechauns. He has decided to mobilize for war. Already his troops are massing in Teamhrach."

Reginald unrolled a map showing the lands around Stoddenferry Castle for some distance. On it was the capital city of Eriu, Teamhrach and Lyon's Gate almost due east on the shores of Lough Greely. "If they march south to siege Tintagel, they will have to come through us first."

"So, we too must call our knights and men-at-arms and prepare to defend the road south." His father was always so matter-of-fact.

Perault knew that the purpose of Stoddenferry Castle from the earliest times was to act as the first line of defense for threats approaching Tintagel from the north and west. Not since the days of the Oak War and the Teuric War had there been a need for its protection; however, over the ages, House Eckert had always been committed to Stoddenferry's upkeep and readiness despite the lack of discord with their northern neighbors.

"And what of Cambria?" Perault almost didn't want to ask.

"King Praeter invited his brother, Duke Banfield Eldorath and Count Terril Djago to Lyon's Gate after the Tourneys. They were to meet and discuss the recent violence on their respective border. Count Djago's retinue was ambushed in route to that meeting. He and a few of his men barely survived and escaped to reported that the attackers wore Yorwick uniforms." Reginald shook his head in disgust.

"Just like the reports from the border," his father added.

Reginald continued. "After that, the count refused to resume the journey to Lyon's Gate and returned to Cambria to recover from his injuries. Worse yet, his generals have called the militia to join his standing forces near the border with Yorwick as if they were expecting invasion."

"Or planning to invade." The words his father spoke sent a thrill of electricity up Perault's spine. Could there be another internal war in Lyonesse?

"So, what do we do?"

"Cambria is the king's problem for now," Reginald replied. "Our most immediate concern is Teamhrach. If the Eriu High-King marches south, he will intend to bottle us in with a siege while the bulk of his forces skirt around to Tintagel. We will send our cavalry to Duke Maruk and the infantry, bowmen, and rangers into the forest to harass the army from Eriu every step of the way south."

"Who will be left to defend the castle? There will be many hundreds of innocents sheltered within our walls from the surrounding farms and villages."

Perault's father barked a laugh. "The Temple Knights. The High-King will not dare attack our home if it is under the protection of the Temple Knights. He would risk a war with all of them!"

"That is true, Father," Reginald agreed, "but High-King Cadeyrn's quarrel is with Duke Maruk in Tintagel. He will not attack us unless attacked by us. Once the High-King and Duke Maruk have resolved their disagreement, both Eriu and Lyonesse will want relations to normalize and trade to resume."

Perault knew pride. He was no stranger to its ability to dull good sense. "Men will still die."

Reginald nodded sadly. "Many men, perhaps thousands. Duke Maruk's pride and honor is hurt, and High-King Cadeyrn has a broken heart for his youngest daughter. The hope is that the army of Eriu will camp outside of Tintagel for a few weeks or months to prove a point and then march home after some accord is reached."

"Or something may happen with two opposing armies in such close proximity – a random decision or errant circumstance that could spark a war that would tear Eriu and Lyonesse apart." Leave it to his father to point out the snares.

"Let us pray Sunna will not allow it come to that." Perault had known only peace his entire life. Tourneys and war-making were only games and abstract notions. This was beginning to feel like anything but a game.

~~~

"You speak for Father more than you used to, has something changed?" Perault walked alone with his older brother Reginald through the dimly-lit corridors under the castle walls. They were surveying the soundness of the foundations, looking for cracks and water, so far they had found none.

"There is something, Perault. I should have spoken of it sooner." Reginald stopped to face him. Perault was second in line to inherit his father's title and he had always been fine with that. He enjoyed the freedom of living where he wished with only himself to be accountable to, rather than the life of an earl always subject to opinion, politics, and critics of his decisions. Maybe it wasn't that bad, but his father rarely left Stoddenferry Castle for more than a few days and always worried about what wasn't getting done while he was away. To Perault it was akin to the life of a slave.

"What is it, Reginald? Is Father ill?"

Reginald looked at his feet. "I'm afraid he is. The druids say he has the Forgetting Disease."

Perault knew this disease. It was not uncommon in older people. It was a slow, degenerative disease that affected their mind slowly over months and years until they could no longer recognize their loved ones or remember things from the past. Eventually, they would waste away unable to care for themselves and often died from asphyxiation when they could no longer remember how to swallow.

"Does Mother know?"

"She was the one who recognized the early symptoms."

"How long have you known?"

"A few months. Father did not want you to know until after you earned the silver-fringed cloak."

Perault paced back and forth, relieving his nervous energy. He wanted to fight something, bang on the shield of an adversary, but there was no fighting the Forgetting Disease. He was helpless against this foe. "What do we do now?"

"There is nothing to do. While we were in Lyon's Gate for the Tourney, the king signed documents transferring title and property to me. I am now the Earl of Stoddenferry."

Heat rose quickly inside Perault, and he lashed out at his brother. "How could you take that away from him? He is not dead yet. Where is the honor in what you have done? Father will be humiliated!"

Reginald grabbed Perault's shoulders in a firm grip and pulled him to his chest. His brother was always taller by at least a head and stronger, often making him feel inferior. He fought to break his brother's embrace until Reginald whispered, "It was Father who wanted it this way, not I."

Perault felt the strength run from his limbs and wiped the tears from his eyes. "I'm sorry, Reginald. I should not have doubted you."

Reginald released him. "No one will know until Father is no longer sound of mind. When that sad day comes there will be a quiet announcement and I will be formally recognized as the Earl of Stoddenferry. The king has agreed to this."

"It is the right thing to do," Perault conceded. "You have my support, brother."

There was the loud bang of an iron gate and steps rapidly moving in their direction from somewhere around a turn in the corridor.

"Assassins?" Perault whispered.

The two brothers silently separated by a few paces and slowly drew their swords.

"Do not hesitate to kill, little brother, this is no game of wooden sticks and blunt swords."

Perault snorted. "You know I have killed before."

Reginald raised an eyebrow but said nothing. The footfalls were close and would soon reveal their owners. Perault held his long sword tightly anticipating the first blows.

Three men charged around the corner and skidded to an abrupt halt, nearly falling over each other. They were dressed in the colors and emblems of Stoddenferry guards all of whom Perault recognized and knew to be good men. Perault and Reginald returned their blades to their scabbards.

"What is the urgency?" Reginald demanded.

Clearly, a little flustered at coming upon the brothers ready to take their heads, the guard stammered, "Y-your father, the earl! He sent us to deliver a message. He said we must hurry."

"Let's see this message then."

The guard handed Reginald a sealed scroll. Perault watched his brother break the seal and unfurl the parchment. Then his eyes went wide. "Tell our Father we are on our way."

Pressing fist to chest in salute the guards scurried back the way they had come.

When they were gone, Reginald, looking decidedly shaken by the contents of the scroll turned to Perault. "Lady Genestra, Countess of Cambria, has been murdered."

"Murdered?" Perault heard himself say. It was surreal. The implications were staggering. "By whom?"

"It says the assassin was killed by Count Djago himself and that he was injured as well, although not seriously. It also says that there is evidence the assassination was ordered by the Duke of Yorwick himself." Reginald handed him the parchment.

"Will there be war?"

"Undoubtedly."

Perault tapped his fingers on the pommel of his sword. "So, spring will end on the wretched news that Lyonesse will be at war internally and with Eriu. This is not how I anticipated spending the warm months of summer."

"Not all of Eriu, just Teamhrach for now. Although there are sure to be some in Eriu who would take advantage of our vulnerability." Reginald began to walk down the corridor that would eventually lead them to ground level. "What will matter more than anything is where the nobles line up in the conflict with Cambria – the king and his brother or Count Djago."

"Where will our family land, brother?"

"That will be Father's decision. But I cannot imagine that he would side against the king. They have known each other for decades, and the duke as well. In their youth, the three of them used to hunt deer and boar on our lands and never have I heard Father say a derogatory word about their character."

Perault hurried to keep up with his brother's longer stride. "What about Count Djago?"

A pained look crossed Reginald's face. "I only met the count once a few years ago when I accompanied Father to Lyon's Gate for a meeting of the Temple Knights. The count was very affable and well-loved by his people and the nobles that serve him. In fact, his father and the Duke of Yorwick were once fast friends."

"It looks like his father's friendship with the duke did not carry over so well."

Reginald chuckled. "You may be correct in that assumption, little brother."

They found their father in his study flipping through a stack of parchment. He looked up when the brothers entered, a stern look on his face. "You've read the news?"

"Yes, Father." To Perault, his father was as strong and mentally acute as he had always been.

"With Cambria threatening a civil war there will be precious few resources available from Lyon's Gate, Yorwick and likely any of the cities north of us regardless of who they choose to support. That leaves Tintagel, and us, on our own to face High-King . . . High-King . . ." His father appeared to be confused about what he was about to say.

"Cadeyrn," Reginald spoke softly.

"Cadeyrn! Yes, High-King Cadeyrn may alter his objectives once he learns that Lyonesse is teetering on the brink of civil war."

Perault pretended not to notice the slip. "How does that change things for us?"

His father sighed. "There will be no Temple Knights from Lyon's Gate and we only have thirty or so we can call on locally. Therefore, our infantry and bowmen will stay with us behind the walls when the Eriu forces arrive and the rangers will do their best to disrupt their army's supply lines. I will still be sending the cavalry to Tintagel where they might be needed in a pitched battle."

"It's a sound plan, father." Perault agreed.

The Earl of Stoddenferry stood from his heavy oak desk. There was no sway in his stance, no hesitation in his voice when he spoke. At that moment he portrayed the regal strength and command of a noble Temple Knight priming for battle. "Perault, get to the rook and send pigeons to the king and Duke Maruk informing them of our plan. Reginald, I leave it to you to prepare the castle for war."

CHAPTER 19

Peace and War

Summer – SY5490

Perault stood on the highest landing on Stoddenferry Castle overlooking the sapphire-blue waters of Lake Virtue. The water was still, lazily lapping over the sandy beach far below while only the hint of a warm breeze touched his face like gentle fingers. He was reminded of Melisende. And how much he missed her. Unfortunately, events in the kingdom would keep him from her a while longer, perhaps the whole summer.

He was not alone. Standing quietly to each side of him, enjoying the warm weather, were his father and brother. The three of them spent a lot of time together these days with so much to do preparing defenses, training the militia and supplying the castle stores for siege. A least that last part appeared to no longer be necessary.

Perault glanced over at his father and immediately felt a pang in his stomach at what he must be going through. So far it was mostly forgetting the names of people he did not see every day, but more and more he complained that he could not even remember the faces of his old friends. It would only get worse over the next few months and Perault knew he was far from prepared to watch his father slowly fade away. The druids recommended keeping his mind active with conversation and activities. At least the fear of war with Eriu and the looming civil war had more than provided ample of both. "Do you think the king intervened in the conflict between Teamhrach and Tintagel, Father?"

His father appeared confused for a moment. "Which king? Oh, yes, King Praeter. I have no doubt he did everything he could to avert the bloodshed and instability it would bring to the kingdom, especially with Count Djago marching on Yorwick."

"Then you are confident there will be no siege?"

His father grunted. "I believe the reports that the High-King has ordered his forces to stand down and that his conscripts are returning to their farms and villages. But I am not a fool and neither is Praeter or even Duke Maruk, despite his poor judgment. It was marrying a woman too young for him that started the whole mess."

"That is why tomorrow morning you and I are taking only the cavalry and Temple Knights to muster with the king's army in Oswalt." Reginald had an edge to his voice which Perault knew had its source with their father. Neither of them was happy about leaving him alone at Stoddenferry Castle while they rode north to fight Count Djago, but the old earl had been adamant that they heed the crown's call. It was only their mother's assurance that she would not leave his side while they were gone that convinced them.

"You two are worse than a pair of skittish house maids flailing at a rat in the kitchen." At least his father still had his humor. "Even if High-King Cadeyrn changes his mind and marches south, I will still have the bulk of the garrison to defend the walls."

Reginald started to say something and then stopped. Perault was relieved, there was no point in arguing again over what had already been resolved.

"What will be my place in the cavalry you lead, brother?" There was no question his brother would lead their forces to Oswalt, but Perault was not sure where he would fit in.

Reginald put his back against the stone crenellations and regarded him uncertainly as if he had never considered the question before now. Perault knew his brother was teasing him and had no doubt he knew exactly what his assignment would be. "You will lead one of the regular cavalry units. I can't put you above a gold-cloaked Temple Knight since you have not earned yours yet, but the regulars will follow you.

Perault nodded, he was fine with that. The regulars of Stoddenferry were not a disorganized rabble, they were highly trained professionals that knew their deadly craft well. He would be honored to lead them.

The next morning Perault was awake before daybreak. After washing and dressing in his riding clothes he walked into the grand hall to find Reginald and his father breakfasting with a score of Temple Knights. He sat next to his brother and almost immediately a servant placed a bowl of sweetened porridge along with a cup of warm ale in front of him. Perault wasn't particularly hungry, but he tried to eat a little anyway since he would not see another warm meal until later that evening when they set camp.

"There is some good news from the north," Reginald informed him between bites of porridge.

"Count Djago has had a change of heart like our friend in Eriu and we can all return to our warm beds?" Perault jested hopefully.

His brother snickered at that. "I wish that were the case. Count Djago is well into the Duchy of Yorwick now and will soon lay siege to the city. Probably before we arrive in Oswalt."

"How is that good news?"

"That wasn't the good news. Apparently, the count is not burning and pillaging villages on his way east as most armies are wont to do. He seems to be going out of his way not to cause harm to Yorwick property and citizenry."

"Will that help him earn goodwill if he succeeds in tearing down the walls surrounding Yorwick and deposing Duke Eldorath?" Perault could appreciate the humane treatment, but he couldn't see the benefit.

"Don't you see boys?" Perault's father joined in. "The count can only be planning to annex the Duchy, take the title, and add their resources to his own. Then he will turn on the rest of Lyonesse without much worry of dissension among those he has already conquered.

Reginald stood from his chair and patted his father. "We shall see." Then he turned his attention to the rest of the room. "It is time to ride," he called out, propelling the Temple Knights into motion.

Perault said his farewells to his father and followed Reginald out the door. It was a wonderfully cool pre-dawn morning under a clear sky twinkling with a sea of stars that always reminded him of his childhood. Often, he would watch the stars with his mother on the same landing where he stood with his father and brother the evening before. She told him that each point of light was a sun like their own except that it was far, far away with worlds and possibly people like themselves that lived their lives by the grace of its warmth. At first, he thought his mother was telling him fairy tales, but when he was older she confided that she had learned this truth from an Enlightened One from the Emerald Isle. Perault had rarely seen an Enlightened One as they were respectfully known in the Western kingdoms. They were Atlantean scholars, priests, and wizards who maintained strange towers capped by unusual pyramid-shaped red crystals that rotated slowly at their apex. They cast crimson illumination that shown bright even in the daylight hours. Every major city Perault had ever visited in Lyonesse had one such tower, and he heard that they could be found throughout the Western kingdoms and lands far beyond.

A groom brought his horse, and Perault quickly mounted. He would be traveling at the head of the column of Temple Knights and regular cavalry next to his brother. Their armor and supplies would follow in wagons at the rear. Oswalt was a little over half the distance to Lyon's Gate and would only take them a few days to cover the distance if the weather held. Perault was eager to arrive at the camp, he had never seen an army gathered together, and it was rumored that this one would be the largest assembly of Temple Knights and soldiers Lyonesse had ever fielded.

The hours crawled by as slowly as their pace. They could have traveled much faster, but Reginald did not want to leave the supply wagons alone and unprotected. Perault passed the time conversing with his brother, listening to him give periodic orders or review an occasional message. Perault marveled at the complexity of the king's messenger service and wondered that there must be an army of scribes and riders to support it.

"What is going to happen when we arrive in Oswalt?" Perault always liked to ponder his future as far in advance as possible, especially when there was more uncertainty than usual involved.

Reginald glanced over at him. "That will be decided by General Alwyn Urec. Although I suspect he will send your unit to join the other silver-fringed cloak knights and regulars."

Perault was taken aback. "We won't stay together?"

His brother laughed in a way that sounded just like his father. "I will take the knights and report to the Master of the Temple of Sunna from Tintagel. You are still under the authority of the king until you earn your gold-fringed cloak."

There was an unusual dynamic between the Temple of Sunna and the King of Lyonesse that Perault did not fully understand. While the Temple Knights were organized and based in Lyonesse they were not exactly under the authority of King Eldorath. The Knight Commander of the Temple Knights served alongside the Arch-Druid of Sunna as the king's chief advisors and helped guide domestic policy and foreign relations from the capital, Lyon's Gate. It was an informal triad, as he understood it, and although the king could act unilaterally in any manner he wished, he would have to do so without the support of the Temple Knights and the druids. This was rarely an option the king pursued, considering that the Temple Knights controlled nearly all the trade and most of the merchants while the druids controlled religion. The strange thing was that nearly every generation of male royalty were not just kings but also Temple Knights. How that worked in the larger scheme of politics not even Sir Aldeman could explain adequately.

Of course, every child from across all economic strata dreamed of becoming a Temple Knight when they grew up. It was an inseparable part of the culture of Lyonesse with the social framework to support it. Any physically capable male child could be squired to a knight when they came of age and unless the druids chose them or their family decided to retain them in the family business or farm, these apprenticeships formed the structure of education in the country. Girls had educational paths as well and Perault had even heard talk of a select group of female apprentices being considered for taking the traditional path to knighthood. It was a strange concept that was disturbing to many of the older knights, but the experiment was championed by Queen Penelope herself so much of the grumbling was kept to themselves. So far he had never seen a female Temple Knight and knew of no one who had. Perhaps the rumors were unfounded, or perhaps one would show up at the Tournies one day and surprise them all.

Perault's mind wandered as the leagues ticked by and he was glad for it. Anything to keep him from pining away for Melisende. Before leaving Stoddenferry Castle he penned a letter to her expressing his love and devotion, his unwavering dedication to their union and peppered it with promises of a happy future together. He prayed that Sunna would see him through the coming conflict to deliver on those promises.

~~~

Mounted on his night-black stallion, Count Terril Djago looked southward across the Thayre River from atop a rise in the terrain watching the great walled city of Yorwick. Their gates stood open to admit streams of panicked citizen who had abandoned their villages in the face of his massive army's approach. He'd brought twenty-thousand infantry and bowmen supported by over five thousand cavalry. Cambria was capable of fielding a substantial host, far larger than any other single city in Lyonesse for that matter, including Lyon's Gate. As first line of defense against the denizens of Fomoire, Cambria maintained a large standing ground force to protect the northern borders including the ground approaches to Lindpoole whose resources were spent primarily on the northern navy to guard the coastline from the Sea of Dragons all the way to the Primal Sea.

Commander Ouza came riding fast to stop beside him. "My lord, Jarl has captured Lindpoole. The city is ours."

That was not surprising. It was mostly Cambrian soldiers who manned the walls and garrisons around Lindpoole. It was the navy he was after. "How many ships were captured?"

Ouza skimmed over the missive in his hand. "Twenty were safely captured in port and only three were burned. The rest are out to sea on patrols and may not return for a few weeks."

"Good," Djago nodded. "Send a reminder to Jarl that I need as many ships intact as possible. Tell him I will be displeased if any more ships were to burn."

"There is another bit of news you will not wish to hear."

"What is it Ouza? Just say what the matter is."

"Teamhrach and Tintagel have reached a peace accord. The conflict has been resolved."

Djago pounded his fist on the side of his leg causing his stallion to shift irritably. "Damn. I was counting on the southern forces to be distracted while I swept through the north."

"King Praeter Eldorath has already ordered the southern forces to assemble in Oswalt, my lord. Our spies anticipate that they will be prepared to march north in less than a month."

Djago wanted to strike Ouza in the mouth for all the bad news it was spewing. Somehow he was able to hold off the urge. "Send word to Cug that I am calling upon him to repay his debt."

"I anticipated as much and sent the message before I left the main column this morning. On my request, his clans have stayed in the vicinity of the Ice Coast since they drove Kumida out of Fomoire last spring. If he leaves immediately, they can be here in three weeks."

Djago nodded his approval. Ouza had managed to redeem himself. "Good. Make sure the Fir Bholg arrive in time to relieve our siege so we can meet the king's forces without the worry of an army from Yorwick on our heels."

"Anything else, my lord?"

Djago paused a moment. "Where is Naamah? I need her assurance that the druids will not interfere."

"I don't know, my lord. Should I open a portal?"

"Not here, fool. There are too many humans around. If she does not appear by this evening then we will open a portal in the privacy of my tent."

"Very good, my lord. I shall see to my orders now." Commander Ouza rode north to where the bulk of the army was still trailing a league or two behind the advance guard. By the next morning, his army would be surrounding Yorwick, cutting off all supplies and news from outside their walls.

Djago considered his options. If the Fir Bholg did not arrive in time to relieve the siege, he would be forced to retreat to Cambria. It would be humiliating, but he would survive. If the Fir Bholg did arrive in time, then the druids would certainly join the war against him. Naamah had a plan to deal with the druids, but she wasn't here to give him an update on her progress. The Atiod-Bherto had been in hiding since their defeat in the Oak War centuries ago and Djago wasn't convinced that they would or could take on the druids of Sunna. Fear and the need to survive often trumped hatred and the desire for revenge.

The best scenario would be a pitched battle between his forces and the king's in open terrain. In addition to his regular soldiers, Djago had one thousand gold-cloaks and a dozen battle wizards – he doubted the king could muster as many of either. Plus, he was sure that he could cajole Cug into providing him with at least a score of his Fir Bholg warriors to serve as shock troops. Djago sighed. There were decidedly too many variables that might not go in his favor. He would have to think of something new to tip the scales in his direction.

Djago dismounted and sat on the cool, damp grass. He watched Yorwick until the sun set and lights began to flicker to life all over the city. Still, there were hundreds of refugees making their way through the gates. There was nothing he could do about it. He found out quickly that his men would not slaughter the local farmers or burn down their villages. If he tried to force them to do so he would quickly lose his army. It was clear that they believed their fight was with the duke and the king by relation, but their hatred did not extend to the common people who were still citizens of Lyonesse despite whose territory they lived within. Djago let it go for now. He would have time to corrupt their souls with the spoils of plunder and women later.

With little left to see, Djago made his way to the main camp where his tents were erected. When he entered, he was relieved to see Naamah waiting for him. "I hope you have better news for me than Ouza today."

She did not smile or greet him warmly, she never did; joy was not an emotion she would ever feel, but nor would he. "The Atiod await your command."

"Good news then. I'm impressed." He stood close to her and began to remove her clothes. She did not protest or seem to notice at all for that matter. "Anything else I need to know?"

"That is all I came to say."

"Well, I have had a very tense day and you have shown up at a very convenient time to help me relieve some of that stress." He gestured toward the bed.

Her clothing in disarray, Naamah smiled seductively and pulled him with her to the sheets.

Morning arrived quickly and his troops were already on the move to surround Yorwick. No one needed to bother him, and they dared not, his generals had their orders. They would be there, staring at the walls of Yorwick and bared asses upon them for at least three weeks if the Fir Bholg arrived on time. There was no need for him to hurry, not yet.

Ten days passed and Djago once again stood in the same spot he stood every day since the siege of Yorwick began. So far, the greatest excitement was when the messenger pigeons left the city and his archers did their best to bring them down. No real intelligence had been gained from the dead birds, but there was no secret as to what was happening either. The city was surrounded, food was in short supply, and help was desperately needed to break the siege.

"Ouza, what news from our spies in Oswalt?" He must have asked his commander the same question every day and the answer was always the same.

"The king still gathers troops to his banner, my lord."

The response was not disappointing, quite the contrary, status quo was good for the time being. Once the king's troops began to move north it would only be a week or two before they faced one another across a battlefield somewhere. So far, time was on his side.

Djago studied the fortified walls and knew he could never take Yorwick unless he starved them out. He didn't even bother to order the construction of siege engines. The walls were too high and too thick with trenches and towers surrounding the city and a substantially more extensive defensive network of walls inside Yorwick surrounding the Keep. It was a city designed to withstand the most withering of assaults. There was a time, only a few weeks ago, that he demanded his generals form a plan to take the city within two weeks. Try as they might, there was no easy way and after some convincing he agreed that their best strategy would be to take them out of the fight with a perpetual siege. That's where the Fir Bholg would come in handy.

Another week passed and Ouza arrived with the news that Cug and his Fir Bholg were only a few days away. Better still, the armies of the south were still in Oswalt. It was time to set Naamah's plan into motion with the Atiod-Bherto, for once the druids of Sunna realized the Fir Bholg had left Fomoire they would move quickly to stop the advance of the Giants. And with the king's armies ready to march north any day, Djago could afford no more delays.

It was time to roll the dice.

"Inform the Arch-druid Cateteric that now is the time for him to take his vengeance upon the druids of Sunna." Djago addressed Naamah in his tent.

"Yes, my lord. I will leave immediately and return soon with news of our great victory." Naamah promised. Then she pushed through the tent flap and out into the dark night beyond.

Djago tapped his fingers on the arm of the wooden chair where he sat alone in thought. A Succubus in her natural form enjoyed the advantage of flight, which meant Naamah would arrive at whatever rock the Atiod-Bherto were hiding under at about the same time the Fir Bholg arrived to relieve his army. Once there, she would instruct Cateteric to immediately attack the Enclave of the druids of Sunna in the forest off the northern coast of Lough Greely before they had a chance to react to the news of the Giants entering Lyonesse. When word was out about the attack on the Enclave, every druid of Sunna, and possibly Eriu, within a thousand leagues would think of nothing but rooting out the Atiod-Bherto, especially if they had met with some initial success. The Fir Bholg would be nothing more than a distant irritation.

He walked over to the table that held the maps of the Western kingdoms. There was Yorwick and the figure that represented their forces and to the south was another figure representing the army of the king. Then there was Eriu with their scattered and fractured kingdoms, followed by Ys and Courth to the south alone and vulnerable. None of them would have time to organize a proper defense against him, especially once he was crowned king.

Crowned king.

Yes, once he defeated the combined forces led by the current king, Praeter Eldorath, Djago would depose him and take the crown for himself. The cities of Lyonesse would have no choice but to submit to his rule and legitimize it. What remained of their forces would ultimately join his own and they would go on to dominate the whole of the Western kingdoms.

Or, Lyonesse would degrade into bitter civil war.

Djago smiled to himself. Either outcome would serve him. Time would soon be nothing more than another element for him to exploit for strategic purposes. What was time to a thing that could live forever, jumping from one body to the next? His own son Pen would likely be his next host. It was a very convenient system the nobles of Lyonesse utilized to choose their future leaders by birth and blood.

CHAPTER 20

Grim Preparations

White tents, their narrow door-flaps fluttering in the mild evening breeze, stood in perfect rows broken only by the occasional corral for livestock or cooking-fire for preparing meals. After three days at camp, Perault still marveled at how they covered the wide expanse of fields outside of Oswalt, too numerous to count. The men he brought from Stoddenferry Castle joined King Praeter's larger force of around ten thousand cavalry, bowmen and infantry along with a score or so wizards trained for military combat.

His gaze traveled south where a smaller group of tents stretched over the countryside. These were remarkable by their colorful variety with streamers and pennants identifying their owner's House and station. His brother, Sir Reginald Eckert, camped among the one thousand Temple Knights assembled from mostly the southern cities of Lyonesse. Perault felt a momentary pang of jealousy. He wanted to be there with them, charging into battle beside them and bringing glory to Sunna, temple, and crown. His time would come, he knew it, but would there be another battle in his lifetime to exalt his future fame and reputation? He could only hope so.

"We will be leaving in the morning."

Perault nearly jumped, startled by the unexpected voice beside him. It was his friend Davin of House Jeutemont. "Are you trying to make my heart jump from my chest?"

"Sorry, Perault. I'll stomp louder next time." The big man grinned.

Perault felt embarrassed. Davin was as big as an Auroch; he should have heard him approach from ten paces. "I guess I'm a little distracted right now."

"Who isn't?" Davin shrugged his big shoulders. "Yorwick is under siege by Count Djago and King Praeter's army is set to march against him in the morning."

"Will Yorwick hold out until we get there?"

Davin snorted a laugh, "Yorwick's walls are in no danger of falling. According to the last report, Count Djago has merely surrounded the city without bringing any siege equipment as if they had all the time in the world to starve them out."

"That's odd." Perault kicked at the grassy earth with his boot. "It was my understanding that Count Djago was quite astute in the tactics of warfare."

"It is, indeed. Even the generals are confounded by his actions."

Davin had the envious position of having been appointed to General Urec's war-staff, a glorified messenger perhaps, but among the few in the know of what was happening big picture.

"How many days to Yorwick, then?" Perault had no idea how an army this size could get anywhere fast.

"The generals are pushing to cover ten leagues each day, so that's about eight days, give or take."

Perault nodded. "I am eager to get underway."

"Do not be too eager, Perault. We will be standing against our own people when we get there and many will die." Davin clasped Perault's arm in friendship. "I'll come by later for a drink or two."

Perault watched his big friend walk along the line of tents and wished he had asked him if the generals thought they were fighting a civil war or a rebellion. He supposed time would tell. Either way,

Davin was right, when the two armies met it would be men of Lyonesse dying on both sides.

Flavorful scents from a multitude of cooking fires indicated that it was almost dinner time. So busy was his training schedule that he had eaten little during the day. Perault planned to remedy that shortly, and his stomach rumbled in agreement. If he were lucky, there would be some version of meat in the stew that evening, but not if he arrived late to the chow-line. With distinct purpose, Perault turned on his heels and headed quickly to his camp, every other step punctuated by a gastral grumble.

Morning came far too early for Perault after a long night of drinking and swapping stories with his friends, Davin and Edwin. He rolled onto his back, pressing his fingers against his tender temples. Just what he needed, a hangover to keep him company the rest of the day.

The sounds and shadows that played against the side of his tent in the dim light indicated that the men outside were well along the way packing their tents and camping gear. Perault was far behind and would have to eat a cold breakfast in his saddle if he was to leave with the rest of his unit. He slowly stood on wobbly legs and walked to the slight opening in his tent to poke his head out.

Thousands of tents were in various stages of dismantling and packing away on numbered carts to be retrieved later that night. Perault almost wished he could climb in with them and sleep the day away. Unfortunately, that wasn't an option with men to lead. Wasting no time on wishes, Perault quickly changed his clothes and packed his belongings in a travel sack before tying up his tent and placing it beside the others in a nearby cart.

"Number nine." He chuckled quietly to himself. The number on the cart reminded him of a children's story his mother used to tell him about nine ducklings that were warned to stay close to mama duck. The tale did not end well for those that did not heed her wise instructions.

Perault retrieved his mount from the corral and rode to catch up with his men forming with the main column. He had hoped to find Dorlik and Hanlin somewhere in the tent city in the days before they struck camp, but there were simply too many tents and not enough time. Maybe he would come across them along the way north.

It didn't take him long to find his unit riding parallel to the infantry about midway down the long, winding column of men. He immediately regretted rushing to catch up. The column was moving so slowly he could have slept in until mid-day and still reached them before it was his unit's turn to go on patrol.

In the distance ahead the Temple Knights led with the king and his generals. They were too far away to recognize, but he knew they were there. Behind them came the squires and infantry, then the bowmen followed by a league of supply carts. The regular cavalry ranged in units far ahead and to the sides in organized patrols that would rotate every few hours. It reminded Perault of something like a mobile beehive with a stream of riders coming and going with messages and the cavalry patrols orbiting in wide circles. And despite the slow pace and anticipated boredom of the journey, it was one of the most exciting times of his life.

~~~

Count Djago sat upon his powerful war steed and surveyed the siege of Yorwick from the same hill where he had waited every day the past four weeks. From his vantage point, Djago could watch the northern and southern approaches to the city. Nothing had changed.

On this day, like so many before, Commander Ouza sat quietly on his horse awaiting the next order when he suddenly pointed to the forest north of their position.

"They have arrived, my lord."

It was nearly mid-day with the warm sun shining down from almost directly above and despite the still air around them, the trees swayed in a long column that stretched at least a quarter of a league into the distance as if caught in some wicked, unnatural breeze.

Djago watched the massive forms of the Fir Bholg materialize from the thick deciduous forest. Many of them were nearly as tall and twice as thick as the trees they pushed aside. They appeared to be powerful creatures covered in furs and hides, with long red or blond hair and heavily bearded faces under thick, protruding brows on sloping foreheads. To a man, they were armed with long spears and clubs studded with metal or the occasional battleax slung over their shoulders.

The Fir Bholg's rough line stretched onto the rolling green lowland below them. Djago was not surprised that there was no discipline in this group. He guessed that when they fought, it was a chaotic charge, fierce and unrelenting, the basest form of hand-to-hand combat. His soldiers, by now aware that the Giants would be joining them, had not likely actually seen one other than in a painted image, let alone the hundreds of them pouring out of the forest. They scattered quickly out of the way of the Fir Bholg's lumbering march, no doubt fearful of becoming a convenient snack.

The group was led by a particularly large Fir Bholg Djago knew must King Cug. He was surrounded by several warriors and what appeared to be a female shaman. That was the one Djago had spoken to through the portal. He was sure of it.

"Let's go down and meet this king of the Giants." Djago spurred his mount forward at a quick pace with Commander Ouza following a step behind.

By the time Djago reached the base of the hill, Cug had led the majority of his warriors out of the forest and into a meadow where they stopped to rest on the soft grass. As he rode closer Djago realized that there were many Cyclopes among them that he did not notice before. They were considerably smaller than the Fir Bholg, dressed similarly in furs and, of course, distinguished by a single eye were there were normally two. The sight of them filled him with apprehension. He expected that Cug would have slaughtered every one of them or at least forced the Cyclopes into slavery rather than allowing them to join his forces. This clemency suggested that Cug was more than just the strongest brute among the Fir Bholg and therefore their leader. Perhaps their king was more intelligent and cunning than he expected. That was never a good thing, Djago preferred stupid and predictable allies.

"I am Count Terril Djago," he addressed the Fir Bholg king without dismounting. Even on his horse he was less than half the height of the colossal Giant. "You have done well to keep our bargain and answer my command."

Cug pulled his red eyebrows together in a scowl. "And you are an arrogant little man to address me like a servant. You would do well to take care with your words before you find yourself a stain under my boot!"

Djago lifted a hand into the air and over two thousand bowmen rushed to stand atop the hill behind him. "Now that we have both demonstrated our willingness to use force against one another, perhaps we can sit as friends and discuss why you are here."

Cug, clearly not pleased with the situation, nodded curtly and sat on the ground with his legs crossed. "Tell me what you want of us so we can fulfill our obligation and return home."

Djago dismounted and sat on the ground facing Cug. To look him in the eye, his neck was bent at an uncomfortable angle that left him feeling oddly vulnerable. This was not how he imagined this meeting. "Your task is simple – keep Duke Eldorath bottled up in Yorwick while I take my forces south and defeat his brother, King Praeter Eldorath."

"So, you want us to camp outside the walls and do nothing until you defeat the King of Lyonesse?" Cug did not look convinced. "And then what? Wait for the druids to punish us for leaving Fomoire?"

A barking laugh escaped Djago's lips. "The druids will no longer be a concern of yours after today. And as far as Yorwick is concerned I don't care if you burst through their walls and boil their people for stew. When I am done with King Praeter you may return to the dreary life you led in Fomoire or serve me in triumph and prosperity."

Djago carefully probed Cug's mind. The Fir Bholg was uncertain and distrustful, yet intrigued by the possibility of escaping the perdition of Fomoire.

The Fir Bholg shaman, Thrakel, pulled her hood from her face and leaned close to stare into Djago's eyes. Her penetrating red orbs might have been mesmerizing to anyone else, and he quickly erected mental defenses to keep her out of his consciousness. She was unexpectedly powerful. Djago would have to deal with this one eventually. "Why should we believe that the druids will do us no harm? What assurances do we have?"

"I owe you nothing, witch!" Djago lashed out and immediately regretted it. He was angry that she had the audacity to test him with her psionic ability just as he was doing it to her king.

"Answer her," Cug rumbled irritably.

Djago glared at them both while he struggled to get his anger under control. He was not used to placating allies and fostering alliances. He expected to have absolute control and to be obeyed absolutely. "The Atiod-Bherto are my assurance." Djago did not want to admit their involvement and assistance, but he saw no other way to adequately answer the Fir Bholg's demand.

Cug pulled on the cloak of his shaman and she returned to her original position. "Thrakel will soon find the truth of your words. If it is how you say, then we will stay and complete our obligation. Further, if you do prevail in the conflict against King Praeter, it is possible that we may support you further with adequate incentive. Otherwise, we will leave this place immediately and return to the north."

"That is not our agreement!" Djago stood angrily. Rage poured through him and he nearly raised a hand to signal his archers and kill them all.

Cug appeared to remain impassive. "Our agreement was to come to your aid if you ever called. We are here and you are clearly in no danger. We will not stay longer if you attempt to keep us here with lies." Cug stood, towering above Djago. Thrakel and the rest of the Fir Bholg stood with him.

Forcing his impulses aside, Djago took charge of his bearing and projected an outwardly cold detachment. "Very well. Once your shaman confirms what I have told you," he flashed a sneer in Thrakel's direction, "I expect your forces to relieve mine sieging Yorwick."

Cug nodded. "Agreed."

The Fir Bholg king slowly circled around and ordered his warriors to set camp. Djago smiled. The Giants were setting up camp in full view of the masses standing on the walls in Yorwick. He could imagine how terrifying the sight of over five hundred Giants outside their gates must look to them. His archers would have their hands full with all the pigeons that would surely be released that evening.

Djago regained his mount and rode to his own tent with Ouza. When they arrived, a messenger was waiting for them. By the way the young soldier was drawing heavy breath, Djago guessed that he had only just entered the camp after a long hard ride.

The messenger bowed quickly to Djago, "My lord," then removed a small, tightly rolled scroll from his leather satchel and handed it to Ouza. "A message from your man in Oswalt."

Oswalt took the small scroll and dismissed the messenger, before breaking the seal to read its contents. Djago watched closely as Commander Ouza read the missive and could almost guess at the substance even before he announced it. "The combined armies of the south are on the move."

Quickly, Djago strode to a wide square table littered with maps. "They will have to travel up the river nearly to Yorwick before they will find a suitable place to cross. How soon will they be here?"

Ouza dropped the scroll into a nearby brazier where it flashed with yellow flame as it burned. "Three weeks at best."

"Good, we will let the men rest for a few days and then we will meet them here." Djago pressed his finger on an open area on the map west of their current position. "The Dormonts."

It was a fitting plain of hard ground and soft grass to fight a pitched battle, especially given its ironic history. Through Djago's memories the demon knew that this place was the host of the decisive battle that determined the fate of Lyonesse as a unified land early in its history. In a time when Lyonesse was split in two, House Dormont controlled the north and House Monmouth controlled the south. Both Houses descended from House Teuric and both claimed the right to rule all of Lyonesse. For years the Houses and their allies fought what amounted to a civil war until their armies met on the plain that would become known as The Dormonts in honor of the bones of the fallen house buried there. It was fitting that history would come full circle and Djago would bury the descendants of House Monmouth – House Eldorath – on the very plain where they had won the right to rule all of Lyonesse so long ago.

Ouza bent low to study the details of the map. "Do you have a plan, my lord?"

"We will take advantage of the terrain at the southern end of The Dormonts. Their greater numbers of cavalry will not be able to outflank us with the river on our left and the forest on our right." Djago traced his finger along the line of the forest. "I want bowmen and rangers in that forest to ambush any surprises the king might think to send against us and barges with more bowmen and infantry to harass their right flank from the river."

Ouza nodded thoughtfully. "Very wise, my lord. And how should I position the main force?"

"Keep it simple. Infantry in the center, cavalry to the flanks, bowmen behind them and wizards interspersed among them." Djago thumped the table. "I want King Eldorath to believe I have no imagination."

"What if the Giants join us?"

"I will keep them hidden with our reserves until the battle is fully engaged." Djago didn't care to hide the evil smile that crept across his face. "Imagine the terror and disbelief that will ripple through their ranks when hundreds of Fir Bholg descend upon them!"

"It appears we cannot lose, my lord."

"I have one more trick up my sleeve." Almost gleefully, Djago slapped his commander on the back. "The Atiod-Bherto will attack the Enclave of the Sunna druids tonight. Once the slaughter is over and the druids are no longer a threat, the Atiod will make their way to The Dormonts and attack the king's rear. The chaos will be historic."

Ouza frowned. "That will require precise timing, my lord."

Djago shifted his gaze away from the maps and fixed his intense glare firmly on his commander. "Naamah will succeed or suffer impressively for her failure. As will you."

To Djago's satisfaction, Ouza looked at the map submissively and uttered, "Yes, my lord."

"Now tell me about your spies in Lyon's Gate. How would you characterize the effectiveness of their disinformation efforts?"

"Mixed," Ouza, still staring at the map on the table, shook his head in evident frustration. "No one believes the rumors that the king has taken a mistress, least of all the queen. Corruption has been no more believable. The only vulnerability we have found to exploit is the possible collusion with his brother, Duke Eldorath, against you. Such an opening presents some promise of creating doubt, if not an open rift that would splinter factions for our spies to turn in our favor."

Djago stepped over to a small table at the edge of the tent and poured himself a cup of wine. "Stay with that, but I want more," Ouza said nothing while Djago drained the cup and filled it again. "I want King Praeter to be looking back over his should toward Lyon's Gate with every step that he travels further away from it. Send in more men, more gold and silver, whatever you need, but there must be chaos in Lyon's Gate to the point of distraction."

"I will leave tonight, my lord."

"Ouza, get it done and get back here before King Praeter arrives with his army. When he finally faces me, I want him concerned just as much with what is happening back home as he is with what is happening across the battlefield."

~~~

Perault spied Davin riding toward him on a warhorse that looked small under his large frame. It was almost comical to watch and even more so when Davin's face stretched to display his wide, silly grin.

"How are you, my friend? I worried you might still be asleep in your tent at Oswalt!"

Perault mocked a wide sway in his saddle. "I don't know what I was thinking, to try to keep up drink-for-drink with a man your size!"

"You bet a gold on it." Davin held out his hand. "I think I won."

"Bah!" Perault slapped his friend's palm. "You still owe me two from last year!"

They shared laughed before Perault led Davin a short distance from his men to speak privately. "Any news from the north?"

"The army will camp along the coast of the Thayre River tonight, but we will not be crossing tomorrow as planned, or at all," Davin replied cryptically.

"Something has changed." Perault did not state it as a question, he knew by Davin's serious expression that it was true.

"Count Djago has abandoned the siege of Yorwick and crossed the river into The Dormonts. That's where the battle will take place."

"The Dormonts!" Perault felt the hair on his neck rising. "That place is said to harbor the wandering spirits of the last civil war in Lyonesse."

Davin eyes took on a haunted look. "There will be more spirits to wander the hallowed ground soon, I fear."

Perault suddenly realized the folly in the count's plan. "Won't Count Djago's rear be vulnerable to attack from Duke Eldorath with the siege lifted?"

Davin leaned in close. "I tell you this only because you are my friend and I have confidence that you will not repeat what I say and spread fear among the men – the siege continues, just not by the forces of Cambria."

Perault was confused. "Then who?"

"The Fir Bholg," Davin sighed heavily. "Count Djago has allied with the Giants and they continue the siege of Yorwick."

It was unbelievable. Perault was struck dumb with shock.

Davin didn't seem to notice. "Come find me when camp is set. I'll find a way for you to hear the details yourself."

Kicking his mount into motion, Davin disappeared into the forward ranks leaving Perault with a sinking feeling in the pit of his stomach.

~~~

Perault stood with Davin outside the wide opening to the tent known as the War Room. Generals followed by flocks of staff along with a slew of nobles were pouring inside to debate the latest news affecting the king's war strategy. He expected his brother to be in attendance representing Stoddenferry Castle, but so far had not caught sight of him.

"When we get inside, stay close to me and act like you're supposed to be here," Davin whispered.

Perault followed Davin. It was the largest tent he had ever seen, easily accommodating the massive oak table that stood at its center surrounded by dukes, generals, the Arch-Druid of Sunna, the Knight Commander of the Temple Knights and, of course, the king.

The lesser nobles and military staffers, like Davin, were crowded an arms-length behind them to give the servants room to buzz about keeping everyone's cups filled with ale. And then his eyes locked on his brother, Sir Reginald, standing on the other side of the tent. He stared hard at Perault with a slight tilt of the head seeming to ask what he was doing there. Perault shrugged and turned his lips in the barest of smiles. It didn't appear to lessen his brother's anxiety at his presence.

Scanning past his brother, Perault gaze landed on many knights and nobles that he recognized. He couldn't believe he was standing in a room, tent even, with so many notable figures and silently thanked Davin once again for the invitation.

"General Urec." The king was standing over a map nearly the size of the table that appeared to show every detail of The Dormonts terrain in amazing detail. "Have you been able to ascertain the count's force structure?"

"I have, your majesty." He glanced over at the arch-druid. "Although it would have been much easier if the arch-druid would have lent a few of his druids to gather the information."

Arch-druid Filberzh the Risen stood impassively in his hooded robe, making it impossible to see the expression on his face, and raised his hand as if dismissing the complaint. "We are only here to observe. You know we cannot take a side in this matter unless provoked." His raspy voice sent a chill up Perault's spine, and he wondered if it had the same effect on the general

"Leave it be, general," the king commanded gently. "Tell me what you know."

"Yes, your majesty. As far as we can determine he has around three thousand armored cavalry, two thousand bowmen, and five thousand heavy infantry. We are unclear about the number of battle-trained wizards, but our best guess is less than twenty."

The king looked around the room, clearly irritated. "Where is Myrllin when I need him?" he grumbled. No one offered an answer.

"There is one more thing." The general's face was stern, but just for a moment Perault swore he detected a hint of . . . Fear.

"What is it general?"

"Count Djago has at least two hundred Fir Bholg and Cyclopes with him."

The room erupted in shock. Davin had told him that very few knew about the Fir Bholg taking up the siege at Yorwick. Now everyone would know that the Giants had aligned themselves with the enemy. Perault sensed that the king already knew this bit of news and planned for the general to let the news come out in this precise setting.

"Quiet down!" General Urec shouted over the commotion. "The king will speak!"

Almost immediately the tent went quiet. The king took a step back from the table with the maps and began to slowly pace the room, weaving between the members of his audience as he coldly, quietly spoke. "It should be clear now, to anyone who may have had doubts before," he paused near certain individuals as he spoke, causing them to shrink back and display their guilt plainly on their faces, "that Count Djago has contrived this conflict with my brother and brought traitorous rebellion against our kingdom!"

The king walked between two nobles and was suddenly looking Perault straight in the eye. Perault knew that the king knew he wasn't supposed to be here and prepared himself for whatever was going to happen next. It was the least expected thing. The king's features remained stern except that his eyes softened just a little and he winked, exactly as he had done after he laid the silver-fringed cloak on Perault's shoulders months ago. He turned quickly then and walked to the map table. "We will not soon forget those who remained staunch friends of the crown in the kingdom's darkest time of need. As for the others, they may well be forgotten all too soon."

Perault dared not move, no one did. If a glass had dropped, he was sure the entire room would clear in panic. The king let the mood carry for a moment; it was an awesome display of control and power that he wielded over everyone in the tent.

The king turned his gaze to his general. "Alwyn, when do you expect the count will be ready to attack?"

"Despite his loyalties, he is a good general and I would not expect him to wait a moment longer than he had to. His troops will be rested and in position to attack the morning after next."

"And ours?"

"The same, your majesty."

The king drew a hand over his long, dark beard. "I see, finalize your battle plans and have them for me by . . ."

The king's words stuck in his throat as a large Gray Owl glided into the tent and transformed into human form next to the arch-druid to the cries of startled astonishment from those nearby. It was a druid, dressed in the traditional long hooded robe with clusters of feathers, beads, and shells hanging from thongs sewn into the seams. The hood came down revealing a beautiful red-haired woman with tattoos on her face and hands that identified her to those who knew their meaning. Without introduction, she leaned in close to the Filberzh the Risen and whispered a few words. Then she waited quietly for his response if one was forthcoming.

For the second time that night, the tent was deathly silent with everyone waiting for someone to say something. Finally, the Filberzh spoke quietly and calmly words that would set the night aflame with activity, "The Enclave near Matu Mountain has been attacked by the Atiod-Bherto. I must go." Barely had he completed the sentence when he and the red-haired druid shifted into owl forms and darted out of the tent.

No one said a word. They all must have been thinking the same thing as Perault. The Atiod-Bherto were a thing of mythology. Ancient druids who practiced human sacrifice in defiance of the laws of nature. They were decimated by the druids of Eriu and Sunna during the Oak War over five hundred years ago. Or so they all thought.

Concern and worry rippled across the King Praeter's features. "We must leave the druids to their own affairs and focus on the danger before us." Without another word, the king walked out the tent, trailed by General Urec.

Murmurs of agreement rippled through the assembly as they departed, but to Perault's ears they were less than confident. Once outside, Perault pulled on Davin's sleeve. "Until tonight, I had no idea what real power was in this world. It's like I have been living in a bubble my whole life."

"I feel the same," Davin agreed. "So much has happened tonight that my head feels like it might burst."

"What were you doing in there?" Reginald suddenly showed up between them. "Don't you know the harm you could have caused to our family's reputation?"

Davin jumped to Perault's defense before he could speak. "The king was fine with your brother's presence at the meeting."

Reginald eyed Perault closely. "Is that true, Perault?"

"I believe it to be true."

"Very well, I have to go. The Knight Commander has called for a gathering of all his commanders. We'll speak more of this later." Reginald turned in the direction of his camp and disappeared into the crowd of soldiers.

Perault clasp Davin on the shoulder. "Thanks for that. Will the king require your service this evening?"

"No," Davin smiled. "But there is a cask of ale somewhere that will."

"Great, let's find Edwin and that cask. I think I'll be sleeping in late tomorrow."

~~~

"I tried to reach Naamah again through a portal this morning, but she has yet to respond, my lord."

Djago was furious with his Succubus. She should have contacted him soon after the Atiod-Bherto attacked the druids of Sunna in their Enclave. The Fir Bholg shaman, Thrakel, confirmed that a battle took place at the Enclave, but she either had no further information or wouldn't tell him what the results were. Whatever she knew it was good enough to convince King Cug to take over the siege of Yorwick, freeing his own troops to march against King Eldorath on the southern tip of The Dormonts as planned. That was two days ago and still there was no word from Naamah.

"She better be dead or near to it." Djago sat atop his sable charger observing the movement of his adversaries' soldiers in the distance. They had just arrived and appeared to be tired from the long march north. He considered calling for forces to attack immediately since his own men were well rested from lounging in camp the past few days.

He looked at the falling sun. There were only a few hours left before sunset. It would be unwise to call for an attack that would stretch into the night. "Tell the generals that we will attack at dawn. And when you are done with that, fly over the battlefield and its surrounds. I don't want any surprises."

Ouza brought a fist to his chest in salute and galloped off to do his bidding. Djago watched him go, annoyed with himself for not sending Ouza to find Naamah and confirm the success of the Atiod-Bherto. Now it was too late. He would need his commander in the battle the next morning and either the Atiod-Bherto would arrive or they wouldn't.

There *was* one thing he was pleased about and that was the brutal enthusiasm with which the Fir Bholg where conducting the siege on Yorwick. By the time Djago led his forces away from the siege, the Giants were well on their way building siege engines and running down foraging parties foolishly sent outside the walls. It was doubtful that the Fir Bholg knew anything about assaulting walls, yet somehow, they managed to erect their massive constructs despite their natural chaos and disorganization.

The last message he received from the soldiers he left behind to monitor the Giants' progress was from three days before and at that time it was claimed that the walls were teetering on collapse. Djago was more than a little annoyed that there had been no more updates. For all he knew, Yorwick might well be defeated already. If that were true, he could have another three hundred Fir Bholg and Cyclopes reinforcing his troops before the battle ended. He could hope anyway, although he was more than pleased with the two hundred Giants he cajoled Cug into releasing to take with him to The Dormonts. Currently, they sat resting out of sight along with his uneasy reserves awaiting his command.

Djago pulled the reins of his mount and returned to his command tent. The idea of looking over his maps again was repulsive. Instead, he slumped heavily in his pillow-padded chair and poured himself a tall mug of red wine. He had men ready in the northern forest, men ready in barges on the river in the south and men ready on the battlefield. His men were ready. Djago was surprised at how exceptionally good the wine was today. It must be a new batch. He looked closely at the barrel it was poured from and sounded out the name, "Mekali Red". It had the mark of a vineyard on the Emerald Isle cultivated by a prominent Atlantean House.

The Atlanteans.

He would have to deal with them eventually. Fortunately, they never seemed to interfere with the internal affairs of a kingdom unless asked and even then, they never took sides. They were peacemakers. When he ruled the Western kingdoms he expected that the Atlanteans would be more than willing to negotiate peace in trade for recognizing his leadership. Even so, he despised them. If it wasn't for them and the Tuatha Dé, he wouldn't have spent centuries imprisoned within the confines of a pithos. Djago would have his revenge one day, he assured himself. Until then he would drink their fine wine.

Djago filled his mug twice over and then closed his eyes to give them a brief rest. The light breeze that found its way through the tent flap carried the scent of wildflowers and the ambient sounds of camp. The body he inhabited relaxed and a sense of comfort and content came over him that he had not often felt.

Then he was being shaken vigorously. "My lord?"

Djago's eyes popped open. There was darkness all around him except where light flickered from the small candle Ouza held in his other hand.

"Get off me!" he demanded and slapped the offending hand away from his shoulder. "What is the meaning of this?" His meditation must have been deep. At least his host would be rested after a few hours of sleep.

"I could not wake you, my lord." Ouza shrugged. "I feared you had departed."

"Feared? Ha!" Djago stood from the chair and stretched sore muscles. "Is it midnight yet?"

"Just past."

"Very well, still a few hours before the men take their positions." He cast his gaze around the tent for a water basin to wash his face. "What do you want?"

"Eldorath is positioned exactly as you expected and there is nothing to indicate they are aware of our presence on the river or in the forest."

Djago located the washbowl and splashed water on his face before responding. "That is a simple reconnaissance, why are you here so late?"

"I roamed further to the north and west and scanned the forest for any significant movement, and I found something interesting." Ouza walked over to the map and pointed. "Here. There is a herd of at least one hundred animals moving quickly in our direction."

Djago felt his mood improving at the news. "The Atiod-Bherto druids?"

"I believe so." Ouza nodded. "They are on schedule to arrive before dawn. But I did not sense Naamah among them."

"Then she must be dead." Djago was annoyed about losing his trusted and beautiful Succubus. How stupid must she have been to get herself killed by a bunch of sun-worshiping wildlings. At least she had come through in the end. "Send a patrol to welcome our new allies and guide them to the rear of the king's lines. I want absolute chaos at dawn from every angle when we attack."

"I will go myself, my lord, as I know their general location and I will return before dawn to stand beside you leading your armies to victory."

"Very well, commander. Get on with it." Djago waved Ouza away. The next few hours would be busy while he prepared orders for his generals.

Djago sat heavily in his padded chair again. He didn't want to be Djago anymore. He didn't want to play a part to satisfy the earth-dwellers that he was so desperate to fit in among. He wanted to be Mamon, Demon of Greed, as he was before. His physical form, once powerful and fearsome, was long ago stripped from him by the Tuatha Dé, forcing him to live within the fragile figures of others.

The demon explored the jumble of emotions that welled up inside his host's body. It was not difficult. Some were reflections of the life Djago once led. Where they came from, he did not know, others were his own. He felt a stirring in the black void of his inner-most core - anticipation. Thousands would die by his command the following day, rivers of blood would saturate the field and by this time tomorrow, his domination of Lyonesse would be nearly absolute. The thought of it finally made him smile.

CHAPTER 21

A Child's Fate

Myrllin didn't have time for this foolishness. All he had done was try to gain access to the Keep in order to speak with the count or countess. Turns out neither were at home. One was dead and the other was leading an army against Yorwick. Apparently, he had been away from Lyonesse for far too long.

"Why don't you put away those weapons and let me be," Myrllin eyed the six soldiers that surrounded him. "We surely don't want anyone getting hurt, do we?"

"He must be a spy from Yorwick!" The youngest guard chirped.

"Yeah, he wanted inside the Keep," another chimed in. "Maybe he's an assassin."

"Well, you've been warned." Myrllin sighed heavily. To his extreme annoyance, the guards ignored him.

"He looks like a street vagrant. Throw him in the dungeon, he's probably just drunk." At least the captain of this sorry crew had a sliver of sense, although it wouldn't be much help to him tonight.

A loud crack, like the splitting of hard stone, rent the air from somewhere behind the guards facing Myrllin. The startled men whirled around and desperately scanned the darkness for the source of the abrupt noise. Quickly it was followed by a succession of popping and crumbling rock that seemed to draw closer and closer in the darkness. The guards found themselves involuntarily backing away and moving closer together.

"Stand firm!" the captain ordered, holding his trembling light-globe out to try and see further down the corridor.

With all of their attention focused in the opposite direction, Myrllin gripped his heavy staff tighter, cast a quick spell that levitated his body an arm's length off the ground and waited.

Seconds later a wide crack appeared in the pavers. Two of the men jumped to the side to avoid falling into the rift while the others scattered to the edges of the hallway. When it reached the place Myrllin had been standing, it stopped and the floor around the entire area began to heave impossibly as if something were trying to escape from below.

This was the moment Myrllin had been waiting for. Expertly twirling his staff, he connected one end of it to the jaw of one of the distracted guards and then spun to thrust the butt of his weapon into the unarmored sternum of another.

The captain, stunned for a moment by Myrllin floating a span in the air, urgently barked orders at his men, "Run the bastard through!" but the violently shifting ground underneath them made it nearly impossible to stay on their feet.

Myrllin, perfectly balanced and unaffected by the shifting earth he levitated above, brought down the end of his staff on the head of the nearest guard knocking him to the ground unconscious. One guard managed to fall forward close enough to lash out with his sword narrowly missed Myrllin's right leg. Realizing his vulnerability, Myrllin struck quickly at the man's neck, causing him to fall to the floor gulping desperately for air. Twisting once more in the opposite direction, two quick steps brought him close to another guard fully unprepared to take the rapid succession of blows rained upon his head. The guard collapsed quickly leaving only the captain and Myrllin facing each other five paces apart.

Myrllin took a step in the air toward him, confident in his own stability when, without warning, the rumbling ceased. "Damn," he muttered and steeled himself for the captain's attack.

"No more tricks then, wizard?" The captain drew himself up from the crouch he was in a moment before.

Myrllin answered by causing the ends of his staff to erupt in flames. The look of stunned surprise on the captain's face was priceless. Myrllin nearly burst into unconstrained laughter at the sight of it. For his part, the captain must have recognized the mockery at his expense and his cheeks reddened with rage.

With the ground still again, the captain quickly covered the distance between the two leading with a furious assault that set Myrllin on his heels. They traded blows for what seemed like an eternity. Myrllin deftly countered every strike, feint, and slice until he found himself gaining the upper hand. The captain was a talented swordsman, but his endurance was failing, probably due to lack of regular exercise and excessive drinking. Myrllin made a mental note to bring it up with Djago the next time they met.

The captain dropped back a step, sword held forward and high, trying to catch his breath. "What manner of wizard are you to wield a staff so skillfully."

"I thought I told you already," Myrllin needed to finish this and get moving. "I am a friend of Count Djago and Lady Genestra. Perhaps I didn't mention my name, I am called Myrllin."

The captain's jaw dropped in astonishment and his sword lowered a little in suddenly lax hands. Myrllin saw the opening and planted the edge of his staff firmly against the captain's temple dropping him like a pithos of rats.

Myrllin carefully stepped over the captain's limp form. "Sorry old boy, I'll put in a good word for you." Then he hurried out, leaving the broken stone pavers and crumpled bodies far behind.

The nursery was three levels up and down a long corridor not far from Lady Genestra's suite of rooms. At least Myrllin hoped that's where they were still, it had been a few hundred years since he was last here and he didn't have time to search the entire keep for the boy.

The visions during his long sleep had been persistent and unusually vivid regarding the child, Pen Djago. Myrllin was to retrieve him on the night of the seventh full moon in the year the Sylvan called 5490 and hide him away until after the battle of The Dormonts. It was all very confusing at first, considering that there had already been a battle of The Dormonts centuries earlier, but now it was beginning to become clearer. While he and his brother, Wodanaz, had been fighting demons and trying to convince the Assembly of Nine that a real threat existed, chaos reigned in Lyonesse. Myrllin couldn't help but wonder if a demon was involved somehow in this conflict as well. There was no time to dwell on it. He had to protect a bloodline that his visions promised would change the world.

In the dim light, a stairway leading up appeared on his right. Myrllin ascended to a landing and then another as he took the steps two at a time. Nearly to the third landing, his foot slid on something slick, and he barely caught himself from tumbling down. He stooped to inspect the stairway and found a slow crimson flow from some dead thing above. Rather than announce his presence with a light-globe, Myrllin cast a spell to enhance his night-vision and carefully climbed the rest of the way up.

On the third landing, he found the source of the blood; a guard lay face down in a sticky red pool. The spear he once carried lay beside him where he dropped it and his sword was still secure in its scabbard having never been drawn. This guard was dead before he hit the ground. Myrllin rolled the guard over and his suspicions were confirmed. The man's throat was completely ripped out.

Myrllin sucked in a deep breath. Whatever had done this must be extraordinarily strong, fast, and silent. And almost certainly unnatural. He doubted any human was capable of such a perfect execution. Surveying the corridor ahead, it was almost completely devoid of light, and his night-vision found nothing to cause alarm. Still, Myrllin proceeded with caution casting protective spells on himself along the way.

There were three doors ahead of him – two on the left and one on the right. Both doors on the left shown no light escaping from the slight gap at their base while the one on the right flashed dimly from time to time as if the light source was in motion. Myrllin paused at the door and listened. The door was heavy and well-constructed within the stone frame, allowing no hint of sound to escape. This was no servants' quarters. Casting a quick enchantment to boost the acuity of his hearing, he pressed his ear to the door once more. This time he detected faint steps, the scuff of a shoe against the floor and the unmistakable cooing of a content infant.

Myrllin paused. Whoever was in there had to be the monster that murdered the guard. He reasoned that if the child still lived, which it obviously did, then the creature's objective was not to kill, but to abduct it. There was an ironic absurdity to his characterization of the thing inside, for they were both here at the same time for the exact same purpose.

Not knowing what to expect, Myrllin did what he always did. He opened the door.

Inside, an old woman in druids' robes stopped and turned, startled at his entrance. She cradled the small infant-child of Count Djago and the late Lady Genestra with the care and confidence of an experienced nursemaid. Anyone else entering the room would have thought exactly that and quickly excused themselves, feeling foolish for their error.

Not Myrllin.

He was unaffected by her illusions and could see the reality of who she was and feel the evil that resided in the void that was once her soul. Except that there was something else there, something leftover . . . . Myrllin was momentarily distracted by her exceptional physical perfection and unparalleled beauty.

"Why have you disturbed us?" she hissed angrily. "Can't you see I am trying to walk the baby to sleep?"

Myrllin was unperturbed. "I know what you are."

She turned to face him fully. "I am the druid, Naamah, personal healer to Count Djago and his son. Who are you?"

Myrllin pulled back his hood revealing long, jet-black hair and skin tanned from long hours walking outdoors. "My name is Myrllin, and I can see the truth of what you are, Succubus."

Naamah glowered at him and dropped the illusion. If it were at all possible, she appeared even more beautiful without the hazy lens of the mirage that she hid behind. Myrllin felt a distinct attraction to her that he knew would undo him if he allowed himself to be overcome by it.

"I have heard of you, wizard." She smiled sweetly, seductively. "There isn't a soulless creature of the Infernal Planes who does not crave your still-beating heart in their hand."

"It gives me a measure of joy to know that my name is so famous in more than one world." He flashed his most impertinent smile.

She took a few steps forward, swaying her curvaceous hips salaciously in her progress, then stopped a single step away from him. The fragrance she wore, a tincture of lily of the valley and jasmine, was ludicrously enthralling. Myrllin steeled his mind against her advances.

Naamah wet her lips with her delicate tongue. "Why are you here Myrllin?" Her tone had changed from forceful and demanding, to a sultry whisper.

"I am here for the child, just as you are, I presume?"

"The count wants to ensure his son's safety while he campaigns in the south. Perhaps you have not heard about the assassins?"

"I have heard." Myrllin probed her mind with his psionic abilities. He could kill her easily with a blast of fire or lightning, but there was no guarantee that the child would not be injured. It would be better if he could dominate her mind if it were possible. "Wherever you are taking him will not be to his benefit. If you have heard of me, you know of my visions. He has a much larger role to play in the history of this world. Hand him to me and I will let you live."

The Succubus pursed her lips and fluttered sad, baby-doll eyes at him replying in a high-pitched whiny, almost child-like voice, "Nobody loves me."

"Naamah, the child." Myrllin released his staff to stand on its own beside him while he held out his hands toward her. "Give him to me."

Without warning, she threw back her head and laughed a heavy, throaty laugh, which she cut off prematurely, setting her dead eyes upon him. "I can't go to Djago without securing his son safely into the hands of the Atiod-Bherto. He will kill me if I give him to you. This child is key to my survival."

Myrllin was unable to penetrate her mind. She had protections that would take more time than he had now to overcome. "Your choice is not with Djago right now, Naamah. It is with me." His voice became a low growl. "You will not leave this room alive with that child. Hand him over."

"So you would determine my fate as well?" It wasn't really a question. "Will you allow me to leave unharmed?"

"I will," Myrllin nodded.

She looked dubious. "You know I must kill again to feed and some of those might be innocents. What is it about this child that you would sacrifice so much for his survival?"

Naamah was beautiful and seductive, stirring feelings within Myrllin that he had not experienced in centuries. It had to be an effect of what she was, part of her nature, like a spider that consumed its mate after conception. He didn't know much about her demon species, but he knew enough to fear the strength of her attraction.

"I don't know exactly and even if I did why would I confide in one of your kind? My word is good. You will not be harmed if you hand me the child. I will not ask again."

Their eyes locked for an eternal moment while she tapped her forefinger on her cheek with indecision. Her perfect lips red and pouty, her soulless eyes searching his for an answer. Myrllin could not fathom what manner of scheme she might be deliberating.

"Fine, take him." Naamah abruptly shoved the sleeping infant into Myrllin's arms. "Don't forget me," she whispered as she passed, lightly trailing her long fingernails against his cheek. It felt invigorating.

"Naamah," Myrllin called to her without turning.

"Yes?"

"We should never meet again. The next time I will be compelled to kill you."

"Your feelings tell me otherwise . . .." A heartbeat later, she was gone.

~~~

"It has been decided; the Temple Knights will not take a side in this battle." Reginald's strong words matched his stern visage. "The Knight Commander has commanded all gold-cloaks to withdrawal to their camps and refrain from joining the battle in the morning."

Perault wasn't sure how he felt about that decision. One the one hand, why should the Temple Knights be dragged into what amounted to a conflict between men and not kingdoms and on the other, were they abandoning their king? "What about the Temple Knights with Count Djago?"

"They are under the authority of the Knight Commander. Of course, they will obey."

Disappointment filled Perault. He'd been looking forward to his first pitched battle. "Very well, I will gather the silver-cloaks and join you at your camp in an hour.

"Hold on." At first confusion and then understanding crept over his brother's features. "You will stay here, brother. The king has authority over the silver-cloaks until they graduate to the gold. You should know that."

Perault did know that he just assumed that the circumstances would be different in times of war. He wasn't disappointed by the segregation as much as he was envious of the exclusive nature of the Temple Knight Brotherhood that he so desperately wanted to be a part of.

Reginald embraced him briefly and then slapped him on the shoulder. "You alone carry the honor of our family on this occasion. I am proud of you, and I know our father is as well. Don't cause our mother heartbreak by going out there and getting yourself killed. She would make me suffer for it."

Perault smiled, knowing that the jest was probably true. "I promise to do my best not to put you in that position. From where will you watch the engagement?"

"From that hill yonder." He pointed to a rise about a quarter-league away and then pulled himself onto his mount. "Watch out for yourself, boy."

Perault watched his brother depart in the direction of his camp and wondered if they would ever see each other again.

~~~

Myrllin was on his fourth exhausted horse in two days. Despite the magical enhancements that allowed his mounts to travel twice the distance, twice as fast, he would be lucky to arrive at The Dormonts before the battle ended. It was a desperate situation that required desperate action. He wasn't particularly concerned about the outcome of the battle, either way his visions would come to pass. What *did* concern him was the fate of Count Djago.

After the bizarre encounter with Naamah in Cambria, Myrllin was convinced that Djago was not what he seemed to be. Notwithstanding the fact that he was able to conjure a Succubus to do his bidding, there was no other explanation for his unusual behavior and the tragic circumstances that surrounded his life over the past year. Knowing this, it was up to Myrllin to put an end to the demon permanently, but he would have to face Djago if he was going to have a chance at it.

From the time the demons began to appear, perhaps two years ago, Myrllin had been researching ways to rid the world of them for good. His father, a powerful Tuatha Dé of the Blood, managed to imprison them all with the aid of powerful allies almost fifteen hundred years ago, but they must have known it could only be a temporary solution. Now that they were free again, Myrllin was determined to destroy them, and he thought he knew how.

In the time of his father, they learned that greater demons could be sent back to the Infernal Planes if one knew their True Name. Unfortunately, the demons were never stupid enough to record their names anywhere in this world and the hosts they possessed could not be compelled to reveal it. And then, a few months before, he discovered a technique that he successfully employed on a Chaos Demon that possessed a healer called Aja. With a little modification, he thought it might work on a Greater demon as well. But he would have to be present when the demon was at its most vulnerable and that only occurred when its host died. If Djago died in battle before Myrllin arrived, then the demon would be free to find another host, and it could be decades or even centuries before he was able to catch it again.

If he didn't succeed, at least he had managed to save the boy and place him with druids in a safe location until this business at The Dormonts was done with. Assuming his visions were correct, and to his great discouragement they always seemed to be, then Pen Djago was perhaps the most important life on this planet and it was up to him to make sure it was preserved.

Seventy leagues to go, it was almost dawn and he needed a new horse. If he made it in time it would be a miracle and these days miracles were far and few between. Myrllin cast an enchantment giving the exhausted horse a burst of energy – there was a chance it would kill it, there was a chance it would run faster. He always teased his brother Wodanaz about his habitual gambling, but it seemed to Myrllin that he gambled just as much.

Except instead of gold, he gambled with lives.

CHAPTER 22

Battle of The Dormonts

Dark banners fluttered in the gentle morning breeze awaiting the first glimmer of light to bring color to their symbols. Each one represented a House or the king, held steadfast and determined in the hands of a man kneeling below it. Dawn was approaching, the light of Sunna, and only the insignificant clink of an armored plate or stomp of hoof betrayed the silent anticipation of ten thousand souls awaiting her arrival.

A quarter of a league from where they faced, another ten thousand mirrored their quiet attendance to the Sun Goddess. Except one. He cared to pay no reverence to any god or goddess that men would serve. If he had his way, he would have ordered his men to attack at that moment, taking advantage of his adversary's weakness gesticulating to a powerless goddess credited with the capacity to affect the passage of the sun across the sky. He didn't have a choice in the matter. Count Djago's army were men of Lyonesse, just like the ones they would be killing that day, and only the supposed blessing of a supreme being would grant them the license to do so.

Djago sighed. Where was Naamah? Where was Ouza? Neither had returned when expected. It was disturbing how much he depended on their council and their action, leaving him dependent upon his generals to carry out his explicit orders and uncertain about their competency to do so. Ever more challenging, he had just lost five hundred Temple Knights the night before because of some baffling principles separating their loyalty from rightful liege and goddess, represented by a Knight Commander of their Order that controlled who they would support and under which circumstances. Djago was sure he would have to kill that man at some point. The only solace he took from the whole situation was that King Praeter had lost over one thousand of his number with the Temple Knights departure. Even now, he could see them by the torches they held lining a faraway hill positioned to observe the outcome of the day's events. Five hundred of his own behind and a thousand of his foes ahead, none of which were under his control, didn't give him a very good sense of security.

"Is everything ready?" Djago peered at the older man, Sir Mainx of House Oberland, whom he had assigned as general of his armies in Ouza's absence.

"They are, my lord." He seemed competent and experienced, as far as Djago could tell, but he sensed a vein of fear that was so often misinterpreted as loyalty. "Our bowmen have been positioned forward to take advantage of their range to counter both infantry and cavalry as required."

"Beware, Sir Mainx," Count Djago met the general's eyes, "our bowmen alone will be minimally effective against their cavalry charge which you know will come against our infantry first thing."

General Mainx bowed. "Lord Ouza prepared our infantry with a special surprise to counter their greater numbers of cavalry.

"Then let them come."

~~~

Perault admired the Temple Knights lining the higher elevation behind him – a string of a thousand torches glittering off polished metal armor, gold-fringed cloaks wafting lazily in the chill morning breeze, regal war horses as still and calm as a summer dew pond – was an image he would never forget. He wanted to be there with them. Instead, he was leading a unit of cavalry from Stoddenferry, men he knew well, in a rear-guard for the king's right flank. It was a frustrating position to hold that would only see conflict if the battle became desperate for his side. Otherwise, like the Temple Knights, he would be a spectator in this epic struggle for the fate of a nation.

From his vantage on a low hill that overlooked the battlefield, Perault counted four thousand infantry arranged in ranks for the crown, flanked by four thousand cavalry and one thousand bowmen. It was a formidable force that would be met almost equally by the opposition. Still, he knew the fighting prowess and determination of a man from Lyonesse would work well in their favor, except that they faced the same from across the field. That was the rub. Men and women of Lyonesse giving their lives in battle against each other. No matter the outcome, this day would be marked among the darkest in the history of the kingdom.

The slow clop of hooves and jostling of metal and leather alerted Perault to the approach of men from behind. It was Duncan Pentager, silver-fringed cloak trailing dramatically in the wind behind him, leading a unit of a hundred cavalry toward a forward position at the front of the lines. "I see you have managed to place yourself in a safe station for the coming conflict."

Perault wanted to knock the arrogant fool from his horse. "Lead your men well, Sir Duncan, and keep solace that I am here watching over our king. His majesty may yet send me to save you."

Duncan just sneered at him and kicked his horse into a quick cantor with his men close behind. No doubt Perault would have felt much the same if he were going to be among the first to engage his countrymen across the field. No one felt good about this fight.

"Perault!"

Davin rode up in a hurry from Perault's left. In the distance behind his friend he could see the lights from the wide-open tent set up for the king to observe the battlefield and consult with his generals. It was surrounded by ranks of the royal guard both mounted and on foot flying the banners of the Gold Lyon.

"What is it, Davin? You look upset."

Davin removed his helmet, revealing his long dark locks soaked with sweat. "A patrol has discovered a small force moving down the Thayre under cover of darkness. They will land and present a threat to our rear if not stopped. The king is sending you and your men to deal with them."

A thrill of excitement shot through Perault. Finally, some action! He slammed a fist against his armored chest in salute and buckled on his helmet. "Tell the king he has nothing to fear. We will run them down."

"You must hurry, Perault. We are set to charge, and even a small number of the enemy behind our lines could prove disastrous."

Wheeling his horse around, Perault raised his metal-clad fist into the air. "To me!" he shouted and urged his horse into a gallop. The river was nearly a league due east; a fair distance that would take nearly an hour to traverse in the darkness.

Before Perault and company could cover a tenth of the distance, the first rays of the sun fell upon The Dormonts; glinting off metal armor like diamonds floating on a sea of green grass. Horns echoed across the open space from the King Eldorath's lines and answered almost immediately by those of the Cambrians. Perault glanced back to see the ranks of infantry and cavalry beginning the first steps of an advance that would end in an ocean of bloodshed.

Perault drove his heels into his mount's flanks, pushing it harder.

Horns blared a second time announcing the inevitable charge, and thousands roared, followed by blistering cracks of lightning and explosive booms of thunder. It became a constant sound like the howl of the wind in a hurricane or the crashing of waves on the beach. Not even the clamor of the hundred men on horseback behind him could drown out the cruel reverberation proclaiming the limits of the combatants' mortality.

Mortality that would be tested this day.

They rode east at a fast cantor toward the Thayre River. Although visibility was good now that the sun had fully risen and the land devoid of large tracts of trees, it was a rolling landscape where large numbers of men could easily hide unseen from a distance. Minutes passed and Perault feared they might ride right past the enemy if they weren't diligent.

Gazing intently ahead, Perault noticed movement between two copses of dense trees. A flash of metal out of place followed by something dark moving slowly across the ground. It had to be a lookout cautioning a larger force following behind. If these were the count's men, then Perault had found his quarry.

He brought his company to a stop and addressed his second-in-command, a silver-cloak he knew as Sir Maldwyn, "I spotted movement on that ridge between the trees to the east. When we charge, take half the men to the left, I will go over the top with the rest. Be ready."

"Yes, my lord." Sir Maldwyn saluted, then rode off, conveying the orders to the rest of the men.

When he returned, Perault resumed the advance at a trot knowing that if the enemy was on the other side of the ridge, then they knew Perault and his men were coming and would surely be ready with an ambush. He spied no further activity anywhere along the ridge and except for the low roar of battle in the distance behind him and the pounding of their own horses' hooves, it was quiet.

"Make ready!" Perault called to his men. They responded by setting their shields and unsheathing swords from sheaths. He picked up the pace, slowly building to a gallop as they neared the base of the ridge.

"Now!" he shouted and Sir Maldwyn immediately broke to the left with fifty men in tow.

Perault charged up the slope. It wasn't too high; he could already see the tops of trees in the near distance beyond. His men no longer trailed behind him; rather, they moved forward to fan out to either side. Once they crested the ridge, they would charge together down the other side in a wedge formation wherever the enemy was formed up.

At least that was the plan.

The war steeds that carried the mix of silver-cloaks and professional cavalry barely lost a step charging up the incline. They were strong, with unmatched endurance bred for this work over centuries, even with the extra weight of armor. Still, their flanks expanded with each heavy breath, puffing hard to reach the summit where their labor would be rewarded in the descent that followed. These beasts were trained for war and craved the deadly application of their natural weapons – tooth and hoof – as much as their masters with sword and ax.

What lay on the other side of the ridge was exactly what Perault expected; a formation of at least one hundred infantry with shields locked and swords drawn, ready to face the headlong charge.

Perault smiled to himself. *This was going to be easy.* He led his men down the other side of the mild slope, gathering speed with each plot of soil rent from the earth beneath their horses' hooves.

Only a few strides away Perault could see the wide, fearful eyes of the infantrymen through the eye sockets of their helmets and it felt satisfying. They should be afraid, he thought, few of them would see another sunrise. He braced for impact, tightening the grip on his sword, anticipating the crunch of metal armor under the hooves of his warhorse and the crack of his Dvergr steel blade on one of those helms.

And then the sun was eclipsed by a cloud of arrows from out of nowhere.

~~~

"They are advancing, my lord."

"I can see that, General. Signal our forces to advance at half-step."

"Yes, my lord." General Mainx saluted and rushed away to carry out his orders. Moments later, the cry of horns across his battle line signaled his men to move forward.

Still more than a little vexed that both Naamah and Ouza were either dead or had abandoned him, Djago was left alone with generals he barely knew to carry his forces to victory. So far, he wasn't overly inspired by their aptitude. If things took a turn for the worse, he would take direct command of the army himself.

A messenger ran over and bowed deeply before speaking. "My lord, the advance company on the Thayre departed during the night and should have already made landfall."

"Any news from our forces concealed in the forest in the north?"

"None so far, my lord." The young boy's eyes were steady and confident. "It is possible the messengers you sent were unable to locate them in the night."

"What is your name, boy?"

"I am called Tomos."

"Go yourself then, Tomos, and report to me no matter where I am on the field when you return."

"Yes, my lord. I will not fail you." The boy ran off nearly at a sprint.

Djago looked over his advancing lines. It would not be long before blood turned the tall green grass his forces trampled into crimson mud.

"They will be at the stone soon." General Mainx was beside him again.

Djago nodded. "Everything is as Commander Ouza instructed?"

"Yes, my lord. All is prepared."

The line of the count's infantry advanced to a stone monolith standing in the middle of the field and stopped. The monolith supposedly marked the spot where Lord Dormont fell in battle nearly three hundred and fifty years before during the first civil war in Lyonesse. Commander Ouza must have chosen that particular spot out of some morbid appreciation of history.

Djago smiled when the king's cavalry broke from the flanks of their army and charged toward his seemingly vulnerable infantry position with the Cambrian cavalry too far out to effectively counter. "They have taken the bait."

Four thousand heavy cavalry stampeded toward Djago's five thousand infantry. Under conventional circumstances, the infantry would be slaughtered and the battle lost in a single charge. Djago was anything but conventional.

"Almost there . . ." General Mainx uttered as he watched the cavalry draw closer.

Djago swore to himself that if his plan failed, he would kill the general where he stood.

"Almost there . . ."

The cavalry was bearing down on the infantry at full speed, in heavy armor, the banner of the Golden Lyon leading the way.

"Now!" General Mainx whispered to himself, but Djago heard him.

As if on cue, the front five ranks of infantry picked up long spears previously hidden in the long grass at the position of the lone monolith and set their butts into the ground against the charging cavalry presenting a bristling, deadly barrier.

The front lines of the cavalry attempted to turn or stop in the last second, but they were too close and too late and those that could stop in time were pushed into the deathtrap to flail upon their sharp ends. The entire charge broke upon the spear wall like a wave slamming against the base of a cliff and when it was over, nearly a third of their number lay broken and dying on the line under the shadow of the fateful monolith. Those that survived turned to retreat and regroup.

Djago cackled wildly at the spectacle. "Send our cavalry to finish them!" he shouted.

General Mainx pointed to the field. "See, my lord? They are already in motion."

It was true, Djago's cavalry had begun their charge as soon as the infantry lifted their spears and were nearly upon what remained of the King Praeter's mounted troops. Before they could arrive to support the infantry, lightning crackled across the battlefield and huge balls of fire boomed into existence against Djago's infantry leaving burning and smoking holes where men had stood a moment before. Countering the strike, magical shields blocked most of the second wave of magical energy hurled against them and Djago's wizards mounted a strike of their own against the king's infantry still advancing across the plain at a steady pace.

A balance ensued for a time where no magical attacks gained advantage over the other, leaving the gallantry of men to fail or prevail across the chaos of the battlefield. Djago watched as his cavalry engaged their counterparts, desperately attempting to re-form. The clouds of arrows sailed over the center of the field in both directions thinning the ranks of opposing infantry, and the magical storm of fire and electricity raged above them all.

It was time to tilt the balance in his favor.

Without averting his gaze from the details of the battle that played out before him, Djago issued the order that he believed would bring the conflict to a decisive end, "Send in the Giants."

~~~

Two hundred combined Fir Bholg and Cyclopes entered the field of battle. They towered over the chaos of infantry and cavalry that no longer formed clear lines of battle. Pockets of men attacked or defended one side or the other and the magical assaults no longer attempted to target groups and masses. It was impossible to tell which side held the advantage.

Until the Giants arrived.

Wading into the mass of men, the Giants quickly overcame the staunch defenses of the king's army wherever they stood their ground. Like the divine hand of Sunna, the Giants led a slow charge from the east edge of the conflict pushing west and laying waste to any fool enough to stand in their way. Breaking the bones of men and beasts, striking terror into their souls and sending them fleeing to their faltering line was only the start of it. The Giants were nearly indiscriminate in their rage and lust to kill, even those who cheered them on frequently found themselves victims of the Giants rampage across the battlefield.

Djago laughed with pure joy at the plight of his rival. The king's army would be in full rout once the Giants began to press south; he was sure of it. But he wasn't about to take a chance.

"General Mainx, send in the balance of the reserve. It is time to overrun their position. And I want you to lead them. Tell the men it will be ten thousand gold to anyone who brings me the head of King Praeter Eldorath!"

"Yes, my lord." The general departed without enthusiasm, leaving Djago with the impression that his orders might not be exactly followed.

His sour mood was quickly eliminated by the sight of the Fir Bholg plucking Eldorath's men from their mounts and tearing their bodies into pieces. Sometimes they would throw them away like broken parts of a rag doll and other times they would stuff the disjointed bits into their mouths and consume them raw. It was a horrifyingly beautiful perfection of creatures led by primitive emotion. Djago admired their innocent cruelty and considered that when he returned to Yorwick he might just crush Cug's head and take control of the Fir Bholg and Cyclopes tribes as his own.

The Eldorath's forces brought forward their reserves. Djago stood unperturbed.

It was their last bastion of hope composed of infantry in formations that absorbed the renegades that fled the earlier ranks in fear. They were an impressive group to be sure, holding off even the Fir Bholg advances at least for a while, but Djago was confident it was a defense they wouldn't be able to sustain for long. The battle was won, the Giants and his own reserves would make sure of it and soon the forces he sent to flank from the river and the forest would fall upon the enemy leaving no doubt as to the outcome.

He drew his sword and marched determinedly toward the bulge in the line created by the Fir Bholg. Djago would not be left to watch from the sidelines. It was time for him to draw blood

CHAPTER 23

Fog of War

Perault felt a harsh impact that penetrated deep into his thigh. He knew he was hit, but there was no pain. Glancing down he was disappointed to see the long shaft of an arrow protruding from his leg through armor that should have deflected the projectile. More horrifying was what was happening to his men. All along the right side of his line horses screamed and fell, tossing their rider to injury or death while some men were shot dead in their saddles leaving their war steeds to continue the charge alone. The arrows fell like rain, indiscriminately, gaining no pleasure or satisfaction in what they struck.

Then Perault understood the ugly truth to their effectiveness. Bowmen, hidden behind nearby trees fired their deadly projectiles at point-blank range rendering the cavalry's armor nearly useless. Perault was too close to divert the charge or assess his losses. He had no choice but to complete the action he began with whatever men remained with him.

Seconds later Perault crashed through the line of infantry trampling men four ranks deep, leaving a trail of crumpled bodies and twisted metal. They tried to strike at him, but they were ill-prepared to fight cavalry with barely a spear between them. The Cambrians blows with sword and ax were half-hearted at best as the bulk of their attention was focused on avoiding the crush of the massive war steeds' sharp hooves.

Perault's first pass easily broke through to the other side. Immediately after he and his men were clear of the infantry, more arrows descended upon them, some finding their mark, others planting themselves harmlessly in the black soil. Rather than give the bastards another shot at them, Perault turned his mount sharply and led his men toward the infantry. They would lose the advantage of speed, but at least they would be safe from the arrows. Clamoring to have his men to keep up with him, Perault was surprised at how many of them had been lost to the ambush. Barely half of their number remained to fight. It would have to be enough until Sir Maldwyn joined them.

The next pass through the infantry stalled before they could break through and they found themselves fighting in a free-for-all from their saddles. Perault kept his warhorse moving as fast as it could wade through the press of infantry. If he stopped, even for a second, they would drag him down. It was the same for the men that followed him. They were a well-trained, stout Stoddenferry breed that somehow managed to stay in some semblance of formation around him. Shield low and swords high, they protected the man next to them as well as if they were forming a shield wall on the ground. It was the correct strategy, but it wouldn't last long before the Cambrians flooded in behind and ripped them from their saddles.

A flash of movement beyond the crush of men drew Perault's attention. It was Sir Maldwyn racing past the melee with a cluster of silver-cloaks bound for the tree-line where the bowmen were hiding. The rest of his men crashed into the rear of the infantry scattering them away from the knot they were forming around Perault and his remaining men.

They were just in time.

It didn't take another pass by the cavalry before the Cambrian infantry buckled altogether losing what endured of their formation. Yet, they still fought on valiantly until their commander finally called for withdrawal. These were solid men of Lyonesse who barely knew the meaning of retreat and against any other foe would likely have fought to the death. Perault suspected that the fire to continue the fight was gone from their adversaries and ordered his men not to pursue.

Sir Maldwyn rode up a moment later followed by two of his men. "The bowmen have scattered into the forest, my lord, after we killed the first few of them. They won't be a threat again."

"Good." Perault looked around the field at the dead and dying. "Tend to the injured. All of them, Maldwyn, not just our own, and send out patrols to ensure there are no more Cambrians within a league."

Sir Maldwyn turned to convey the orders to his men while Perault dismounted, nearly falling to the ground in pain when he put weight on his right leg. The shaft of the arrow had snapped off during combat and Perault did not realize the extent of his injury until now.

Sir Maldwyn quickly dismounted and rushed to help Perault to a sitting position. "Are you injured, my lord?"

"One of those damned bowmen got me in the leg on our first charge. I'll be fine. I just need clean linen from my saddlebag if you would." With his adrenaline fading, Perault began to feel the throb of pain course down his leg.

Carefully, he unstrapped the metal greave and inspected his injury. He was relieved to find that it was shallower than expected and he was able to use his dagger to cut out the tip of the arrow. Fortunately, it was not a traditional barbed arrowhead--that would have caused him to dig a hole the size of his fist. Maybe the Cambrians weren't as cruel as he imagined, he mused while gently wrapping his thigh in the linen Sir Maldwyn retrieved for him. It would require stitches later, but that would have to wait. Right now, he had to help tend to his men.

"Help me up, please." Perault extended his hand toward Sir Maldwyn, who slowly pulled him to his feet.

"Can you walk?"

Perault put a little pressure on his right leg and then took a few steps. "I'll be fine as long as . . ." The blast of a horn sounded far in the distance where the main battle continued to rage interrupted him. The pattern was distinct and not like the others that sounded before. Its call was answered by the same unusual sound from further away.

Perault looked at Sir Maldwyn who stared at him with a look of surprise on his face. "Those were the battle horns of the Temple Knights. The Knight Commander has ordered a charge."

~~~

Myrllin heard the distant horns that announced the beginning of the second battle of The Dormonts and it brought back memories from a time that he would have sooner forgotten. Nearly everyone alive today knew the story of The Dormonts from popularized writings of House Monmouth and their allies that prevailed in the battle. It was said the victors determined what history recorded and it was no different in this case. Myrllin experienced a very different truth and it was a source of shame that he would never forgive himself for. He felt it acutely even now, almost three hundred and fifty years later. He knew it intimately because he'd been there.

Determination fueled him now. This time it would be different, and the proper line of succession would be established. No matter the cost, no matter the lives that would suffer in its wake. His visions assured him of it and he knew that once revealed, they could not be undone.

The path he followed was trampled with the stampede of animals the like of which he had never seen before. He guessed that they had to be the druids, moving in a hurry, toward the battle ahead. Myrllin hoped that they were the children of Sunna although he knew they could have just as easily be the Atiod-Bherto rushing to reinforce Count Djago. Whichever they were, it would be best for him to avoid them. The druids, regardless of the deity they served, rarely looked kindly upon his breeding. They regarded him—and his brother—as nothing Tuatha Dé, which admittedly a large part of them was. But they were both more, much more and the druids sensed that too.

And for reasons he knew well, it made them very afraid.

Myrllin didn't have time for a stroll down memory lane, he had to get to The Dormonts before Count Djago managed to get himself killed. He would have only one chance at the demon, but only if he was near when, and if, the count died. The odds were long of any of that happening, either way, and he still had a distance to go yet.

He urged his mount forward as fast as he dared. The forest was thick around him and one miss-step along the rugged path and he would end up with a lame horse and his own two feet for transportation. Images played through his mind of the exploding trees and cry of dying men that had played itself out here once before. They were so real and vivid in his memories that he could see them as if they were truly there, all around him, impaled in trees or sunken into the earth by tangles of roots that only left an errant foot or hand visible above the surface.

Myrllin shook his head to clear his vision. What he was seeing was real, not a centuries-old image conjured by his hyperactive imagination. Everywhere he looked, there were bodies overtaken by the environment as if they were ancient structures reclaimed by nature. Except that these men were only an hour or so dead. So mangled and disfigured their appearance, Myrllin could not make out from which side they hailed.

Except for one.

This one lay on the ground. He was not suspended in the trees nor sucked into the ground. There were no apparent injuries, other than the unnatural twist of his neck that indicated some force of strength had ended his tyranny. To that, there was no question, on both accounts. Myrllin knew enough from his study of demons to know that this one only showed its true form in death and considering the creatures current misfortune, it was most certainly dead.

When Myrllin met Naamah, he could easily see through her illusion as a Succubus, a minor demon conjured by a Greater demon from the Infernal Planes. Now, with no ability to see through illusions required, lay her male counterpart, an Incubus if Myrllin remembered correctly, with leathery wings like a bat, a tail that was long and obscene, claws such as seen only on an eagle and a maw full of sharp, jagged teeth that had likely ripped the life from uncalculatable numbers of humans. It was how they survived in this world; the life-force of others absorbed into their own.

The creature wore the uniform of the top-ranking Cambrian military commander. It was another confirmation that Count Djago was merely a host for a demon spreading chaos and strife. Myrllin wondered how many more of Djago's demonic minions he would eventually have to track down.

Furtive movement nearby sent Myrllin spinning around with a lightning spell set to release on the tip of his tongue. The forest around him was still. Then the sound came again, and this time Myrllin observed faint movement from a body steps away. He approached it cautiously and found himself taken aback by its severe condition. A root, easily as thick around as Myrllin's arm and three times as long, impaled the body through its stomach and out the back. Blood covered the uniform to such an extent that only the barest hint of color at the collar was left to reveal that it was another soldier of Cambria.

Myrllin knelt close over the body. No, not a soldier, nor man, nor demonic creature. Just a boy, probably a messenger. As if the child could somehow sense Myrllin's presence, his eyelids fluttered open weakly exposing clear blue orbs that focused on him intently.

"Are . . . are you a friend?" he whispered hoarsely.

Myrllin leaned closer and cradled the boy's head between his hands. His soft brown locks had not lost their innocence to the coarseness of a man's. "I am a friend."

"Tell Count Djago I have failed. Ask him to forgive me."

Myrllin nodded. "What is your name, boy?"

"Tomos."

Blood no longer flowed from Tomos's wounds, there was precious little left to give and Myrllin silently lamented that he could do nothing to save him. "I will carry your message to the count, Tomos. You have my word."

A slight smile appeared at the edges of Tomos's delicate lips. He would soon be at peace. With a swift twist and a snap, Myrllin ended the child's suffering, then lay his head gently on the ground and closed his eyes with his fingertips. War was a cruel past-time brought about by those in power with no care or understanding of its true consequences.

Myrllin stood and returned to where his mount stood quietly waiting for him. Pausing for a moment, he regretted that he didn't have the time to bury Tomos. He deserved more than being left in the forest to be ripped to pieces by scavengers. If he survived this day he promised himself to return and properly inter Tomos's remains.

Myrllin spurred his horse away from the tragic scene with haste. He felt seething anger rising within him at what he just experienced. He knew the druids were to blame. It may have been the druids of Sunna or the Atiod-Bherto, and the way he felt in that moment it hardly mattered. If either group were encountered before he arrived at The Dormonts, he might just kill them all.

~~~

Djago swung his heavy two-handed broad sword in powerful arcs like the hand of death harvesting a field of grain with a scythe. The bloodlust was upon him, unstoppable in his advance and invulnerable to the heroics of the humans brave enough to stand against him. He was the point of the spear, followed by the ferocity of the Fir Bholg and Cyclopes, that cut through the ranks of the king's men like they were so many rag dolls.

First, Eldorath's reserve cavalry was sent against them. It was a pleasure rending man from horse, cutting their bodies in half and watching as the Giants tried to consume them like unshelled nuts in their armor. Djago laughed with glee at the sight of it. At least a hundred cavalry died in their first charge with barely a casualty to their own. Not that he cared if a Giant died, he was just enjoying the hell out of the slaughter and the Giants made it so much more interesting.

Next came their infantry. If nothing else, they were precise and disciplined. More than a few Giants died to their spears, especially the Cyclopes who were intentionally blinded before they were overcome. Djago was impressed by the Eldorath's improvised strategy. The first wave killed a quarter of their number, still, one hundred Fir Bholg were a considerable force and Djago led the survivors north toward the forest where he expected the Atiod-Bherto to reinforce him at any moment.

Already the ground was slick with the blood of men and the going was slow with the renewed efforts of the king's footmen. Djago was frustrated at the slow pace, but they were still advancing north. The rest of his army, led by ineffectual generals, were hopefully pressing the enemy west. Not a single messenger survived of the twenty who'd trailed him into battle alongside the Fir Bholg. Maybe some had been eaten by the frenzied Giants or died like cowards to an enemy's blade. Whatever the case, Djago was frustrated that communication was cut off from the rest of his army. His intuition told him he should have been more careful.

The boom and crackle of magic echoed farther away than he expected from the distant south and Djago sensed that he and the Giants had outpaced the battle wizards. The fifteen or so that fought for him were tasked with countering the wizards supporting the king.

Considering that the Giants were minimally affected by magic, the king had likely reprioritized his wizards' targets.

Djago paused to assess his immediate situation. The Fir Bholg had effectively pushed deep into the enemy infantry creating a massive bulge in their line that threatened to split the king's northern force from the main. If that happened, the battle would be all but won after he swung around and attacked from the rear. All he needed was the appearance of the Atiod-Bherto from the nearby forest to give them the final push they needed to break through the line.

He twisted in his saddle to ascertain the position of his infantry. To his right and left they pushed forward slightly behind the Giants. After they had witnessed a few of their own torn apart by their supposed allies, not a single man left the formation in their eagerness to fight beside the deadly creatures. Djago wasn't about to get upset over it. The Fir Bholg were barbarians for him to use as just another tool among so many others.

A horn blew from behind him and to the south. It was a tangle of a half-dozen mounted men making their way toward him through the press of bodies. None of them wore armor and few carried only a sword at their side for protection; messengers from the look of them.

"My lord!" one shouted. "We lost track of you in your fast advance!"

Djago wondered if he wouldn't do better with a flock of pigeons. "What news do you have?"

"The generals report that we are advancing at all points along the line . . ."

"Arrows!" someone shouted.

Djago lifted his shield from where it hung on the rear of his horse and raised it high enough to protect his back and head. "Continue," he urged the messenger.

Arrows pelted Djago's shield like heavy shards of hail and sprinkled the ground around him. One found its mark in the chest of the messenger that was about to speak, leaving his report unfinished for eternity.

Djago looked on impassively. "Can one of you tell me the rest?"

"Yes, my lord." A thin young man stepped forward. He had a wild look in his eyes like he might bolt off at any moment and continually glanced at the sky as if expecting more arrows to fall at any moment. It was very likely they would.

"The king has apparently committed so many of his men against you and those . . .Giants," he shuddered when he glanced over at them, "that it has cost him ground along his entire line."

"Where is my cavalry?"

"Harassing the southern flank of the enemy, my lord." He picked up a shield that lay next to a fallen infantryman. The other messengers, clearing thinking it was a good idea, quickly followed his lead.

Djago nodded with approval. "Take word to the generals to push harder." He glanced behind and noted with satisfaction that the bulge had moved further away from him in the time he had been standing there. "Once the Atiod-Bherto join us, we will advance and the day will be ours!" Not waiting for a response, he swung his mount around to rejoin the fray.

There was something intriguing about the carnage that surrounded him. Something intoxicating that he could never explain to a human. Death and dying were in evidence all around him, blood and bile covered the bodies of fallen heroes stretching like crimson honey beneath the hooves of his horse where he crossed over it and the tang that coated his nostrils and tongue tasted sweeter by far than any fruit he ever tasted. A fatal end had found these poor soles in a variety of methods that fascinated him. Djago enjoyed studying the aftermath of killing nearly as much as the act of it. He paused to relish in the collage of death around him. The Fir Bholg, for all that they lacked in organization and discipline, were very efficient executioners on the battlefield. Certainly, they cleaved their victims with massive axes and clubs like any human might, but a Giant could just as well tear a human into pieces with his bare hands. And the most beautifully grotesque part of that was the not-so-unusual practice of consuming the tenderest pieces of their victims raw without skipping a step.

Djago smiled wickedly at the various limbs gnawed to the bone and hollow torsos absent of their innards. Mamon, the demon inside of him, was no stranger to the taste of human flesh and he yearned to familiarize himself with its flavor once again, but it was not the time or place. No need to horrify his men. There would be an opportunity for that kind of feast later.

Moving along the line of Fir Bholg fighting ahead of him, he noticed a gap opening between the Giants and his infantry to their left. It was a deliberate action as they moved in perfect formation at the command of their senior officer. Djago was infuriated. The fool was obviously afraid of losing a few of his precious men to errant blows from their Giant allies, not realizing the larger danger of opening a hole in the line for the enemy to exploit. He spurred his horse forward intent on killing their commander and taking control of the unit himself.

It was too late.

Easily two hundred of King Praeter's soldiers poured through the opening. More would follow once their commanders realized what had happened. Djago was incensed and was about to order the Fir Bholg to break off their advance to defend the gap when a long shadow caught his attention. He snapped his gaze upward and watched a flight of hundreds of arrows descending on the men charging through the breach. Behind it soared a second wave and then a third. When the sun shone unimpeded again, their adversaries progress had stalled, and Djago's infantry fought the depleted forces in perfect formation back to their original position, plugging the opening once more.

Brilliant. That commander would be a general when this battle was won.

"Yeah!" Djago rode near their line and raised his fist in the air, pumping it over and over several times urging his men on. They responded with cheers and the clapping of spears against their shields.

It was nearly over. The Fir Bholg were expanding the bulge in the enemy's line to the point of breaking, his infantry was progressing at every point with the support of his bowmen and cavalry, and at any moment the soldiers he sent down the Thayre would be causing chaos behind their lines in the south. At this rate, he might not need the damn Atiod-Bherto, Djago laughed to himself.

Spinning his horse around, he raced north to join the right flank where the Fir Bholg were at their weakest. A formation of his infantry pushed the line between the Giants and the tree-line with a hundred or so bowmen following close behind. He glanced at a rise about a quarter-league behind him and snarled. Five hundred Temple Knights sat passively watching the battle from atop their mounts. They should have been beside him. They would have been the decisive factor on his northern flank, crushing the king's poorly defended position and freeing the Fir Bholg to break around and overrun their infantry.

Djago would not forget the Temple Knights treachery. They were Cambrians. How could they claim neutrality? When the Master of the Temple in Cambria informed him of the Knight Commander's decision to stay out of the fight, Djago almost killed him on the spot. Had he done so, his own citizens might have risen up against him and his cause would have been lost. It was a miracle that he was able to control his rage. These people were so sensitive about the temple and their whore of a goddess. He would enjoy dismantling every brick of their beliefs and corrupting their precious Temple Knights before he was done.

He tore his gaze away from the ridge and toward the battle. The noise of it – the cries and screams, the clash of steel and metal, the roar of a Giant and the distance crackle of magic – was a deafening cacophony that played like sweet music in his ears. The last time he commanded a battle was also the day he was imprisoned by the Tuatha Dé. Instead of human soldiers, his infantry was a horde of mindless demons willing to die at his command. That was almost fifteen hundred years ago. He wielded such power back then, power that had been ripped from him and the others of his kind and never restored. He wanted that power again. Maybe it would return, maybe not. Being cut off from the Infernal Planes for so long had taken its toll and even returning there might not bring it back. Djago shuddered at the thought. He would never return to that place! He would rather live through the fragile bodies of these humans than go back to being the slave of an arch-demon for eternity.

He gripped the reins of his horse and prepared to thrust himself into the fray, driving his men forward. And paused. A flicker of movement on his periphery caught his attention, something was happening at the edge of the forest where the trees began to thin. A broad smile stretched across his face.

Forms emerged slowly from the dark background of the forest. Scores of painted faces under hooded robes adorned with decorative feathers, shells and beads flickered into shape from all manner of beasts, while others maintained their animal form. Humans, deer, owls, and eagles stared back at him with emotionless expressions ignoring the obvious carnage that should have captured the attention of any natural being. There was no question they were druids. The Atiod-Bherto had finally arrived.

A rush of adrenaline coursed through Djago's body, filling him with excitement. This was it. He was about to play the final pawn in his battle plans, the move that would bring his enemies to their knees. Using his psionic ability, he sent instructions to the druids. He knew many of them had a similar ability of their own that would allow him to direct their assault.

There was no response.

He sent his mind out to them again, this time probing like invisible tendrils to find one who could communicate with him. To his surprise, he was blocked by everyone that he found.

A low rumble shook the ground beneath his horses' hooves and vibrated all the way up to where he sat uncertainly in his saddle. Something was wrong. The rumbling grew in intensity causing stones to jump and jiggle and soldiers to lose their footing. Even the Fir Bholg stopped their advance and struggled to remain steady.

Djago fought to keep his horse under control, finding it increasingly difficult to stay mounted. He spared a glance toward the druids. The earth was not moving under them. Many stood chanting with their arms extended forward and parallel to the ground. For the first time, Djago noticed that more than a few bore the iconic gold medallion in the shape of a sun.

The symbol of Sunna.

The distraction proved costly as Djago lost his grip and was thrown from his saddle landing hard in the blood-saturated mud.

Doing his best to regain his footing, he called to his bowmen, "Target the druids yonder!"

It was a hopeless command. The bowmen were sprawled on the ground unable to stand, let alone launch an arrow with any semblance of accuracy. The situation was no less dire with his infantry. Everywhere he looked, only the ground under his men moved violently leaving a discernable line between chaos and calm with the king's soldiers on the other side. The only thing that prevented a slaughter was that his enemy dared not step over the invisible line and get caught up in the vicious earthquake. Even the Giants barely managed to stay on their feet and when they took a step forward, the shifting earth somehow traveled with them.

Djago felt hopeless. How could this be happening? Where were the Atiod-Bherto? Where was that bitch Naamah?

A fierce bellow of rage and anger drew his attention back to the Fir Bholg. With an explosion of earth, thick, snake-like vines sprouted out of the ground beneath the Giants climbing up their legs and entangling their arms where they stood. As strong as the Giants were, the sheer mass of vines was stronger, inhibiting the Giants movement, pressing their limbs tight against their torso.

Djago stared enraged as the bellows of fury altered to screams of agony.

Not missing the opportunity to strike at the immobile Giants, the King Praeter's men thrust at them with long spears that punctured the soft places between the tattered armor they wore, their eyes and their necks. Soon the vines were dripping in crimson, and one by one the desperate flailing of the massive forms ceased.

Thinking the worst was over, Djago was surprised when the earth unexpectedly heaved upward accompanied by a resounding *crack* that rent the air around him. A fracture ran through the ground under his infantry and bowmen still striving to escape to safety. The appearance of an expanding fissure caused panic, more so when it began to separate into a widening gap that consumed hundreds in its wake. Men crawled and stumbled to escape in every direction. Many made it to stable ground only to be run through by the king's soldiers, while others ran toward the forest where webs of lightning cooked them alive inside their armor.

It all happened in a matter of a few short minutes, and then the rifts in the earth closed entombing men forever when the rumbling finally ceased. Djago bounced to his feet and surveyed his surroundings. The din of battle still raged to the south, but around him, it was eerily quiet. Whatever infantry and bowmen of his northern flank that survived were scattered and disorganized. The Fir Bholg still hung like massive bloody cocoons in a tangled forest with very few still showing signs of life. Smoke from lightning obscured the druids, but Djago knew they would be coming.

There would be no salvaging his gains in the north.

Djago released a wild scream into the still air. He had been minutes away from victory! What happened to his men in the forest? Why had they not warned him? There could only be one answer – they were all dead. Just as he knew both Naamah and Ouza must be if the druids of Sunna were here. Djago quickly pulled himself together. There was no time to rage over their failures now, he had to regroup.

Taking advantage of the brief pause in the battle. Djago ran to the nearest horse standing about a hundred paces away. He would join his infantry that formed the southern flank of the Fir Bholg bulge and retreat with them to his larger forces further south. If he could rally his army into a defensive position and put his wizards to the task of countering the druids there might still be hope. He would also need reinforcements from the Fir Bholg sieging Yorwick, every Giant they could spare, and they would have to hurry.

His mind was spinning with strategic options, calculating the chances of success of one over another and assessing the remaining strength of his forces when a strange horn sounded far to the south. Djago's memories revealed to the demon inside of him that it was the unique blare of the Temple Knights. Seconds later the sound was echoed by the five hundred Temple Knights on the ridge behind him. They had finally determined where their allegiances lay and were preparing to charge.

CHAPTER 24

Challenge

A lone eagle coasted high above the green plains that surrounded the besieged city of Yorwick. Even from this distance, the bird looked larger than a typical eagle, and Cug might have considered shooting it down if it wasn't so high. Instead, he watched it fly over the city and begin a spiral descent as if it too had considered the possibility of having to avoid an arrow. Soon it disappeared somewhere behind Yorwick's high wall. Cug shrugged, it was probably just after the rats that must be abundant in a city of that size. He knew that humans often used birds to carry messages from one place to another, but it was done with pigeons, not eagles, as far as he knew.

He shook his head to clear the fog. This damn siege was causing him to daydream like some waste-about lout. He had better things to do at his home in Fomoire than watch the grass grow and eagles fly around a human city that he didn't give one piss about. Cug was sure the three hundred or so Fir Bholg and Cyclopes camped around Yorwick probably felt the same way.

"Aengus," he glanced over at his friend and second-in-command. "Do you have confirmation that the battle has begun?"

"Not yet. Maybe this afternoon."

"We should leave then, before any more humans die." Cug ordered his people to steer clear of any humans they encountered from the first day they marched into Lyonesse. It wasn't that he cared a whiff for the life of a human, he enjoyed eating them as much as the next Giant. They didn't need to give the druids, or the Tuatha Dé, a reason to punish them more than that idiot Kumida had already. Unfortunately, isolated farmsteads and foraging parties from Yorwick had become incidental victims that Cug could not control. Just to keep busy and to put on a show for the soldiers Djago left behind, he had his warriors building siege equipment that he and Aengus alone knew they were never going to use.

"I advise that we wait for confirmation that the battle has ended, my king." Thrakel, his Elder shaman, had a thin, shrill voice that cut through the air like a rusted knife. "If he is victorious, he will become master of all of Lyonesse and a very powerful enemy if he finds out we deserted before the battle ended."

"And if he is not victorious?"

Thrakel cackled at something only she found humorous. "Then we leave, and nothing changes."

"Very well. Although I fear the longer we stay here, the more our people are at risk for another man's benefit.

The call of horns echoed through the city and figures appeared on the thick wall where the main dual portcullis was located. At first, there were only a few which quickly resolved into hundreds as the insistent blare of the horns continued.

"Something is happening," Aengus sharp eyes could resolve details at a distance despite his advanced age. "Those men on the wall are bowmen."

Cug squinted through the distance; his eyesight was not what it used to be. "Is it a distraction to draw us away from the east side of the city?"

Aengus scratched at his long gray beard. "It's hard to tell."

"I'll bet that eagle knows," Thrakel cackled.

"Gather our men," Cug placed his hand on Aengus's shoulder and squeezed hard, "but leave a reliable force to watch the east gate."

Aengus nodded and set off at a lumbering run. Moments later, the blast of a mountain ram's horn sounded along the perimeter of the siege drawing groups of Giants to Cug like wolves to the scent of blood. They didn't know why they came, all they knew was that there might be blood to spill and fresh meat to eat and for hungry bellies the size of a mammoth, that was inspiration enough.

Cug was sure something more was going on than a show of force to intimidate them. Humans were clever creatures and as far as he knew, rarely suicidal. "Thrakel, check the surroundings. I need to be sure there is not another army approaching from behind."

"Yes, my king." The shape of her body wavered and then reformed into that of a large raven. She took off straight into the air and within seconds was out of sight in the morning haze.

Cug doubted the Tuatha Dé were conspiring with the humans. The Tuatha Dé would never have allowed the humans to announce their arrival with the fanfare of horns and the clamor of soldiers on walls. They would have simply arrived and attacked. He had witnessed their methods firsthand when his father, the king before him, decided to build a settlement south of the Arges River. Cug was a young boy then, yet he remembered with a chill to this day the terrible magic the Tuatha Dé employed to destroy the settlement and send them running across the border into Fomoire. He shook his head at the memories, now it was he standing in Lyonesse acting as big a fool as his father had been.

Fir Bholg and Cyclopes streamed around him forming into loose ranks with the smaller Giants up front. Aengus returned a little while later with over one hundred Giants from the far side of the city.

"Twenty Fir Bholg and thirty Cyclopes remain to guard the east gate. There was hardly a hair of movement on the walls when I was there, but that doesn't mean anything." Aengus reported.

Cug nodded his approval. "I've sent Thrakel to make sure we are safe from any surprises at our backs, she may not return for a while."

Aengus grunted sourly. "Then we wait and see what these little pissers do next."

They didn't have to wait long. A series of horns inside Yorwick's walls blasted a second time and to Cug's astonishment, the portcullis rose to allow a column of lancers, five abreast, to exit the city. The morning sun reflected off their metal armor and helmets in blinding flashes while they moved into formation with long yellow streamers waving in the gentle breeze at the tips of their lances. Cug secretly admired how impressive they looked in comparison to his rabble of warriors in mismatched leather and metal armor, damp furs and wild hair.

"They are arranging themselves to charge us." Aengus sounded incredulous.

Cug shared his view. Maybe the humans were suicidal after all. Even with more than double their number, the Giants would decimate any cavalry charge head-on. "Make sure we have shields upfront and spears behind."

"Already done."

A charge against a shield wall backed by Giants would be as effective as charging the wall that surrounded Yorwick. It didn't make sense. The humans must know that. Cug smiled. "They must be trying to tempt us to attack them. We would be in range of their bowmen if we did and that's just what they want."

"Do you suppose they think we are that stupid?" Aengus chuckled gruffly.

"Look at us." Cug swung his arm out to encompass all the Fir Bholg and Cyclopes in sight. "I might think we were that stupid if I were them."

The double portcullis closed behind the last ranks of cavalry leaving them stranded on the outside of the city walls. It was a bold move that Cug begrudgingly respected. Their soldiers knew that there was no going back so they would fight that much harder to defend their lives and their homes.

"There is that eagle again." Aengus pointed to a larger-than-normal bird in flight over the wall where the bowmen stood.

Cug half expected one of them to shoot it out of the air, but it flew safely on, over the lines of cavalry and the flat, grassy plain beyond. It was on track to fly close overhead, but it landed on the branch of a small leafless tree about two-thirds of the way to them. Cug found it strange that he had never noticed the tree before. There, a moment later, it was joined by a large snowy owl.

"Shall I have the archers kill those birds?" Aengus asked.

Cug shook his head slowly. "No, leave them be."

A horn suddenly blared from the line of cavalry prompting them to move forward, sending all thoughts of birds into the ether. They plodded toward the Giants slowly at first, picking up speed gradually in their advance until they were in full gallop charging across the field toward Cug's line.

From beside him, Aengus shouted, "Shield wall!" and two rows of shields, bristling with the long shafts of metal-tipped spears materialized with surprising discipline.

The double line of almost three hundred Giants braced for the impact of a thousand armored cavalry. Cug noticed that many of them wore the gold or silver cloaks of men the humans called Temple Knights, a religious Order of some sort that worshipped a sun goddess. The Fir Bholg had little use for gods except for one who lived far off in Aitva that never bothered to listen to their prayers. Most, except the Cyclopes, had forgotten about the deity centuries ago.

The Yorwick cavalry charged across the open plain with not a man in their formation missing a step. It was a thing of beauty to watch and to fear if you were anyone other than a Fir Bholg. Cug almost felt sorry for them. None of those fools would see another sunrise and most would end up as shit from the ass of a Giant in a few days. Cug doubted any of them considered that as part of their immediate future.

Just before the cavalry crossed the path of the tree, they skidded to a stop. The eagle and the owl sat impassively as if nothing unusual were occurring around them. They did not startle or take flight, rather, they kept their eyes firmly set on the Giants before them. Cug was sure they were staring at him more than any other.

"What's happening?" Cug glanced over at Aengus, confusion riddled his features, and then at the cavalry . . . and the birds.

Aengus remained silent.

Every eye watched as both birds hopped to the ground and transformed into hooded forms the size of humans covered with lengths of feathers, shells and beads. Cug recognized them easily as druids of Sunna – one wore the ancient symbol of their goddess in gold – a medallion in the shape of the sun. They walked together toward the shield wall and stopped a pace away.

The one on the right pulled down her hood revealing long red hair framing a painted face, pale skin and bright green eyes. "I am Grian, Elder in service to the light of the world, Sunna.

Elder? Cug was surprised that a woman so young, and beautiful held the status of Elder. She was quite the opposite of his Elder shaman, Thrakel. Where in the Infernal Planes was she anyway?

The druid standing next to Grian pulled the hood from his face. He was taller with a tanned complexion and brown hair and eyes. "I am Buadhach, Elder shaman in service to the light of the world, Sunna."

They stood there as if expecting a reply. None followed.

"We seek the Fir Bholg king that goes by the name of Cug the Conqueror."

They knew his name. At least a name he was known by when he united the Fir Bholg tribes under his rule many years before. That part was more than a little unsettling. Regardless, he stepped forward, he was no coward. "I am Cug," he announced.

"King Cug, Arch-druid Filberzh the Risen commands that you answer for the incursion of your warriors into the undisputed territory of Lyonesse and the unlawful siege of Yorwick."

Cug did not like the girl's tone or her commanding nature. Still, he knew that if she were an elder druid then he would have to tread lightly. "We are not here to kill and destroy, Elder Grian. We are here simply to keep the human soldiers inside Yorwick while Count Djago wages war against the King of Lyonesse on The Dormonts. Any human deaths that have arisen due to our presence have been purely incidental."

"Incidental?" Her tone was condescending. "What if these brave men had valiantly charged your shield wall and died unnecessarily upon it defending their home? Would that have been incidental?"

"We would simply be defending ourselves," Cug countered. "There was no need for them to come out of Yorwick to attack us."

Grian looked at Buadhach and Cug was sure something passed between them. "Because of your consideration bringing the four Dryads to us alive and with their health, Filberzh the Risen will consider this matter settled if you withdraw from this place and return to your lands peacefully."

Cug was not about to be dictated to by the little druid bitch. If he did, he would not be King of the Fir Bholg long. He had no choice but to stand up to the Elder druid and not lose face with his clans. "I have an agreement with Count Djago to maintain the siege of Yorwick until the battle of The Dormonts has come to an end. I will keep that promise and chew the head from any human, or elder druid, that tries to force me to do otherwise."

Grian stared hard at him and Cug felt as if his fate was being decided. How these tiny creatures could command so much power was beyond him. The only solace he maintained was that few of her magical tricks would work on his kind thanks to the Tuatha Dé.

And then there was a fluttering at his side and, startled, he turned in time to see Thrakel transforming beside him. "There are twenty druids concealed in the hills behind us," she whispered.

With some satisfaction, Cug noticed that Grian's eyes enlarged just a little at the appearance of his shaman. "Yes," he confirmed, "we have shaman equal to your druids and more so. I know about the twenty druids behind us and they will all join our stewpot if the next few minutes go badly."

Grian glanced again at Buadhach and something was decided. "King Cug," Grian addressed him formally, a good sign. "We will accept your presence until the battle of The Dormonts is done on one condition."

"What is your condition?" Cug could barely keep the contempt from his voice.

Grian smiled. Or was it a smirk? "You must prove yourself in the light of Sunna against five of Yorwick's finest."

"One against five?" Cug scoffed. "Is that truly fair?"

"Are five humans too much of a challenge for Cug the Conqueror?" Grian crossed her arms in front of her breasts subconsciously.

Cug stepped forward, towering over the tiny druid. "I meant to say *only* five humans. I accept your challenge!"

He spoke quickly and quietly to Aengus and Thrakel. "If I should fall, my last wish is that you kill every druid in the vicinity and break every stone that was the city of Yorwick."

They both nodded their agreement and then Thrakel placed her gnarled hand on his forearm. "Use your club. I have enchanted it with a spell of hardness that will keep it from splintering."

That was the problem with many Fir Bholg weapons, they often broke or split into a thousand pieces under a Giant's power and strength. Thrakel's gift of this enchantment would allow him to use all of his strength against the humans without tempering it in deference to his weapon.

"And be mindful of your heels," Aengus added. "Humans always go for the heels."

Five men were standing with the Elder druid Grian when Cug turned to face them. To a man they all wore serious expressions on their faces and gold-fringed cloaks with the golden symbol of Sunna at their breasts. One, the man in the center, wore four gold knots on his shoulder and bore an air of command.

"These are the five that will die for your custom?" Cug smirked at Grian contemptuously.

"These honorable Temple Knights will defend the sovereign rights of king and country against invasion," Grian announced more for the soldiers of Yorwick's benefit than himself.

Cug strode toward them loosely adjusting his grip on the massive club that must have been carved from a five-hundred-year-old oak, and when he was close enough, swiftly brought the club down on the head of the Temple Knight standing in the center of the group. The other four dove away, scrambling out of the Giant's long reach as quickly as possible.

"Now there are four!" he roared, sweeping the club in a backhanded arc narrowly missing the druids who instantly transformed into their flight forms and careened away in a spray of feathers to avoid the deadly weapon.

The four Temple Knights wasted no time recovering from their initial shock and edged into positions around the Fir Bholg. Cug was unconcerned, slamming his club again into the earth between two of them. The concussion sent waves of energy through the earth enough to knock them from their feet. With swift action, Cug snatched one of Temple Knights from the ground and drained the blood from his limp body in one mighty squeeze, before tossing him into the line of mounted knights that watched their brother's violent death in horror.

"Three!"

A stab of pain brought Cug's attention back to his right where a knight dug his sword deep into the Fir Bholg's heel in an attempt to cut it through. Aengus had warned him about this tactic. Fortunately, Cug had skin as tough and thick as tree bark causing the blade to stick fast. It was all the Temple Knight could do to pull it out, but he claimed it with little consolation as it could do nothing to deflect the heavy club that splattered his innards across the tall green grass.

"Two!" Cug howled with laughter.

His laughter was abruptly cut short by a sharp stab penetrating the inner part of his thigh between his legs. It was a vile sting that barely missed his scrotum, forcing an involuntary yelp of pain and shock from his throat. Twisting fiercely, Cug stomped the ground hard to dislodge the spear, inadvertently trampling the Temple Knight that desperately held fast to it.

"One." Cug gasped as he jerked the spear free.

He cast around looking for the last remaining knight and turned just in time to put out his hand to block the onrush of the man bearing down on him with his upraised broad sword. Expecting to grab him, Cug was surprised when the knight fell on his knees, skidded under his grasp and disconnected the Giant's small finger from his hand with one cruel strike.

Cug roared in agony and pressed his hand to his chest to the stem the pulse of blood that followed. Stumbling back a few paces to keep his last adversary out from under him, the Fir Bholg felt a slice across the back of his calf before the Temple Knight danced out of reach of his kicks and stomps.

"Come now, for a Giant, you squeal like a fat sow in labor. Is this how you wish to be remembered?" The knight was smiling from beneath his open-face helmet like a hungry cat that caught a bird.

How arrogant the little pisshead was. Cug decided he would ruin that smile before he killed him and tried to remain calm. The knight wanted him to charge in a rage, but Cug was too experienced to be goaded with words.

"Have you ever heard the sound that a human head makes when it is crushed between a Fir Bholg's teeth?" Cug smiled back. "Your friends are about to find out."

The knight's complexion lightened a shade or two, yet to his credit, he kept his smile. Cug lifted his club and slowly strode toward him while the mounted Temple Knights shouted encouragement to their comrade. The Giants roared, hurling insults and rude gestures.

Still a few paces away, the knight picked up a nearby spear and hurled it at Cug's head. The human was strong and fast, Cug would give him that, but he easily avoided the missile with a quick bob of his head and it streaked past harmlessly. Cug responded by flicking his club at the knight. The head of the club landed just in front of him, the rotational force of the spin turning it to the right and around the knight side stepping to the left.

"Ha!" he shouted triumphantly and then the handle of the still spinning club flipped around like a wobbly top and smashed into his back, knocking him to the ground.

Cug was on him. He picked up the disoriented, breathless Temple Knight with one hand and plucked off his helmet. One thick thumb pressed into the knight's mouth, breaking his jaw and shattering his teeth.

"Not smiling anymore, are we?"

The knight could only respond with gurgling screams, eyes wide with fear, blood pouring down the front of his surcoat. Cug held the dying man up to the now silent Temple Knights, silent now with the exception of a few hollow curses. Cug did not smile, he did not taunt them. The challenge was over and there would be no battle. Nearly dead, the knight hung limply in his upheld fist, his body twitching with the occasional spasm. Cug, not one to go back on his promises, shoved the knight's head between his teeth and bit forcefully, crushing it into a salty tang that washed over his tongue. The Giants howled with cheers at the sight of it.

He tossed the headless body at his feet and turned to face his people. "We go home now," he shouted to be heard over the rumbling thunder of their merriment. "These humans are not worth the life of a single one of ours. Let them fight their own battles!"

Aengus joined him, slapping him hard on the back. "Are you ok?"

Cug leaned on his friend a little as they walked to their camp. He didn't care to watch the Temple Knights collect what was left of their dead. "My ass and my leg hurt. Mostly my ass," Cug smiled weakly. He was tired. "The little pisser nearly pierced my fruit."

Aengus laughed. "He might have done you a favor. You have too many bastards as it is o' king!"

Cug forced a chuckle. All he really wanted was to get back to Fomoire and find a chunk of ice to sit on.

CHAPTER 25

Last Stand

Perault crested the final grassy incline and stopped. His mount was slick with lather and puffing heavily from the hard ride, he could feel its flanks heaving under his saddle desperate for respite. As much as he loved his horse, all of that was secondary to the scene that played out in the distance. It was almost too much to comprehend and nothing like the tapestries or paintings in books that he had studied so eagerly growing up. Battle was supposed to be glorious and honorable, a proud tradition of kings and nobles and knights that made heroes out of men whose exploits would be penned and sung over countless generations. What he witnessed here was nothing like that at all.

He was first struck by the sound – loud and confusing. Individual cries and screams from human or horse could be heard periodically over the jumbled roar of noise that formed the solid baseline of resonance. Perault could hear it almost a league away over the jostle of horse and armor when he rode and it became no less clear the closer he came to it. Joining the sound with sight was nearly overwhelming. He could never have expected what his eyes refused to believe before him.

The field of lush green grass that once separated the opposing armies were now churned and muddy, saturated with the blood of thousands. Broken bodies lay everywhere with no effort by either side to retrieve them while clusters of wounded sat or crawled to safety while others cried in agony where they fell. If there was ever the semblance of two cohesive lines of ranks facing each other, it was gone now. It looked more like a brawl with almost no command structure making it difficult for Perault to discern the difference between one soldier and another. The Temple Knights stood out among them, their gold-cloaks flashing in the morning sunlight. They maintained their organization and discipline. One thousand of them, including his brother, had charged into the forward ranks of Djago's army decimating what remained of their fractured line. Likewise, another unknown number from Cambria had smashed into them from the rear. Whatever their reason for joining the fray, Perault was glad for it.

It was clear that the southern line of Djago's force was crumbling and soon to be overrun if they did not retreat. Further north, the situation was different. Through the haze, Perault could barely make out the stag emblem of Djago's house fluttering erratically on banners. Around them, thousands of men and at least a score of Fir Bholg were valiantly defending the count. Strange, tentacle-like vines as thick as oak trunks sprouted here and there from the ground in their midst slowing the Giants and killing men until they were ripped to shreds and periodically, arcs of lightning and shafts of fire would rip into one side or the other. Sometimes the deadly magic was blocked by the opposing wizards, sometimes they would scorch dozens in a fiery death. Somehow, Count Djago was holding his line and even gaining ground in a few places.

Perault turned to his captain. "Have our injured men taken to those tents over there." He could see druids tending the wounded. "Everyone else, follow me."

"What about you, my lord? You are wounded as well."

Perault coughed a laugh. "I was denied the start of this battle; I will not miss the end of it!" He kicked his tired horse forward into a steady gallop followed by seventy cavalrymen from Stoddenferry. This was the charge they had all been waiting for.

They rode fast behind the lines north to where Djago made his stand. He could have joined in the south, but a charge might have run down their own men and it didn't look like they needed his help anyway. The battle would be won or lost in the north, so that is where Perault would be.

Angling closer, Perault spied a knot of cavalry about to break through the line of the king's infantry not far from Djago's banners. He drew his sword and pointed it at the impending breach. "To me!" he shouted to his men. Instinctively, they formed a delta formation with Perault at their head.

Seconds later, the last of the infantry failed, and Djago's cavalry poured through. Perault was there to meet them. The crash of metal armor and scream of horses echoed in his ears as if from a great distance. All he knew was how to work his sword, deploy his shield and press his horse forward instinctively. He sliced the arm of a man clean off, ripped through the neck of another, deflected a blow, then another and smashed the face of one more with the pommel of his sword. No thoughts entered his mind other than to kill and not be killed. He was a warrior of death in the clothing of a knight of Sunna plying his deadly craft against all comers.

Perault pressed hard, dealing death all around him, until suddenly there was no one left to fight. Regaining his senses after the brief shot of adrenaline, he took in his surroundings. His charge had penetrated to the rear of the Cambrian line followed by hundreds of the king's infantry advancing into the opening behind them. Djago's entire line was breaking down because of it. Only a stone's throw away the count's banners marked his location and Perault urged his mount forward for a better look. His men protected his flanks as they progressed, trampling infantry from behind or slaying the few that came against them until they were in sight of the count himself.

Perault gasped. There were no less than a hundred men dead at his feet. So many that anyone that tried to assault him had to first climb over the bodies. They may not all have died by Djago's hand, but Perault was willing to bet that most had. The count stood holding his broad sword in a two-handed grip, breathing heavily from exertion and shouting orders to soldiers that loyally battled to defend him despite the fact that there was no doubt the battle was lost.

To Perault's left, Djago's last cavalry unit made a desperate charge against a formation of Temple Knights that had just arrived. To his right the last Giant, a Fir Bholg, bellowed with pain and anger, wrapped in vines and immobile, fell to the King Praeter's spearmen. Only a few hundred infantry remained along with a handful of his personal guards, fighting in a rapidly constricting circle around Count Djago.

"Dismount!" he ordered. There was no room to maneuver any closer on horseback. "Stay close and watch your back!"

Perault led his men around to the northeastern side of the perimeter where the king's men were making little headway and pressed in close among them. Here, the fighting was close and personal. He pushed with his shield and lashed out with his sword killing men who eyes were blue or brown or green with gray mustaches or brown or none at all. Those faces he would remember for the rest of his life.

With the men of Stoddenferry on his left and right, Perault drove forward. He could see Count Djago standing almost frozen in place staring at something in the distance while the maelstrom of death surged around him. Perault followed the count's gaze to his right and was startled to see a man, a man he knew, suspended in the air upon a gray cloud wearing flowing robes and bearing a long staff in one outstretched hand. It was the man he once met in a tavern. He called himself Myrllin and he stood as frozen and transfixed as Count Djago. Whatever was happening, there was a silent battle waged between the two as deadly as any sword or spear.

"Perault!" It was one of his men who brought his attention back to the battle just in time to block a powerful blow. It stopped him in his tracks.

He and his men were no longer battling regular foot soldiers, a score of battle-hardened soldiers of Djago's personal guard faced them. Perault had to take care, any one of them was likely equal to his own skill or better. The man on his left went down, Perault rewarded the guard with a blade through his throat before one of his own men filled the gap. Their advance ground to a halt against the guards leaving them vulnerable to a counterattack if any of Djago's infantrymen were held in reserve. The elite guard pushed back on Perault and his men hard, forcing their heels to slide a pace in reverse.

"Hold the line!" Perault shouted to his men. They had the numbers, but Perault worried they might be outmatched in skill.

A Stoddenferry soldier took a violent blow to the head and stumbled disoriented. It was everything Perault could do to keep the guards from breaking through the opening before more of his men could fill it.

"Move up! Move up! Move up!" he howled at his men. It was too late. Four guards shoved past him and into their ranks.

"Regroup!" he shouted, but there was no hope for it. The advance had disintegrated into one-on-one and small-group combat. Chaos reigned on the field in every direction.

Perault found himself trading blows with a stout guard more agile than he could have imagined. He feigned to his right and punched with his shield only to be solidly blocked, sending him back on his heels. The big fella was strong and fought much like his friend Davin. A dangerous foe on a crowded battlefield.

Steading himself for another assault, Perault crouched and was nearly blindsided by the rush of a blade a thumbs-width above his head. He pushed himself backward swinging recklessly at whomever nearly separated his head from his neck and connected solidly with the man's thigh. A sharp scream rent the air, but Perault never saw who it was he had permanently crippled. He was on his butt, with his sword out to one side, his shield behind him and the big guard standing nearly on top of him with his sword above his head and a satisfied smile on his face.

Perault was finished and he knew it.

The guard inhaled sharply standing frozen for what seemed like an eternity. And then the point of a blade erupted from his sternum. Perault couldn't believe his eyes. He barely rolled out of the way when the stout man fell dead on the blood-soaked earth in his place. Behind him, a Temple Knight nodded to Perault quickly and then turned to engage another. The Temple Knights had finally arrived. A hundred of them were crowding in from every direction to finish off the count's guards.

Perault stood and quickly regained his bearings. Fierce combat raged all around him, the Stoddenferry man that had taken the hard blow moments earlier had somehow survived and was back in the fight, the guards were all fighting for their lives and Count Djago still stood frozen and alone.

Count Terril Djago.

The count was alone and unguarded without a soul between them. Perault had to take the chance to put an end to this mad man's tyranny. He ran as fast as he could through the slick of carnage and over the scattered pile of corpses into the clearing where Count Djago stood. Carefully he circled around to face the count, but he might as well be invisible for all the count noticed.

Conflict clouded Perault's mind; could he strike down a defenseless man even if he was an evil despot? It didn't feel right, it felt like murder. The oath of his order played over his mind sounding almost sinister and taunting rather than pure in the light of Sunna as he had always thought of it before.

"I hear the call from darkness and come into the light

I am born once again unto Sunna, to live in her sight

To defend her teaching and follow her faith

And never reveal the secrets of the Order to which body and soul I am endowed

Ne'er to commit murder, deceit, or lie

To honor and serve my king and my lord

Upon pain of death and ruin upon my soul

In her Grace, I shall serve with bone and blood and spirit

With every breath within me to the end of days."

There was nothing ambiguous about that one line, 'Ne'er to commit murder . . .". Would Sunna judge him harshly and expel him from her service if he killed Djago like this?

As if in answer a voice spoke breathlessly into his ear, "Kill him. Kill him now . . ."

It nearly startled Perault out of his boots. He turned to see the man called Myrllin standing next to him, his eyes firmly on Djago, his face flushed with strain and his beard and hair drenched with sweat.

"Do it now, you cannot know the evil that resides inside," his failing voice whispered with what sounded like desperation.

Perault lifted his sword in line with Count Djago's chest.

"Do it . . ."

A voice spoke through Count Djago's lips, one that seemed unearthly and disjointed, unaccustomed to a human's natural speech, *"Napeai ipamis allar nanaeel caosg!"*

"Sunna forgive me." Perault thrust the sword forward with everything he had.

The Dvergr steel blade sliced cleanly through the space above the count's breastplate, into the front of his neck and through his spine. Eyes wide with disbelief, rage, and hate burned deeply inside those dark orbs making Perault want to turn away. And then his body twitched convulsively and slowly sank to the ground.

Perault managed to keep his gaze firm and watch the life depart from the body of the count. He felt nothing – no pleasure, no satisfaction, no regrets – until a dark shadow rose from the lifeless form like a wisp of smoke, congealing into a black orb dense with evil so pervasive that fear drove Perault to his knees, trembling uncontrollably in its presence. If he had use of his legs, surely he would have run in terror from it. Perault could barely breathe. He was so fearful and ashamed that he barely noticed the calm voice of Myrllin speaking words he did not understand next to him.

"Zir Kures. Geh ozien."

Why was the wizard not afraid? Perault wanted to scream. He *would* scream if it continued much longer. It took every ounce of control he possessed not to let his terror vocalize.

And then it was gone.

There was no more fear, no more terror, only shame at his reaction. Perault glanced around expecting everyone on the battlefield to be staring at him, bearing witness to his shame and found that nothing had changed. The battle still raged on in small pockets as far as he could see. No one had seen, no one cared.

Except Myrllin.

Perault spun around. To his shock, Myrllin was nowhere to be found.

~~~

The haze of morning dissipated, the roar of men in armor was replaced by deafening silence, the cries of death no longer echoed across the once beautiful plain of grass. Yet, death still remained. It was present in the blood-drenched ground where they stood, the bodies that lay silent and alone, and in the eyes of thousands that watched King Praeter Eldorath, unclean with blood and grime himself, slowly plod to the highest point on the battlefield to address his realm's defenders.

"Until today, I always believed that Lyonesse would never repeat the sins of the past. Yet here we are, spilling our blood on The Dormonts just as our ancestors did centuries ago. It makes me feel ashamed to be your king."

A general grumbling cascaded through the thousands that watched their king hang his head and many spirited cries of encouragement rang from voices unrestrained. The soldiers still believed in him. Perault knew the truth now, had witnessed it in its raw form and nearly been undone by it. He prayed to Sunna that the king would enlighten the people with the truth.

"There is no honor in what we have done here today!" Tears flowed freely down Eldorath's face. "No matter the cause or reason! We have defiled this land with the blood of our brothers once again. There can be no celebration of victory, no conference of rewards or honor for justly valorous deeds. We can only pray that Sunna will forgive our ignorance, the limits of our intellect, the frailty of our morality."

If Perault hoped for this war to be the vehicle that earned him his gold-fringed cloak, it was not to be; that was clear enough from the king's words. It didn't matter. Perault would have felt forever stained to receive it as a reward for killing his kinsmen.

"I order and decree that no man here or anywhere in my realm call any person from Cambria anything other than brother or sister. There shall be no revenge or retribution. Anyone who violates this order shall be dealt with harshly. I forgive this transgression for the sake of the kingdom and the sake of all of our souls."

No one spoke a word among the thousands that witnessed the historic moment and Perault wondered if the famous poet/historians Vyvyan or Penhallow were somewhere nearby to record it.

King Eldorath pointed to the ground where he sat on his horse. "On this spot the druids will build a stone monument for all who have fallen on this day. It will be a place of solace and remembrance that will last through time and become a mystery to those who come after we have gone. The stones will keep the memories of this time for all eternity. It will be known as Bane Hinge."

Perault could see the king was weary, barely keeping his head erect and his seat on his mount secure. It saddened him to see a regal man of dignity and grace brought so low by the events at hand.

"Go home to your families. You have my leave. And report back to your regular posts in three weeks. Together we will build a new and stronger Lyonesse that will become a beacon of strength and beauty for all to see."

Quietly, and without fanfare, King Praeter Eldorath of Lyonesse departed The Dormonts, leaving his subjects with the deep sensation that they had been a part of something monumental. At least Perault felt that way. He looked at the second sword he carried; a fine blade of Dvergr steel with the crest of House Djago, the silhouette of a stag, prominent on the hilt.

What should he do with it? Present it to the king? Destroy it?

Perault would keep it for now. He knew there was a son of Count Djago in Cambria or, more likely, in hiding that might value his father's blade one day. Count Djago was a good man once before whatever had taken his soul and forced him to do terrible things. It was unfortunate that the people of Lyonesse would only remember the last of him.

Epilogue

"How can you say I will have no children? How can you know for sure?"

"Don't be a fool, Praeter. Look at you. You are nearly an old man and you think a child of your own making is still in your future after all these years?" Myrllin did not mean to be cruel, but he didn't have time for ridiculous notions.

"Your damn visions!" King Praeter Eldorath threw his cup across the room spilling fine Mekali wine all over the floor.

"Relax, brother," Banfield cautioned. "Myrllin is here to help our kingdom. Neither of us will ever sire a child at our age. This is a viable solution to the succession of our family line."

"This is Djago's child!" Praeter howled. "How do we know the child will not grow up half-demon?"

"The child was conceived before the count was taken by the demon. That much I am sure," Myrllin countered. "What he needs is a mother and a father who will love and protect him. You need an heir. The match is perfect."

Praeter spun on his heels to face Myrllin. "I am not a fool, Myrllin. What are you not telling me?"

Myrllin sighed. "You must take this child as your own and pronounce him as your heir. He will take your name and keep his own. You may decide on his first name yourself. All I can tell you is that this child will father a bloodline that will alter the course of history a hundred generations from now."

The king laughed genuinely from the depths of his abdomen. "And they call me king? I cannot even provide my kingdom with an heir of my own blood. Instead, I stand here with my brother and a five-hundred-year-old wizard who looks half my age dictating the future of my realm. My realm!"

"Enough of your tantrums!" Banfield slammed his fist on the table and stood to face his brother. "You know it is the only way and we both know you are going to do it. And it's not just for yourself. It's for the security of *your* realm's future. Not to mention the obvious, but taking this child will also go far to bring Cambria back into the good graces with the rest of Lyonesse."

The brothers stood staring at each other intently for a long moment nearly toe to toe. The tension was so high that Myrllin was sure they would come to blows, rolling around on the floor like children. No doubt they had done it before, many decades ago.

Finally, it was the king that relented. "I will leave it for the queen to decide." He opened the door of the chamber and spoke to a guard outside, "Summon the queen."

Praeter refilled his cup with wine and returned to his seat. No one said much as they waited, mostly studying the contents of their cup or finding sudden interest in a tapestry on the wall until the air between them became awkward. Myrllin wondered why it always took women an eternity to come when they were summoned and he concluded that their delay was almost certainly deliberate.

Praeter was the first to break the silence. "Where is your Wodanaz? Normally you and your brother aren't too far apart."

Myrllin looked inward for a brief second before he replied, "He's on the northwestern coast of Vikja chasing another demon."

"Another demon raising an army?" The king sounded more than a little alarmed.

"No, this one has taken the form of a Phoenix ablaze with fire. I will join him to hunt it down as soon as I am finished here."

"How will you find him?" Banfield asked.

"Wodanaz and I always know exactly where the other is in this world as well as each other's general condition."

"How curious." Banfield glanced at his own brother. "Is it some peculiar magic you share?"

Myrllin chuckled. "No, no. It's because of the Liafal Stone."

King Praeter leaned in clearly surprised by his admission. "The Liafal Stone? I thought that was reserved for the High-Kings of Eriu?"

"It is," Myrllin nodded. "Our father was the first High-King. It was he who brought the Stone to Eriu in the first place. It conveyed much more power then, or perhaps it only seemed so because my father was Tuatha Dé. In any case, my brother and I touched the Stone through him when we were infants."

Both Praeter and Banfield stared at him in stunned silence.

Myrllin shrugged. "Some say a Tuatha Dé should sit on the High-King's throne again."

Praeter blinked in surprise. "I doubt anyone in Eriu would agree with that."

"I'm sure you are correct," Myrllin agreed. "The Tuatha Dé aren't what they used to be. Far from it. Those of The Blood concern themselves with playing god and staying far above the affairs of men."

"Is that what you and Wodanaz are, Myrllin, gods?" Banfield looked him over with a skeptical eye.

Myrllin nearly choked on his wine at the thought of himself as a god. "I assure you that I am a creature of man. I can't speak for my brother though; I think he enjoys being worshipped by the women. Especially Vikja women!"

They all laughed at that, but inside, Myrllin was not sure how much of a jest it really was.

"What is so funny?" The distinct timbre of a woman rang through the room. The queen had arrived.

"Nothing, dear," Praeter rose to greet her with a kiss on the cheek. "Just Myrllin and his stories."

Both Banfield and Myrllin greeted her and kissed her hand before Praeter offered her a seat.

She declined. "I pray this will not take much time? I have an appointment with the decorator that I do not wish to postpone."

Praeter took her hand gently and spoke in a mild voice. "There is a delicate matter we must discuss. It involves our inability to produce an heir that will carry our name. Please sit. Myrllin thinks he has a solution and it may take a while for you to understand."

The queen pulled her hand away, glared at Myrllin with mock scorn and shook her head. "You have such humor, good wizard." Then she folded her arms under her breasts and addressed her husband. "Myrllin and I have already worked it all out. We will adopt the boy and raise him as our own. In three days we will bring him before the council and then before the people and announce him as our heir. The day after, Arch-druid Filberzh the Risen will bless him in the light of Sunna."

A dark look came over the king's face as he slowly turned his head to glare at Myrllin. "Sometimes, I wonder who the real demons are in this world."

Myrllin just shrugged. What could he say?

"Don't blame Myrllin, my dear," the queen lightly chided. "He knew rightly that there was no way you would agree to bring a child into our family without my consent."

Praeter spread his hands apart in surrender. "I suppose all that's left is to decide on a name."

The queen smiled sweetly and gently kissed her husband's cheek. "We worked that out as well. Now, I must go. I want everything to be perfect when the druids arrive with our child." She left the men staring at her in utter silence as she briskly departed the room.

Praeter turned to face Myrllin once again. A look of exasperation dominated his otherwise regal features. "So, Myrllin, what will I call my heir?"

Visions swirled in Myrllin's mind. Visions about the boy and the significance of what his descendants would become. One in particular. When he replied, his voice sounded haunted and unearthly, even to his own ears. "The child will be called Artur Pendjago Eldorath."

~~~

A black raven was waiting in the open window of Zracul's second-floor room at the inn when he walked through the door. Unlike any typical bird, this one did not immediately turn to flight at his entrance, rather, it appeared to anticipate his arrival. Zracul had been anticipating such a bird as well, for he knew it carried a message from his brothers in Tintagel, Vadim and Fain.

He sat in the chair adjacent to the window and locked eyes with the raven. The message was not the usual kind that was written and strapped to the poor creature's leg to ferry. This was a message imprinted upon the raven's mind that only someone with Zracul's talents could decipher.

Zracul stared deep into the raven's eyes, past those black orbs and into its mind. In full control, he calmed the bird and allowed the images and sounds placed there for him to find wash over him. The message was simple and brief:

"Esiasch gohia brin iadnamad a Kiltullagh. Niiso tia do Ys."

Ys? That was unexpected. Zracul assumed he would meet his brothers in Tintagel where they would carry out their plans, but Ys would work just as well. Maybe better. He heard a lot of interesting things about that city since he had arrived in the Western kingdoms and he was eager to find out if any of it were true.

Zracul released the raven, allowing it to take flight. The sun was nearly set with darkness falling fast behind. He decided that there was no reason to wait until morning to depart. In stark contrast to Vradesti, the roads between cities in the Western kingdoms were clear and wide, and he did not fear bandits. He grabbed his saddlebags and stuffed them with his clothes and other personals, then set off to the stables to find his horse. Lyonesse had been quite an adventure for him, but it was nothing compared to what he had in store for Ys.

~~~

Waves beat the hull of the square-sailed longboat that carried Kumida and what remained of his loyal followers along the coast of the Great Sea toward their destination. So far, the journey had been long and perilous. They sailed the Arges River to its end, then trekked through the treacherous lands called The Wilds and over snowcapped mountains into otherwise unknown passes until they reached the coast of the Great Sea. Many lands they navigated, many people he knew and was able to avoid only because of the Chaos Demon subjugating what he once was, what he would never be again.

Luck was with them when they arrived on the coast as a longboat full of Vikja had camped for the night on an isolated beach. By morning the Cyclopes were sailing east in that same longboat leaving behind thirty dead Vikja warriors to be plucked to pieces by sea birds and crab. So far, that had been the highlight of their journey.

Once they reached the Great Sea, it would only be a few days to reach the coast of the Sicans and from there a day or two to reach Aitva. His people believed Aitva was the home of the great Cyclops god Arges. The demon inside Kumida didn't believe in this world's gods, he knew the truth of gods in this age and it only gave him more contempt for the creatures that worshipped them. All he cared was that he was getting away from Fomoire deep into the lands where humans resided. From Aitva, he could rebuild his clan from two dozen into hundreds that would eventually conquer and enslave every kingdom within one thousand leagues. It might take two or three hundred years before he was ready, but what did he care? He had the time.

Briefly, Kumida wondered what had become of Steropes and Brontes. They'd fled the Ice Coast in ships into the Sea of Dragons when Cug attacked. He cursed their betrayal and hoped they were all rotting at the bottom of the cold depths of the sea. Better yet, maybe they would find their way to Aitva as well, it would be an unforgettable reunion.

He stared out over the water contemplating the many ways he might torture and kill the traitors when something far off attracted his attention causing a rare smile to stretch across his face. "There! There in the distance is our destination! Can you see it? The spire of darkness that rises from the depths of the earth and enrobes our god in warmth and comfort! It is Aitva! Our new home."

Kumida's voice carried to all the Cyclopes who followed, lending courage to their resolve and encouraging them to row faster. That was their new home, the place where they would start afresh and rebuild their population. That would be the place where the first Empire of the Cyclopes would be born.

~~~

"Welcome home, Perault." Melisende wrapped him in a hug that was tighter than he would have given her credit for and then her soft lips were pressed against his with a passion he had all but forgotten since last they met.

This was the informal greeting with her in private after the formal welcome he had received from his family and the Brighams when he first arrived at Stoddenferry Castle with his brother. It was the moment he looked forward to as soon as he realized that his lover had come to his home to await his return.

"I am so happy to be in your arms," he told her between kisses.

She pulled back a little and held his face between her hands. "If I have my way, we would never be apart again."

"You are so right, my love." He kissed each of her palms in turn. "I am here, your family is here and the war is over. I will tell my father I wish to be married within a fortnight!"

Her eyes widened with joy, before concern flashed across her delicate features. "Are you sure, Perault? I know how much you want the gold-fringed cloak and the honors that come with it."

Perault shook his head slowly. "I have seen enough of death and fighting. The gold cloak will come when it comes, and if it never does, I will be all the happier that I have not wasted my days away from you."

Their lips came together again, her body warm and inviting against his. Since his return, the passion between them seemed all the sweeter. He wanted her badly, wanted her now. They should have retreated further than the trophy room to a quieter part of the castle. Maybe they could go there now . . .

"Ahem."

Perault and Melisende separated faster than two feral dogs doused with a pail of water. His brother Reginald stood a pace away with a satisfied smirk on his face. Perault would pay him back for that later.

"Father wishes to see you. He says it's a matter of some urgency. Shall I tell him the two of you are attending a matter of urgency as well?"

Perault, cheeks red with embarrassment, punched him in the shoulder. "Is it a private meeting?"

His brother rubbed his sore shoulder, still smiling. "No, little brother. Mother and the Brighams are with him. Melisende may join us as well if she is up to it."

She took Perault's hand in her own and squeezed tight. "I am fine, thank you."

"Very well, follow me then."

Perault would never hear the end of this from his brother. The next few days would be a torture of knowing smiles and kissy sounds that wouldn't end until they were rolling around on the ground like children. Hopefully, he and Melisende could simply avoid him until he no longer found it amusing to harass them.

When they arrived at his father's office, it was just as Reginald had said it would be. Melisende hurried to sit with their mothers on a divan near the wall while he and Reginald stood before their father's desk. He looked up from a conversation he was having with Mr. Brigham, sitting in a lounge chair nearby, when they entered the room.

"Ah, my boys. Sit down."

Reginald took a seat next to Mr. Brigham, leaving Perault to sit in the only chair fully facing his father's desk. It was at that moment that he knew this meeting was going to be about him.

His father leaned forward over the papers scattered on his desk. "King Praeter Eldorath sent an emissary in advance of your arrival with a message for you. Not a pigeon, but an emissary!"

Perault felt fear rising along his spine. He wasn't sure where his father was going with this.

"He wanted me to know, you to know really, that what you did in the battle of The Dormonts was not unnoticed by him." The Earl of Stoddenferry rose from his great chair and around his desk to kneel beside his son.

Perault was taken aback by the entire display. His father had never acted this way before. It was probably one of the most uncomfortable experiences he had ever endured in his life. He wanted to stand up, tell his father to stand up, say something. Instead, he stayed silent.

"The emissary and your brother told me everything. What you did saved thousands of lives, maybe even turned the course of the battle. You stood before a man possessed by a powerful demon and fearlessly thrust your blade through his neck."

Perault sighed, "Father, I only knew him as a man. There was no way for me to know what he had become."

"Still, you fought through countless infantry and his personal guard to end the life of a tyrant. King Praeter will not let that service go unrewarded despite what he said after the battle that day."

"What sort of reward?"

His father smiled with pride. "You will receive your gold-fringed cloak."

"It was a fight with no honor against brothers of our own kingdom," Perault protested. "How could I accept such a hollow reward?"

His father's face reddened with anger. "Hollow reward? How many of the dead, or the ones you slain would consider it hollow? You have earned this reward not only by spilling your own blood but by the blood you spilled of others. Don't you dare dishonor their sacrifice."

Perault bowed his head. "You are right, Father. I am ashamed."

His father lifted Perault's chin with his hands. They felt calm and gentle. "There is no shame, son. Our king reached a similar conclusion. Already he thinks of you as a true knight of Sunna and the realm, but even he must justify it with more than your heroic deeds in this battle. So, he asks one more service from you."

"What is it, Father?"

"There are strange rumors out of Ys. Something to do with the royal family that the king is concerned might be destabilizing to the

Western kingdoms. He wants you to go and investigate, find the truth of the matter, and report what you find."

"Father, I have pledged to marry Melisende within a fortnight."

Twisting his neck to face Melisende, the earl spoke in true gentle form, "Will you extend my son's commitment to three months to do as King Praeter requires?"

Melisende looked like a bird trapped in a cage. "Yes, my lord. I will gladly relieve his obligation and extend the date of our marriage to three months from today for him to achieve his dream."

Perault's eyes welled with tears. Melisende had truly shown him the depths of her love that day.

"Very well," Perault announced. "I will go to Ys and uncover the source of unrest and return here to marry the woman I love within three months."

He walked purposefully to where Melisende sat between their mothers and knelt before her, taking one beautifully delicate hand in his. "On my honor, I will return to marry you, Melisende, and nothing under the light of Sunna will stand in my way."

GLOSSARY AND CAST

Aengus – Fir Bholg clan chief and close advisor to King Cug

Aine – Nursemaid to Pen Djago

Arges – One-eyed god of the Giants. He is purported to live in the depths of Mount Aitva in the Sicans lands

Arid Fellowship - A professional guild of assassins based in Eriu

Arthfael – Corrupt banker and gambler in Lyon's Gate

Atiod-Bherto - Cult of druids defeated in the Oak War by the combined forces of the druids of Sunna and Eriu and the allied cities in both Eriu and Lyonesse. The Atiod were infamous for ritual sacrifice of animals and humans on stone altars and wickerwork structures. Their stone circles are identified by the center recumbent stone and flankers used for astronomy, ritual, and sacrifice. Now outlawed by the Western kingdoms, they continue to practice their dark arts in seclusion. The Atiod are chiefly located in the extreme north and south of Eriu

Bale – Dog-handler in service to Sir Aldeman

Baron Morcant – Lady Genestra's Father

Boeger Penhallow – Famous author of myths and fairy tales

Brontes – Clan chief of one of the three tribes of Cyclopes in Fomoire

Buadhach – Eriu druid

Cateteric – Arch-druid of the Atiod-Bherto

Count Terril Djago – Ruler of Cambria and its surrounds

Count Temprest – Count of Lindpoole

Cug – Fir Bholg king of all the Giants in Fomoire. Clan Chief of the mining Giants who are sometimes referred to as the Sack-People because they are known for carrying ore from the mines in sacks

Davin of House Jeutemont – Squire to the aged Sir Grethin and long-time close friend of Perault

Dhroghan – Legendary hero of the Tuatha Dé and founding member of the Five

Dorlik – Apprentice blacksmith in the King's army, squire during the Tourneys and friend to Perault

Duke Banfield Eldorath – Duke of Yorwick, brother of King Praeter Eldorath of Lyonesse

Duncan Pentager – Squire and long-time Tourney rival of Perault

Earl Fineas Eckert - Lord of Stoddenferry Castle in Lyonesse, husband to Lady Rhoswen, and father of Sir Reginald and Perault

Elian and Yorlik Brigham – Older brothers of Melisende

Enlightened Ones – The formal name applied to the Atlanteans by the people of the Western kingdoms

Erol and Lyra Brigham – Wealthy grain merchants in Tintagel, close family friends of the Eckert family, parents of Elian, Yorlik and Melisende

Eriu – Prominent kingdom within the Western Kingdoms and also the name of the Moon Goddess worshipped by a sect of druids and throughout Eriu and Lyonesse

Filberzh the Risen - The Arch-druid of Sunna

Fraken – Dvergr captain of the Mountain King's personal guard

General Alwyn Urec – Commanding General of the armies of Lyonesse

Geoffrass – The Mad Wizard of Tintagel banished to The Wilds by the Duke of Tintagel. He had a Dvergr Dwarf apprentice named Firolin

Genestra – Countess of Cambria, wife of Djago, and mother of Pen

Grian – Elder Eriu druid

Hanlin – Groom in the King's cavalry, squire during the Tourneys and friend to Perault

Jaria and Daria – Succubus sisters devoted to Zracul

Jarl – Captain of the guard, reporting to Commander Ouza

King Praeter Eldorath and Queen Penelope Eldorath – Rulers of Lyonesse from the capital city of Lyon's Gate

Kiltullagh – Ancient city where, according to legends, the Sphere of Elements is hidden

Kumida – Cyclops possessed by a Chaos Demon

Mamon – Demon of Greed who took possession of Count Terril Djago

Medes – Military Captain reporting to Commander Ouza.

Melisende Brigham – Love interest of Perault

Metis – Goddess of wisdom

Myrllin – The Mad Bard, the Prophet, the Sage, the Steward of Hy Brasil. He has the ability to foresee the future with varying degrees of clarity. He is a powerful wizard with an obscure past. Myrllin lives in a castle on the mystical island of Hy Brasil, which is not always visible. When he is not needed, he has the ability to hibernate without aging for hundreds of years at a time. Son of the legendary Tuatha Dé hero Dhroghan and a Nymph, and twin to Wodanaz, whom he is older than by one minute

Naamah – A Succubus, or minor demon, summoned by Djago to serve as a spy among the druids in Cambria

Ouza – A Incubus, or minor demon, summoned by Djago to serve as Minister of the Military and Commander of the Guard in Cambria

Ourea – Active volcano in the Atlas Mountains located on the Emerald Isle

Perault – Squire and youngest son of Earl Fineas Eckert, Lord of Stoddenferry Castle, and Lady Rhoswen

Phaos – The young Fir Bholg clan chieftain of the Logger Giants

Pithos – A traditional vessel for transporting wine, olive oil and other liquids in Hellas

Prince Zracul – From Vradesti in the Eastern Kingdoms, possessed by Ornias, Greater Demon of Greed

Purple Porphyry – An extremely expensive purple marble from TaShemau that appears 'dusted with the stars'

Sefrick – Squire defeated by Perault in the Lyon's Gate Tourney

Sir Aldeman – Famous knight of Lyonesse who took on Perault as his last squire

Sir Beldham – Champion lancer of many Tourneys

Sir Geremy – Knight Champion of the Tourney in Yorwick

Sir Mainx of House Oberland – General of the armies of Cambria

Sir Maldwyn – Silver-cloak and second in command of the regulars from Stoddenferry Castle

Sir Meldecamp – Tourney Champion of Lyon's Gate

Sir Reynfrey – Commander of Count Djago's Personal Guard and Minister of the Military in Cambria

Squire Edwin Finbrat – Squire to Sir Geremy of House Talowin

Steropes – Clan chief of the Melanochroti clan, one of the three tribes of Cyclopes in Fomoire

Sulyen the Breaker – Lord of the Dvergr Dwarves, Protector of Tirnan Yog

Sunna – Sun Goddess served by a sect of druids in Eriu and Lyonesse and worshiped throughout the Western Kingdoms. Patron Deity of the Temple Knights

Tala – Lady Genestra's lady-in-waiting

Taudrick – druid in Cambria with healing powers dedicated to Count Djago and his family

Terril Djago – Count of Cambria, married to Genestra, taken by the Greater demon Mamon

The Wilds – The expansive, densely forested region between the Western and Eastern Kingdoms.

Theod – Supply Captain reporting to Commander Ouza

Tomos – Messenger in the army of Cambria

Thrakel – Fir Bholg shaman

Tuatha Dé - A mysterious, magical race of people who reside in a kingdom of four cities far to the north

Tuatha Dé Blood – The pure race of Tuatha Dé that comprises the leadership, scholars, and wizard class of their people

Turgik – Arch-wizard of Tirnan Yog

Vadim and Fain – The two younger brothers of Zracul

Valiant Keep – The massive fortified manor-house at the heart of Tintagel where the Duke and Duchess reside

Vyvyan – Famous poet and lyricist

Wodanaz – The Wanderer, Famed Poet, and Minstrel, Seeker of Wisdom, Chronicler of the Fourth Age, Son of legendary Tuatha Dé Dhroghan and a Nymph, and the younger twin brother of Myrllin

Wynne – Lady Genestra's lady-in-waiting

ENOCHIAN TRANSLATIONS

"Blior do ialpvrg." – Have comfort in the flames.

"Lonsh zien a nanaeel oddooain ol iolcam aboapri fafen priaz!" – In (the) power exalted of my hands and name I bring forth those that serve!

"Micma, aziazor cnila, teloch, telocvovim, iadoiasmomar a iadoiasmomar!" – Behold, in the likeness of blood, of death, of him that is fallen, of him that is and shall be crowned with hell fire!"

"Mer-lin. Gi biab ixomaxip pambt." – Myrllin, you are known unto me.

"Napeai ipamis allar nanaeel caosg!" – O your swords cannot bind my power upon the earth

"Zir Kures. Geh ozien." – I am here. You are mine.

"Esiasch gohia brin iadnamad a Kiltullagh. Niiso tia do Ys." – Brother, we have the location of Kiltullagh. Find us in Ys.

ABOUT THE AUTHOR

Born in Homestead, Florida, Ravek Hunter grew up in the United States and Belgium. He earned a bachelor's degree in marketing from Florida International University and went on to become a sporting goods executive. He currently serves as a consultant in the same industry and occasionally assists his wife of fifteen years at her floral design company. The proud father of two boys, Ravek counts reading, exercising, and family travel among his leisure hobbies.

Over the past thirty-five years, Ravek's passion has been researching ancient civilizations with a focus on the origin stories behind their mythology. His writing style attempts to immerse the reader into the story by bringing to life historically accurate and rich details of the culture and time period that frame the narrative.

Inspired by classic fantasy authors like Robert Jordan, Terry Goodkind, and R. A. Salvatore, Ravek writes to entertain and provoke his readers, who, he hopes, share his fondness for mythology.

CONNECT WITH RAVEK HUNTER

Thank you for choosing this work of blood, sweat and tears by *Ravek Hunter*! If you enjoyed reading this novel, please consider posting a review, telling me what you think on one of the social media platforms listed below or reach out via my direct email:

Friend me on Facebook:

https://www.facebook.com/Ravek-Hunter-Literary-LLC-238417183579740/

Follow me on Twitter:

https://twitter.com/RavekHunter

Subscribe to my blog:

https://www.goodreads.com/author/show/17885196.Ravek_Hunter

Visit my website:

https://www.WorldsofAtlantis.com

Email: Ravekhunter@gmail.com

www.ingramcontent.com/pod-product-compliance
Lightning Source LLC
Chambersburg PA
CBHW050920030726
47503CB00007BB/2386